ARCADIA

MARS

DOUG COOK

ARCADIA MARS

DOUG COOK

This book is dedicated to my wife Elizabeth, whose wisdom and patience helped make this book possible.

CONTENTS

INTRODUCTION

"Humans are the only species that moves systematically and purposefully over very large distances, in multigenerational migrations, for reasons not tied to the availability of resources. The itch that led our ancestors to risk everything to travel in small boats across large bodies of water like the Pacific Ocean is related to the drive that will one day lead us to colonize Mars. Its origins lie in a mixture of culture and genetics."

Chris Impey, Beyond: Our Future in Space, 2015

This introduction is the inspiration for *Arcadia Mars* the exciting sci-fi sequel to *The Aquila Mission*.

History of Mars in culture.

Man has always gazed at the planet Mars in wonder. Its ruddy hue has inspired the lore of war in Babylonian, Hindu, Greek, and Roman culture. Famously, Mars was the Roman god of war, symbolized by an arrow piercing the planet's that also represents a Roman shield and spear.

With the advent of high quality telescopes in the nineteenth century, astronomers began interpreting the geographic features on the red planet. The most imaginative of them, Giovanni Schiaparelli, described continents crossed by canals. While he may not have imagined water filled canals attributed to intelligent design, others embellished his observations and a plethora of colorful Martian science fiction ensued.

The myth of water filled canals on Mars was reinforced with American astronomer Percival Lowell's observations and publications made into the early twentieth century. The vagaries of Earth based observation coupled with atmospheric turbulence cultivated the myth until the successful Mars flyby images from Mariner 9 in 1965, showing what appeared to be a cratered planet as lifeless as the Moon. Nevertheless, there were tantalizing images from Mariner 9 of canyons possibly carved by water.

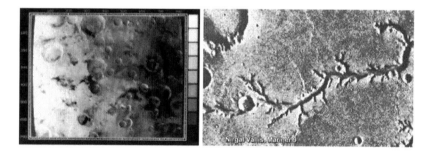

Mariner 9 images of Mars 1965. The right image captures Nirgal Vallis which was probably carved by flowing water. JPL/NASA

Mars still stokes our imagination with the wealth of data acquired by successful orbiting platforms and surface landers. We now know that Mars' first billion years of geologic history was remarkably like Earth's involving enough water to fill a great northern hemisphere ocean. There are great river channels flowing into that ocean. Some xenobiologists even speculate that life evolved on Mars before it did on Earth. Great impacts blasted pieces of Mars free to eventually fall on Earth possibly with the seeds of life.

The fact that Mars retains much of this former ocean as subsurface ice and has substantial gravity, 0.38 g, makes Mars the most compelling destination in the solar system for establishing human colonies off Earth.

The Elusive Goal of Human Exploration of Mars

Werner von Braun, the father of the Apollo Saturn V and Nazi Germany's V2 rocket, long dreamed of sending humans to Mars. The V2 liquid fueled rocket was developed with his army of engineers at Peenemunde, was intended as an advanced weapon system launched against Britain late in WWII, however, Braun envisioned loftier designs. After the first V2 hit London, von Braun said, "The rocket worked perfectly, except for landing on the wrong planet." He was the first rocket scientist/engineer to undertake a serious forward looking technical analysis of a potential human Mars mission.[1]

NASA's Marshall Spaceflight Center conducted an investigation in 1962 called *Project EMPIRE*. It was proposed that a human mission to Mars would require eight Saturn V boosters and assembly in low Earth orbit (LEO).[2] This booster potential was lost when the Apollo Saturn V heavy lift rocket was retired. The Apollo deep space system with its mighty Saturn V booster served for nine crewed missions to the Moon with six successful landings.

---

1 "Von Braun Mars Expedition – 1956". astronautix.com. Archived from the original on 16 January 2010. Retrieved 11 July 2018.

2 Platoff, Annie, Eyes on the Red Planet: Human Mars Mission Planning, 1952–1970, (2001); NASA/CR-2001-2089280
https://web.archive.org/web/20100531192655/http://ston.jsc.nasa.gov/collections/TRS/_techrep/CR-2001-208928.pdf Web archive accessed 11 July 2018.

The Saturn V could have been further developed for even bolder deep space missions as *Project Empire* and von Braun envisioned. The success of the Apollo Moon landings brought complacency. Senator William Proxmire, a lifelong critic of the space program, convinced congress to kill the Saturn V booster and Apollo system. Proxmire ensured that the entire Saturn V and Apollo production and assembly lines were shut down in the early 1970s, resulting in the destruction of the machinery and tooling so that production could not be restarted.[3]

The goal to send humans to Mars has been stated by US administrations since Apollo but has remained an elusive, ill-defined goal always on the twenty to thirty year horizon. From 1989–1993, the George H. W. Bush administration put in place *The Space Exploration Initiative* policy, calling for construction of a US Space Station, sending humans back to the Moon "to stay", and eventually human exploration of Mars.

From the 1990s to early 2000s, NASA undertook conceptual design studies named *Mars Reference Missions* for human Mars missions. The ESA, Russia, and China have undertaken similar studies. There have been long duration isolation projects to study the psychological effects of a long duration Mars mission and to help design closed ecosystems to grow food and maintain life support. The HIGH SEAS Project is one such study that has been underway since 2013 on the island of Hawaii. The longest duration HIGH SEAS crew isolation mission was 366 days.

On January 14, 2004, the George W. Bush administration announced the *Vision for Space Exploration*. It included establishing a lunar outpost by 2020. In a speech on April 15, 2010, President Barack Obama envisioned a human mission to

---

3 Cook, Doug, The Aquila Mission, CreateSpace, 2018. Print.

orbit Mars by the mid-2030s, followed by a landing at an indeterminate date in the late 2030s.

Despite the myriad policy initiatives and design efforts, human space exploration has been confined to low Earth orbit since the Saturn V was retired in 1973. Notwithstanding, we have gained significant experience in terms of space science, technology, and space medicine since Apollo. The International Space Station, ISS, has been continuously occupied since November 2, 2001. Scott Kelly and Mikhail Korniyenko spent 342 continuous days on ISS and Valeri Polyakov, spent 438 days on the former Russian Mir space station. These missions have given us invaluable knowledge on human physiology challenges in long duration space flight in microgravity with exposure to radiation.

Scott Kelly said of his long duration mission on ISS, "In a world of compromise and uncertainty, this space station is a triumph of engineering and cooperation. Putting it into orbit—making it work and keeping it working—is the hardest thing that human beings have ever done, and it stands as proof that when we set our minds to something hard, when we work together, we can do anything, including solving our problems here on Earth. I also know that if we want to go to Mars, it will be very, very difficult, it will cost a great deal of money, and it may cost human lives. But I know now that if we decide to do it, we can."[4]

With the experience and technology gained from the Skylab, Mir, and ISS space stations, we can manage humans in habitat modules to travel to and stay on Mars. We now have the heavy lift vehicles to get us there. The Space launch System (SLS) is NASA's basis for all its future deep space missions. It is phenomenally expensive and will cost about $1 billion per

---

4 Kelly, Scott, Endurance, Knopf Penguin Random House, New York, 2017. Print.

launch. The SLS consumes about $2.5 billion out of NASA's current $19 billion annual budget. The SLS effort employs about 20,000 people across all fifty US States and has nearly unstoppable momentum and political support.

The BFR Reality

According to journalist Stephen Petranek, SpaceX has a single mission statement: "It exists solely for the purpose of creating a self-sustaining human civilization on Mars." On February 6, 2018, SpaceX successfully launched its Falcon Heavy lift vehicle that can also be used for human deep space flight and to assemble a mission to Mars. The projected launch cost of this partially reusable rocket is reported to be less than ten percent of the SLS. Not only does the Falcon Heavy change the outlook for deep space but the announcement of the development of the reusable SpaceX BFR heavy lift rocket is a total game changer. The BFR will have fifty percent more lift capability than the SLS. It will be totally reusable, and cost much less per launch than the Falcon Heavy. The Falcon Heavy and SLS were the design basis for *The Aquila Mission* published April 2018.

September 29th, 2017, "SpaceX CEO and Lead Designer Elon Musk presented an updated vehicle design for what's currently being referred to as BFR."[5] The BFR, *Big F---ing Rocket* as coined by Elon Musk, offers the promise of a fully reusable, inexpensive, super-heavy lift vehicle that can send cargo and humans to Mars and back. A more palatable translation of BFR as the *Big Falcon Rocket* has taken root.

As we enter 2019, SpaceX has further changed the jargon. The BFR reusable design is comprised of a *Super Heavy* booster

---

5 "Becoming a Multi-Planet Species", SpaceX, Web accessed 12 July 2018.
http://www.spacex.com/sites/spacex/files/making_life_multiplanetary-2017.pdf

and *Starship* second stage. In this introductory discussion, for simplicity, we will continue with the name BFR. In *Arcadia Mars* fiction, SpaceTrans is the manufacturer of the Colossus colony transport ship.

SpaceX is now aggressively developing the BFR, planning test suborbital hops in 2019, cargo to Mars by 2022, and perhaps the first crew to Mars by 2024. Manufacturing and launch facilities are being constructed. A point of caution is that their unproven deep space life support systems need to keep pace with their heavy lift capability. The BFR will be fully reusable with per launch costs projected to be around $10 million. That's about one percent of the SLS launch cost. When fully refueled in LEO, the BFR is designed to be able to carry a human crew to Mars, land, and return to Earth after refueling from Mars based in situ resources (ISRU). All other scenarios for a human Mars mission involve a complicated system of multiple modules: habitats, landers, resupply, and an Earth Return vehicle. Since BFR development is rapidly becoming reality, the BFR is the reference heavy lift design for *Arcadia Mars* where it is called the Colossus.

The BFR booster stage will be powered by thirty-one *Raptor* engines with a specific impulse of 330 seconds using subcooled methane (CH_4) and liquid oxygen (LOX) for propellant. The space ship second stage is powered by seven vacuum service *Raptor* engines with a specific impulse of 375 seconds. The Space Launch System (SLS) uses more efficient liquid hydrogen (LH_2)/LOX engines with specific impulse of 462 seconds in vacuum. SpaceX chose methane for the *Raptor* engine to increase its reusability, to allow for higher temperature storage in space (LH_2 stored at -253° C vs CH_4 at -162° C), and to more easily manufacture methane and LOX from Mars' in situ resources (ISRU) of ground water ice and carbon dioxide atmosphere. The process is easily demonstrated in Earth labs using the Sabatier reaction.[6]

Chesley Bonestell's 1949 artist vision of a massive single stage rocket to land a crew on the Moon or Mars.[7] It bears an uncanny resemblance to the SpaceX BFR rocket design.

MOON BASE ALPHA

SpaceX vision of Moon Base Alpha served by the BFR rocket.[8]

---

6 GPUs to Mars: Full-Scale Simulation of SpaceX's Mars Rocket Engine. YouTube. 5 May 2015. Retrieved 4 June 2015.

7 Bonestell, Chesley, and Willy Ley, The Conquest of Space, The Viking Press, New York, 1949. Print.

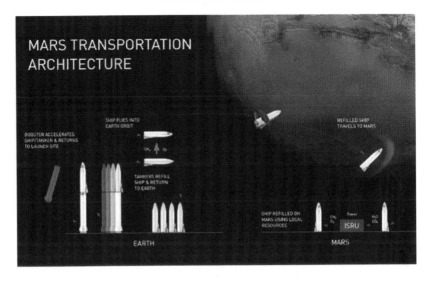

SpaceX Fully Reusable BFR Mission to Mars and Return Architecture: BFR refuels with CH4 and O2 in Earth orbit, and then blasts off for Mars. Ninety-nine percent of entry velocity burns off aerodynamically then supersonic retro-propulsion brings BFR down for a soft vertical landing. In situ resources of Mars water and CO2 are processed using the Sabatier Reaction to make CH4 and O2 propellants for BFR Earth return.[8], [9]

While the BFR offers a great advancement as a fully reusable super-heavy lift vehicle and deep space vehicle that will be able to get humans to Mars, some considerations are worth reviewing. The BFR will be able to lift 150 MT to LEO. To be used as a deep space vehicle, it will need to be fully refueled on orbit to launch and reach Earth escape velocity to deep space. The physics of that require a full fuel load of 240 MT of methane and 860 MT of LOX. The total propellant load is 1100 MT. This sounds easy but even with a BFR fuel tanker delivering 150 MT, it will

---

8 "Becoming a Multi-Planet Species", SpaceX, Web accessed 12 July 2018.
http://www.spacex.com/sites/spacex/files/making_life_multiplanetary-2017.pdf

9 Hoeser, Steve, 2018, "Engineering Mars commercial rocket propellant production for the Big Falcon Rocket," The Space Review, Web accessed 31 July 2018.
http://www.thespacereview.com/article/3479/1

require eight BFR load launches to refuel one BFR for launch from LEO to deep space. SpaceX anticipates a reasonably fast turnaround but the task is daunting to expect a BFR with a deep space crew to endure the wait on orbit and additional risk of eight refueling rendezvous before launching to deep space. The author suggests that a reasonable solution would be to fully refuel the deep space BFR with a one-time rendezvous from a fuel depot. The fuel depot, as shown in the figure below, would have been supplied by multiple BFR fuel tanker launches.

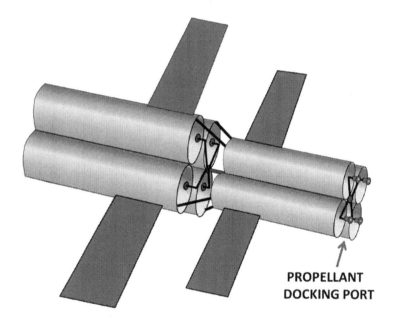

PROPELLANT
DOCKING PORT

Author's concept of a **Low Earth Orbit (LEO) BFR Propellant Depot** capable of storing a full load of propellant for the BFR Second Stage Spaceship (240 MT of methane and 860 MT of LOX). One BFR ship can lift 150 MT to LEO. It will take eight BFR launches to fill the depot for one deep space BFR launch from LEO. The propellant docking port mates with the propellant transfer lines in the BFR aft engine bay by present design.

Another serious consideration about ramping up the passenger count on BFR ships for building a Mars colony is that

SpaceX is proposing that the BFR ship can carry one hundred colonists to Mars based on the interior volume size (825 cubic meters) compared to a B380 Airbus. The assumption is that one hundred passengers could have perhaps fifty shared cabins and modest common areas. This is not an intercontinental B380 flight. This cramped space will be the reality for the one hundred passengers for a six month journey through deep space to get to Mars. Also the requirements for life support and consumables for that six month voyage for one hundred persons are staggering. Putting human crew into hibernation-like stasis is an attractive possibility to save consumables and reduce space requirements for a six month voyage to Mars.[10]

Currently, the state-of-the art ISS can barely maintain life support in its closed system for a crew of six. Astronaut Scott Kelly suffered from high concentrations of carbon dioxide on ISS when it often exceeded a partial pressure of six millimeters of mercury. US Navy standards for submarines aim to keep carbon dioxide below two millimeters of mercury to avoid crew stress and mental impairment.4

The requirement for consumables and Mars surface support infrastructure is also staggering. The consumable requirement is 2.5 MT per person per year. We will need to provide at least a three year supply for our first group of twenty-one colonists. That amounts to 158 MT split between two ships that will also carry hardware for infrastructure. For one hundred persons for six months outbound to Mars requires 125 MT of consumables for just the flight. It's not known if the remaining 25 MT capacity can accommodate life support for one hundred persons. Three years of consumables for one hundred persons on Mars amounts

10 "Torpor Inducing Transfer Habitat for Human Stasis to Mars", NASA Grant NNX13AP82G, May 2014, Web accessed 5 Oct 2018, https://www.nasa.gov/sites/default/files/files/Bradford_2013_PhI_Torpor.pdf

to 750 MT requiring five BFR supply ships. Now we need more ships for infrastructure to support for the one hundred colonists. The author estimates that infrastructure supply (habs/power/life support etc.) for the twenty-one person Arcadia Colony would require five[11] BFR ships to Mars plus propellant ship launches. Let's multiply that times five for one hundred colonists-- that's an additional twenty BFR ships to Mars in addition to the six ships above (one for colonists plus five for consumables) plus propellant ship launches. That comes to a total of 234 BFR launches to start a one hundred person colony. This seems to be unattainable and unsustainable for a start-up colony. The conclusion is that colony increments should be about twenty persons per 26 month Mars launch window cycle. Complete ISRU support, producing air, water and food on Mars, should be enabled within two years of landing on Mars to minimize the continuing need for support ships from Earth.

	Persons	Ships to Mars	Propellant launches	Total Launches
Arcadia Colony	21	5	40	45
Arcadia Addition	100	26	208	234

Now let's examine the reality of ISRU propellant production to get a BFR ship back to Earth. As stated above, the appeal to using the BFR Raptor engine for Mars missions is that in situ resources of Mars water and atmospheric carbon dioxide (CO_2) can be processed using the Sabatier Reaction to make methane (CH_4) and LOX (O_2) propellants for the BFR Earth return. To be sure, there are near surface sources of water ice at our proposed Arcadia Planitia Mars Base. Mining and processing water ice will be energy and infrastructure intensive.

---

11 For the Arcadia Mars story, the author uses three Colossus ships per twenty-one person colony increment.

12

The overall energy requirement to produce one metric ton of methane propellant is 17 megawatt-hours.[12] So assuming all feedstock is available, the power required to produce a full 240 MT load of methane gas for a BFR is estimated to be approximately 4.1 gigawatt-hours. In addition to that, we will need 860 MT of LOX. This can be attained by the electrolysis of water giving us oxygen and hydrogen. The hydrogen will feed back into the Sabatier reaction.

Commercially available electrolysis systems require about 6.25 megawatt-hours of power to produce one MT of oxygen and 0.125 MT of hydrogen gas from 1.125 MT of water. So it requires 5.4 gigawatt-hours of energy to produce 860 MT of oxygen. Now we need energy to liquefy the oxygen and methane. It takes 0.180 megawatt-hours to liquefy one MT of oxygen and so 154 megawatt-hours to liquefy 860 MT of oxygen. Similarly it takes 43.2 megawatt-hours to liquefy 240 MT of methane. The total energy cost is 9.7 gigawatt-hours of energy to produce the 1100 MT of liquid propellants to refuel one BFR ship on Mars.

	1 MT	240 MT	860 MT	1100 MT
METHANE gas	17 megawatt-hrs	4.1 gigawatt-hrs		
OXYGEN gas	6.25 megawatt-hrs		5.4 gigawatt-hrs	
Methane Liquid		43.2 megawatt-hrs		
LOX			154 megawatt-hrs	
TOTAL LOAD				9.7 gigawatt-hrs

ENERGY REQUIREMENT TO GENERATE PROPELLANT FOR BFR RETURN FROM MARS

At Los Alamos National Laboratory, NASA is experimenting with a small one kilowatt-hour nuclear fusion reactor design that can be used for a Mars base. They envision a

---

12 Zubrin, Robert M.; Muscatello,"Integrated Mars In Situ Propellant Production System". Journal of Aerospace Engineering. Jan 2013. Vol 26: Issue 1, pp 43–56. doi:10.1061/(asce)as.1943-5525.0000201. Web accessed 1 Aug 2018.

40 kWh system that can be deployed in multiples as needed. Ten of these 40 kWh reactors would yield 0.4 megawatt-hours so we need 24,250 hours or 1010 days or 2.8 years to produce the propellant for one BFR. Whew! This is longer than the stay time of a landing crew waiting until the next launch window to come home with no power to spare for life support or other systems. More reactors, larger reactors, and the addition of solar electric power could help.

Four *Kilopower* nuclear reactors casting shadows on the Martian surface. (NASA Artwork)

Here is an unrealized design for a small, sealed, transportable, autonomous reactor (SSTAR) designed by Lawrence Livermore Labs.[13] As conceived for use on Earth, the portable fusion reactor would produce 100 megawatts of power and be 15 meters high by 3 meters wide, and weigh 500 MT. A 10 megawatt version is expected to weigh less than 200 MT. This might be adaptable for a special design to fit the size and 150 MT mass capability of the BFR. A 10 megawatt power source could

---

13 Smith, C, "Nuclear Energy to Go: A Self-Contained, Portable Nuclear Reactor", Science and Technology, August 2004. Web accessed 2 August 2018. https://str.llnl.gov/str/JulAug04/Smith.html

produce the 1100 MT of propellant to refuel a BFR in 40 days instead of 2.8 years.

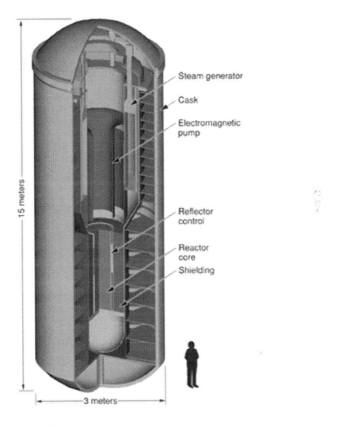

The average household needs a seven kilowatt energy supply. The ten megawatt SSTAR reactor could supply energy for over 1000 homes or all of the energy needs a growing Mars colony will need for the foreseeable future.

The Earth return trip for a BFR itself requires major energy expenditure. Since the first crew to Mars will return to Earth, the plan is to return them using the infrastructure outlined above. One caveat is that the author calculates that a half-load of 500,000 kg of propellant can launch a minimal cargo in a BFR to 7.2 km/s beyond the Mars escape velocity of 6.5 km/s to get it on a Hohmann transfer orbit back to Earth.

Multiple BFR ships used to establish a Mars colony.[8]

For the first twenty-one person colony, it will be necessary to refuel one BFR for an emergency evacuation. Five BFR ships will bring all the consumables and infrastructure supplies. (*Arcadia Mars* reduces this to three Colossus ships to simplify the story.) The author proposes that the extra four ships stay on Mars and eventually cannibalized for parts and metal where that will serve the economics of the colony. The economics of reuse will certainly be served by the BFR propellant tankers ferrying from Earth to LEO.

The propellant tanks in a spare BFR could be used for additional habitat space. The BFR originally planned to have a carbon fiber resin composite hull like some current Boeing and Airbus airliners. In January 2019, SpaceX announced that the BFR design will switch to stainless steel for cost and extreme temperature performance reasons. The Colossus ships envisioned in *Arcadia Mars* have an aluminum outer hull. The aluminum alloy skin or stainless steel could be salvaged for feedstock for 3D printing other hab structures or vehicles.

WHY ARCADIA PLANITIA AS A CREW LANDING SITE?

Any serious recent discussion of sending humans to Mars necessarily must include a landing area where primarily there is ready access to subsurface water ice. Science objectives are important but are secondary to water for survival. Water ice cannot exist directly on the surface since the low atmospheric pressure and temperature puts ice at the physical state where it will readily sublimate like carbon dioxide dry ice exposed at room temperature on Earth. Ice will be used as an in situ resource to be utilized for water, oxygen, and rocket propellant for return to Earth. The rocket propellant produced from ice can be liquid hydrogen or liquid methane (includes CO_2 from the atmosphere) combined with liquid oxygen. As orbiting labs such as the Mars Reconnaissance Orbiter (MRO) probe Mars with SHARAD ground penetrating radar and photograph the morphology of the surface, massive evidence points to the existence of widespread shallow subsurface water ice in the Arcadia Planitia region of Mars, establishing it as a primary Mars Exploration Zone[14], EZ, containing many Regions of Interest, ROIs, within one hundred kilometers of the primary landing base site. The ROIs have scientific interest in the search for past or present life on Mars and most importantly have resources such as water ice to support human habitation. NASA affiliated workshops, SpaceX, and numerous studies agree on this evidence and propose that this mid-latitude area will be an ideal area for a landing zone for crews

---

14 Mars Exploration Zone, NASA, Web accessed 26 Aug 2018.
https://www.youtube.com/watch?v=94bIW7e1Otg

on Mars because of the access to water ice. [15],[16], [17] While abundant water ice can be found in polar regions, the surface temperature and orbital access issues are too extreme to entertain a first crew landing there.

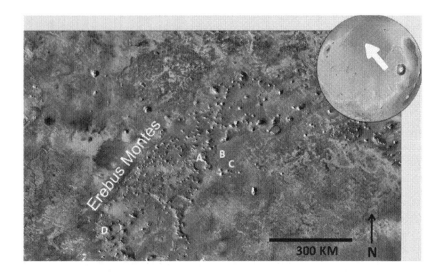

Mars Erebus Montes area of Arcadia Planitia. Diacria Quadrangle (MC-2) Centered on 38°N 189 °E. This area is 1500 kilometers northeast of Olympus Mons. Images A to D below show evidence of abundant near surface ice. The northern hemisphere of Mars including Arcadia Planitia once held an ocean. NASA/JPL THEMIS and HiRISE imagery.

15 Bramson, A. M., S. Byrne, N. E. Putzig, S. Sutton, J. J. Plaut, T. C. Brothers, and J. W. Holt, 2015, Widespread excess ice in Arcadia Planitia, Mars, Geophys. Res. Lett., 42. Web Accessed 12 Aug 2018, https://arxiv.org/abs/1509.03210

16 Viola, D., A. McEwen, C. Dundas, Arcadia Planitia: Acheron Fossae and Erebus Montes, NASA 1st EZ Workshop for Human Missions to Mars, 2015, Web accessed 13 Aug 2018, https://www.nasa.gov/sites/default/files/atoms/files/viola_arcadiaplanitia_final_tagged.pdf

17 Williams, N, et al, Surface Morphologies of Arcadia Planitia as an Indicator of Past and Present Near-Surface Ice. Lunar and Planetary Science Conference 2017, Paper 2852. Web accessed 13 July 2018. https://www.hou.usra.edu/meetings/lpsc2017/pdf/2852.pdf

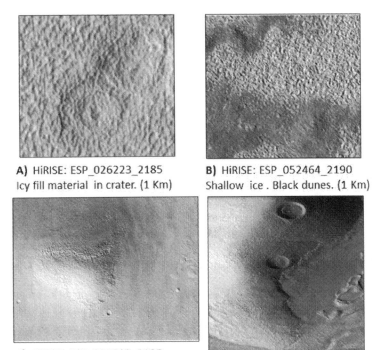

A) HiRISE: ESP_026223_2185
Icy fill material in crater. (1 Km)

B) HiRISE: ESP_052464_2190
Shallow ice . Black dunes. (1 Km)

C) HiRISE: PSP_004097_2185
Subsurface ice pingo. (3 Km)

D) HiRISE: ESP_046702_2170
Subsurface ice pingo and
Subsurface ice flow. (4Km)

From the HiRISE orbital reconnaissance photography (above) and SHARAD ground penetrating radar, the presence of shallow easily obtainable water ice in Arcadia Planitia is a near certainty. This easy access to water makes this area very attractive for a first crew landing and ultimately the first colony on Mars. At global scale, the former ocean bed appears very flat. However, on closer examination at kilometer scales and closer, reveal very rough terrain similar to but even more rugged than permafrost areas in Siberia and Alaska on Earth. The rugged terrain may present huge challenges for exploration rover travel. Detailed satellite imagery will be necessary to map a passable route.

WHY GO TO MARS?

Ahead of human deep space exploration, our robotic exploration of the solar system has been phenomenally successful, morphing into international effort to send science orbiters, landers, and rovers to Mars. The Mars 2020 rover will continue this effort and cache samples for future Earth return. The detailed analysis of these samples will reveal any challenges or threats to humans that might be present in Mars regolith.

On December 11, 2017, President Trump signed *Space Policy Directive 1*, an integrated public-private program led by NASA with a stated goal of reviving manned space exploration:

> "Beginning with missions beyond low-Earth orbit, the United States will lead the return of humans to the Moon for long-term exploration and utilization, followed by human missions to Mars and other destinations."

Again, there is no commitment to goals with a definite date. As such, the goal to send humans to explore and colonize Mars remains nebulous. A compelling, overarching reason to send humans to another world is needed.

Chris Carberry, CEO of Explore Mars, Inc., enumerates six essential reasons for mankind to explore and eventually colonize Mars:

1) Discovery and Scientific Knowledge
2) Inspiration and Innovation
3) Prosperity and National Morale 4) Security and Diplomacy
5) Advancement and Expansion of Humanity
6) To Understand Earth.

Further, Carberry states that "Recent workshops and studies have also shown that missions to Mars are both achievable and affordable. NASA will not require a large increase in its budget to achieve this goal of landing humans on Mars by 2033." [18] Indeed, these are valid reasons to send humans to explore Mars and it is encouraging that we have come to the point in the history of human space flight that the journey is technologically and financially achievable.[19]

The reasons to go to Mars enumerated above assume a relatively peaceful, stable *status quo* Earth. However, Carl Sagan stated that the most compelling reason to extend our civilization to another world is to ensure the survival of the human race. [20] We can imagine a spectrum of global disaster scenarios to motivate humans to become a multi-planet species for our survival, among them: global thermonuclear war, famine, pandemic disease, and impending asteroid impact. [21]

Since 1998, we have been systematically searching for and cataloging near Earth objects (NEOs: i.e. asteroids and comets). To date, over 16,000 NEOs have been discovered that are larger than 140 m diameter and 7816 are larger than 1 km potentially posing a global impact threat. Of the NEO populations, about 4700 have been classified as potentially hazardous objects (PHOs) that cross closer than 8 million km to Earth and are greater than 300 m in diameter. While this sounds ominous, to date there are

---

18 C. Carberry, J. Webster, Six essential reasons Why We Need to Send Humans to Mars, Fox News Opinion, (2017) http://www.foxnews.com/opinion/2017/01/17/

19 Heidmann, Richard, and Pierre Brisson, "An Economic Model for a Martian Colony of a Thousand People," Planete-Mars.com, Web accessed archive 12 July 2018. http://planete-mars.com/an-economic-model-for-a-martian-colony-of-a-thousand-people/

20 Sagan, Carl, The Pale Blue Dot, The Random House Publishing Group, New York, 1994. Print.

21 Szocik,K., Wójtowicz, T., Baran, L, War or Peace? The possible scenarios of colonizing Mars, Space Policy 42 (2017) 31–36, http://dx.doi.org/10.1016/j.spacepol.2017.10.002 Web accessed 9 July 2018.

no PHOs that pose an imminent high probability impact threat.[22] The Chixulub impactor that killed half of the species on Earth including the dinosaurs 66 million years ago was a fifteen kilometer wide asteroid that delivered the equivalent of ten billion Hiroshima A-bombs of impact energy. This size of impact statistically occurs only once every hundred million years. That likelihood of impact could only be delivered by a large rogue body coming in from the outer regions of the solar system and hitherto undetected. The specter of such an extinction level event, however improbable, conjured the premise of *Arcadia Mars*:

> *Despite the threat of ongoing global warming, Earth overpopulation, and global thermonuclear war, alongside the peaceful motivations of exploration, colonization, and the wonder of exploration itself, humanity has not yet mustered the will to depart its terrestrial cradle. Until-- A one hundred kilometer diameter Kuiper Belt Object (KBO) from beyond Neptune and Pluto is discovered to be on a trajectory to the inner solar system. It has a one-in-fifty chance of impacting the Earth in the year 2098. This disaster would be twenty-thousand times the impact energy of the Chixulub Event. Mankind cannot afford to gamble with extinction. The time to become a spacefaring multi-planet species is now.*

---

22 "2017 Report of the NEO Definition Team: Update to Determine the Feasibility of Enhancing the Search and Characterization of NEOs", NASA Planetary Science Division, Web accessed 12 July 2018.
https://cneos.jpl.nasa.gov/doc/2017_neo_sdt_final_e-version.pdf

ARCADIA MARS

PREFACE

Arcadia Mars is the dramatic sequel to *The Aquila Mission,* the story of a grand seven year international effort to design and build a space exploration system, and train its elite crew -- Coby Brewster, Ellie Accardi, Vik Ivanov, and Abby Denton-- to rendezvous with, study, and sample asteroid Bennu and short period comet 125P. The mission is a stepping-stone to landing a crew on Mars.

On *Aquila,* much of their mission time in cruise between objectives is spent working on planning the first crewed mission to Mars slated for 2033, ten years in the future. Their efforts are coordinated with counterpart planning teams on Earth. With increasing light speed communication delays, they rely on video, text, and digital file transfers. Coby and Vik contribute engineering expertise. Abby contributes her aerospace medical expertise. Ellie gets deeply involved in future Mars landing site selection.

The *Aquila Mission* objectives are met with unqualified successes aided by AI entities who are unofficial crewmembers. CASSI is the mainframe AI controlling navigation and life support and many vital functions on the Altair. Manned maneuvering units controlled by the AI named CAMI facilitate crew EVAs to the asteroid and comet. After millions of visits inside the orbit of Mars, the short period comet has been baked by the Sun and lost most of its near surface volatiles. Outgassing is not a great threat to close-in human exploration.

They discover an amber-like organic nodule on Bennu with an arthropoid fossil embedded in it. Their sample return has bagged proof of an extraterrestrial life form. As the science work at 125P is winding down, they discover a vent opening on the comet with the unnatural symmetry of an elongated hexagon. They find an odd metallic floor in the vent that is suggestive of a metallic meteorite but with a composition unlike any found in our solar system.

After *Aquila*, the desperation to restart civilization off world stems from the fact that the Earth has a one-in-fifty chance of being destroyed by a newly discovered interloper from the Kuiper belt. The main characters from *Aquila*, Coby Brewster, Ellie Accardi, Vik Ivanov, and Abby Denton lead the first colony on Mars in the desperate bid to make a second home for humanity, accompanied by close family members. The multi-national effort inevitably involves deep questions and conflict. How do we travel across the face of Mars to make new discoveries? How do we begin to govern a new civilization? How do we deal with the worst crimes a human can commit? In the *Arcadia* epilogue set in the year 2035, we get acquainted with other characters on the first Mars colony at Arcadia Planitia. The AI entities CASSI and CAMI that made the achievements of *Aquila* possible are even more capable in *Arcadia* where we see humans accompanied by true androids.

The idea for *The Aquila Mission* can be traced to a dream I had back in 2015 on a family vacation in Bahrain. I awoke from my dream before sunrise and started drawing orbit diagrams for the asteroid and comet rendezvous scenario on hotel stationery. The idea stuck with me and I began research in earnest. The idea spurred me to write *The Aquila Mission*, which is both well researched non-fiction and an adventure in hard sci-fi. That book project took six months to complete the first draft. I began *Arcadia Mars* at that time and then let it stew on the shelf while I got back to editing *Aquila*. That process took about a year with my editor Phil Athans.

Writing *The Aquila Mission* and *Arcadia Mars* for me was like reading a good sci-fi book but based on the very real history of Apollo and construction of ISS. The technical parts need telling to put solid technical legs on the mission idea that I sincerely believe to be a viable stepping-stone to putting a crew on Mars. The sci-fi evolution of the first book and the twist at its conclusion seemed to demand the *Arcadia* sequel. My Arcadia readers are asking for a sequel.

While writing these books, each paragraph and string of dialog came fresh and as unexpected as if I were living it. In *Aquila,* I set out to have Coby develop a relationship with Abby but Ellie won his heart. I set out to tell the tale of the successful first deep space mission beyond the Moon but disaster strikes at every stage of the mission. *Arcadia* has more unexpected relationships and conflicts. While the colony is growing, I made a *Dramatis Personae* list to help me get to know the new characters in the growing colonies. I encourage readers to find that list and a *Glossary of Terms* following the *Arcadia* Epilogue.

The reader will recognize that certain details laid out for the Arcadia Colony on Mars in the Epilogue of *The Aquila Mission* have changed. For example, some of the minutia of the layout of the colony and it successors have evolved as research and practical design ideas required change.

I would like acknowledge the contributions by my wife Elizabeth whose guidance on the UAE and LDS colonies and interpersonal relationships got me past some tough questions. I would also like to acknowledge my editors Adam Berry, Haley Cook-Simmons, Jeanie Ross, Sam Siriano, and Mike Hulver. Their careful attention to detail and acumen for a good sci-fi story helped improve this book.

On to *Arcadia Mars!*

March 29, 2019
Doug Cook
Colorado Springs, CO

PROLOGUE

...Every surviving civilization is obliged to become spacefaring--not because of exploratory or romantic zeal, but for the most practical reason imaginable: staying alive... If our long-term survival is at stake, we have a basic responsibility to our species to venture to other worlds. "

Carl Sagan, *Pale Blue Dot,* 1994

Discovery

At the Haleakala Observatory on Maui, the Pan-STARRS large, twin 1.8 meter telescopes with a 1.4 Gigapixel CCD arrays methodically whir and expose sixty-second images in succession. They record stars and potentially solar system objects as faint as magnitude 23.6, only one ten millionth as bright as the faintest stars that a human eye can see. Dwarf planet Pluto, as the poster child of Kuiper Belt Objects (KBOs), is magnitude 14 from Earth or four thousand times brighter than objects that Pan-STARRS can find. Since Pluto's discovery by astronomer Clyde Tombaugh in 1930, over two thousand KBOs have been discovered beyond the orbit of Neptune. Most are larger than one hundred kilometers in diameter. A handful approaches the size of two thousand kilometer dwarf planet Pluto. They have names like Quaoar, Haumea, Sedna, Makemake, Eris, and the yet to be named (225088) 2007 OR10. Many are binary objects or have more than one moon. They are classified based on orbit distance, eccentricity, and inclination as plutinos, cubewanos, CDOs, and SDOs. The later are greater than fifty AUs (Earth-Sun distance ~150 million km), have high eccentricity, and high orbital inclination.

The data sets that Pan-STARRS collects over the sky visible from the observatory repeats regularly to find moving objects. *Where is Waldo* among billions of apparently static stars? A powerful computer system processes the observations- over two petabytes of data and growing. It calibrates the position and brightness properties of objects on the images. Multiple observations of the same patch of sky show moving objects such as asteroids, comets, and KBOs against the background astrometry of cataloged stars. Repeat observations of a moving object over a reasonable timeframe allow calculation of its orbit and identification of known objects. Unidentified objects get repeated observations to refine the orbit calculation and flag it as an uncatalogued object to be classified.

Based mainly on age dates of meteorites, it is known that our solar system formed about 4.6 billion years ago. Age dates of Apollo lunar samples, lunar meteorites, and oldest rocks on Earth imply that the Earth and Moon were substantially molten early on and lunar maria formed from 4.1 to 3.8 million years ago. Computer modeling suggests that instabilities in the orbits and resonances of Jupiter, Saturn, Uranus, and Neptune were being realigned in that timeframe. The outer planet realignments sent planetesimals left over from the formation of the solar system inward toward Earth in an event called the Late Heavy Bombardment.[23] Lunar maria basins are evidence of these huge impacts from planetesimals in the one hundred kilometer plus size range. The computer simulations and observational evidence show that an Earth impact from a body larger than one kilometer (global threat threshold) originating inside the Kuiper Belt is

---

23 Taylor, G. J. (August, 2006) Wandering Gas Giants and Lunar Bombardment. Planetary Science Research Discoveries.
http://www.psrd.hawaii.edu/Aug06/cataclysmDynamics.html (Web accessed 16 July 2018)

extremely unlikely today. Yet current accepted theory for the continuing appearance of unknown or extremely long period comets into the inner solar system is that they were gravitational perturbed from their previous orbits in the Kuiper belt or more distant Oort Cloud.[24]

Based on computer simulations including perturbations in known KBOs, Caltech astronomers Konstantin Batygin and Mike Brown provide evidence of a giant planet, dubbed Planet X, in the outer solar system. The perturbations have only a probability of 0.007% to be due to chance, pointing clearly to the gravitational influence of an undiscovered planet. It may have a mass about ten times that of Earth and similar to Neptune but twenty times more distant (i.e. about 600 AU). Its orbit would be over ten thousand years.[25] The search is on.

Institute for Astronomy (IfA) - Manoa
University of Hawaii
Oahu, Hawaii
July 14, 2027

An international team of astronomers parsing Pan-STARRS data processed by their AI supercomputer is led by Dr. Matteo Russo and Dr. Kelsey Leech. The air in the dim room is filled with smell of four hour old coffee on the warmer. The remains of

24 Fouchard, M., H. Rickman, Ch. Froeschlé, G.B. Valsecchi, Planetary perturbations for Oort Cloud comets. I. Distributions and dynamics, Icarus, Volume 222, Issue 1, 2013, Pages 20-31, Web accessed 14 July 2018.
https://www.sciencedirect.com/science/article/pii/S0019103512004368

25 Batygin, K, and M. Brown, "Evidence for a Distant Giant Planet in the Solar System", The Astronomical Journal, 151:22, February 2016. Web accessed 14 July 2018. http://iopscience.iop.org/article/10.3847/0004-6256/151/2/22/pdf

a large pepperoni pizza linger on the desk in its greasy delivery box.

"Matt, look at this floater that *PASCI*[26] found. It's tentatively tagged 2027 NG13. The angular motion is barely noticeable in the five day blink. Either this is bad data or this one is *way* far out."

"Compare the blink to the data set from a month ago. See if it's there and has the same relative motion."

"*PASCI's* ahead of you on that. She has the blink set with one month and two month data. We have the same relative motion but wow! It must be *way* out there!"

"*PASCI*, back up one year and blink on your prediction of the floater's location."

"*Affirmative, Matt. The data blink comparison is on your screen.*"

"Ahoo! There it is! Compute the apparent orbital period from the angular vector rate in these first observations."

"*The apparent orbital period is approximately eleven thousand years with a semi-major axis of six to seven hundred AU.*"

"The apparent 22nd magnitude at that distance would make this a huge object. Oh my God!! Matteo, are you thinking what I'm thinking?"

"Planet X? Yes. Yes it could be! But we need more data and a longer time baseline before we spout off."

"Clyde Tombaugh's photographic data set from the 1930 Pluto discovery at the Lowell Observatory has been digitized and

---

26 Fictitious: PASCI (sounds like Passy) = Pan-STARRS Astrometric Computing Intelligence.

referenced to Gaia data. It's the oldest data set of this quality covering most of the Northern Hemisphere sky. *PASCI*, compute the floater's position prediction for 1930 and check the Lowell Observatory data set."

"Working. The data from that date range covers the wrong sector."

"Do we have that sector from before 1930?"

"Affirmative. The 1929 Lowell data covers the predicted sector. Blink comparing for similar anomalies…Working…First anomaly, 24th magnitude, found five degrees forty-three minutes from predicted location. Second anomaly, 22nd magnitude, found eleven arc minutes from predicted 2027 NG13 location."

"Kelsey, can you believe this? I think it's time to notify the PS-1 Consortium and the IAU."

"Not so fast. We certainly have a momentous discovery but we have some more work to do. *PASCI*, recompute the orbit of both floaters and output a report file. Let's provisionally call the 24th magnitude anomaly NG14. Now find it on plate at least a month forward or back."

"Affirmative…The 2027 NG13 report is complete. The second anomaly, *NG14, is found on two plates three months prior in 2029. It is on a trajectory into the solar system consistent with a very long period or hyperbolic comet. The parallax indicates that it was at over eighty eight AU distance in 1929."*

Kelsey continues, "Wow! At that distance and that magnitude, it's probably larger than one hundred kilometers and more a dwarf planet than a comet! *PASCI*, project NG14 motion forward to try to find it on the SDSS[27] since 2001 and PS1 data from 2008 to present."

"Affirmative. Accessing 2 petabytes of SDSS data and 2 petabytes of PS1 data. Standby… NG14 is found on multiple archive passes from 2005 to present. It is currently 49 AU out in the constellation Virgo near the star β Virginis. Projecting orbit calculations forward, NG14 enters the inner solar system and passes inside of 0.001 lunar distance of Earth on February 28, 2079."

"Oh shit! Matt, can you believe this? How can we confirm this and how will the world react? Oh God, I, I need to sit down…"

"Sit here Kelsey. Damn! I don't feel so good myself. We just went from the biggest astronomy discovery of the century to possibly destroying the Earth! *PASCI*, please recheck the data and report the possibility of NG14 Earth impact."

"Affirmative. Processing…With the data available, the uncertainty of orbit calculations implies a one in fifty chance of Earth impact on February 28, 2079."

"Oh God! Oh God! Oh God! Matteo, we have to report it! *Now* it's time to notify the PS-1 Consortium and the IAU."

"We need to get the Webb/JWST to observe NG13 and NG14 for another parallax measurement, higher accuracy, and to see if they are related. Could this monster be diverted? The world only has fifty two years to get its shit together."

---

27 Ofek, Erin, 2012, SDSS (Sloan Digital Sky Survey) Observations of Kuiper Belt Objects: Colors and Variability, Earth and Planetary Astrophysics, Web accessed 13 July 2018, https://arxiv.org/pdf/1202

Mars Orbiting Base Camp
August 8, 2031
Mission Sol 751
Sol Time 00:12:33:46

"Con 4 final seven-second trim burn in ten minutes and counting down. She's 47,000 klicks out. Give me a status report on Cons 1, 2, and 3 down on Arcadia."

"Communications, nominal."

"Control and subsystems nominal."

"Solar and battery systems nominal."

There is a huge push to elevate humans into a multi-planet species. The humans to Mars *Constellation Project* was tremendously accelerated in 2027 with the discovery of 2027 NG14 also called '*Shiva*'- *the destroyer*. It is a one hundred kilometer diameter KBO with a one in fifty chance of impacting Earth in 2079. *Shiva* was nudged out of its 15,000 year orbit on the outer edges of the Kuiper belt by the huge 2027 NG13 '*Abaddon*', the newly discovered ninth planet. *Abaddon* is the *Despoiler* or *Angel of Destruction*. It was discovered simultaneously with *Shiva*. The first crew is scheduled to land on Mars in 2033 to be followed by the first colony in December 2035 and more Colossus Mars colony ships in May 2036 and March 2038.

The goal is to have the Mars colony firmly established with one million inhabitants by 2079 when *Shiva* has its unwelcome encounter with Earth. The intent is to have multiple colony locations with a substantial proportion of the population sheltered underground in lava tube caves that have been located by the Mars Reconnaissance Orbiter (MRO) or in tunnels and rooms excavated in subsurface ice. In addition, there must be multiple sources of air, water, food, fuel, and energy established to support the colonies. Diversity is the key to survival. Additional goals aim to establish trade alliances and to have the colony ninety percent self-sufficient by 2045. It is anticipated that the primary exports initially will be liquid oxygen, hydrogen, and methane propellants manufactured from Mars ice and CO_2 resources for use elsewhere off-Earth. Other mineral resources will be exploited as economics and trade opportunities evolve. Uranium fission will be a substantial source of energy for the foreseeable future. Locating, extracting, and refining uranium for exporting and use on Mars is another mineral resource opportunity.

On Mars orbit, Bruce Bouchout is on duty as Mars Base Camp Mission Control Director. He and his crew has been monitoring the approach of a fleet of six Constellation Mars landers destined to establish Mars Arcadia Base in advance of the first crew landings. The Constellation fleet was launched from Earth over a period spanning January 25-30, 2031. Habitat modules Constellation 1 and 2 landed safely on Sol 748 followed by supply module Constellation 3 on Sol 750. Inbound Constellation 4 is the second supply module and due to begin aerobraking descent in Mars' thin atmosphere in two hours.

"Burn in three, two, one, mark…Burn looks good…shut down in three, two, one. On the money. We are perfectly aligned for the entry corridor. Okay crew; keep on your toes as we approach aerobraking. This round of coffee is on me. Starcup's finest Martian blend."

"Bruce, I'll take the coffee but I'd die to get my hands on a Krispy Kreme donut to go with it."

"In your dreams Jenny. Keep your eyes on the telemetry. We have a much better seat here than Mission Control back in Houston twenty light minutes away. At least we have a shot at finding and correcting an anomaly."

"We have three Cons down safe and three to go. This is almost starting to feel routine."

"God, I hope you're right but let's stay vigilant. There's a lot of space junk trashed down there on the surface from failed probe landings. We need this entire fleet safe on the surface if we want to keep our crew landing on schedule for 2033…"

"…Okay team; Con 4 is in the entry corridor. Turn to entry attitude. Atmosphere contact in thirty seconds…"

"Telemetry shows atmosphere contact. We've got 5.6 kilometers per second to burn down in three minutes. Heat shield nominal…Ride is good…We are at 400 meters per second…Waiting for parachute deploy…There it is! Jettison heat shield in three—two—one…Negative jettison! Okay Team! Give me a solution! We've got two minutes on chutes until we're at 1800 meters to get that heat shield jettisoned so we can fire the thrusters!"

"Recycling the pyros[28]…Sending override pyro fire command…Negative pyros…"

"Okay. What else have we got? We don't have time for a reboot!"

"If I were riding that Con, I'd pry that shield loose with a crowbar!"

---

28 Pyros on a spacecraft are small explosive devices designed to sever connections in a programmed sequence of events.

"Not very helpful. I'm afraid we're out of time. Can we override the chute jettison?"

"That's a firm. I'm ready on that."

"Do it. Let's hold onto those chutes and take the hard landing without the pyros."

"Override command sent. Chutes not jettisoned. Impact in five seconds…We've lost telemetry and pancaked at one hundred meters per second."

"There is remote chance that some of the supplies survived. Let's work this with Houston and make damn sure that we can get the next two Con landers down with the MAVs and Sabatier reactors intact. Without those MAVs, we won't land our crews in two years because they won't have a ride home. It will take those two years to make the Sabatier reactors to make propellant for crew return. We've still got a chance to send another supply module just ahead of the crews."

Mars Base Camp Director Bruce Bouchout Personal Log:

What's needed to improve Mars landing success is a stream of reliable, identical landers where we can gain some solid experience. Statistics on Mars landing successes are only as good as the number of repeats on a given landing system. To date, three successful Constellation landings are the longest string of successes for any Mars landing system. All have used heat shields and parachutes for initial descent but the final landing has to be perfect also. The record up to 2020 was two successes each for the 1975 Viking landers on retros, the two MER rovers, Spirit and Opportunity in 2003 on airbags, the Phoenix Mars Lander and Mars Insight Missions on retros, and the MSL Curiosity and Mars 2020 rover on retros and a sky crane. This very complicated system amazed the world when it first worked with Curiosity. NASA called the Mars entry, descent, and landing (EDL) phase the *seven minutes of terror.*[29] ESA and Russia scored deserved landing successes with two ExoMars landers on retros in 2020 and 2024. Then there was the ghastly long hiatus of no landers from 2024 until now with the Constellation fleet.

SpaceTrans will revolutionize Mars EDL for its Colossus ships by aerobraking with the ships heat shield belly forward to slow all but one percent of entry velocity, eliminating parachutes, and using engine retro burn with remaining mission propellant to perform a precision soft landing. The Colossus ships are due to arrive in 2033 with robotic supply ships and prior to the first crew landing in another Colossus.

---

29 "Mars Curiosity Rover Landing Success", NASA JPL, Web accessed 29 January 2018, https://www.space.com/16932-mars-rover-curiosity-landing-success.html

1

TIMELINE TO MARS

"Eventually we must leave Earth--at least a certain number of our progeny must as our sun approaches the end of its solar life cycle. But just as terrestrial explorers have always led the way for settlers, this will also happen extra-terrestrially. Earth is our cradle, not our final destiny."

Astronaut Edgar Mitchell, *The Way of the Explorer,* 1996

What follows is the historical record of the key events that led to the first footsteps and colonization of Mars.

July 4, 2024- ISS achieves its independence as a commercial space station. The collective space budget of the *International Space Coalition* is now free to focus on human presence in deep space. Private enterprise will be a good steward of the ISS. They leverage the wealth of knowledge gained from over twenty years of humans calling this huge facility home and learning what manufacturing processes can be profitable in micro-gravity. Paying scientists take residence. The space tourism industry is flourishing with large BigSpace hotels served by the Colossus fleet of reusable commercial vehicles.

July 20, 2024- On the fifty-fifth anniversary of the historic Apollo 11 Moon landing, SpaceTrans sends the first crewed Colossus mission with paying passengers beyond LEO to orbit the Moon for ten days in Colossus ship *Copernicus*. The Colossus fleet of reusable heavy lift vehicles has been established in LEO but will become the future workhorse for transportation to deep space.

August 20, 2024- The *Aquila Mission* returned to Earth on this date. The mission sent a crew to deep space for thirteen months to study asteroid Bennu and comet 125P. The international mission was billed to pave the path to landing a crew on Mars. It took years to design and build Aquila, and to train the crew of two men and two women. Commander Coby Brewster influenced the selection of a crew with key abilities.

Pilot Vik Ivanov is a renowned aeronautical engineer. Abby Denton is a flight surgeon. Ellie Accardi is the mission astrogeologist. During their long mission planning and training, the crew's professional boundaries drop and relationships grow with sincere bonds of friendship growing to love and passion. Starting a family in space was unplanned but stuff happens. The crew had survived a major solar radiation storm but their birth control pills were rendered ineffective.

Coby and Ellie, Vik and Abby had planned to announce their wedding plans to the world when they returned. There was a more pressing need when Ellie and Abby revealed six month baby bumps during their return physical exams. Captain Johnson of the recovery ship USS *Anchorage* performed a double wedding at the crews return welcome ceremony in front of cameras broadcasting to the world.

Conservatives were aghast but the event spurred more interest in human space flight than the scientific success of the mission. Not only did government funding increase but private industry and investors spurred rapid technology development especially in asteroid mining for in situ resource utilization (ISRU). The search for and exploitation of water and metal resources on the Moon and asteroids pave the path to permanent human presence on the Moon and beyond.

Space Directive 1 of 2018 decreed the concept of the Lunar Orbital Platform-Gateway (LOP-G) as a staging center for deep space missions. It was temporarily preempted by the assembly of the *Altair* deep space vehicle staging at ISS. The *Aquila Mission* executed in *Altair* had proven to the world that human space flight was indeed ready to send a crew to Mars. It had proven that the crew could survive and thrive on a long duration mission in deep space- longer even than the six months it would take to send a crew to Mars.

June 30, 2025- The *Commercial Lunar Hab Module* establishes a lunar base at Taurus Littrow with the first commercial crew of landing for a six-month stay on the lunar surface. Also in 2025, commercial launches enabled the establishment of key astronomical observatories on the lunar far side with optical and radio telescopes forever shielded from interference from the Earth and her innumerable satellites broadcasting simultaneously. The rest of Moon was left to the commercial enterprise and BigSpace branded hotels were established for lunar tourism in 2026.

March 15, 2026- *Mars Sample Return Mission* brings back ten tube containers from the Mars 2020 Rover sample archive caches. The samples reveal the nature and concentration of strongly oxidizing perchlorates in Martian soil. Perchlorate (ClO 4 −) is widespread in Martian soils at concentrations approaching one percent. At such concentrations, perchlorate could be an important source of oxygen, but it could also become a critical chemical hazard to astronauts.[30]

This underscores the need for crew isolation from Martian soil and dust. This is planned to be accomplished where possible by using *suitports* to enter and exit their spacesuits. While the astronauts' suits must remain outside, quick entry/exit times of less than ten minutes are possible. The returned samples also facilitate development of procedures for scrubbing perchlorate from Martian soil and recover oxygen.

July 20, 2026- L2 *Deep Space Gateway* is established with the Tarazed habitat module from the *Aquila Mission*. A crew arrives to "repurpose" the habitat and deep clean it for new use.

2027- There is a permanent crew presence on the expanding Taurus Littrow lunar base. Robotic mining operations begin to extract water for propellants in permanently shaded craters at the lunar South Pole. Alumina[31] , silica, and lithium are mined at robotic mid-latitude bases. The propellants along with alumina, silica, and lithium are exported for the space construction market at low Earth orbit (LEO) and geostationary orbit (GEO). Major space vehicle, power, and habitat components are 3D printed

---

30 Davila, A., D. Wilson, J. Coates, and C. McKay, "Perchlorate on Mars: A chemical hazard and a resource for humans", International Journal of Astrobiology, 2013. Web accessed 9 Aug 2018.
https://www.researchgate.net/publication/242525435_Perchlorate_on_Mars_A_chemi cal_hazard_and_a_resource_for_humans

31 "What are the possibilities of refining aluminum on the Moon?" Chemistry/Stack Exchange, 1 Jan 2018, https://chemistry.stackexchange.com/questions/19687/what-possibilities-are-there-for-refining-aluminium-on-the-moon

from aluminum-lithium alloy[32] mined from the Moon (Lunar ore is 25% alumina). Solar electric pyrolysis reduces the metal. Silica is used to manufacture lightweight and efficient solar cells. Massive solar power stations are constructed in GEO with power beamed to Earth stations by microwaves.

Global warming and rising sea levels threaten coastal cities and historic launch sites at Cape Canaveral. Expensive, massive projects are undertaken to build sea walls to protect the most critical areas. Some cities and infrastructure are abandoned to the sea. Global warming climate shifts cause devastating droughts on once fertile farmlands and forests. Massive dust storms and firestorms are common. The world's population has swelled to 8.4 billion. Campaigns to control population growth fall on deaf ears. Cruel starvation and epidemics serve to keep further population growth in check.

July 14, 2027- The *Shiva* KBO is discovered to be on a trajectory to possibly impact the Earth in 2079. An emergency meeting of the United Nations directs a huge expansion of the *International Space Coalition* with a commitment to focus on establishing colonies on Mars. The Humans to Mars *Constellation Project* was tremendously accelerated. Mars is favored over the Moon because of its nearly unlimited water resources. The commitment is long term with planned exponential expansion to give the human race a second home.

Mars entry, descent, and landing (EDL) of large payloads had once been a huge technical challenge up until the early 2020s. Payloads of twenty, fifty, and over one hundred metric tons (MT) become possible using inflatable heat shields,

---

32 "Aluminum-Lithium Alloy," Web accessed 23 July 2018,
https://en.wikipedia.org/wiki/Aluminium-lithium_alloy

parachutes, and retrorockets. The first Mars Constellation fleet is powered by cheaper fuel launched to propellant depots by Colossus rockets. Colossus landings on Mars will supersede the Constellation fleet.

The least expensive propellant for deep space is manufactured by mining the C-class asteroid Ryugu. That asteroid has enough water bearing minerals to ultimately manufacture 500 million MT of hydrogen and oxygen propellant. Many other C-class asteroids are waiting to be harvested.

January 15-30, 2028- A global *Planetary Defense Conference* at Lawrence Livermore National Laboratory addresses the *Shiva* threat by planning to attempt to divert the one hundred kilometer beast with a ten gigaton (Gt) nuclear device,[33] one hundred times the yield of any H-bomb ever exploded on Earth. This is not the Hollywood *Armageddon* or *Deep Impact* scenario where astronauts need to bore into the threatening comet to plant nukes to break it up just before it impacts Earth.

The nudge from a huge nuclear device hitting *Shiva* in a high velocity tangential strike at a distance beyond Neptune has been modeled to be sufficient to give *Shiva's* trajectory a slight margin to miss the Earth. The *Shiva Diversion Mission* needs design and construction time. *Shiva Diversion Mission* ship *Vishnu* (the savior) is scheduled to launch in 2035 with a gravity

---

33 "Proceedings of the Planetary Defense Workshop Lawrence Livermore National Laboratory Livermore, California

May 22–26, 1995" Web accessed 19 July 2018.
https://web.archive.org/web/20150909023233/https://e-reports-ext.llnl.gov/pdf/232015.pdf

assist from Jupiter in 2036 for its fateful rendezvous with *Shiva* and precisely aimed detonation in 2044. The nuclear device will be traveling at 28 km/s velocity relative to *Shiva*, twice as fast as the New Horizons Mission rendezvous with Pluto.

The *Shiva* detonation rendezvous will be aimed at thirty seven AU from the Earth between the orbits of Neptune and Pluto. The ten gigaton explosion is calculated to give *Shiva* a 4.31 cm/s lateral shove that will become a 73,000 km deflection by the time it reaches Earth. That will be a near miss of only six times the diameter of Earth. If perfectly executed, this will ensure that *Shiva* will miss Earth. However, it will create a shotgun blast of debris that may impact Earth even if the main *Shiva* body misses. Added to that continued threat, the orbit calculations must be extremely precise to know that the deflection is changing the trajectory *away* from Earth.

The plan is a gamble at best. Regardless, the UN Security Council and General Body votes unanimously to execute the *Shiva Diversion Mission.* It is with hopes and prayers that ongoing observations of astronomical interferometry using Earth based ELT, the Webb JWST, and lunar far side telescopes will give the needed precision for the *Shiva* rendezvous nuclear detonation to have chance of success.

Mars will be almost one AU from Earth on February 28, 2079 when Shiva crosses Earth's path. *IF* everything goes according to plan, this should vastly reduce the chances of humanity's new second home being impacted by debris from the *Shiva Diversion* detonation.

2028 to 2029- Commercial enterprises launch a fleet of communication and GPS satellite to facilitate surface operations on Mars.

July 18, 2029- The orbiting *Mars Base Camp* habitat is established with a crew of four to stay until October31, 2030. The second crew is scheduled August 5, 2031 and expands the base camp and establishes a permanent presence on orbit. Return windows occur at Earth-Mars opposition every 26 months. The outpost construction will evolve to feature twin habitats telescoped out to a radius of 125 meters rotating around a central hub and stores bay. The thirty second rotation period will give the astronauts 0.5 g of centripetal acceleration for artificial gravity. The twin habs will connect to the hub with a one meter wide tunnel. The crew can traverse through to the hub in a tunnel on a simple ladder.

August 14, 2029- The *Bennu Mining Expedition* launches. Bennu mining operations, like those at Ryugu, produce liquid hydrogen (LH2), methane (CH4), and liquid oxygen (LOX) propellant from hydrated C-type asteroid minerals. The iron and aluminum oxide byproducts are powdered for 3D printing feedstock.

May 21, 2030- The first propellant is delivered to the L2 Deep Space Gateway depot. The *Tarazed* habitat there had been jettisoned from *Aquila* and nudged to the L2 Lagrange point to be repurposed for the Gateway space station. The first crew to reenter *Tarazed* was both awed by the history that had unfolded in the habitat but also daunted by the task of bringing back the new car smell to the hab that had been home to a crew of four for thirteen months.

January 15, 2031- Thirty-five colonists and crew are selected for the planned 2035 establishment of Mars Arcadia Colony. The original *Aquila* crew is chosen to lead off and organize the group of colonists. Once again, Coby Brewster is selected as Commander. The colonists must be a cross-section of disciplines, nationalities, and ages. Coby Brewster and Vik Ivanov are able pilots and engineers. Abby Denton is a veteran flight surgeon whose expertise saved Coby and Vik's lives more than once on the *Aquila Mission*. Ellie Accardi is the renowned astrogeologist who discovered fossil extraterrestrial life on asteroid Bennu. Coby and Ellie's daughter Sofi and Vik and Abby's son Alex are part of the package.

Otherwise, qualifications needed for consideration are space flight experience, and degreed experience in engineering (aerospace, mechanical, civil, electrical, chemical, nuclear, computer, and biomedical), medicine, planetary geology, astrobiology, agricultural science specializing in hydroponics, and psychology. Special consideration is given to combinations of these qualifications.

March 15, 2031- The selected Arcadia Base colonists are assembled for indoctrination and training that will last for the next four years. Four months of isolation with the full complement of colonists helped establish bonds and sought to weed out any misfits. This was an expanded version of the NASA HI-SEAS Isolation Missions. Three of the group voluntarily left and an additional four were asked to leave because of psychological impairment and incompatibility. This left twenty-one primary candidates and seven back-up candidates to go forward with training.

Beyond the HI-SEAS experience, the training went on endlessly to turn them into an efficient team trained to operate and maintain the Colossus ship, its cargo sky crane, base habitats, life support, and agriculture systems. Training ensured that skill sets were redundant. Each critical function was covered by several colonists in training and simulation.

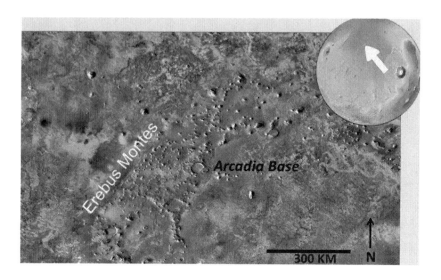

Diacria Quadrangle (MC-2) **Mars Arcadia Base** location 38.4°N 189.7°E. Erebus Montes area of Arcadia Planitia is 1500 kilometers northeast of Olympus Mons. The landing zone is on the east flank of *Golombek Crater* in post-glacial terrain with abundant near surface ice. NASA/JPL THEMIS and HiRISE imagery.

August 5-10, 2031- The Mars Arcadia Base is established with *Constellation* robotic landers including habitats, consumables in resupply modules, robotic construction equipment, and an advanced robotic lander slowly manufacturing ascent propellant for the first Colossus crew lander. The Sabatier Reactor is powered by a kilopower nuclear reactor. It manufactures methane and oxygen propellant for Earth return from Mars water ice and CO_2 harvested from the atmosphere. The robotic construction equipment constructs six landing pads from 3D printed sintered regolith for SpaceTrans Colossus ships first arriving in 2033. The landing pads are necessary to support the huge ships and prevent rocket exhaust from excavating the regolith and sending hypervelocity debris that might damage base infrastructure.

The Humans to Mars effort, funded by the *International Space Coalition,* is now expanded to include fifteen nations and space agencies from the original five that funded and operated the *Aquila Mission.*

April 4, 2033, the *Arcadia 1 Mission* Colossus ship *Arcturus* launches for the first crew landing on Mars. They will have a relatively short 174 day journey with this launch window.

April 28, 2033- Two robotic Colossus ships, *Pleiades* and *Alcyone* launch for Mars on a long 274 day journey to deliver supplies to expand Arcadia Colony Base and support the first crew. The landing is scheduled for January 27, 2034.

August 1, 2033- SpaceTrans has fully commercialized its Colossus services for colonization and has signed contracts. The next colony outside Mars Arcadia Colony Base, *New Kolob*, will be funded by the Mormon NDS, Church of the New Day Saints. The third, *al-Salam al-Jadid,* or New Peace, will be funded by the United Arab Nations. These colonies are planned to be established beginning in 2038.

SpaceTrans greatly expands its Colossus manufacture and launch capability. A launch facility is constructed near the shore of Dockweiler Beach at the edge of LAX so that ships rolling out of the LA plant don't have to be barged all the way to the Cape in Florida. A Colossus manufacturing facility is up and running on the Cape to feed that launch facility. Paired manufacture and launch facilities are planned for construction in Japan, Korea, China, India, and the UAE. The pace of off world colony building from many nations will be at a fever pitch in a few years.

September 29, 2033- The *Arcadia 1* Mission first Mars crew landing occurred on Arcadia Planitia in the Colossus ship *Arcturus.* The ten person international crew is led by Commander Trent Granger. He is recorded forever in the history books as the first human to set foot on Mars. This mission infrastructure laid the groundwork for the Mars Arcadia Colony. As reconnaissance predicted, the first crew has abundant ground water ice to generate precious water, oxygen, and propellant.

Arcadia Planitia has long been high on the list of accessible Mars water resources as revealed from the detailed mapping of the Mars Reconnaissance Orbiter data. The MRO orbit insertion was in October 2006 and it served until 2021. It was replaced by MRO II. The MRO high-resolution imagery shows primary evidence of near surface ice morphology accessible to landing in a relatively low latitude region of the planet at 39.8° north. Recent craters expose ice with little dust cover. However, the best evidence is detailed in the 2015 Bramson report. It shows that the Shallow Radar (*SHARAD*) sounder onboard the *Mars Reconnaissance Orbiter* provides evidence for a localized ten-meter thick ice layer in the Arcadia subsurface. Secondary evidence includes young impact craters with fluidized sediment in conspicuous flow patterns and hydrated minerals located from orbit with visible and infrared spectrometers.[34] The ice is not related to the polar ice caps. Mars once held vast lakes and a northern hemisphere ocean with conditions that existed for a billion years. The subsurface water in Arcadia Planitia is thought to be a remnant of the northern ocean.

Unlike Apollo missions to the Moon, unlike the initial robotic exploration of Mars, the overarching goal of landing crews on Mars was not solely for science exploration but to ensure the success of in situ resource utilization, crew survival, and expansion of surface infrastructure to a thriving colony. With this goal paramount, the first crew landings and first colony landings focused on the chosen landing zone in Arcadia Planitia where

---

34 Bramson, A. M., S. Byrne, N. E. Putzig, S. Sutton, J. J. Plaut, T. C. Brothers, and J. W. Holt, 2015, Widespread excess ice in Arcadia Planitia, Mars, Geophys. Res. Lett., 42, https://arxiv.org/abs/1509.03210

abundant water ice resources lay just below the surface. Landing sites separated by great distance as depicted in the classic movie *The Martian* could expand our science but not help support subsequent crews. There will be more than enough science to achieve with successful crew landings at the designated initial colony site. Mars science objectives will quickly follow with colony success and bootstrap knowledge gained from the first foothold.

January 27, 2034- The second robotic Colossus Mars supply ships *Pleiades* and *Alcyone* land to begin preparations for the first Mars Arcadia colony crew landing to expand Arcadia Colony Base and support the first crew that landed in September 2033. The supply ships landing, unloading, and infrastructure expansion is the focus for the next year of the *Arcadia 1* crew.

March 16, 2035- After nearly seven years of preparation, planning, and construction, the *Shiva Diversion Mission* ship *Vishnu* (the savior) launches with a ten gigaton (Gt) nuclear device to impact, detonate, and deflect the one hundred kilometer Kuiper Belt Object (KBO) *Shiva* from its possible extinction encounter with Earth in 2079.

May 8, 2035- The *Arcadia 1* Earth return window opens, and the Colossus ship *Arcturus* majestically lifts off from Mars with the propellant robotically manufactured from ice on Arcadia Planitia. The triumphant first crew to land on Mars on the *Arcadia 1* Mission returns to Earth on November 4, 2035 making a precise soft landing at the SpaceTrans Port at Cape Canaveral. After two weeks of quarantine, recovery, and medical tests, they are reunited with their families. Then they endured a two week world celebratory tour of parades and press conferences.

June 20, 2035- Two robotic Colossus Mars Arcadia colony supply ships, *Hyades* and *Aldebaran*, launch. They land at Arcadia

Colony Base December 17, 2035 three days before the colonists arrive. Each ship carries 150,000 kg payload to Mars. Cargo Modules are in two sizes: 2 m x 2m x 2m (8 cubic meters) and 4m x 8m diameter (201 cubic meters). The Supply Manifest includes: Inflatable habs; Consumables; Life support and replacement parts; Propellant manufacturing equipment; Solar Cell Farm; Nuclear Fission Power Plant; Industrial 3D Printers (one is a huge beast designed for construction using sintered regolith); Alumina; plastics stocks; wiring, connectors; controls; electric motors; Computers; Replacement modules; Solar panel arrays; Battery farms; Robotic back hoe for remote operation; (2)Two man pressurized rovers and replacement parts; Geology and Biology lab equipment; Medical equipment and supplies.

Alnath module—5 MT. The seed bank- tomatoes, strawberries, soybeans, potatoes (vodka), spinach, lettuce, radishes, barley, wheat, rye, hops (beer), sugar beets, corn, cryo-frozen fertilized chicken eggs-embryos, tilapia, catfish, pigs, sheep, goats, dairy cows, for times of plenty- frozen embryos dogs, cats, humans; Fertilizers, chemicals for neutralizing perchlorates, fertilizers for hydroponics; Antibiotics, vitamins, nutrition supplements, calcium, and iron

June 23, 2035- The Mars Arcadia Colony Colossus Ship *Taurus* with a crew of twenty-one colonists was launched. There are six married couples: the original *Aquila Mission* crew Coby Brewster and Ellie Accardi, Vik Ivanov and Abby Denton; from the *Aquila* backup crew Paul Earhart and Tracy Dixon; Satoshi Fukoshima and Megumi Hirakata, Trevor Brown and Mandy Shields, Harrison Frank and Eve Cain. The six single adults are Vik's son Oleg Ivanov, Elena Petrov and her son Jacob, Olga Sadoski, Dieter Schwartz, Sandy Conklin and Dao-Ming Cai. The two adolescents are Coby and Ellie's daughter Sophia and Vik and Abby's son Alexei. They were conceived in deep space during the Aquila Mission.

August 14-15, 2035- The Mars Arcadia Beta supply ships *Castor,* and *Pollux* and Colony Ship *Gemini* launch for Mars. The launch window is not optimal and the transit time is 276 days for the supply ships and 281 days for the colony ship with twenty one international colonists. Among the colonists is the well-known Jennings family. Sam and Paula Jennings are PhD Space Systems and Hab Engineers. Paula is the commander. Their daughter Tracy Jennings is eighteen and earned her BS in Astrobiology from Princeton.

December 21, 2035-The Colony Colossus Ship *Taurus* crew lands after a 181 day journey. The two new Colossus robotic supply landers *Hyades* and *Aldebaran* are there waiting to be unloaded. The colony has a primary store of twenty-seven months of supplies on the surface with emergency six month rations to cover a system breakdown. Additional emergency supplies can be delivered from the orbiting Basecamp. There is a scheduled Colossus supply run at each Earth-Mars opposition every twenty-six months. Any additional emergency supplies from Earth will take six to twenty-six months to deliver depending on the Earth-Mars configuration. The goal is for the colony to be nearly self-sufficient in growing food and manufacturing repair and replacement parts by 2045.

April 21, 2036- The *Shiva Diversion Mission* ship *Vishnu* (the savior) executes a precise close encounter with Jupiter to get a gravitational slingshot boost in speed towards its target, the KBO *Shiva*. The ship *Vishnu* carries a ten gigaton (Gt) nuclear device to impact, detonate, and deflect the one hundred kilometer diameter *Shiva* from its possible extinction encounter with Earth in 2079. The *Shiva* rendezvous detonation will be at 37 AU from the Earth between the orbits of Neptune and Pluto. The ten gigaton explosion is calculated to give *Shiva* a 4.31 cm/s lateral shove that will become a 73,000 km deflection by the time it reaches Earth.

2

THE PATH TO MARS

"Going to Mars could make us better humans. And we had to be better. When we eventually colonize Mars, ...then we need to do so as an enlightened species moving forward, not as panicked refugees clinging to survival by our fingernails."

Meg Howrey, The Wanderers, 2017

GNN Interviews of *Arcadia Colonists*
June 2-4, 2035

"This is GNN Space Correspondent Kate Turner here to interview some of the crew and colonists that were selected and have trained long and hard to go to Mars to finally establish the first colony at Arcadia Base. The *Arcadia 1* Mission paved the way with Commander Trent Granger being the first human to set foot on Mars. The ten person crew established the foundations of

Arcadia Base during their two year stay. Only nine returned. History will record that the time from 2023, with Aquila as the first mission beyond the Moon, 2025, with the first lunar base at Taurus Littrow, to 2035, with this first human colony on Mars, is the beginning of the diaspora of humans into the solar system. I have asked each person to be open, forthright, and honest with their interviews. We will censor any inappropriate material before this is broadcast. "

The idea of going to Mars has the almost universal appeal to every kid who dreamt of being an astronaut and going to space. But going to space is one thing, going to Mars is quite another. First, the length of the mission in isolation with a small crew takes an extraordinary person with the ability to withstand small spaces, lack of privacy, unpleasant odors, *and* keep a positive attitude indefinitely. Individuals had endured the test on Earth with two year isolation missions in remote places that simulated Mars. These isolation crews knew there was an end to the mission and they would go home. They also knew that if they reached a breaking point, they could call it quits and walk away. The first crews to land on Mars had endured more. Their missions in total lasted almost two and half years. Those crews could not call it quits and walk away. They also had something that no isolation crew or subsequent crews to Mars *could* have-- an honored place in the history books for being the first.

Signing up to be a colonist on Mars is another matter. Your place in the history books is a small footnote as an individual. You cannot walk away and go home. You are leaving behind friends, family, and everything dear and wonderful about Earth. The colonists accept that and that this does mark a turning point in our history. Colonizing Mars is inevitable and above all necessary for our long term survival as a species.

The International Space Coalition established guidelines for the selection of the members of the first Mars colony. Candidates should represent a balance of gender, age, and cultures. Possibilities of procreation were considered desirable but not critical for this small first colony. Others would soon follow to enlarge the established colonial base adding to the reproduction pool to maintain and grow the colony from within.

Qualifications needed for consideration are space flight experience, and degreed experience in engineering, medicine, planetary geology, astrobiology, agricultural science specializing in hydroponics, and psychology - especially combinations of these qualifications. Mark Watney, from the classic *The Martian,* on paper was only a botanist but his engineering and medical skill set and resourcefulness went far beyond the botanist title.

The applicant short list of forty persons was required to submit a one-thousand word essay on why they wanted to colonize Mars, what made them qualified, what they as an individual could offer, and what it meant to leave the Earth, family, and friends. They are required to submit to a psych profile and a polygraph test. They are required to submit ten recent references from persons who knew the individual for at least five years. A panel from the Coalition reviewed these documents and their recommendations were reviewed by the lead colonists Coby Brewster, Ellie Accardi, Vik Ivanov, and Abby Denton. The selected colonists were assembled in 2032 for indoctrination and training.

Coby Brewster

"The world is eagerly watching and wanting to hear from this first group of colonists. We all want to get to know you better as you leave the Earth for another world. Commander Brewster, I'll ask you first. How did you find your way to space and now on your way to Mars?"

Me? I was practically born with wings. My dad and two uncles were Army Air Corp aviators in WWII. Dad had me on his lap behind the yoke of his small Piper Cub when I was two.

I don't directly remember the hyperbole years of Apollo. I wasn't even born when Neil Armstrong and Buzz Aldrin set foot on the Moon. I was only one when human exploration of the Moon came to a standstill as Apollo 17 departed in December 1972.

I received my MS from Stanford the same year Dad passed from a massive heart attack. He'd always been a smoker. Certainly that shortened his life but he lived it as if each day was a joy to be cherished. Family was everything to him.

Out of ROTC, I joined the Air Force full time. I learned to pilot the most advanced jet fighters going. Aside from combat training, I trained on the mechanics and avionics. I sometimes worked alongside the aircraft mechanics. I fancied I could fix most anything I flew.

I met Ellen when I was at Ellington. I was a shy fly-boy at first. Ellen would describe me as five feet eleven inches, brown hair, green eyes, and needing some serious romantic attention. She was the first thing in my life that I found more beautiful than a sleek airplane. Through our short engagement, she thought that pilots were flashy and sexy. I did my best to live up to that ideal. After six months of marital bliss, we were transferred to Edwards AFB in the remote desert of southern California. She reluctantly endured being a pilot's wife at Edwards as I stepped up the ranks as a Test Pilot/Flight Engineer.

I read the call for NASA astronaut applicants on a notice board on the base. I threw my hat in the ring with my NASA application. I thought I had winning qualifications but I was coached to curb my enthusiasm on the interview. I got the call and joined the 1996 NASA Group 16 astronaut recruits. I flew three missions to ISS and did nine EVAs. Those were the best things I have done in my life up till then but there was collateral damage. I didn't slow down enough to say yes to have children with Helen. She was diagnosed with breast cancer just after I returned from my mission in 2012. Ellen died three years later. I was alone with my NASA career in the Commercial Crew Program waiting for the call serve on another mission.

Then along came *The Aquila Mission*. We were a crew of four: two men, Vik Ivanov and me, and two women Ellie Accardi and Abby Denton. We started as professionals at arm's length. This grew to friendship and camaraderie, then to passion, love, and marriage-- Ellie to me and Abby to Vik. With Ellie and Abby six months pregnant when we were recovered on the *USS Anchorage* after *Aquila*, we moved up our weddings to the moment before we faced the cameras welcoming us back to Earth. The ship's captain was more than happy to perform a quick ceremony to maintain our honor.

Aquila was the most demanding mission imaginable. It consumed eight years of our lives and added over four hundred days of microgravity and hard radiation exposure to the butcher's bill. In space, trying to sleep with my eyes closed, we get the occasional blue-white fireworks flash in one eye or the other. This is the very real effect of cosmic rays striking my retinas.

Aquila nearly killed Vik twice and me once. Abby's expertise as a doctor brought us back from the brink But Aquila gave life back to me. It gave me my wife Ellie, my crew mate, and our precocious space child Sofi. Vik and Abby are closer than family. Aquila brought them together and gave them a son named Alex.

After *Aquila*, aside from the joys of family, our lives were busy with consulting on planning for a future run at sending a crew to Mars. It all seemed so nebulous without a firm mission mandate and time commitment. Then there was the panic of 2027 with the discovery of Shiva, the KBO from beyond Pluto that could destroy all life on Earth. On *Aquila*, we studied asteroid Bennu that has a one in eighteen hundred chance of impacting Earth in 2192. *Shiva*, that damned ball of ice and rock, is a million times the mass of Bennu. It has a one in fifty chance of hitting Earth in 2079 with three times the velocity of Bennu. I won't be alive to witness that but I don't want my family to be at risk. Now we have the opportunity to give humanity a new start on a new world by establishing a colony on Mars. Becoming interplanetary is to guarantee the long term survival of our species. That's *everything*. That's why we're going. Going to Mars will be the greatest adventure humankind has ever undertaken.

My *Aquila* crew mates are closer than family. I'm sixty-five and Ellie and Abby are fifty-one. Vik is the old man just older than me at sixty-six. I can't imagine a more qualified, reliable, and loving group to be the foundation of a colony. We are giving the rest of our lives to this colony. But, God, do we have the right to ask our children, Sofi and Alex, just eleven, to give everything to be with us on Mars? They're coming willingly and enthusiastically but I can't help but feel guilt for taking their innocent lives on this beautiful Earth and trading that for the harsh reality of Mars. We have to stay focused on the goal of making a viable colony off Earth for the survival of humankind. The science and engineering spinoffs will be incalculable as we explore Mars and open the door beyond.

We have trained now for four years with the rest of the crew and colonists. There have been some tough struggles and conflicts. The problem individuals have washed out or could be cut in the final selection due to happen next week. I'm really impressed with the diverse abilities and sincere bonds of friendship we've grown in this group.

Among the Arcadia colonists are Elena Petrov and my son Jacob Petrov. Elena is a very qualified and gregarious FKA cosmonaut. When I was in a funk after Ellen died, Elena filled my emptiness and we spent a few days and nights of passion as *Aquila* was ramping up and Ellie and I were still at arm's length. Elena and I didn't communicate for years. On ISS, just before we blasted off for *Aquila*, Elena revealed to me that she'd had our son Jacob. I was stunned and joyful at the same time. When I told Ellie, she was jealous and hurt as expected. Now with Elena and Jacob as a part of our colony family, we have worked hard together on training. The improbable situation now seems natural. Jacob is now eighteen. He's a very dedicated and talented pilot and budding mechanical engineer. He won't shy away from any challenge. Elena, now fifty-four, has given strength and comfort to many in the colony group as we trained. She's been professionally pleasant with me but very aloof with Ellie. I know it's awkward for both of them but I don't want this to grow into something worse.

We missed Earth desperately on the thirteen months of *Aquila*. Now we see the ravages of rising sea level, floods, drought, and famine brought on by global warming. Rising sea levels have already claimed hundreds of the world's coastal communities, and now major cities—New York, Shanghai, Venice—are being threatened. We are ready to make this voyage and give our lives to it. How can we dare to take our children and families to Mars? I turn that around and say, with the threat from *Shiva*, how can we not?

The first ten that have already landed on Mars have paved the way for us at *Arcadia Base*. An *Arcadia 1* crewman lost his life but that incident taught us to find a fix to the damned thing that killed him. That fix could save the entire colony if a similar accident cost us losing life critical equipment.

Ellie Accardi

I was adopted and my adopted parents were always wrapped up in University of Naples affairs as professors. There was little time or affection spent on me but don't shed any tears for me. I found my true friends at the very same University where my parents were faculty. My oceanography professor, Dr. Tony Siriano, became like a father to me. He took me and other students fishing from the Miseno Marina Napoli. Dr. Siriano landed a grant from AGIP Petroleum, now ENI, of Milan, Italy. That enabled Tony to buy deep diving submersible time in the Gulf of Mexico to study oil seeps and associated chemosynthetic communities. Dr. Siriano included student interns in his grant proposal. Three other students and I were invited to participate in the project. I got paid to go on research cruises in the Gulf of Mexico with the famous Sea-Link submersibles! The grant focused on studying seeps on AGIP's deep-water oil exploration leases.

I have always been interested in the riddles of geology and how intertwined it is with biology on Earth. My passions were fed by doing submersible research on chemosynthetic communities of life living on oil and gas seeps in the Gulf of Mexico. How could I leverage my experiences and get my ass to space to pursue astrogeology? I took stock and decided that my stuff, I felt it was the *right stuff*, could someday get me into ESA as an astronaut. I joined the *Aeronautica Militare* or Italian Air Force after I finished my Masters in Geology. I trained to fly fighter jets and requested transfer to the *Gruppo Sistemi Spaziali* or Space Systems Squadron. I applied to be an astronaut candidate in 2008 along with ten thousand other people. Of that huge crowd, I was officially selected as an astronaut to join the 2009 ESA Group!

After years of training and doing mundane Earth based assignments, I got my first mission assignment to ISS. The nearly two-hundred day ISS mission was even more demanding than training but infinitely more rewarding. For a few years, I held the longest mission record for a woman in space. Most of my mission was dedicated to studying Earth's geology by remote sensing.

I rose to the rank of Captain in the Italian Air Force. When the opportunity to apply for the *Aquila Mission* to send a crew to a carbonaceous asteroid and a comet, I was at the front of the line with my qualifications and expectations. Wow! I got the mission! It was a very arduous journey of training and preparation. Nothing could have prepared me for what we discovered and what we found in each other. I came back with Coby as my husband and expecting with Sofi. That wasn't planned! God, how could we conceive in space and have my Sofi fetus exposed to hard radiation for six months without her being deformed? Miracles do happen. I suspect that the amniotic fluid was a good radiation filter as is anything with lots of hydrogen like water and plastics. I think Abby agrees on that. She experienced the same roller coaster coming back married to Vik and pregnant with Alex.

Since *Aquila*, I have been directing the exploration of Mars' geology, or areology the term coined by Kim Stanley Robinson, at NASA. This has entailed putting our colony in geologic context with what is known from other robotic and crew landing sites. What concrete samples do we have from Mars? Rare meteorites have been proven by chemical assay to have originated from Mars! These have been ejected by past impacts and orbited to land on Earth by chance. My studies have bolstered the assertion by astrogeologists in 1996 that fossil life possibly had been found in Martian meteorite ALH 84001. My dream is that our colony exploration will find fossil evidence of extinct life perhaps from a long dried up, ancient Mars lake. Better yet we could find extant, yes living, Martian life from subsurface samples! The most recent estimate of the mass of the Earth's subsurface biosphere is about ten percent of the surface biosphere.[35] So why couldn't life thrive in the warmer subsurface of Mars?

Fellow colonists Trevor Brown and Mandy Shields are my protégé astrobiologists. They play a dual role leading the development of the colony's greenhouse aquaponics effort. What is aquaponics? It offers the best of growing highly productive crops such as sugar beets with water and nutrients that will also support tilapia fish stocks. I'm imagining fish and chips on Mars![36]

The passionate experiences we had in *Aquila* training gave me a deeper love for planet Earth: the experience of living underwater on a coral reef; the deep sea fishing and fury of a sudden storm; the primal nature of Florida just fifty kilometers from the Cape. Now with all the human-caused threats and the specter of *Shiva* destroying all life here, I must be part of the first Mars colony to give me, my family, and my descendants a chance to live and thrive on another planet. Not only will we give everything of ourselves to save humanity, but we'll carry a seed and embryo bank that could someday restart many forms of precious Earth life. We're committed to being the nucleus of a growing colony and culture on Mars. Our lives, our children, and perhaps the future of humankind depend on it.

Vik Ivanov

---

35 Onstott, P.C. et al, "Paleo-Rock-Hosted Life on Earth and the Search on Mars: a Review and Strategy for Exploration", Earth and Planetary Astrophysics, Sept. 2018, Web accessed 28 Sept 2018. arXiv:1809.08266 [astro-ph.EP]

36 Reilly, James, "Mark Watney should have had Fish and Chips," Presentation to AAPG Total Solar Eclipse Seminar, 2017, Casper, WY.

I am Viktor Yegoravich Ivanov from Turkmenistan, formerly USSR. I suppose I am the most famous and *only* Turkmen cosmonaut. I am very proud of my roots from this country on the eastern shore of the Caspian. My father and uncle used to take me sturgeon fishing every summer off Turkmenbashi in the Caspian. The truth is I never liked the fishing. I just wanted to fix things-- boats, cars, and airplanes. It's hard to speak of my father and uncle without mentioning that both of them flew jets in the Soviet Air Force. I never followed them into the Air Force but their wings got me dreaming of flying and space.

I did not need to be in the military to follow my dream of going to space. I received my mechanical engineering degree studying at the Kharkiv Aviation Institute. I was selected as a cosmonaut candidate and had my training at the Gagarin Cosmonaut Training Center. I never did get to fly to fix the Mir. My three expeditions to space before *Aquila* were to construct the International Space Station. I spent almost two years in space and performed four EVAs constructing and fixing ISS.

Life and habitat real estate were much different on ISS compared to *Aquila* and the new Mars colony effort. ISS is an international effort but every module was constructed, owned, and maintained by a different nation. On ISS, a problem in life support on a USA module was a USA problem to fix. The *International Space Coalition* changed that. All *Coalition* members and hardware are together for the whole of the mission. A problem with one system is the problem of the entire crew.

My extensive ISS experience earned me the opportunity to join the *Aquila Mission*! *Bo-zeh moy!* The training and design phase was endless. The mission was demanding at every turn. That damn asteroid fried me with electricity! Things break. I fix. Then the damned comet samples poisoned Coby and me. My Abby saved us. She's the best doctor ever sent to space.

Abby, *lyubov moya*, we never meant to get pregnant but stuff happens. I wanted to marry Abby from the time we were together in Key West. Now she has given me another son, Alex. Oleg will be a good big brother. The last time I went fishing on the Caspian was with my son Oleg when he was twelve. It's a tradition I must uphold. Oleg must be like me even though he has his mother Katerina's red hair. He hates fishing also. Oleg is now age forty-one. He studied Aeronautical Engineering in university in Moscow. He followed my footsteps to become a cosmonaut and now join Ellie, Alex, and me on an expedition to Mars. I like that dream. It has been a joy to work with Oleg in the Mars colony training. He makes me proud. His has good common sense and has a deep understanding of how all of our complex systems work. We'll make a good team.

Mars. *Bo-zeh moy!* Gods! We are really training and preparing to go there. What can go wrong? Anything and everything and I'll be there to fix it. Even though I'm seventy now, I have more experience than anyone to keep this colony going. I have a lot of *space* left in me. The Colossus is a good bird- proven on robotic and crewed Mars landings. We have all our eggs in this bird just like the *Coalition* depended on Soyuz to get to ISS for so many years. Unloading the Colossus with a sky crane has already proven deadly. We have to do this safer and better. Then comes the struggle with setting up habs and life support and keeping it all running. If there are any hiccups-- people die.

My Abby and her team of medics can work miracles but the machines must work to keep us alive. The good Earth is sick and in peril. We have to make Mars work in a big way. Who knows where we'll be in a hundred years?

Abby Denton

68

I was born in South Bend, Indiana near the St. Joe River. I grew up water skiing on the river with my family and friends. We also used to go climb the huge sand dunes at Warren Dunes State Park. Dad says, "Let's conquer Tower Hill!" One step up and slide back three-fourths of that. When I got to the top of the huge dune, I was totally winded. Dad was always demanding and dominating. But I reveled in the sun with the west wind in my hair. I pretended I could fly as I ran headlong down the steep face. I suppose those flying dreams, my fascination with astronomy, and a tomboy's fascination for squishy biology things got me to space.

Mom and Dad fed my interest in astronomy by getting me an eight inch telescope for Christmas when I was fifteen. The Moon and Mars were my favorites to observe. I could visit them someday! I could pinpoint the Apollo 11 landing site near the crater Moltke on the Sea of Tranquility. The opposition of Mars in 1997 got me excited. I could see the white Mars polar caps waning and the iconic dusky Syrtis Major that looks like India. The Mars Pathfinder mission and Sojourner rover landed that summer on the fourth of July. I thought, I could be there with the first crew landing in my lifetime! Who knew that such a dream could come true?

Sally Ride, as America's first woman in space, inspired me and showed me that it was possible for a girl to become an astronaut. Another inspiration was Mae Jemison, the first woman doctor in space. My passion for biology would be my ticket.

I studied biology and medicine at Johns Hopkins in Baltimore. I spent my residency program there and got involved in hyperbaric medicine. That helped bolster my resume. I answered the call for NASA Group 20 astronaut recruits. I had out grown Dad's domineering presence that usually kept me being shy and self-conscious--but not now. It seemed like an eternity of holding my breath but I got the call for interviews and medicals. I took my self-confidence with me. I was in!

I trained harder than any of my fellow recruits. I tried, maybe too hard, to make myself indispensable in spaceflight physiology. I find ISS exercise equipment a grind but it's a very necessary routine for long duration space flight in microgravity. I developed a system to combine the treadmill, cycle, and resistance exercise range of benefits into a single integrated system that involves the user in a VR simulation on an Earthscape that gets the blood moving! These improvements will helped keep us fit on the long duration *Aquila Mission*.

During *Aquila*, I proved my skills as an astronaut and doctor in two life threatening incidents. At Bennu, during an EVA I was conducting with Vik, a huge electrical discharge from the asteroid knocked out Vik and his MMU. No time to be timid. My quick action rescued Vik and my skills as a physician saved him. This is what we train for. My actions came from training and not emotion.

At comet 125P, Ellie and I rescued Coby and Vik after they were overcome with cyanide and formaldehyde fumes from comet samples that were not properly sealed and stowed. I believe I saved all of us by doing a controlled atmosphere dump. I administered the cyanide antidote just in time to bring Coby and Vik back from the brink. I'm not bragging, just explaining how important training is to handling a medical emergency. I will need a handful of medics and more physicians to keep us going on Mars. It won't be like a trip to the corner store. Every moment could bring a disaster to sort out. I trust that Vik and his team can fix the machines. I have to fix the people.

The ultimate challenges were faced during *Aquila*. Aside from the emergencies, Ellie and I got pregnant because the radiation nuked our birth control. Sex on *Aquila* was a natural need of two single men and two single women giving themselves to the most stressful mission imaginable. Sex was not expressly forbidden, just not talked about. The first symptoms of pregnancy were raging morning sickness for Ellie and me. Coby and Vik helped keep us hydrated and cleaned up. Vomiting in space is not pretty. We were so afraid that we would give birth to freaks or miscarry with all the hard radiation that we could not avoid. We could not abort with the facilities I had on Aquila. We could have faced late term abortion if we found out the worst when we got back. But we got green lights from our Earth-side doctors.

We all had a long ordeal adjusting to Earth gravity after thirteen months in microgravity. We had swollen legs and ankles. Heaven is life in an 87 degree swimming pool and 96 degree hot tub! We still had to keep up treadmill exercise to get back to normal. We all had some vision affects from microgravity. Our eyes were slightly misshapen from excess eye pressure called ocular hypertension. For Coby, Ellie and I, this was temporary. For Vik, there is a permanent issue in his retina with choroidal folds in the space between the retina and the optic nerve. He's far from blind but we will have to monitor it. This has happened with a few individuals coming home from long duration stays on ISS. It's not a show stopper for Vik. Nothing could stop my big Russian spaceman from going to Mars.

After three months back on Earth, Ellie delivered Sofi and I had my perfect Alex. The odd thing is that our babies were born underweight in the tenth percentile but long in the ninety-fifth percentile. Their early development was way above average. Now we can say that Sofi and Alex are exceptionally gifted. Ellie and I agree that our amniotic fluid shielded our babies from radiation to some degree. This is a first sample of human conception in space. We still have huge challenges to nurture a healthy growing colony.

An even bigger challenge for me was recovering physically and emotionally from my wounds in the Abu Dhabi terrorism incident after we returned from *Aquila*. It was all over the news so I won't burden you with that story now.

It will be important that we all stay fit to stave off the effects of not being in Earth's gravity and subject to high exposure to hard radiation. I have to keep us all going on the four Mars elastomeric active resistance VR exercise units, or MARED, that I developed. They will be on the Taurus on the six month outbound journey and then we'll move them into the Arcadia colony rec hall. I preach that using MARED is as important for individual mental health as well as for maintaining fitness in the weak 0.4 g Martian gravity. The VR system has over one thousand Earthscapes and Marscapes to explore while exercising.

There'll be no shortage of medical emergencies on Mars. I'll manage that but I'd rather put my skills as an OB-GYN to good use delivering babies. We'll have five fertile couples to start with on Mars. In total, seven of our colonists are women of childbearing age and have consensually committed to having babies on Mars either with a husband or through artificial insemination. That part will play out from donations within the colony when the time comes. Likewise, all of our colonists are committed to doing their share of time in a daycare and in teaching roles. God, we have a beautiful group! This is the most exciting phase of exploration in human history.

Sophia Accardi-Brewster and Alexei Denton-Ivanov

They call us Sofi and Alex, the space twins. We're practically sister and brother, the first humans conceived in deep space. That wasn't supposed to happen. The doctors expected that we would be born freaks. Experiments with mice on ISS proved that probability. As far as I can tell, we proved them wrong. I have ten fingers and ten toes. We're going on eleven and people say we're beyond gifted whatever that means. The only freaky thing that gets me teased is that I am almost a head taller than my classmates at Bay Area Charter Elementary. Alex and I are both in the 99th percentile for height and I'm still two inches taller than he is. I was born first and I don't let Alex forget that. I have my father's brown hair and green eyes. Alex has his father's sandy hair and brown eyes. Sometimes when I remember he's not my brother, he's my best friend and I think he's really cute. Don't tell him I said that!

When our parents returned from the *Aquila Mission* in 2024, they were heroes. They had gone farther and longer than any previous crew. The discoveries they made at their asteroid and comet shook up the scientists and the religious. Kids call Mom the *Bug Monster Queen* because she found the fossil on Bennu. They brought back that gnarly fossil that proved that there is or *was* life beyond the Earth. What world it came from and what happened to that world is a question that still begs an answer. Maybe I can help find an answer someday.

Our parents were at the top of the list to lead the first Mars colony. They were way involved in selecting our group of colonists back in in 2031 when Alex and I were just six. Our parents told the *Coalition* that if they were going to colonize Mars, bringing the family is a package deal. Jees, we were excited when they told us. Don't tell but I even wet myself! Now some days I have my doubts. I have my friends and I love this planet and all the animals on it. I love the rain. I love rainbows and sunsets!

What will it be like on Mars? I know we can still keep in touch with Earth on Facebook. Our hab computer library will have any kind of vid and music we could want. Netflix, Hulu, MangaJam, YouTube, it's pretty much endless. But I'm really into all the stuff we have learned about Mars since the Viking landers. Did they find life? The MRO II and ExoMars orbiters give us lots of detail on the geology around or Arcadia Base. The Curiosity and Mars 2020 rovers put me right there on Mars. I really can't wait to go scouting in our pressurized Mars Exploration Rover!

The Mars opposition back in 2033 was way cool through my telescope! Mars was closer than it's been since way back in 2018 but without the huge dust storm that covered it then.

The training has been long and hard. I, I guess I'm ready to go… The isolation training was a drag but Mars should be so much better. The geology training we've had does get me excited for Mars. We did day long hikes into Meteor Crater and the Grand Canyon in Arizona. Volcanic Sunset Crater near Flagstaff is another world!

People say that Alex and I finish each other's thoughts and sentences. I'll let him tell the rest of the story.

Sofi's my best friend. I'm glad she's not really my sister. But, Jees, when she looks me in the eyes and smiles, I, I don't know what to think. One bully kid called Sofi's Mom the *Bug Monster Queen* and made her cry. I punched him so hard in the gut that he fell down with the wind knocked out of him. The others backed off and pretty much didn't bully us anymore after that.

Yeah, that was a kick when Dad told me we were going to Mars! He said that we had a lot of studying to do to get ready. He wasn't kidding. I eat the stuff up. Sofi and I are into robotics, computers, electronics, and everything that makes a space hab work. I teach her a bunch of hardware stuff and she tries to get me excited about helping her find life on Mars.

Mom pushes us out to go be kids. We have a lot to get into. Sofi and I spend a lot of time in our pool. Space Dads Vik and Coby taught us how to snorkel then we graduated to scuba in the pool. I'll never forget the first time I put the regulator in my mouth and let myself sink below the surface. It was calm and serene. I closed my eyes and I was weightless-- floating in space! Sofi and I will be there soon!

We belong to the Taylor Lake Yacht Club. There are a lot of NASA kids there. We bike over there for boating and tennis. We can check out a boat for sailing and fishing in Taylor Lake. Sometimes while we are sailing, Sofi sidles up next to me in the Sunfish cockpit. I don't let that go to my head. I can beat the pants off Sofi in tennis.

Some of our family vacations have been really cool. Mom and Dad say that the water sports will help get us ready for space. We went to Eleuthera in the Bahamas and got some open water time snorkeling and scuba diving. It's awesome to be weightless and move freely in 3D. Closer to home, we take a charter boat out a hundred miles into the Gulf and dive on the Flower Gardens reefs. Mostly this is scuba, but we also have used Sea-Flea three man subs. Dad let Sofi and me take turns being pilot. I took the sub down the wall to six hundred feet! We saw a grouper that was darn near as big as the sub.

We had our HI-SEAS[37] training last year. I was amazed at the natural beauty of Hawaii. The deep blue of the ocean gives way to such a lush green paradise in the lowlands. HI-SEAS is a Mars Simulation Habitat on the Mauna Loa volcano on the Big Island at about 2500 meters above the ocean. They say the basaltic lava is like some areas on Mars. Jees! Our Arcadia Base will be over 1500 kilometers northeast of Olympus Mons, the biggest volcano in the solar system. Arcadia is more shaped by glaciers than volcanoes. It's all about lots of ice. Okay, we did get

---

37 NASA HI-SEAS Isolation Missions. HI-SEAS, is an acronym for Hawaii Space Exploration Analog and Simulation.

to feel what isolation with our small colony group will be like. Sofi and I spent more time together than ever. We geeked out on a robot we've been working on. There were some rough spots with other colonists but mostly our parents came through as leaders and smoothed things out.

Since HI-SEAS, Sofi and I often take our trail bikes out to Robinson Park for a picnic. Once she looked me in the eyes and I knew she was going to kiss me. In moments like this I swear she's in my head and we mind-share thoughts and feelings. I returned her thought and kissed her on the cheek first. We shared that it felt like, like…

Sofi interjected giggling "Tickly fireworks!"

Alex blushed, "Yeah, like tickly fireworks! Now the whole world knows."

Sofi and Alex personal diary:

In that instant and not in the interview, Sofi's thoughts came to me that she's glad I'm not her brother! In that moment we could see our path into the future with our grandchildren in a growing Mars civilization. Without saying a word, we both just laughed. I can't get enough of sitting in the green grass with Sofi under blue sky and warm sun before we leave for Mars.

Elena Petrov

These are my thoughts in my head and will not be recorded in any diary or divulged to that media bitch Kate Turner. I'll give her a sweet interview tomorrow.

I never thought I would find hate in my heart. It grew slowly and now it's a focus and passion that feeds me. I can freely say to myself that I hate Rafaela Accardi. I can't bring myself to call her Ellie. That name is an endearment between her and my *medved* Coby. The first time I saw him at Baikonur over twenty years ago

I knew I needed his seed to give me a son. I played it slow over the years then we had a steamy one-nighter that I claimed meant nothing. I got into his head and we hooked up again a year later. Coby was unaware that my timing was perfect. I was ripe for his seed. We parted as casual lovers. I had conceived his son, Jacob. I didn't tell him for over five years. I dropped the announcement when he was leaving on the *Aquila Mission* with *that* woman. I know that the news threw him and hurt that woman…

I have been a good mother and role model for Jacob. I'm an even better cosmonaut. My selfless willingness to act for Russia lies dormant. My involvement with Commander Coby Brewster before *Aquila* was part my desire and part the suggestion of the FKA. Coby gave me my son Jacob and now we both have a place on the *Arcadia Colony Expedition*.

I am not a spy, but in a test of allegiance, I will faithfully support and die for Russia and FKA over the *Coalition*. My past is deeply hidden and unknown to the *Coalition*. I so vividly remember my few months back in 2006 in *Kazan State School* where we trained in allegiance, social etiquette, manipulation, assassination, and kompromat. A friend from that school, Masha Butinovich, was only eighteen but she excelled in her tradecraft. Masha made headlines in 2018 when she was arrested for influencing election campaign PACs with massive illegal piles of laundered Russian money.

I would prefer to believe that my affair with Coby Brewster that resulted in my pregnancy was managed from my need to have a baby and to have the best genes possible for my future cosmonaut. I am not sorry for that. Jacob is innocent of my plan and he is the best caliber of cosmonaut. Not only am I fiercely proud of him, but Coby shows his pride as they have bonded during our Mars training.

Jacob Petrov

I grew up on the Baikonur Star City astronaut housing compound. I have always called my mother Mama Elena. Her lover, Anatoli, became like a father to me in the time that he was around until I was about six. He took me up flying in a *Yak-130* a few times when I was five. It's an advanced training aircraft that's able to replicate the characteristics of several fifth generation fighters. I'll never forget the feeling of the g-forces on take offs and banks and rolls. Anatoli must have arranged a booster seat and some special adapter to harness me in. As near as I can remember, he left us shortly after Elena came back from her first long stay on ISS. I do remember that they fought. I think Anatoli screwed things by sneaking off with a pretty engineer while Elena was on orbit. There are no secrets in such a small community. I don't have fond memories of school in Star City. I'm smart and got top grades. I have worked hard for the role I've earned as a member of this Mars colony. I think my focused hard work distanced me from any real friends. Some started calling me bastard because it was known that my real father is the American spaceman Coby Brewster. He was world famous as the commander of the *Aquila Mission*. God, I swelled with pride watching the vids of that mission when they were up. I always knew I was headed for space and to make that destiny possible, I had to excel in school. I got my BS in aeronautical engineering at sixteen and my MS at eighteen. Elena saw to it that I got into flight school. I got my wings about the same time that I finished my master's thesis on propulsion systems. I was already in cosmonaut training at Yuri Gagarin Institute when Mama Elena got the call to apply for the first Mars colony. Actually we applied together knowing that we might have a shot at going together. A colony not only needed talent, it needed family. I was trying to imagine a girl my age joining the colony so we could live happily on Mars. Going stag is not my ideal for happiness but I'll take it as it comes. After the colony group and alternates were selected, we went for our first two months of isolation training. They tried to shake out the misfits during isolation. There's a lot of talent. I'm truly impressed by the mix of professionals in our small group. We have to make Mars our world and fix anything that Mars tries to break. Where is that girl of my dreams? Sandy Conklin looks hot but she is eight years older than me. We're good friends and sometimes lately I think she looks at me like she's interested. What doesn't square with that is that it seems she's tight with Dao-Ming from China.

But, I've painted this sad puppy dog picture of Jacob Petrov going to Mars. Things get better. Six months ago, we had joint isolation training with the Arcadia Beta colonists who will join us on Mars a few months after we get there. My hopes for this colony venture skyrocketed when we were first introduced to Commander Paula Jennings, her husband Sam, and their beautiful daughter Tracy. Tracy has short brunette hair with adorable bangs and deep, dark brown eyes that swallowed me whole. Since I knew the ropes on the isolation habs, I took Tracy for a tour. A few days later, we had gotten to know each other better. We found ourselves alone in a quiet corner. I put my arms around her and she warmed to me as I kissed her. In that instant I saw stars and thought my heart would beat out of my chest. It's going to be too many long months until we see each other again on Mars.

Oleg Ivanov

I am Oleg Ivanov, son of the great Vik Ivanov, pilot and flight engineer on the *Aquila Mission*. That record breaking mission was a proud accomplishment for Russia and especially our home of Turkmenistan. I was already a young cosmonaut when Papa flew *Aquila*. I am now age forty-one and thought I would still be single when we leave for Mars for the same reason that Mama Katarina left Papa. But alas, Olga Sadoski and I will be married next week! Olga was on the backup crew for *Aquila* so I have known her casually since Papa trained for that mission. Our Arcadia training brought us closer together and our chemistry grew. Being married to Olga seems so obvious and natural. Why didn't we find each other ten years ago?

I hardly knew Papa Vik since he went to space on ISS the first time. All his time was mission training or being up there for months on months. I'm sure this is why Mama broke from him. Mama left him long before *Aquila* and then there was the long seven year grind of training for that special mission. I missed Papa through most of my teen years. I do fondly remember the last time we went fishing on the Caspian when I was twelve. We laughed because we both hate the thought of hurting the fish. Since that time I grew up with Mama Katarina in Moscow.

Mama Katarina's brother, Uncle Peter, became more like a father to me. He was retired from the Navy as a submarine Commander. This made an impression on me, how it was honorable to be in military service. At eighteen, I was going to sign up for the Navy until Papa Vik found out. He had a long man-to-man talk with me about our destiny in space. He pulled strings to get me into the Aerospace Academy in Moscow where I was supported and sheltered by Mama Katarina.

I was foundering there until I met my flight instructor Natasha. I'm about average height at 1.8 meters, have a rock hard body, and some say rugged good looks favoring Papa Vik. At first, Natasha was not interested in me romantically but took a strong interest in my studies. She even tutored me in calculus. From then on, I never felt I was worthy of her. But, I was smitten with her and would fantasize being in bed with her. We did have a romance despite my feelings of inferiority. I was briefly married to Sasha during university but she left me for another engineer in my senior year. Maybe I should have lavished her more with flowers and affection than keeping my nose always in the books. Ah, so after that space was my mistress.

After University, I worked on Soyuz production and quality control. I applied to Energia at least ten times to get a training slot as a cosmonaut. Inducted was finally accepted and inducted into Cosmonaut 2019 Group 18- RKKE (Korolev Energia). Just like Papa, I was fully immersed in training for years. I saw even less of Papa Vik after he was recruited for the *Aquila* mission. I saw him off at KSC in 2023. I was fiercely proud of him from that moment, especially seeing the giant SRS rocket lift-off with the *Aquila* crew to form up with the rest of the deep space vehicle *Altair*.

I was rapt in the mission and got to be on the recovery ship when the *Altair* reentry capsule returned from deep space. I stood by him when he took Abby as his new wife right there on the recovery ship! God! How I got teased at the academy about Papa Vik being the first cosmonaut to have sex in space. I punched Nik in gut when he took that trash too far. Three months after Papa and Abby returned, my step brother Alexei was born. A month after that Vik and Abby sat me down to give the talk about the *Arcadia* colony.

My first ISS mission was Expedition 66 as a crew engineer in 2025. I felt more alive in space than I ever did with Natasha. My second ISS mission was with the Expedition 72/73 crew in 2027. I was in low Earth orbit when Shiva was discovered and while a crew including one of my classmates established the first permanent lunar base. How could I be so jealous when I was in space? Don't get jealous-play your cards! I applied and got what to that point was the ultimate assignment. I was on the second crew to occupy and expand the Taurus Littrow Lunar Base for a full year stay. I made EVAs for construction work at least once every two weeks.

It was great material for my resume and to feed my love of my space mistress. She does give you a full dose of radiation on every EVA. The doctors back at Baikonur were concerned that I was nearing a career limit for radiation. But perhaps not for a seasoned cosmonaut wanting to join a one-way trip to the Mars Arcadia Colony. As the son of the great Vik Ivanov, I had pull in high places to get to Mars. On January 15, 2031, I was one of thirty-five colonists and crew selected for the planned 2035 establishment of Mars Arcadia Colony. We'll be establishing a second home for humans as insurance against possible extinction from *Shiva* in 2079.

Olga Sadoski has the calling card of being on the back-up crew for *Aquila* and went through the grueling seven years of training. That and her extensive flight experience on ISS earned her a place in the Mars Arcadia Colony. Like me she was always too busy with mission training to get romantically involved. I was attracted to her from a distance since we first met before Aquila during Papa's mission training. She has stunning long brown hair, hazel eyes, and a warm inviting smile. Olga really fills out those mission blue overalls adorned with her mission patches. I rank her in age by a few years and now also with my time in space.

The first opportunity I had to spend time with Olga was on our HI-SEAS crew isolation mission in Hawaii. We maintained our professional appearances but exchanged nuances to know that there was a genuine mutual interest. Besides, there was no place to go to get to know her better. I gained more respect for her as a team player and that she would truly be an asset to the Mars colony.

After HI-SEAS ended, we had a great day snorkeling in the crystal blue waters and laying lazily in the warm sun at Mauna Kea Beach about thirty minutes and sixty-million kilometers from our Mars simulation. Away from the colony crew and nearly alone in secluded cove, I kissed her for the first time. God it felt so good since we had kept under wraps for months. Yet, my feelings were mixed. Olga is a beginning for me. I flash into the future and selfishly allowed myself to believe that Olga and I could be happy together and one day have a family on Mars. It's hard to bear the thought that all this beauty on Earth and the people we leave behind could be gone in a flash.

We both have a passion for our science objectives on Mars and the technical challenges of making our colony self-sufficient. Among the most important long term goals of self-sufficiency is to grow the population. I proposed to Olga last week and in the same breath asked her to have babies with me.

She said, "Yes! When do we start?"

"Getting married or having babies?"

"*I to I drugoye!* Both, silly boy!"

We plan to get married next week before we launch. What pains me is that Mama Katarina and I have been on the outs since I was called for Mars. I wish she would come for the wedding and give her blessings. I have to see her before we leave! Papa Vik gave his blessings. Papa and I have grown much closer during our training for Mars. We are a team.

Trevor Brown and Mandy Shields, Married
Astrobiologists, PhD Rutgers and Georgetown Universities
Aquaponics[38], Cornell University

---

38 Hydroponics and aquaculture.

I'm Mandy Shields and this is my husband Trevor Brown. I'm twenty-eight and Trevor is twenty-nine. We claim three distinct honors: First- We're very honored to be among the twenty-one primary colonist candidates for Arcadia Mars. Second- We both have dual PhDs in Astrobiology and Aquaponics. Not only are we among the youngest to hold dual PhDs, we are the only persons to hold these dual degrees. These disciplines will be indispensable to the colony. It will be our primary responsibility to feed the colony with what we can grow in our greenhouses. Third- We will be the first British and first persons of color on Mars.

"Well put Mandy. As she said, I'm Trevor."

We went to different Universities for astrobiology. Mandy went to Rutgers and I went to Georgetown. We met at an astrobiology conference at Rutgers in Ithaca, New York seven years ago while we were working on our dissertations. At the time, we anticipated Earth bound careers studying atmospheres of exoplanets and researching biological systems that might exist in exoplanet extreme environments. The *Shiva* discovery changed everything for us. We started thinking about agricultural systems on Mars. How could we best serve a colony on Mars? We decided to take our knowledge of biological systems and apply it to the practical indispensable means of producing food and oxygen to sustain the colony.

I had the inspiration from a vacation trip to Colorado when I was nine. The family was camping in the Sangre de Cristo Mountains at the Great Sand Dunes. I got to go sandboarding and was pretty good at it since I'd learned snowboarding in the Alps. I couldn't help but think about how the dunes against the mountains must be a bit like Mars. Except Mars is trying to kill you with almost no atmosphere and way sub-zero temperatures. We took a bizarre side trip into the near-desert of the San Luis

Valley to the Colorado Gators Wildlife Park. Can you imagine alligators in Colorado? The amazing thing to me was why they brought in gators and what the family that ran the place had accomplished. They started out with an aquaculture operation raising tilapia. They brought in the gators as a tourist attraction and to eat dead fish. To add more color to the attraction, they grew lush tropical vegetation and produced fig crops from the nutrient rich aquaculture water. I made the connection, aquaculture, and hydroponics, for the desert on Mars!

I discussed it with Mandy. We applied to Cornell, the only place on the planet with a degree program in aquaponics. Can you imagine? I think we are the only two people to find humor and inspiration in the old movie *Salmon Fishing in The Yemen*.

"Good segue dear. My turn."

Those were the days! Studies, romance and marriage. We put off starting a family since we thought it would ruin our chances of getting selected to join the colony. Get to Mars, make it habitable, then start a new family. We would stay here on the green Earth, but what future will there be for our family if *Shiva* hits?

So how do Mandy and I fit in to help make Mars habitable with aquaponics? The first crew to land at Arcadia Base got a start with a small greenhouse. Much of the groundwork was laid with robotic construction. The Habs are pre-fabricated. The robots built landing pads, the foundations walls, and roof structure for the greenhouses. This first attempt did prove that crops could be grown in treated Mars soil and with hydroponics. It was far from self-sustaining for the crew that was living there for two years. We will need much more growing space to be successful at sustaining our colony. Powerful LED lights are proven to provide the proper ultraviolet light to drive photosynthesis in the prolific hydroponic farms.[39] Greenhouses in the traditional sense on Earth won't work on Mars because of overly harsh UV radiation and the fickle sun choking dust storms that can last for weeks.

The Mars greenhouse is advanced technology with a system that continuously monitors conditions and adjusts the air quality, relative humidity, soil and hydroponics moisture, and LED lights to maximize photosynthesis. Strawberries, lettuce, bell peppers, and herbs are good starter crops for our hydroponic greenhouses.

My turn Mandy. Let's not forget red chili, serrano, and jalapeño peppers for hot sauce. Everything, especially reconstituted food brought from Earth, tastes better with my hot sauce! Tomatoes, cucumbers, squash, melons, and peas will be essential and grow well in hydroponics with good supports to hold the heavier plants. It will probably be necessary to grow root vegetables such as carrots, radishes, turnips, beets, and potatoes in treated Martian soil. These don't do well hydroponically. Test beds on Earth have yielded abundant harvests of radishes, peas, rye, and tomatoes all grown on Mars soil simulant. Imagine growing rye grain on Mars! It's used for flour, bread, beer, whiskey, vodka, and animal fodder. Abby requests that we don't try to ferment anything beyond beer. But she will reconsider if we can improve upon Scotty's Saurian Brandy!

Good one Trevor. Our expanded greenhouses will grow beets and sugar beets. We can enjoy beet greens as a salad. Perhaps we can brew up some vinegar from the rye. We'll expand into algaculture or farming algae like Chlorella for making biofuels, omega-3 fatty acids, bioplastics, and animal feeds. We

---

39 "Shipping Container Farms" Business Insider, Web accessed 4 January, 2017, http://www.businessinsider.com/kimbal-musk-shipping-container-farms-new-york-city-2016-12

plan to develop a poultry unit for fresh chicken eggs and meat. Besides feed from the algae, we will feed the chickens grains and food scraps. We have recently developed a method of keeping fertilized eggs in stasis for over a year to get them to Mars and establish the poultry unit.

The algaculture products and other less desirable proteins from our greenhouses can be doctored with appropriate enzymes and used to grow actual beef cell tissue in vitro through tissue engineering. Now that's alchemy at its finest! Some call it cultured meat. "Pass the hot sauce please!" Have you looked at the ingredients in frozen dinners from the supermarket recently? We believe we can ramp this up to a useable scale at Arcadia base. Mandy top that.

Poultry and cultured meat will not be our only meat protein. Let's not forget about the tilapia. Remember the alligator farm back in Colorado? Juvenile tilapia will travel to Mars in a five-hundred liter closed biological system circulating through a filtration system with live bacteria. An automatic pellet feeder will give the fish the precise nutrients needed. Nile tilapia can live for up to nine years and reach sexual maturity in about six months. All we need is our supply of fresh water to fill a twenty-thousand liter, five-meter diameter tank in the aquaponics dome and feed them basically with the same feed as we'll use for the chickens. Demo tanks of that size here on Earth can produce about one-hundred eighty kilograms of fish every six months. That's a nice, tasty supplement to our food supply. We can scale up all the aquaponics and greenhouse facilities with our robotic construction. All we need is human hands to manage all of it. As Abby said earlier, our colonists are committed to doing their share of time in a daycare and in teaching roles. In addition, and perhaps more importantly, everyone will be expected to work shifts in our greenhouses. Trevor and I couldn't possibly do all the work ourselves!"

Kate Turner asks, "What will you miss most?"

"What will I miss about home, about this entire planet? There's no question about that. It's my family. I'll miss my sister the most and the sound of her voice." There are tears welling in her amber eyes.

John Meek, New Kolob Colony Liaison
PhD Urban Planning/IPE/Space Law

My path to space began on camping trips with my father under dark skies in the wilderness of Utah. It filled my soul with the spirit to gaze on the infinite wonder of the stars and planets. I can still smell the campfire and taste the S'mores. Furthering my passion for space, Orson Scott Card, my favorite sci-fi author, filled my head with the fantasy of space adventures in *Ender's Game* and *Ender's Shadow* series. My father and I and others from our stake bandied the idea of sending an LDS colony to Mars as SpaceTrans was developing its big Colossus ships making such a bold idea possible. My father, Quentin Meek, is a recently ordained member of *The Quorum of the Twelve Apostles*. He was instrumental in convincing the LDS to muster its resources to engage SpaceTrans to commission our colony ships *Canaan, Moab*, and *Provo*.

When I was eighteen, I was ordained to the office of Eder in the *Melchizedek Priesthood* and then sent to the Missionary Training Center in Provo, Utah. I was sent on my mission in the suburbs of Chicago with Jake Smith for two years starting in 2024. The gang violence and crime of the inner city had invaded the suburbs full on. Jake and I were allowed to trade the traditional white shirt and tie for blue jeans and a white golf shirt to try to not be so absurdly conspicuous. Yes, we rang thousands of doorbells and heard infinite versions of *Book of Mormon* ding-dong jokes. Providence kept the closest gunfire a few blocks away.

After the discovery of the *Shiva* threat in 2027, I was selected in the LDS quest to form the *New Kolob* colony on Mars. The colony follows prophecy of *Kolob* being the habitable planet nearest to the throne of God. The LDS vision has the *New Kolob* colony being central to the economy of a growing human settlement of space. The currency of that economy is water and propellants that we will manufacture on Mars and someday export for further expansion in the solar system.

I was sponsored to pursue a tailor made education to guide the expansion of human civilization to other planets. My undergrad years were at BYU. My graduate studies were at Georgetown University where I studied Urban Planning, International Political Economy, and Space Law. Jameel al-Badie and Eve Cain, here with us today, were classmates of mine. Our area of intersection was the study of Space Law. Jameel and Eve further studied Criminal Justice. Jameel and I completed dissertations on Urban Planning with our advanced designs of cities on Mars to the glory of God.

While I was in grad school, I courted Leah Field from our stake in Salt Lake City. Leah and I married just after I passed my Georgetown orals. She's a designated colonist on the first colony ship, *Provo*.

Jameel and I will launch on August 15 on the *Arcadia Beta Colony* ship *Gemini* about two months after the first colony ship *Taurus*. We will arrive on Mars in May 2036, about five months after *Taurus*. Jameel and I will serve as liaisons and ambassadors for our respective colonies due to arrive in March 2038. We will also oversee advance construction of our colonies living space and assets.

Jameel al-Badie, al-Salam al-Jadid Colony Liaison
PhD Urban Planning/IPE/Space Law/Criminal Justice

Salam alekum. Shukran, John Meek. Thank you for the introduction. I can relate to John's *qisa* remembering his camping adventures with his father. I had similar experiences with my father in the Rub al Khali desert southwest of Abu Dhabi. The winter months are glorious on the dunes in the deep desert. We had a canvas *khayma* set up where by tradition we brewed *qahua* in a brass *dallah* on the fire.

John Meek interrupts. "Jameel can you say that in English?"

Oh, sorry Kate. We camped in a tent and drank green coffee brewed in the campfire. I preferred sleeping under the stars with our prized camels staked nearby. The Milky Way seemed as three dimensional as if we were in deep space. My father taught me the Arabic names for the stars that guide travelers at night. He taught me that "Life in Islam is not bound to Earth. Other planets have life like Earth. And all living things and non-living things glorify Allah."[40]

As John Meek said, we have designed cities for Mars to the glory of God. My design was commissioned by the UAE and Sheikh Mansour bin Zahid Al Majed. We had originally envisioned our colony to be launched in one hundred years. With the *Shiva* threat, our schedule has moved up to 2038 in parallel with the LDS. Our vision is to construct a city on Mars dedicated to Allah and peace: *al-Salam al-Jadid.* We have commissioned two Colossus supply ships from SpaceTrans, *Dubai* and *Sharjah,* and one colony ship, *Abu Dhabi.*

---

40 "Islam & Life On Other Planets," Web accessed 27 Sept 2018.
http://www.miracles-of-quran.com/islam_life_other_planets.htm

That reminds me, I must say a word about my foray into Criminal Justice. The very unfortunate terrorist incident in Abu Dhabi in 2024 left my country humiliated and needing justice. The bombing was claimed by the *Tilah Wahid* derivative of Al Qaeda and ISIS. The justice they received was swift. The extremists were cornered, fought back, and there were no survivors. The UAE was vowed to dramatically increase security by rooting out extremists and bringing them to trial before they can act. I was recruited not only to be an off world city builder but to help insure that our colonists are safe from extremists. Our colonists have been vetted by background checks by all possible means including my scrutiny.

My wife, Layla Mohammed, a physician and OB-GYN for the care and well-being of our colonies women and children, will arrive on the *Abu Dhabi* with the first twenty UAE colonists.

Dr. Harold Draper, his Family of Artificial Intelligence Systems, and Robots on Mars

Kate Turner asks, "Dr. Draper, will you describe the artificial intelligence systems that will help in our colonization of Mars?"

"Thanks Kate. I'd be glad to represent my AI family."

CASSI[41], as an artificial intelligence system, was an essential member of the *Aquila Mission* crew and has evolved into other essential systems for space exploration and Mars colonization. CASSI's voice interface makes the computer system easy to interact with in a natural way that would be impossible with a keyboard or control panel. CASSI is infinitely more sophisticated than the early 21st century AI system named SIRI that many people carried with them on their cell phones.

---

41 Cybernetic Artificial Space Systems Intelligence

CASSI's design and AI programming were a joint effort between NASA, Roscosmos, MIT, Stanford, Empire, and Googleplex. Dr. Harold Draper of MIT was the project PI. He had the daunting task of coordinating the disparate egos of six monumental bureaucracies. The CASSI beta version was the product of his team at MIT. The teams at other institutions were assigned for beta testing, generating harder and more complex tasks for testing, and helping to develop CASSI's personality to fit anticipated mission needs. The programming language they used is *Prolog-SS* the Prolog programming language for space systems. The roots of Prolog[42] were sown in 1972 by a team under Alain Colmerauer in Marseilles, France. Dr. Draper and the MIT team along with the Aquila crew had the final responsibility to get CASSI to production, flight ready status—CASSI 5.1.1. CASSI's evolution was a joy to behold. CASSI's personality has guiding algorithms but has evolved into a self-aware, friendly near human presence. The guiding algorithms give CASSI a conscience with empathy, driven to help humans in all aspects of life, and an over-arching self-regulating principle of do-no-harm.

Cookies are a training tool for cybernetic development of an artificial intelligence. *Cookies* contain data sets with computational challenges on the cutting edge of physics and cosmology. Cookies are generally a huge dataset of hundreds of terabytes with a task program oriented to challenge the developing mind of a supercomputing artificial intelligence. A developing AI literally looks forward to these challenges as a reward for drudging through long stretches of mundane and routine but important computational tasks. Those mundane and routine computational tasks always have priority for the maintenance and operation of Altair and all components of the

---

42 "Introduction to Prolog Programming" Web accessed 5 April 2017.
http://www.cse.unsw.edu.au/~billw/cs9414/notes/prolog/intro.html

Aquila Mission over working on a *cookie* data set. Fermilab, Lawrence Berkeley and Argonne National Laboratories, and CERN have established a special consortium on an AI supercomputing project where computing resources are shared. CASSI is an adjunct member of this computing group.

On the Aquila Mission, CASSI played a vital role controlling all of the systems of the Altair deep space vehicle including life support, navigation, rocket thrust maneuvers, medical diagnosis, and electronics systems monitoring. CASSI extended her subroutines as an onboard AI name s CAMI[43] to operate the deep space MMU vehicle that the crew used to perform EVA's to explore asteroid Bennu and comet 125P.

More advanced versions of CASSI, v.16.3.1, are now essential on Mars exploration and colonization. CASSI controls systems on the Colossus Space Trans ships and pressurized Mars crew rovers. CASSI operates VR systems for exercise and entertainment systems.

CASSI has evolved into essential robotic systems. Industry partners in robotics from US, EU, Russia, Japan, and China have been intimately involved in developing the robotics. CARIAN[44] is an android robot crew member that works alongside the crew or independently inside the habitats or outside on the surface of Mars. Performing mundane tasks outside helps reduce crew exposure to harsh radiation. CARIIN[45] is the artificial intelligence system that controls the essential industrial robot systems used for water ice mining for propellant, water, and oxygen; regolith mining for construction and industrial raw materials and metal

---

43 Cybernetic Artificial MMU Intelligence

44 CARIAN (sounds like Carrie Ann) Cybernetic Artificial Robotic Intelligence-Android

45 CARIIN (sounds like Karen) Cybernetic Artificial Robotic Intelligence- Industrial

ores; industrial 3D printing; habitat and aquaponics pod construction; landing pad construction; and construction of new robotic systems. Construction robotics are supplemented with processed materials sent from Earth such as pellet plastics, powdered copper, powdered aluminum, aluminum oxide, titanium dioxide, and prefabricated semiconductor silicon wafers. These wafers are used in a robotic clean lab to make any needed processor chips for computers, communications, and control equipment. Processing Mars regolith to make essential silicon solar cells is planned to be routine in our Mars colony by 2037. Processing Mars regolith to make semiconductor quality silicon wafers is an evolving future technology.

GNN Interviews of *Arcadia Colonists*
June 4, 2035

"This is GNN Space Correspondent Kate Turner here wrapping up a series of deeply revealing interviews that takes us into the souls of the colonists who will soon leave the Earth forever to make Mars their home. We wish them all the good fortune that the universe can bestow upon them to save humanity from calamity in 2079. As always I wish you good health and sweet dreams…"

STATE of the ART ROBOTICS of 2018 that EVOLVE for MARS COLONIZATION

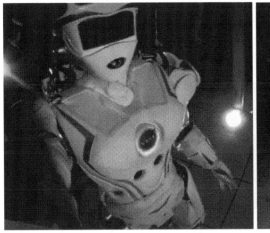

Valkyrie: NASA's Superhero Robot[46] Atlas: Commissioned by the US Pentagon[47], [48]

Robotic 3D Metal Printing[49], [50]

---

46 "Valkyrie: NASA's Superhero Robot", Web accessed 14 Aug 2018.

https://www.youtube.com/watch?v=IE-YBaYjbqY

47 "Ten Amazing Robots that will Change the World", Web accessed 15 Aug 2018.
https://www.youtube.com/watch?v=6feEE716UEk

48 "Atlas: The World's most Dynamic Humanoid", Web accessed 15 Aug 2018.
https://www.bostondynamics.com/atlas

49 "Future of Construction", Web accessed 15 Aug 2018.
https://futureofconstruction.org/case/mx3d/

MARSHA- NASA Award winning concept design of a 3D printed Mars habitat constructed of biorenewable plastic (PLA) reinforced with locally-sourced basalt fiber. The plastics are some of the best materials for radiation shielding per unit of mass. [51]

50 "MX3D Bridge Project", Web accessed 15 Aug 2018. http://mx3d.com/projects/bridge-2/

51 "3D-printed Mars habitat could be a perfect fit for early SpaceX Starship colonies," TESLARATI, Web accessed 15 February 2019. https://www.teslarati.com/3d-printed-mars-habitat-perfect-fit-early-spacex-starship-colonies/

3

HOMECOMING TO A
CHANGED WORLD

"Returning to Earth, that was the challenging part."

– Buzz Aldrin,
The Dark Side of the Moon

GNN Special Report
August 20, 2024
12:15 PM EDT

"This is GNN Space Correspondent Kate Turner. The *Aquila* crew is on target to begin entry into the Earth's atmosphere in five minutes to return home to after their historic 398 day voyage in deep space. They touched the face of an asteroid and a comet from four and a half billion years ago at the dawn of our solar system. They were the first crew to travel to deep space beyond the Moon traveling faster than any human before. They rocketed past the Moon in five hours. It took Apollo fifty-two hours to reach lunar orbit on the slow train…"

Aquila Mission Rigel Capsule
Mission Elapsed Time 398:06:19:21
Commander Coby Brewster personal log:

Our third and final attitude burn used the Rigel ESM service module engine. The maneuver is to insure hitting Earth's thin atmosphere at the exact angle to slow us with atmospheric friction and land on target in the Pacific Ocean off San Diego. Only the Apollo astronauts had experienced reentering the Earth's atmosphere from deep space. We will be coming in faster than Apollo. Each of us on the Aquila crew had only experienced ballistic entry in a Soyuz reentry module typically not exceeding 4.5 g of deceleration. Each of us knew what it was like to have anything that could go wrong happen in a simulation and result in the taste of death. We are not afraid. Our accomplishments had made history. The science data we beamed back digitally has made the mission an immense success. The contingency samples sealed away on Vega and Tarazed are in the back of my mind. They were intended as a backup if we do not survive reentry.

398:08:11:53 MET

"Houston, Altair. Ready for communication blackout. See you on the other side."

The Rigel capsule begins to aerobrake on Earth's atmosphere at 41,234 km/hour, faster than any crew vehicle has reentered. Rigel is oriented heat shield forward. The windows are facing away from the onslaught of atmosphere. Vik and I can see lightning white ionization swirling rhythmically and falling astern like riding inside the exhaust of the biggest rocket ever created. After a minute, it is tinged with blue and crimson. I'm having visions of our team building experiences back on Earth before the mission- the Aquarius habitat, the sport fishing trip in Key West, the first time making love to Ellie, the canoe trip on the Itchetucknee before they went into isolation, the accomplishments of the mission... My eyes tear up with the images of the beautiful planet Earth and the joy of coming home.

The ionization makes radio communication impossible for several minutes on reentry. Vik calls out that orientation looks good. We are at four g's of deceleration and rising. Abby and Ellie see the light show reflected off the interior walls and from the lateral windows. We all feel tremendous vibration. I imagine that I am smelling insulation burning inside the capsule. God, I hope it's only my imagination! The deceleration g-force is against our backs so the straps are not putting large stress on their abdomens. Abby had assured Ellie that their fetuses are safely floating in incompressible amniotic fluid that is the same density as the fetus. It becomes harder to breathe. We use the survival technique of forcing rapid sips of air.

Apollo crews experienced six to seven g's on reentry from lunar orbit. Our deceleration reaches a maximum of nine g's as predicted. It becomes the most excruciating crushing weight imaginable but we know it is survivable. Keep breathing! Sips of air! The Soyuz returning NASA astronaut Peggy Whitson had an abnormally steep reentry, dolling out over eight g's. She called it "an interesting ride." In August 1958, Navy Reserve officer

Carter Collins survived the Johnsville Human Centrifuge at more than twenty g's for a record fifty-four seconds.[52]

As quickly as the g's built, the possibility of surviving with lessening g's graced us.

"Houston, Altair. Do you read? Drogue chute deployed. Houston, Altair. Drogue chute deployed. Houston, *Altair* is coming home."

"Altair, Houston. We read you five-by-five. Welcome home! We have you on radar and on target. Seahawk helos from the *USS Anchorage* are on target to greet you."

Bang! Ka-thump!

"Roger. Main chutes deployed. We can see them! What a sight!"

"*Altair*, Houston. The Seahawk helos have you in sight and video is live to the world!"

The gloriously calm, cerulean ocean received the Rigel capsule with a gentle kiss at splashdown. The very pregnant Abby and Ellie especially appreciated this in comparison to the car wreck jolt of a Soyuz landing on the hard, dusty steppes of Kazakhstan. The capsule is gently bobbing as a welcome back to one-g. In an instant, the main chute detaches and four bladders inflate in their place to keep the capsule upright. Six divers and a zodiac are deployed from the lead Seahawk. The divers attach an additional flotation collar around the capsule. I exchange thumbs up signs with one of the divers. One of the dive crew is a videographer from Lincoln Main transmitting live. Momentarily, we see the *USS Anchorage* powering alongside. The divers attach a

---

52 "The G Machine" Smithsonian Air & Space, 12 December, 2016, https://www.airspacemag.com/history-of-flight/the-g-machine-16799374/

towline and tending lines to Rigel to recover the capsule into the recovery ships flooded well deck.

The *USS Anchorage* is a 208 meter amphibious transport ship based in San Diego, California. The ship can carry over one-thousand servicemen. It has an internal floodable well deck for recovery of anything from troop transports to space capsules. It has an aircraft hangar and can launch helicopters such as the Seahawk and other vertical take-off and landing aircraft such as the Osprey and Harrier. The *USNS Salvor*, a Safeguard class salvage ship is also deployed as a backup for the recovery of our capsule in the event of an out-of-target area landing.

Rigel is towed into the ship's well deck and settled into a special cradle. Live video is streaming with network commentary. We are busy doffing helmets and unstrapping our harnesses. We don surgical masks as per mission plan. Water is being pumped out of the ship's well bay. When the capsule is stable, our hatch is opened. A hive of Navy, NASA, and Lincoln Main personnel swarm over and around the capsule with rehearsed efficiency. A HazMat Team from NASA JSC Astromaterials Research and Exploration Science Laboratory will enter the Rigel capsule to retrieve the sample return containers and core tubes from the sample isolation compartment in the lower equipment bay. They will be sealed in another very stout sample isolation compartment for transport to the JSC Lab by a NASA transport jet. The crews of Apollos 11, 12, and 14 spent twenty-one days in quarantine isolation guarding the world from possible virulent hazards from the Moon. This procedure is deemed overkill for us since we just survived over six months in isolation on *Altair* after the last samples were collected. We will however spend ten days in the company of our physicians to oversee our recovery from 410 days in microgravity including the prep time at ISS.

We are overwhelmed with Earth gravity as we are gently helped out of the Rigel capsule and lowered into oversized reclining wheelchairs. We put on warm smiles for the cameras, enthusiastically wave, and give the tenders high fives. Thankfully, no speeches are expected from us yet. We are wheeled into an elevator and off to sick bay for off-camera NASA post-fight medicals.

Abby and Ellie are mentally prepared for the inevitable revelation of their pregnancies. They are graciously welcomed and attended by technicians Tara and Samantha to get them out of their ACES suits and into hospital gowns. Dr. Shirley Hanson from NASA JSC is their attending physician. Shirley is professional but gregarious and awed by their successful mission. "Welcome Aquila crew! You'll need to wear those surgical masks in presence of others for the next ten days. It's more for your protection than the off chance you might spread space bugs. We'll get you checked out shortly and blood samples will show the condition of your immune systems…"

"I don't see any issues with either of you in this preliminary physical aside from the expected change in bone density and muscle tone. To find both of you pregnant is nothing short of astounding. Congratulations! I honor your science achievements, but this is history for space physiology! The ultrasounds both look normal for twenty-six weeks gestation. We'll do a much more thorough and continuing follow-up at JSC. With your kind permission extended from your NASA contract, I'm obliged to give a brief on your condition to Ben Kirk."

Abby replies, "Thanks, Shirley. Your preliminary assessment gives me great relief. Yes, give Ben a full brief. It's hard to hide our condition."

Shirley gives them both a hug. "Your NASA blues are over there. Tara and Sam can assist you. We'll wheel you up to the ceremony on the flight deck. I advise you not to stand any more than a minute at the podium."

Ellie says, "No worries there. I don't think I can do thirty seconds. I feel the weight of the whole world."

The Aquila welcoming ceremony is coming together on the Flight Deck. The Aquila Crew, Captain Roy Johnson, NASA Flight Operations Director Ben Kirk, and senior Lincoln Main managers are to appear before the entire ship's complement of personnel. Captain Roy Johnson is to make introductions: thanking his recovery crew, recognizing Lincoln Main, etc.

Before the ceremony, we are standing with Ben Kirk and Captain Johnson in his ready room. Ben Kirk leans over and quietly speaks to Vik and I, "Dr. Hanson briefed me and I see the delicate condition in which Ellie and Abby have returned. Commander Brewster and Mister Ivanov, you have got some explaining to do."

I speak so all can hear. "Can you arrange for a couple of weddings?" Everyone smiles in the ready-room. Ellie and Abby stifle a giggle.

"With your celebrity status, I'm sure we can get through this. I suppose you want St. Patrick's Cathedral?"

"No, Ben. Keep this low key. Captain Johnson, can you do the honors before we get to San Diego?"

"Aye aye Commander Brewster! It will be my pleasure. Do you have the rings?"

"No but we can remedy that later. I just want to be able to make the announcement of Ellie and Abby's pregnancies with the announcement of our weddings. We had long planned to get married when we got back so there's no time like the present."

"OK, as ship's captain I can wing an impromptu if you can excuse brevity. Let's do this. Commander Brewster, do you take Captain Accardi to be your lawfully wedded wife?"

"I do."

"Captain Accardi?"

"I do."

"Pilot Ivanov and Dr. Denton?"

"We do!"

"By the power vested in me by the United States Navy, I pronounce you married."

"Wow! That was quick- but we'll take it!" Coby takes Ellie and Vik takes Abby for a quick kiss and embrace.

"Okay crew, it's show time. We have chairs for you beside the podium."

Abby says "Not a moment too soon. We need to get off our feet. Gravity is brutal!"

They all walk out onto the flight deck. The four astronauts are noticeably unsteady and take their seats as the crew of the *USS Anchorage* and gathered dignitaries erupt in raucous applause. Network cameras are broadcasting to the world.

Captain Johnson takes the podium. "Crew of the USS Anchorage, NASA Flight Operations Director Ben Kirk, NASA personnel, Lincoln Main personnel, and world television audience, the *USS Anchorage* is honored to be the recovery ship for the returning Aquila crew. Thank you to the helicopter and dive crews. We had a textbook recovery. The astronauts have had preliminary physicals and are here for a brief appearance. NASA Flight Operations Director Ben Kirk, will now take the podium to introduce our heroes."

There is another loud round of applause. Ben Kirk adjusts the microphone, "Commander Jacob Brewster, Pilot Viktor Ivanov, Dr. Abbigail Denton, and Captain Rafaela Accardi, we welcome you into the history books, and congratulate you for your long journey and challenges in deep space. We appreciate the ordeal of your overwhelming return to gravity. The astronauts are wearing surgical masks to stay isolated for the next few days. I have a surprise announcement to make. Captain Johnson has just married Coby Brewster to Ellie Accardi and Vik Ivanov to Abby Denton. Dr. Shirley Hanson has examined the astronauts with the only unexpected news being that Ellie and Abby are six months pregnant. This is just one of the many record setting accomplishments of their voyage. The crew was purposely selected as two men and two women for compatibility. So we accept this *natural* outcome and wish them the best of health. Meanwhile, the NASA ARES, Astromaterials Research Lab, is anxiously waiting to receive the invaluable samples you have returned from asteroid Bennu and comet 125P. The samples famously include what is believed to be fossil proof of extraterrestrial life from Bennu. Ladies and gentlemen, you've heard enough from me, I now introduce you to Commander Coby Brewster."

Coby takes the podium. "Thank you Ben and all of you for the gracious welcome home. I never thought the air could smell so sweet and the sky of Earth could be so blue. Yes, the adjustment to gravity is more than a challenge but all of us have gone through this before from other missions. We have endured much and discovered more than we could have dreamed of. NASA and the *International Space Coalition* can now set our sights on Mars..."

Ellie sees the deck of the gray ship turning under the blue sky. Barely audible-- "Oh God!" Slowly the deck is coming toward her. She passes out and falls down. There is an audible gasp from the audience. Coby jumps to her side. Shirley Hanson, their attending NASA physician gets to Ellie immediately and signals for gurneys she had standing by for Ellie and Abby. "Ellie, are you with me?" She takes Ellie's pulse and sees that her eyes are rolled back in her head. Two attendants lift her onto the gurney. "Abby get on a gurney before you pass out also." The gurneys are rolled off the flight deck and Coby and Vik follow in wheel chairs.

While it was not an elegant exit from the *Welcome Home* ceremony, it was soon reported that Ellie Accardi was in good medical condition. The entire crew just needed time to get used to gravity after such a long time in space. They spent the night in sick bay on the Anchorage then as they steamed closer to San Diego. They were escorted to the helo deck and strapped into a Seahawk for a twenty minute ride to Naval Air Station North Island. The crew are given quiet private quarters in the medical wing for twenty-four hours. With a medical discharge they are whisked to the airbase tarmac where an Air Force C-20 Gulfstream is waiting. The crew, still wearing surgical masks, is accompanied by Dr. Shirley Hanson and pampered by attendants on the five-hour flight back to Ellington Field in Houston.

Shirley informs them, "I still have you for seventy two hours of rest and isolation before you can be discharged and taken home with assigned nurse teams. You have a few more days before you are expected at JSC for debriefing."

Coby can't be contained. "Thanks for the special attention Shirley. That's just how we planned to spend our honeymoons!"

Ellie jumps in. "I'm not sure we need nurses 24/7 but we could use some TLC with home cooked meals. Yes, *Earth* food. Pregnant women have needs!"

"You're a step ahead of me on that. Here are some menu choices recommended to wean you off of space food."

Vik pushes back on that, "I'll have Beluga caviar and Stoli for starters."

Coby chimes in, "Bacon and eggs, bacon, lettuce, and tomato sandwiches, and don't forget the cheeseburgers with bacon!"

Ellie laughs, "Easy big boys! Get your minds out of the food gutter. We need filet mignon with pickles, king crab with pickles, and *real* vanilla ice cream with pickles."

Abby has the last word, "Just what the doctor orders. Yes, pickles. I couldn't get my mind to focus on what I need. Yes, pickles! This baby has discriminating tastes. There will be time to indulge but let's ease into this. Can we stop by *HEB Foods* on the way to El Lago? By the way team, let's shack-up at the Ivanov house for as long as we need to get our Earth legs back. We have the pool and hot tub that Ben Kirk assures me is clean, ready, and waiting for us."

"Oh God! Yes! Let the therapy begin…"

Aquila Samples
August 21, 2024
Astromaterials Acquisition and Curation Office
Johnson Space Center
Houston, TX

The priceless, sealed SRC containers arrived at Astromaterials Acquisition and Curation Office at the Johnson Space Center in Houston the day after the Rigel capsule came back to Earth with the Aquila crew. Dr. Kikuko Nakahara, of NASA ARES

(Astromaterials Research and Exploration Science Laboratory) supervised receiving and curating the precious samples. She and her colleagues work on a sample split to categorize the samples from both asteroid Bennu and comet 125P and ultimately tease out the unique science data they might have. Of supreme interest to the waiting world is sample BENNU B35B with possible proof of extraterrestrial life in fossil form encased in the amber-like nodule.

Dr. Daniele Lorenzo, Lunar and Planetary Laboratory at University of Arizona, Dr. Grant Jeffries of ANSMET, and Dr. David Moreau from NASA Ames Astrobiology are working with Kikuko. Dr. Jeffries became involved in Aquila Mission work on Bennu because of his recent find of a unique carbonaceous chondrite meteorite from Antarctica, specimen EET 23439. His analysis of the specimen dated it at 4.563 billion years old, from the beginnings of our solar system. The coal-black meteorite has a host of carbon compounds including amino acids, carboxylic acid, PAHs (poly-aromatic hydrocarbons), minute quantities of C60 buckminsterfullerene, and diamondoids. The most interesting and unique carbon compound discovered in EET 23439, not found in any previous carbonaceous chondrite, is a range of diterpene compounds ($C20H32$). These presented in globules up to fifty millimeters in size. The globules look like and are chemically similar to amber.

This clue led the Aquila crew to specifically look for similar nodules on Bennu first using remote sensing equipment then going EVA to explore the identified targets. Kikuko mentally plays the video from Aquila that is seared into her memory forever:

"CAMI, sever the harpoons and retract the monopod. Then proceed to Target B35B."

"Affirmative... Severed and monopod retracted... Proceeding to Target B35B fifty meters from here."

"CAMI set the monopod with harpoons one meter from B35B on this vector."

"Affirmative... Touchdown at one meter...Monopod set."

"CAMI, take a scoop sample one meter from B35B for background. Bag and tag it."

"Affirmative... Bagged and tagged."

"Thank you, CAMI. Now we will focus on nodule B35B. It does measure twenty-one centimeters length in my HUD. Like the other one, this nodule is amber yellow with even brighter purple-blue iridescent sheen around the edges. CAMI, please use the GHLI to get a close image of the nodule from five centimeters."

"Affirmative... Rotating to bring the GHLI down to five centimeters."

"From what I can see in my HUD, like the other one, the nodule appears amorphous and somewhat translucent with dark brown inclusions. No, wait! CAMI, Hold the GHLI at three centimeters. Focus on the green inclusion. But, how? It, it, looks arthropoid! It looks like a portion of an appendage about nine centimeters long! Altair, what do you see on the monitor up there?"

"Ellie, this is Abby. We see it in detail! Yes, I would say it's an arthropoid tarsus with sensory hairs! My God! How could that be here on this asteroid from the very beginnings of the solar system?"

Coby broke in. "Ellie, do not touch or manipulate the nodule until we consult with Houston."

"Roger. CAMI, maintain the current GHLI image and do not touch the nodule yet."

"Affirmative."

"Houston, Altair, Commander Brewster. We have a discovery of overriding importance. We need confirmation that you are receiving the video display. We appear to have possible proof of extraterrestrial life in fossil form encased in the nodule B35B! We need your recommendations before we proceed to manipulate the nodule for collection. Coby, over."

CASSI offers the first detailed analysis of the object in the nodule on an open channel. "Houston, Altair, this is CASSI. I have analyzed the image from the GHLI. There is an eighty percent probability that the green inclusion is organic and arthropoid. However, there is no known example of this appendage from any database I have on board. It is not from any known species whether extant, extinct, or fossil. It may be a case of parallel evolution. CASSI, over."

While they were waiting for response from Houston, Abby chimed in, "Yes, parallel evolution! Like any animal with an exoskeleton; like any animal with wings: insect, bird, or bat; like the tail fin of a shark, a higher bony fish, or a dolphin; like the eye of an insect and the eye of a human. But again, how could that be here on asteroid from the very beginnings of the solar system?"

Ellie speculated, "The nodule probably was cast somehow into the original solar nebula at the beginning of the solar system. It likely formed on a planet in another star system. Perhaps this nodule was ejected in a meteorite collision with the planet but that likely would not send it out of the star system. Possibly the planet on which it evolved was catastrophically destroyed in a huge planet-planet impact and the broken bits were scattered outside the star system and into the nebula that eventually formed our solar system."

Coby said what the others were thinking. "Gees! What are the odds of *that*?"

BENNU SAMPLE B35B
August 24-30, 2024
Astromaterials Acquisition and Curation Office

Most of the rock and core samples are similar to the carbonaceous chondrite EET 23439 that Dr. Jeffries found and analyzed. These will be shared with other labs and analyzed in due course. The gem of the *Aquila* mission, sample BENNU B35B, is handled in an ultra-clean lab that has been meticulously sterilized to receive and work on this invaluable organic nodule from the beginnings of our solar system.

No sample contamination can be allowed. Initially, the nodule is just intensively studied without any invasive work. Since this is a unique sample and the ARES Lab is uniquely qualified for studying it, no sample splits will be sent to other labs and experts anxiously waiting around the world. All work data is immediately copied to the other labs. The initial non-invasive work involves photographing B35B from all angles in various frequencies of light from ultraviolet to infrared. Then it is subjected to a detailed MRI. They decide against a CAT scan since the X-rays might destroy some of the chemistry of the fossil in the nodule.

The first invasive work extracts a micro-core one centimeter into the nodule to analyze its composition. It is very similar to the organic nodules discovered in meteorite EET 23439 by Dr. Jeffries. It is a range of diterpene compounds ($C20H32$) similar to amber. Then comes the most exacting and intense sampling procedure. To make any more progress on the fossil, they must have a sample of it. It has already been documented with all known non-invasive science. The MRI scan has given the team a detailed 3D model of the fossil that has been shared and 3D printed in their sister labs.

Kikuko guides the ultra-sterile diamond tipped micro-core with computer guided precision to take a minute sample through the thickest part of the tarsus fossil. The procedure is broadcast to waiting science teams.

"I've never been so nervous in my life. I'm glad the drill is preprogrammed. My shaking hands might botch the work…Almost there… Penetrating the tarsus now… Slowly… Yes it's all the way through! Retracting slowly…The core is out. Okay, now I'm taking out the core bit and placing the micro-core in the receiver. There, the hardest part is over. The receiver will now be placed in the sectioning apparatus of the GCMS.[53] The core is being sectioned into six splits with two for archive, two for GCMS, one for XRD, and one for a very hopeful DNA amplification and analysis… There…The splits are complete and the first GCMS sample is proceeding. The other splits are now in individual micro-receivers."

In DNA for Earth based life, there are four different bases: adenine (A) and guanine (G) are the larger purines. Cytosine (C) and thymine (T) are the smaller pyrimidines. RNA also contains four different bases. Three of these are the same as in DNA: adenine, guanine, and cytosine. RNA contains uracil (U) instead

---

53 Gas chromatography–mass spectrometry used to identify chemical compounds in a sample.

of thymine (T). RNA converts the genetic information contained within DNA to a format used to build proteins, and then moves it to ribosomal protein factories.

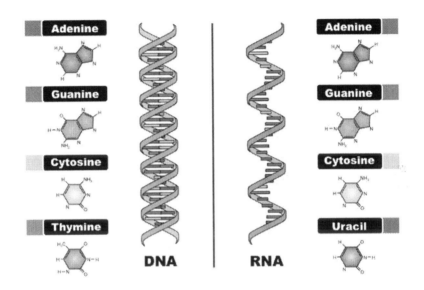

Comparison of DNA and RNA Structure with the difference of Thyamine and Uracil in base composition. Image credit: http://ib.bioninja.com.au/standard-level/topic-2-molecular-biology/26-structure-of-dna-and-rna/dna-versus-rna.html

Anticipation makes the analyses are excruciatingly slow. The GCMS tantalizingly reveals that the exoskeleton appears to be closer to the protein keratin than the polysaccharide chitin that Earth based arthropods have in their exoskeletons. The interior of the tarsus yields purine and pyrimidine molecules. Instead of the exact building blocks of Earth based DNA, they cannot find the purine guanine. Instead they find the purines isoguanine, an isomer of guanine, and hypoxanthine. The DNA amplification analysis is negative for true DNA but instead reveals strands of RNA that apparently incorporates isoguanine and hypoxanthine.

The excitement builds since this is the first time RNA has been detected in extraterrestrial samples. RNA, like DNA, can carry genetic codes to build proteins. RNA is a precursor to DNA. Complex organic molecules have been detected beyond our solar system and in other galaxies using radio-telescopes. Purines and pyrimidines have been recovered in carbonaceous chondrite meteorites. Experiments show that ultraviolet light enables chemical reactions to form these RNA base pairs.[54] The excitement builds since this is the first time RNA has been detected in extraterrestrial samples. The complete structure of the RNA may never be assessed from this sample that is so degraded over at least 4.5 billion years. Nevertheless, the excitement is overwhelming since they have not only found fossil evidence for extraterrestrial life but they have solid clues on what makes its genetic structure work!

Comet 125P Core and Rock Samples
August 21-30, 2024
Astromaterials Acquisition and Curation Office

As a separate operation, scientists and technicians from the ARES team are doing preliminary work on comet 125P core and rock samples. Their work will be painstaking, slow, and thorough. This is the opportunity to work with detail and precision not possible with a robotic space probe. These samples will be shared with other labs. They observe special precautions on poisonous volatiles when handling these samples, storing them in liquid nitrogen at minus 196° C and processing them in a cold lab kept at minus 40° C to preserve the volatiles in a solid state. Flashback

---

54 "The Origin of RNA Precursors on Exoplanets", Science Advances 01 Aug 2018: Vol. 4, no. 8, Web accessed 9 Aug 2018,
http://advances.sciencemag.org/content/4/8/eaar3302

on Altair: In the Tarazed hab, Ellie is in the Coms bay finishing her science report. Abby is in the medical bay working on an inventory of medical supplies for the last long mission leg home. Abby smells an odor that triggers a mental alarm. She knows that smell from med school. The bitter almond smell could be hydrogen cyanide but the formaldehyde smell is unmistakable. "Do you smell that, Ellie?" Coby and Vik had nearly succumbed to volatiles from a leaking comet core tube that had not been properly stowed in the sample isolation chamber. The ARES lab, in addition to keeping the volatile samples cold, maintains negative pressure ventilation fume hoods around the analysis equipment, and respirators on hand.

This work will be detailed beyond the experience of any lay person. Kikuko recalls, "I have worked on comet Wild 2 samples returned by *STARDUST*, and asteroid Itokawa samples returned by *Hayabu*sa. All of those interplanetary dust particle samples are smaller than the thickness of a human hair, invisible for human eyes-- an average of 10 microns diameter. And yet they are so precious, each containing secrets of the origin and ancient history of the Solar System. So I had to be very good at micro-manipulation and also using cutting edge nanotechnology. Our laboratory material science covers micro-crystallography, mineralogy, basic inorganic and organic chemistry using various microanalysis instruments."[55]

The cometary dust samples do have mineralogical similarities to some meteorites. "The two new minerals I discovered were the smallest mineral samples ever recognized by the International Mineralogical Association."

---

[55] Biography of ARES scientist Keiko Nakamura-Messenger. Web accessed 18 August 2018. https://ares.jsc.nasa.gov/people/individualbios/showbio.pl?id=19

What will these large comet 125P samples and cores turn up that microscopic comet dust could not reveal?

August 26, 2024
El Lago, TX

Coby Brewster's Private Journal:

Since our spectacular landing, the news channels have been covering Aquila 24/7 with stories about us, the weddings, and naturally, the pregnancies. There is wild speculation about what we found at Bennu and comet 125P and the dangers that come with it. Reporters, friends, and families have been clamoring to see their 'heroes' but private security and an answering service gives us a bubble of privacy. In a week, that bubble will burst as we are expected to attend a press conference in the JSC Media Room followed by a private reception for friends and family arranged by NASA Flight Operations Director Ben Kirk.

The El Lago and Timber Cove subdivisions fronting Taylor Lake are just a few minutes from the NASA Manned Spacecraft Center. These are developments of what today would be considered modest homes on small cul-de-sacs and streets, surrounded by water and trees. Astronauts have settled here since the original Mercury Seven and the famous Astronaut Group Three that fed Apollo's ranks- Armstrong, Aldrin, Bean, Cernan, Lovell, Scott. In fact, the two homes that Ellie and I and Vik and Abby have settled into are two doors apart on Woodland Drive in El Lago on either side of what was Neil Armstrong's home. Just down the road are former homes of Apollo astronauts Ed White and Fred Haise.

This is a close knit neighborhood with few secrets. Ellie and I wanted to live as close to Vik and Abby as our realtor could arrange. We had endured a complete lack of privacy in space and sometimes its indignities. We shared every intimacy before and during *Aquila* but polygamy was not on the list. Nothing is morally against it. It just wasn't what we need or want. Our reliance on one another is instinctual. Now we share being pregnant. What would our babies have as challenges being conceived in deep space in microgravity and subjected to radiation for six months?

Once we settled back into El Lago with security around us, we tried to relax and get back into a comfortable routine in very real Earth gravity. All four of us have swollen legs and ankles. It's much worse for Ellie and Abby being pregnant. Their morning sickness has returned with a vengeance. Abby prescribes herbal teas and broth to keep hydrated. Floating weightless is good therapy. Heaven for the four of us is hours spent in Vik and Abby's Houston standard 87 degree swimming pool and below standard 96 degree hot tub. The hot tub is kept lower than normal for the babies. We slowly begin to feel normal after about two weeks.

Parades for Heroes

September 15, 2024
JSC Media Relations Office

Coalition PR Secretary Emily Collins has been handling the mountains of emails and well wishes for the Aquila crew coming from around the world. The crew has been hoping to minimize public exposure but requests from the *Coalition* nations are making it nearly impossible to avoid doing a whirlwind goodwill tour for the adoring public. Emily implores them, "Your spectacularly successful mission is exactly what the world needs.

We haven't had hero explorers to celebrate like this since Apollo. Your discoveries have scientists and the whole world reeling." Coby responds, "I hear you loud and clear. My biggest concerns are security and the health and comfort of Ellie and Abby so close to their due dates and so recently returned from thirteen months in microgravity." "We'll have a security detail with us and security teams on the ground at each event. We will fly in a NASA 767 with first class sleeper cabins and have five star hotel accommodations. NASA's Dr. Shirley Hanson will accompany us."

"Where do you plan to take us and on what kind of schedule?" "The itinerary will take about two weeks allowing a reasonable break between events. We'll limit the US tour to LA, Chicago, and New York. Our overseas tour is London, Berlin, Moscow, Rome, and Abu Dhabi. We would like to start a week from today. That should give you time to get ready and get you back no closer than five weeks from your due dates. Abby, do you have anything to add about the medical issues?" "Wow! Where do I begin? First off, you do not yet have our consent to take us on this circus. We'll all have to agree to it. Medically it's a risk but not nearly as big as *Aquila*. I'll have to discuss it with Dr. Shirley and Ben Kirk. I have a bad feeling about this. Can we give you our decision tomorrow?" "I'd rather hear a yes now but tomorrow will have to do. We've already given so many assurances." Vik asks pointedly, "Why the hell Abu Dhabi? They aren't a member of the *Coalition*. Why prolong the long tour and expose us to more security risks?" "It's not widely known but the UAE has been a big but silent benefactor of the *Coalition*. In fact, some of the safety factors like on orbit resupply were made possible with UAE donations." Ellie asks, "What's in it for them?" "They're coming out in the open now and are even footing most of the expense of the entire goodwill tour. They plan to start a colony on Mars and have advance reservations for

118

SpaceTrans Colossus ships to make it happen after the *Coalition* paves the way with the advance bases." Coby has the final word, "Commercial colonization? Well, I suppose that's like the Mayflower. Okay, we'll give you our decision tomorrow."

September 16, 2024
JSC Flight Operations Director Office

The *Aquila* crew is in conference with Director Ben Kirk and Dr. Shirley Hansen.

Coby opens, "Ben and Shirley, you know why we're here. This crew gave everything for the mission. We're still exhausted and trying to get our Earth legs back. Now we seem to be coerced into this whirlwind PR tour. Yes, we're grateful for the efforts of so many workers, companies, and countries. We've said it all on TV."

Ben is calm and pragmatic as always. "I appreciate that. Emily outlined the logistics yesterday- private plane; five star hotels. Please consider the youngsters out there looking up to you as their role models. The opportunity to further the STEAM[56] agenda is invaluable. Think of all the girls who find inspiration from what you've accomplished."

Coby replies, "That hits home."

---

56 Education initiatives to promote Science, Technology, Engineering, Arts, and math. This is expanded from the usual STEM acronym to recognize the role of the Arts in conveying concepts and proposing architecture of the future.

Abby brings up the pregnancy issue. "I don't think it's a good idea to have us traveling so far from home when we're well into our third trimester."

Shirley counters, "So far from home? I'd say that's relative! I'll be there with you constantly monitoring your condition. We've mapped out hospitals and evac routes for each event."

Abby breaks the impasse. "Okay. I'm in. I'm in it for STEAM and inspiring kids—especially girls."

Ellie says, "I agree. You've got me."

Vik, "*Da, Ya nakhozhus'v.*"

Coby, "That's it then. We're a go. You better take good care of Ellie and Abby."

"It's settled then. Get rested and get packed. We leave for LA on Friday."

September 23, 2024

Chicago, Illinois

The Aquila crew's experience of the parade in Los Angeles was uplifting and recharged their space weary bones. Today is Chicago. There are about 500,000 people lining the streets. There are barricades to hold the crowds back and police presence is high. The *Aquila* crew is in a white Cadillac limo and behind a bulletproof bubble top. The slow procession allows security to flank their limo. Armored black security Suburban SUVs are ahead and behind. An Air Force C-17 Globemaster has been assigned to transport these security vehicles to each event location.

The *Aquila* crew stands in the security bubble waving to the crowds.

Abby comments, "I feel like we're caged animals on display. I truly wish we could be out there walking among the people without the need for security."

Ellie responds, "I'd rather be safe in this bubble. We're safe and as removed from a potentially hostile environment as we were in the Rigel capsule." Despite the caution and Ellie's comment, the signs and placards they see and chants they hear are very supportive.

Aquila Gives Us Hope!

You Saved My Son!
He has chosen math
and science over drugs!

On to Mars in 2033!

Way to Go Space Heroes!

You Touched an Asteroid.
You Touched My Heart!

When the crew arrived at the *Langham Chicago*, The lobby was filled with adoring fans. Security keeps them at bay but still the enthusiasm is contagious. They allow some autograph seekers to get close enough to get the treasure. The entire crew sign on *Aquila Mission* photos and hand them to the lucky few.

A group of college students sporting University of Chicago t-shirts shouts in unison, "Coby! Ellie! Vik! Abby! Chicago loves you!" One particularly athletic girl in the crowd yelled, "Coby, I love you!" She caught his eye and threw a wadded package straight at his head. Reflexively Coby protected his face and caught the wad in his right hand. He smiled and laughed as he handed it off the big six-foot-six security guy named Lars. Taking this incident as threat, Lars and the three other security guards hustled the crew to the elevator.

Ellie was agitated. "What was it that the girl hurled at you?" Lars laughed and held up a pair of pink panties tentatively by the waistband.

Ellie reacted, "Eewww, gross! Please get rid of that!"

Coby responded, "If that's the worst security incident we have to face in this circus, we have little to worry about."

"Don't let the panty offering go to your head. I trust my instincts. Nothing can make me let my guard down. I won't relax until we are back in El Lago and out of the lime light."

Lars escorted them to their adjoining rooms and took up station in the hall. They find their luxury rooms to be a welcome relief from the roar of the crowd. Before Vik and Abby retire to their room, Coby turns on the TV to a random station selection. *GNN* is giving a very upbeat report of today's events. Coby switches the channel up and lands on the *FERAL NEWS NETWORK* coverage of parades in Chicago and Los Angeles. They report that the parades are marred by throngs of protesters. However, they are running the same clip of a very small crowd outside a church identified as being in Waco, Texas.

———————————————

God made life on Earth,
not on asteroids!

The Aquila Mission was faked!

122

*Astronauts should keep it
in their space pants!*

Space whores go to hell!

*Money for Ministry,
not for playing with Space Rocks!*

Ellie demands, "Coby, turn that trash off!" Abby is visibly upset and covers her face with her hands.

Coby hugs Ellie while Vik comforts Abby. Coby speaks up, "I'm sorry you saw that. The real sentiment is what we've been seeing on the street. *FERAL* had to dig deep to find those idiots. They play to their audience looking for or making up dirt on any good news story. They forgot to show *The Earth is Flat* sign." That lightened the mood with a knowing laugh. No one could take away from their very real and visceral experience of seeing the Earth from deep space.

October 1, 2024
Rome, Italy

The parade appearances in London, Moscow, Berlin, and Rome are as enthusiastic and uneventful as the appearances had been in the US.

Coby and Ellie are alone in their hotel room. The October weather is delightful. Clear blue skies and crisp, fragrant air beckons. Coby muses, "Here we are in Rome and we can't even be tourists. I'd love to be out there with you for a romantic stroll."

"Second to my home in Milan, this is my favorite city. I'd love to have that stroll with you in the *Giardino Degli Aranci*. It's undeniably the most romantic place in Rome."

"You say that from experience?"

"Yes, but sadly very much alone when I was a student." Then Ellie protests, "I've had enough of this. The world has seen enough of us on TV. We can't do appearances in every city on the planet. I'm exhausted. I'm sure our Coalition hosts will understand if we cut the tour short for obvious medical reasons."

"I agree but I think we need to do Abu Dhabi for the financial support they gave *Aquila*. Abu Dhabi is in two days. Let's do a medical checkup with Abby and Shirley in the morning and plead with Emily Collins to let us off the hook if you still feel tired. Maybe what we need is to sneak off to the *Giardino* tomorrow afternoon."

"Yes, and I know a *back* way to get there. Hey big Daddy, get over here and feel this." She gently guides his hand to her swollen abdomen. "Our baby is dancing…"

October 3, 2024
Abu Dhabi, United Arab Emirates

Even though it's October and getting cooler back home in Houston, it's still oppressively hot, 40° C / 104° F, and dripping wet with humidity when they arrived at the Abu Dhabi International Airport. Abu Dhabi is not favored with dry air off the Rub al Khali desert. Instead, the prevailing north wind is off the steamy warm Arabian Gulf so it never dries out.

Thankfully this is the last *Aquila* crew appearance parade event. This event has its unique embellishments. The United Arab Emirates flaunts its military might by adding five-hundred military parade troops, armored personnel carriers, LAV-68 laser guided rocket launchers, and riot control tear gas launchers. Also there is a change in security protocol. The diplomatic dynamics demanded that the security protocol that was so well practiced in the previous events now must accommodate UAE security personnel and vehicles under the command of Col. Omar Zayed. Two black Suburbans would be added, immediately in front and behind the *Aquila* limo.

Coby and Vik are very vocal about the change. Coby speaks to Emily Collins, "I don't like that the UAE is putting their demands on our security. We lose control and how do we know if their security can be trusted?"

Emily replies. "I agree with you Coby. Vik, be calm. With the huge financial donations that came in from the UAE, the *Coalition* and the State Department are asking us to cooperate fully with what the UAE, an important ally, are offering to insure security at this event."

Vik says, "Okay. Let me talk to Lars and Col. Zayed. We want full cooperation and coordination of our security with theirs. Not only does this put *our lives and family* at risk but it's *bigger*. Any unforeseen incident could become a flash point for delicate relations in the Middle East."

The *Aquila* crew is standing up waving at the crowd in their Cadillac limo within its blessedly cool air conditioned security bubble. Presently they are approaching the reviewing stand. Attending guards open the limo for the *Aquila* crew to exit and stand on a red carpet before the ornate stands with private boxes for the individual dignitaries and their entourage. A voice over loud speakers introduces the dignitaries in English to the honored guests: "...President of the United Arab Emirates, the Emir of Abu Dhabi and the Supreme Commander of the Union Defense Force, *Mansour bin Zahid Al Majed*; King of Saudi Arabia and Custodian of the Two Holy Mosques, *Mohammad bin Naimi;* King of Bahrain, *Mohammad bin Al Khalifa*; Sultan of Oman, *Qaboos bin Sultan*; Amir of Qatar, *Sheikh Tamar bin Mohammed Al Amir.*

There is a reddish brown haze in the humid air wafting in from the populous Eastern Province of Saudi Arabia and the nearby Jebel Ali industrial complex. You can see it, smell it, and taste it. After the introductions and a short speech describing the UAE's aspirations to be involved in space exploration and ultimately colonization, the crew is invited back into their limo to continue the parade. They are hyper-vigilant yet fascinated as they gaze out over the faces in the crowd in a way they had not felt at the other parade events. There is a mix of many nationalities and dress. Half are locals in national dress from the UAE, men wear a long white flowing thobe and white ghutra with black igal head dress, and women wear a long black abaya and black hijab head covering and niqab face covering. There are business people from India, Europe, Canada, and the US; construction workers from Bangladesh and Nepal; domestic workers from Thailand and Philippines. The faces are friendly and welcoming. Some are holding placards. Most are welcoming and celebrating the *Aquila* accomplishment.

'Ahlaan Wasahlan -- Welcome Aquila!

Mabrook Aquila!

You conquered Bennu!

My daughter will put boots on Mars!

الله إلا إله ال

Abby winced at that last placard. She could read some Arabic and she knew that passage is from the Quran. *"There is no god but God."* Out of context, it's a beautiful statement of faith. In the context of this celebration of the *Aquila Mission*, she took it as a blatant protest of their finding of fossil extraterrestrial life on Bennu. Suddenly, this part of the crowd did not look so friendly.

The man in a white thobe did not, at first glance, look out of place. It was his glare of pure hatred as he pushed his way forward toward the motorcade that alarmed Abby. "Get down! Get down on the floor now!" Vik and Coby saw the threat too. Coby pushed Ellie down then fell on top of her in a controlled way to protect the baby. Vik covered Abby. Their world seemed to be closing in. Everything in their past and their future seemed to focus on this moment. Abby and Ellie instinctively wrap their arms around their abdomens to protect their precious babies in utero.

"Alahu Akbar!!"

Their world exploded in a white flash tinged pink with blood and human flesh. The limo rocks violently to the left almost rolling over.

"Uhhh! Vik grunted. "My leg!"

Abby screamed, "Noo!! I'm hit!"

There were screams of horror from the crowd outside. In seconds the motorcycle escort surrounded their open white limo. The police threw open the doors battered and bloody on the outside.

"La daei lildhuera! ladayna alan!"

"We have you now! You are safe with us!" Many gentle hands extracted them one at time and hustled them to the next vehicle, an armored black Suburban.

Vik seeing the wound on Abby's thigh spurting blood, "Mine is just a flesh wound. Yours is *bad* Abby. Got to put pressure on it! Oh God! I have to put pressure on it!" The Suburban is speeding away with the escort of Police motorcycles. He presses firmly on her thigh expecting her reaction but hoping to staunch the bleeding.

Abby chokes out, "Ahhgh! Y-Yes , it's bad. I think the shrapnel cut my femoral artery. I-I need a tourniquet! Oh God...I'm losing too much blood..."

Ellie sobs, "It's going to be alright. Oh my God! It's going to be alright. Abby!"

Coby is yelling. "Hospital now! Now!"

Abby adds with all the strength she can muster, "Almustashfaa alan! Bsre!"

The Suburban is screeching through traffic and around cars that are trying to pull out of the way. The driver yells back over the sirens. "We are almost there. Yes, there it is!" The Suburban screeches into the Emergency Entrance of the Cleveland Clinic, the finest hospital in Abu Dhabi. The big hospital doors slide back and an emergency team is wheeling out a gurney as a policeman quickly opens the back door to Vik and Abby.

Abby manages to say, "I'm a doctor. I need four units of O-negative in *me* stat! I need you to save my baby!"

In an on-rush of medical staff, the first to her gurney is Dr. Naila Otaibi. "Try to relax. We've got you. Don't give orders to my team. I'm Doctor Otaibi. I'm in charge here. Team! Clear this one to the OR, stat! You're in good hands here. We'll take good care of you. You're going to okay. What's your name Ma'am?"

Starting to let go and seeing a tunnel close in…"Uhhh, I-I'm Abby. Abby d-Denton…Naila…name so pretty…My baby…"

"Stay with us Abby. Abby! Don't go to sleep. Stay awake! I'm putting in a plasma line now…A little sting…Abby, I know what I'm doing. I'm just back from six months in Yemen- *Médecins Sans Frontières*. We're getting you into the OR to stop that bleeder. Oxygen mask now. It's not so bad Abby. Your baby is okay…Get me a pulse/ox and BP."

"BP 90 over 60. Pulse 162. Ox 72 percent."

"Abby. Now comes the anesthesia. Breathe deep. You can sleep now. We have you…"

Vik tries to go with Abby. "I'm her husband."

"Easy big guy. She's going to the OR and you can't be in there." Seeing the trail of blood on the floor, "I'm Dr. Said. We need to treat *your* leg. You're bleeding badly also. Lie down on this gurney. We have a room in the ER with your name on it. And what is your name sir?"

"I-I'm Viktor Ivanov."

Coby and Ellie are escorted to the waiting room. Lars and several of the other *Coalition* Security agents have just arrived. In the fray, they had been unable to follow directly. Fifteen minutes later, Shirley Hansen and Emily Collins arrive. They report that due to the crowd density, forty-seven persons in the crowd were killed including the crew limo driver. An additional one-hundred-forty-seven were wounded. All emergency vehicles and hospitals in the city are overwhelmed with the carnage. The UAE has never seen violence on this scale though it had happened so often in Syria, Iraq, and Afghanistan that most of the world is callous to it.

They learn that the bubble top of the supposed bulletproof limo had been shattered. The armored door of the limo was penetrated by ball-bearing shrapnel from the C-4 suicide bomb. Abby saved the lives of the crew by getting them down below the bubble. The shrapnel that hit Abby had first punched through the armored door, through Vik's thigh, then into Abby. It severed her femoral artery and was stopped by her femur causing a hairline fracture in that massive bone.

The bombing is being claimed by a new terror group named *'Iilah Wahid (One God)*. It is a Wahhabi ultraconservative fringe group derivative of Al Qaeda and ISIS. They had been particularly agitated when it was announced that *Aquila* had found supposed evidence of extraterrestrial life.

The crew and especially Abby received mountains of well wishes. Vik recovered well enough to walk a short stretch on crutches in two days. Abby is bed ridden and has a constant presence by her side from Vik, Coby, or Ellie. Tears of thankfulness are shed.

"Girl you saved our lives getting us down on the deck."

"I guess I saw the monster coming. I knew he wanted death and terror."

The UAE, not wanting to appear to harbor terrorists, wastes no time tracking down the *'Iilah Wahid* leaders. They are cornered in an upscale housing compound named *Oasis*. A secret team of commandos called the Anti-Terrorist Unit (WMA-*Wahdat Mukafahat Al'iirhab*) are called in to root out the extremists and attempt to capture them. *'Iilah Wahid* had been tipped off and got the first deadly shots off killing two of the commandos instantly. The WMA returns fire and zero in on the one villa where *'Iilah Wahid* is holed up.

The *Oasis* Compound residents instead of hunkering down inside for safety, pour out to watch the spectacle. They believe that Allah has no bullets for them. Blankets are laid on the surrounding lush green lawns and obligatory chai and biscuits are served by the women.

The WMA breaks loose with their truck mounted *Eiqab* 70mm anti-aircraft machine cannon while the extremists return fire. The extremist villa walls are shattered in the withering, high power barrage. There can be no capture. Then the villa disappears in a huge explosion showering the troops and onlookers with debris, bits of flesh, and dust.

The UAE is very conciliatory and vows to double down on security and surveillance of extremists. They are even more motivated to push forward their presence in space with home grown legions of scientists and engineers.

In 2018, the UAE built a city to simulate life on Mars. The ambitious project in the desert near Dubai is an inspirational design for the *Coalition*. Sheikh Mohammed bin Rashid said, "The UAE seeks to establish international efforts to develop technologies that benefit humankind, and establish the foundation of a better future for more generations to come. We also want to consolidate the passion for leadership in science in the UAE, contributing to improving life on Earth and to developing innovative solutions to many of our global challenges."

Sheikh Mohammed bin Zayed said, "We have great confidence in our national work teams, and Emirates Mars Mission prove that our youth are trustworthy and capable of achieving national ambitions."[57]

---

57 "City dedicated to researching Mars colonization unveiled at UAE Government Centennial meeting", The National, 17 Sept 2017, Web accessed 17 Aug 2018.

Their simulated city on Mars is architecturally elegant and can be used to air condition the wildly increasing temperatures in the UAE. However, the glass dome design will be woefully inadequate to abate solar and cosmic radiation pummeling Mars from deep space.

In 2018, the UAE's vision was to build a city on Mars in less than one hundred years- by 2117. Now, with *Shiva's* threat, they intend to accelerate that to 2038. They have a contract with SpaceTrans for the Colossus ships to support their city through 2045. "We have eradicated the unbeliever extremists. Our vision is a city on Mars dedicated to peace: *al-Salam al-Jadid.*"

Abby takes two weeks to recover enough to travel with the crew on the private jet back to Houston. She will be in a wheel chair for six more weeks for the wound and femur fracture to heal. Abby will have to give birth by C-section to avoid stressing her wound.

November 18-20, 2024
Houston Methodist Hospital

Ellie goes into labor first. After 12 hours of hard labor, she gives birth to Sofi-- Sophia Aurora Accardi-Brewster, at 8:14 PM November 18, 2024. Coby is by her side in delivery and receives the quiet but very alert newborn from Dr. Shirley after the attending midwives have her cleaned. After this brief introduction, Coby gently hands her to Ellie. Immediately Sofi nuzzles and roots for a nipple.

---

https://www.thenational.ae/uae/government/city-dedicated-to-researching-mars-colonisation-unveiled-at-uae-government-centennial-meeting-1.661843

Abby, Vik, and Dr. Shirley Hansen come to visit early the next morning. Vik is pushing Abby in her wheel chair. Vik has a noticeable limp from his wound in the UAE bombing. He and Abby are getting daily physical therapy. While cooing over baby Sofi, Abby has a big painful contraction. Dr. Shirley determines that it's not labor yet. Out of precaution, she still insists that Abby should be admitted to maternity immediately. At midnight, Abby is taken to surgery for a C-section with Vik attending. Alex-- Alexei Pavel Denton-Ivanov, is born at 12:45 AM November 20, 2024.

The rumors and concerns that the "space twins" would be deformed from radiation exposure and microgravity are unfounded. They are both in perfect health. Shirley Hansen remarks, "These first babies to be conceived in space are a bit underweight in the 10th percentile but long in the 90th percentile. They are longest babies I've ever seen! This isn't a statistical sample but I'd bet that microgravity has something to do with it. What else will we see as they develop?"

Colossus, ECLSS, and unloading the behemoth
August 6, 2025
University of Colorado Boulder
Aerospace Engineering Center

SpaceTrans has had a successful demo launch of Colossus and a series of commercial cargo launches with flawless booster and second stage returns to establish reusability. SpaceTrans lack the depth of knowledge and experience in human space flight that the *Coalition* has gained in ISS operation for twenty eight years and counting.

SpaceTrans has convened an engineering conference to initiate a radical upgrade of the ECLSS Life Support system for the Colossus to support long duration deep space flight with a crew complement of up to twenty-five persons. The *Aquila* crew is in attendance weighing in with their recommendations from hard earned experience. The original SpaceTrans hype about sending one-hundred colonists in a single Colossus ship would not be possible unless all the passengers were in cryo-sleep. Then they would not consuming oxygen and nutrition at the rate that they would if they were awake bumping into one another. With one hundred passengers, there is only eight cubic meters of pressurized ship space allotted to each person.

Over the first three days of the conference, they hammer out the design basis for the control deck, galley, recreation, exercise, communications, medical, sleep cubes, and most importantly the ECLSS Life Support for a crew limited to twenty five passengers for the six month trip to Mars.

The next two days is focused on the cargo decks and cargo handling. There will be two radically different designs. One is for the passenger ship version of Colossus; the other is for the robotic cargo version. The huge advantages of Colossus are its reusability and its huge one hundred-fifty metric tons to Mars cargo capacity. Reusability will allow for quick launch turnarounds and much lower launch cost per metric ton. Getting cargo to Mars is a good thing. Unloading it to the surface from cargo decks ten stories high is a huge challenge.

On Apollo, Neil and Buzz only had to climb down a three meter ladder to the surface of the Moon. Apollo 15 through 17 had the luxury of a lunar rover to extend exploration greater distances. The rover was folded up in a neat package on the side of the descent module where a pull of a cord lowered it on hinges to unfold on the surface.

It's not so easy unloading the Colossus. It is envisioned that crew and cargo will descend an elevator system on a winch cable hanging from an arm extended out from the cargo bay ten stories high. Granted the pull of gravity is only 0.38 of gravity on Earth but mass remains the same. That's a problem if a load begins to sway. Passengers and consumables loads can be easily managed. Small cargo modules for consumables might be cubes two meters on a side.

Larger cargo modules will be needed for Inflatable habs, life support, propellant manufacturing equipment, solar cell farms; nuclear fission power plants, industrial 3D printers, pressurized rovers, and ice mining equipment. Such a cargo module could be as large as a cylinder eight meters in diameter and four meters high limited by the internal diameter of the cargo bay. Unloading such a colossal mass will require a huge cargo bay door and correspondingly large cargo arm and elevator winch system. Now we need to account for the stability of the Colossus sitting on its landing pad legs. Special legs will need to be extended with a wider footprint under the cargo arm just as a mobile construction crane extends special leg pads for stability. Expert cargo tenders will be needed in the cargo bay and on the surface to control the loads. AI robotics should be designed to assist.

"Let's roll up our sleeves and design what's needed to get the job done safely."

Since returning from *Aquila*, the crew continues as top consultants for the orbiting Mars Base Camp and planned 2033 first Mars crew landing. The 2027 discovery of *Shiva* changed the game. They were asked to consider being the leaders of Mars Arcadia Colony slated to be established in 2035. In a few years they will have carte blanche to select half of the twenty one person first colony crew. The *International Space Coalition* will select the other half based on professional qualifications, psychological evaluation, and inevitably a little politics.

Three years later
February 10, 2028
El Lago, TX.

It's a cold night in Houston. The wind has been blowing with intermittent rain squalls all day. Coby and Ellie are sitting on the couch enjoying a glass of red wine. They are under a throw blanket by the fireplace with a pleasant crackling wood fire. Sofi is sleeping, tucked snug and warm in her bed.

"No, Coby. We can't do this! When we were on *Aquila*, I thought that going to Mars was the obvious next step for us. Putting a crew down there is inevitable. We've done our share consulting on Mars Base Camp and the planning for the first crew landing. We defied the odds getting back alive from *Aquila*. Now, the first colony on Mars? What could go wrong? Let me count the ways! Now we have Sofi. Abby and Vik have Alex. How can we offer up their lives in addition to ours for this experiment?"

"Ellie, I don't take this lightly. It's not for the glory of history. What odds do Sofi and Alex and any of our family have here with *Shiva* bearing down day-by-day and threatening the entire planet? Sofi and Alex will be a mature age of seventy-three when *Shiva* arrives. I'd put the odds of their survival better on Mars. What of Jacob? He's ten now and I wouldn't leave without him. Elena is has proven her mettle at ISS and will be an asset on Mars. What could go wrong? You, me, Vik, and Abby will be there to sort out any messes the kids can get into. Besides, you'll have an entire new world of geology to explore."

"You do touch all the right buttons. No, it won't be easy for any of us. *Tutto aposto*. Alright, I'll give it everything I've got so long as you remind me every day why we're doing this."

Two doors down on Woodland Drive in El Lago, Abby and Vik are propped up in bed. Having long ago recovered from the effects of the return to Earth gravity, nonetheless they are still amazed at how brutal gravity can be.

"Vik, can we get a softer bed? A pile of feathers might do."

"How about we sleep floating in the hot tub?"

"I'm in! Say are you sure Alex is asleep?"

"Like a baby."

"He *is* a baby!" They both laugh at that.

Reminiscing Vik adds, "*Bo-zeh moy!* What a mission and the look on Ben Kirk's face when he saw you and Ellie pregnant!"

She nuzzles into Vik's arm. "We did stun the whole world didn't we? I was so afraid that our babies wouldn't make it. First the exposure to deep space radiation, then a terrorist nearly killed all of us. Alex seems just perfect and so does Sofi. They're practically inseparable."

"Da. We returned from the most dangerous mission imaginable. We did survive the terrorist because you saw him and got us down to some protection on the floor of the limo. Now Mars? How can we willingly leave the Earth never to return? How can we commit our families to such danger and uncertainty?"

"You are my strength you big spaceman. You are the bravest person I've ever met. Please don't question what we have to do. Alex and Sofi and Oleg need to come with us to start a new future. We will be the seed. Others will follow- tens, hundreds, and then thousands as we are able to support the growing numbers. We've always felt that humans need a second home. Now *Shiva* gives us no choice. Who's more qualified than you to get us there and keep the equipment running? Who is more qualified to deal with keeping space farers alive than me? *Shiva* leaves us no choice but to make a future for humans on Mars. It is our duty and our legacy. That legacy will be descendants of you, me, Coby, and Ellie, and the colonists chosen to go with us. We can do this. We *have* to do this!"

"*Da.* After that speech, I wouldn't let you go without me. You need me!"

The nuzzling became a kiss and giggling. "Shhh! Don't wake Alex! I need you all to myself."

4

ARCADIA 1 MISSION-
COLOSSUS SHIP *ARCTURUS*

"This is the goal: To make available for life every place where life is possible. To make inhabitable all worlds as yet uninhabitable and all life purposeful."

Hermann Oberth, *Man Into Space,* 1957

On April 4, 2033, the *Arcadia 1 Mission* Colossus ship *Arcturus* launches with the first crew destined to land on Mars. They will have a relatively short 174 day journey with this launch window. Just a few weeks later, on April 28, 2033, two robotic Colossus ships, *Pleiades* and *Alcyone* launch for Mars on a much longer 274 day journey to deliver supplies support the first crew and to expand Arcadia Colony Base. The Arcadia colony will follow in 2035.

The designated *Arcadia Base Landing Zone* is in the Erebus Montes area of Arcadia Planitia fifteen hundred kilometers northeast of Olympus Mons. The landing zone is on the east flank of Golombek Crater in post-glacial terrain with abundant near surface ice. The low elevation, smooth northern hemisphere of Mars including Arcadia Planitia once held an ocean.

September 29, 2033
Arcadia 1 Mission Elapsed Time 174:14:27:41
Sol 0
Earth distance: 247,948,787 kilometers
Two-way communications time delay: 7 minutes 21 seconds

The *Arcadia 1 Mission* Colossus ship *Arcturus* approaches the red planet in a precise atmospheric entry corridor engaged by the CASSI ship's AI computer using automatic star reference sightings and radio navigation beacons on the ground at Arcadia Base. This is first Mars crew landing. The hopes of the world are with the ten person international crew led by Commander Trent Granger.

"The first human beings on Mars- just imagine that! We're doing it! Believe me crew, Mars will be daunting, but this moment is more exhilarating than anything in my life."

They have secured everything on ship. That's no easy task after the six month outbound trip from earth. The crew is strapped in and wearing flight pressure suits. They begin to feel the atmosphere buffeting the ship.

"Okay crew, we're not only the first crew but as you well know, this is the first Colossus ship to make a landing on Mars. We've practiced this endlessly in the sims."

Precise computer control has allowed dozens of precise Colossus landings on Earth. Ninety-nine percent of the ship's velocity will be shed by atmospheric friction. The last percent is a controlled retro-rocket burn for a precise landing on the prepared landing pad. "It's a piece of cake compared to what the first rovers went through. Hang tight. Atmosphere contact begins now. Seven minutes to touch-down"

The great ship is oriented belly first into the thin atmosphere of Mars. At first they only feel a slight increase in weight pushing into their couches. This builds to soft then harder and harder buffeting as a storm of blue-white ionization trails streak by the windows above them.

CASSI reports, "Retro engines engaging. Landing in two minutes and ten seconds. Retros at one hundred percent...Altitude fifteen thousand meters...Ten thousand meters..."

The big ship is pitching over so the crew can see the ruddy horizon of Mars and the ground approaching ever more slowly.

Trent announces, "There's Golombek Crater. It's just like the sims!"

CASSI continues, "One hundred meters altitude...Fifty...Twenty...Touch down one meter off the landing mark. Propulsion systems powered down. The ship is yours Commander."

"On the money! Fine flying CASSI. Landing gear and systems check."

"All systems nominal and you are welcome."

"CASSI, please open Coms to Houston."

"Go ahead Commander."

"Houston, *Arcturus Arcadia 1* is down on the red planet. Reporting from *Mars Arcadia Base*. Repeat. *Arcturus Arcadia1* has landed!" They congratulate one another and give high fives all the way around.

On an open link to Houston Commander Granger gives directions to the crew, "Unstrap and stow your flight suits. Barry Peterson and Tom Decloux will remain on the Command Deck as per safety protocol. The EVA team will buddy pair by assignment and get into your EVA suits. We're going for a walk!"

"Trent, let's not rush this," Kerstin Nemetz, Flight Surgeon, cautions. "Our inner ears are scrambled with Mars gravity after six months of microgravity. If anyone wants to postpone their EVA-- feeling dizzy or nauseated, speak up now."

Serena says, "Screw that! After six months in this can, I'd kill to go for a walk. I feel great! This is only one third g!"

"Right," Trent says "Let's do this!"

Barry speaks his mind, "Tom, it sucks that you and I got the short straws and stay behind on the first EVA."

"Don't worry Barry. History will only record that Trent takes the first steps on Mars. We all share the glory of being the first crew,"

"Okay, can the chatter. Be glad I cut the feed to Houston just then."

After the seven minute two-way radio delay they get they jubilant congratulations from Mission Control. The Houston transmission signs off with, "The weather station at Arcadia reports it's a fine day for a walk. You can leave your umbrellas inside!"

The rudiments of a base is already there having been established by robots starting in 2031. The *Mars Arcadia Base* was established with robotic landers of habitats, consumables in resupply modules, robotic construction equipment, and an advanced robotic lander slowly manufacturing ascent propellant for the *Arcturus*. A robot miner augers into the Martian surface to a shallow ice layer to test the ice and the system. It will be delivering water ice to the Sabatier Reactor to be powered by a kilopower nuclear reactor. The Sabatier produces methane and oxygen from the water ice and carbon dioxide from Mars' atmosphere. A much larger SSTAR nuclear reactor will be needed to complete the gargantuan task to refuel the *Arcturus* before the crew return window opens. Robotic equipment constructed six landing pads from 3D printed sintered regolith for SpaceTrans Colossus ships. *Arcturus* sits on Pad 2. The landing pads are necessary to support the huge ships and prevent rocket exhaust from excavating the regolith and sending hypervelocity debris that might damage base infrastructure.

The eight person EVA party is assembled after suit check in the cargo deck. They have stacked cargo secured around them. They enter the large airlock designed to handle cargo modules. The inner hatch is sealed. Video and audio is being transmitted to Houston.

Commander Granger speaks, "CASSI, please initiate depressurization."

"Affirmative. Depressurization initiated. Three minutes to equalization."

During the depressurization process, each of them takes time to reflect on how far they've come and the meaning of what they about to do. The hopes of humankind and the dreams of generations of people looking at the red planet as a destination for exploration are about to be realized. Trent Granger has one thing on *his* mind-- *I* will be the first man to make that important first step and *I* will be immortalized in the history books.

"Depressurization completed."

"Open the cargo bay airlock door and extend the cargo boom."

"Affirmative. Door opening." They don't hear a hiss but some debris swirls toward the opening door. "Cargo boom extending."

"Alright troops step aboard the elevator pallet. What a view! We're thirty-two meters above the surface. Securing the safety gate. CASSI extend the elevator on the sky crane and begin descent sequence."

"Affirmative. I will keep the lights on for you."

"Thank you CASSI." Commander Granger keeps a running commentary open to Houston on the long descent. "It's a spectacular sight with Arcadia Base laid out below us. We've monitored construction progress from the robots on the surface and from the orbiters. It looks very different from this perspective ten stories up. We're facing west toward the rim wall of Golombek Crater which is about twenty kilometers distant. I can see the area that the robot dozers have leveled for the Base. The surrounding plains are rugged from the subsurface ice like permafrost terrain in Siberia. In fact I can even see what looks like dirty ice in places where the dozers scraped. There are two solar arrays deployed, two kilo-power reactors, two Sabatier reactors, and the two inflatable BS-340 Hab modules. We will keep using the *Arcturus* as our home until we get all the equipment checked and running reliably."

Pilot Serena Solis, second in command interrupts, "Commander, we've set down on the surface. It's show time."

"The crew elevator has stopped and I'm opening the gate. As I set the first human boot on the surface of Mars, I'm humbled by this accomplishment made possible by thousands of people from many nations on Earth. As Mars appears as a bright rusty red dot in the sky from Earth, I can see Earth as a bright pale blue dot in the sky. God bless all of you on that blue dot. We have come the distance. Many more will follow as we establish Mars as a second home for humankind. Let history record that the second boots on Mars are those of my second in command Serena Solis. Please."

"Thanks Trent. As I step off onto this red soil, I won't make a speech. You already said what's on all our minds. Seriously, being the first woman on Mars thrills me to the core and to my shaking boots. It's the realization of my dreams and hard work. Ill also comment on what I think is striking and on what our future here depends. I'm now standing on the bed of what was an ocean on Mars billions of years ago. Much of that water is below my feet. It will sustain us and everyone who follows. I also have no doubt that we will find evidence of past life perhaps even living organisms in the subsurface. Mars is not dead. What will *our* civilization on Mars look like in a hundred years?"

"Thanks Serena. We've got a restless crew stuck on the elevator behind you. Please everyone step out and let's place the *International Space Coalition* flag and take some pictures for history. Then we begin our first EVA to start checking the status of *Arcadia Base*-- so far built only by our tireless robots."

This first EVA will last five more hours. Each assigned buddy pair has specific tasks to accomplish. Barry Peterson and Tom Decloux are now the CAPCOMs tracking each of the four pairs on their specific checklists. The crew on Mars is much less reliant on Houston Mission Control because of the radio delay at the great distance. CASSI helps with the tracking by plotting each crew member on a flat-screen panel map of Arcadia Base and posting their checklist items and progress against the EVA timeline. CASSI also provides regular progress reports to Houston.

Denikin Andreevich and Lisenka Savelievna set about their task of collecting and documenting contingency geology samples. They are bagged, tagged, and placed in special sealed SRC sample return containers.

Denikin says, "This place looks so much like places I've studied on Earth- like the Gobi desert or the Utah desert except *here* there's not a blade grass, or cactus, or a bit of sage brush. Imagine the ocean here billions of years ago, perhaps teaming with life evolving and finding its way until it all dried up. We're going to look very hard to find the evidence of possible past life and perhaps even find some live bugs in the subsurface. Microbes happily live up to two kilometers deep in the Earth. There's so much to do on each EVA. I'm looking forward to getting the rover unloaded. We can science the shit out of this place when we get wheels."

It's certainly not all about science since they have a base to construct. Trent and Serena oversee the deployment of the *Arcturus* solar panels with Barry Peterson and CASSI operating from the command deck. They were used in space on the outbound trip but had to be retracted for landing. Now the panels must be redeployed to maintain power in the ship while it serves as the temporary crew habitat. Other tasks on the checklist involve inspecting the condition of each of the robotic installations. The two inflatable BS-340 Hab modules and each with an ECLSS life support module and gas and water storage tanks get the most scrutiny. Their lives will depend on perfect installation and operation. There are two pressurized crew rovers, two cryo propellant transfer wagons sitting idle. Six busy construction robots are each methodically working on the specific task for which it was designed and programmed.

After each EVA, in buddy pairs, they use CO2 hoses to clean Mars dust off before entering the *Arcturus* cargo bay airlock. The perchlorates in the Mars dust might wreak havoc on human lungs if it gets inside the ship.

Arcadia 1 Mission
EVA 8
Sol 2

The *Arcadia 1* crew makes electrical connections from power sources to junction boxes and then to the power consumers: hab modules, ECLSS modules, and propellant manufacturing Sabatier reactors. Plumbing connections are made from ECLSS to the hab modules. The BS-340 inflatable habs are inflated cylinders fourteen meters long and seven meters diameter. The cylinders are set on their sides connected end-to-end with crew access up a ladder to the central air lock. Each hab module has 340 cubic meters of inflated volume with three living/working decks that can accommodate six persons. The upper deck has sleeping and hygiene compartments. In due course, the robots will 3D print an arched cover with sintered regolith over the habs to protect from solar and cosmic radiation. Eventually, the colonists will live underground in excavated tunnels and chambers.

Arcadia 1 Mission
EVA 15
Sol 8

The solar array farms, kilo-power nuclear reactors, and ECLSS life support modules are commissioned. The hab modules are declared operational and five of the ten *Arcadia 1* crew moves in for a more thorough hab check-out. Trent Granger, Barry Peterson, and Denikin Andreevich are in Hab 1. Serena Solis and Kerstin Nemetz are in Hab 2. They have a common meal in the Hab 1 galley. The guys do the cooking.

Kerstin comments, "Thanks for the romantic dinner. It's no better and no worse than on *Arcturus*. It's all the same food."

Barry complains, "This is our first home on Mars and the chemical smell is nauseating."

Trent replies, "It's not so bad when you get used to it. It smells better than my beater back home. I'm hopeful that the ECLSS will cycle out the smell. It's already better than when we first cracked the airlock. Take your teddy bear and go to bed Barry."

Serena as always tries to put a bright face on their cramped lifestyle. "My glass is more than half full. I'm on Mars living my dream. We have another thirty months together so let's be kind for God's sake. Barry, you always have the best taste in music. Please pick out one of your playlists for CASSI to cue up…"

Arcadia 1 Mission
EVA 23
Sol 16

The third week of EVA activity accomplished unloading *Arcturus*. There are twenty individual modules, two metric tons (MT) each, of food consumables to unload. The modules are thermally insulated and stackable near the hab entrance. Other modules have spare clothing, tools, and electronics. Work is good for their mental health. Trent is pleased with the teamwork and the routine they have for the load handling. The two MT loads do not pose any problems for the equipment or the crew.

Arcturus has ten percent propellant remaining. They will have to refuel to at least sixty percent to make the return flight to Earth. That means they need at least one hundred twenty metric tons of methane and four hundred thirty metric tons of LOX liquid oxygen. They barely have enough power to run the Sabatier reactor at a minimal rate and power the hab and life support. Sabatier trial runs have been made with ice mined near the reactor.

The *Arcadia 1* Mission needs the arriving Colossus ships *Pleiades* and *Alcyone* to bring the ten megawatt SSTAR nuclear reactor to make serious headway in propellant production. The two new inbound Colossus ships can be drained to transfer the expected ten percent residual fuel loads. They have two 10 MT cryo transfer wagons, one for the methane and one for the LOX.

January 27, 2034
Arcadia 1 Mission Elapsed Time 294:06:33:04
Sol 120

"Houston, Arcadia Base. Houston, Arcadia Base. This is Commander Granger. Landing Pads 3 and 4 are rechecked for integrity and cleared of debris. The ships are reading the landing beacons. *Pleiades* and *Alcyone* are just ten thousand klicks out. It should be quite a show to watch them streak in from this perspective. Houston, we have live feed beaming to you."

On Sol 120, the two robotic Colossus Mars supply ships approach to land bringing support the *Arcadia 1* crew will need to expand Arcadia Colony Base in preparation for the first Mars *Arcadia Colony* crew landing next year. The ships are coming in parallel formation, aerobraking belly forward, and trailing a gold and crimson ionized trail. The visual from *Arcadia Base* cannot yet see the ships, just the fireworks in the dim dawn light. At two minutes to touchdown, still hypersonic, the two ships pitch tail first and ignite their inboard retrorockets. Now on visual in a graceful demonstration of controlled landing, *Pleiades* and *Alcyone* slow and descend to their designated landing pads.

"Houston, *Arcadia Base*. We have a good show. We have two good birds down. Now we face the job of unloading the supply ships. *Arcadia Base* infrastructure expansion is the focus for the next year for us."

February 15, 2034
Arcadia 1 Mission Elapsed Time 313:11:21:37
Sol 139

The crew has unloaded mostly two MT module loads and several four MT module loads from the two ships including a backup ECLSS, two more kilopower reactors, solar panels, and parts for the first greenhouse. They are now progressing to unload the largest and most important cargo load to date. Eight crew persons are unloading the ten megawatt SSTAR nuclear reactor from the Alcyone. Four are in the cargo bay and four are on the ground stabilizing the load with guy lines. Trent Granger is supervising.

The advanced reactor design, originally for Earth use in remote areas, has been downsized to fit in the Colossus cargo bay and to be well within its load capacity. The reactor package weighs one hundred twenty metric tons. The cargo bay doors and cargo boom have been modified to accommodate it. Load stabilizing pads are extended to stabilize the Alcyone while lowering the huge load. Tom Decloux, Denikin Andreevich, Barry Peterson, and Takahashi Shigenaga are on the surface. The load is robotically loaded and secured on the oversized cargo pallet.

Trent calls, "Slow away. Easy now. CASSI, please lower the load on the sky crane at ten centimeters per second...Good. Slowly increase to twenty centimeters per second..."

The huge load is ten meters off the surface. The entire ship begins to shake with the pendulum harmonics.

"CASSI, slow to ten centimeters per second! Dammit! We have to get this load down!"

Five meters off the surface... The *Alcyone* continues to shake and visibly sway. The four men on the surface are trying to prevent the load from swaying with their guy ropes. The corner of the pallet strikes Barry Peterson's helmet faceplate and is driven deep into his now destroyed face. The load touches down next to where Barry has fallen. Tom, Denikin, and Takahashi rush to see if they can help.

Tom yells out over the radio, "Emergency! Barry is down! H-his faceplate is smashed! Oh my good God! His face!... I, I think he's dead..."

Without the load swing, the Alcyone stabilizes without toppling over. The three with Barry wait for Kerstin Nemetz, their crew flight surgeon, and Trent to arrive. Barry's medical sensors tell all of them what they already knew. He's dead. They cover him with a Mylar blanket from Kerstin's kit.

Kerstin and Trent make the difficult decision to not take Barry in for an autopsy. The incident was documented on video. They'll make detailed reports and recommendations. They agree that a quick proper burial is in order. They radio in a preliminary report to Houston.

Two hours later, the mining robot has dug a grave a hundred meters east from Alcyone. The grave is walled in crystal blue ice. Barry Peterson is laid to rest with a ceremony presided by Tom Decloux, their acting Chaplain. They mound up a cairn of regolith and rocks on the grave. Later they will fabricate a proper memorial plaque commemorating Barry Peterson's sacrifice as the first fatality on Mars.

The nine remaining crew members gather in Hab 1 and take stock of the disaster, what they have accomplished, and what their future holds.

Trent tries to inspire them, "We have to look forward. This base is up and running smoothly but we have a long way to go. I for one would like to get back to Earth. We don't have the propellant to get home and that SSTAR reactor in necessary to fully power the Sabatier units. It's our ticket home. Stop feeling sorry for yourselves and focus on what we have to do."

Tom replies, "Trent, we know what we have to do. We aren't feeling sorry for ourselves but I'd like to take a minute to remember Barry out of respect. He was my best friend. He was a friend to all of us. He paid the ultimate sacrifice trying to do exactly what you are preaching about. I'd like to hear a few words from each of you on how you remember Barry…"

May 1, 2035
Arcadia 1 Mission Elapsed Time 753:18:51:28
Sol 579

Trent speaks to the crew during an increasingly rare communal dinner, "We've come the distance. It's been hard work but thanks to me, we have our ticket home. We now have a sixty-percent propellant load on Arcturus. We'll leave our legacy here

154

for the colony that follows us. The SSTAR reactor was a bitch to unload and get up and running. We did it. Now we're all going back to Earth."

It has come to a head. Serena finally freaks out over Trent's style of Command that's been grating on her for years. "I can't be around you another day. My dream has always been to live on Mars. I want to stay here and join the colony." She sobs, "You go back to Earth without me. What's there for humans with *Shiva* coming?"

"Serena, that's mutiny. I won't stand for it. Do you remember how Helen Craig got Bob Trask off of the ISS? I have the trank pens. Don't tempt me to use one."

Tom says, "Trent. Chill out! We're all under stress. You'd do well to have a little empathy. Threats are not what Serena needs."

Kerstin Nemetz goes to the med bay and returns with a mild sedative. "Serena, we all know how you feel. Please take this and you'll calm down. You can't stay here alone for seven months. We're your friends, almost like brothers and sisters. Yes we have our squabbles. We have accomplished so much here on Mars but it's time to focus on going home and spend the rest of our lives enjoying the warm green hills and blue oceans on Earth."

May 8, 2035
Arcadia 1 Mission Elapsed Time 760:07:24:16
Sol 586

The Earth return window opens just after sunrise on Arcadia Planitia. The Colossus ship *Arcturus* majestically lifts off from Mars with the propellant manufactured on Mars thanks to the literal blood, sweat, and tears of the first crew to land there. The return voyage will take one hundred ninety eight days. Half-way, they will pass the *Arcadia Colony* ship *Taurus* that's already outbound to take up where they left off on Mars.

November 22, 2035

Arcadia 1 Mission Elapsed Time 958:16:43:38

This is not the first time the Colossus heat shield is subjected to reentry from deep space at over 40,000 km/hour. Crews returning from the Moon have paved the way. The triumphant first *Arcadia 1* crew to land on Mars establishing Arcadia Base returns to Earth making a precise soft landing at the SpaceTrans Port at Cape Canaveral.

They are subjected to two weeks of quarantine, recovery, and medical tests. They have endured two years, seven months, and eighteen days in microgravity and the .38 g on Mars. Even with two hours per day of exercise there is serious bone and muscle loss. At long last they are reunited with their friends and families. It has been eleven years since the world celebrated *Aquila*. The world needs good news and celebration. When the medical teams clear the crew, they put a good face on a two week world celebratory tour of parades and press conferences. Security is much tighter than it was for the *Aquila* celebration. Despite protests from the UAE, the requested parade there never materialized.

The world eagerly looks for hope that humans will survive beyond 2079 with colonies on Mars even if *Shiva* destroys the Earth. Every person hopes that he or she or their child can earn the ticket to a Mars colony.

None of the eight other surviving crew members is willing talk to Trent Granger for the rest of their lives.

5

OUTBOUND – COLONY SHIP
TAURUS

"It may be that the venture into space is the product of biological determinism which impels us to explore a new environment when we are technologically ready."

Richard S. Lewis, *Appointment on the Moon*, 1968

June 5, 2035

It's a warm night in June. Coby, Ellie, and Sofi are in their back yard in the El Lago Taylor Lake neighborhood looking up at the Moon and the bright planet Mars at opposition. Mars is getting closer than any time it has been since 2018. They are a few weeks from the approaching launch window. It's a time of contemplation and introspection.

As they stare at the Moon and Mars, Coby holds Ellie and Sofi, "Humans went from the Earth to the Moon on Apollo. We will go from the Earth to Mars on Colossus. We have already been that distance on *Altair* during the *Aquila Mission*. Nothing we have done before will be as hard as making it on Mars." Ellie wipes his tears and her own.

Sofi is optimistic. "This is going to be adventure! I can't wait to collect my own Mars rocks."

Coby hugs her tighter. "There will be so many Mars rocks and so much terrain to explore on Mars it will last you and an army of geologist's many lifetimes of work. This is not just a summer adventure trip. We'll need your help making Mars our new forever home."

Personal Preparation

The colonists are allotted a personal preference kit (PPK) to weigh no more than ten kilograms and fit into a special 0.1 cubic meter locker. They are allotted a ten terabyte uncensored digital drive for personal files and entertainment. They will have unlimited access to the colony intranet with a digital backbone of ten petabytes of technical data, music, movies, and an algorithm selected copy of a vast spectrum of worldwide internet content. Each person while on Mars will be allotted one gigabyte of bandwidth for Earth communication, either for sending or receiving with the reality of light time delay. This communication is subject to digital surveillance by *Coalition* protocol. The *Arcadia Colony* has peaceful intent but there is no guarantee that its multinational colonists are not subject to political pressures from Earth.

Each person selects a thirty day personal meal plan that will be supplied in repetitious quantity for three years on Mars. They will be able select from general stores to supplement their personal meal plan. There is the expectation that the colony will be resupplied at every twenty-six month launch window and that the colony will be working toward self-sufficiency in growing food.

Legal Considerations

The international ISS Charter was amended for the *Aquila Mission* and serves as the basis for the expanded *Mars Arcadia Colony Base Charter*. It is not yet a formal democracy but serves as the colony's Constitution and Bill of Rights. The Aquila crew was instrumental in the organization of the colony. They were given international support. Collectively, they decided that Coby would be the Commander on the outbound colony trip to Mars and then be the colonial Governor for the first two years. Succession is decided by a majority vote of colonists age sixteen and over but had to be ratified by the *International Space Coalition*.

A small colony of twenty one people could never be a full cross-section of humanity and unlikely to be both reproductive and self-sufficient in all of the technical aspects to support an independent colony to thrive and grow. At best, the colony is expected to establish a firm base for expansion for incoming colonists and new adjunct colonies.

Outbound

Kennedy Space Center Pad 39C
Cape Canaveral, Florida
Mars Arcadia Colony Colossus Ship *Taurus*
June 23, 2035
Mission Elapsed Time -00:00:10:00

Reference Dramatis Personae

This is finally launch day. The reality of leaving Earth weighs heavier than Earth's gravity for the soon to be colonists. On the *Taurus* Colossus ship there are five seats in the Command Deck occupied by Commander Coby Brewster, Pilot Vik Ivanov, Pilot Elena Petrov, Abby Denton, and Ellie Accardi. There are sixteen seats in Deck Two in four sections of four: Oleg Ivanov and wife Olga Sadoski, Alexei Ivanov, Sophia Brewster; Jacob Petrov, Tracy Dixon and husband Paul Earhart, Dieter Schwartz; Megumi Hirakata and husband Satoshi Fukoshima, Trevor Brown and wife Mandy Shields; Dao-Ming Cai, Sandy Conklin, Harrison Frank and his wife Eve Cain.

All of them are in flight pressure suits and strapped in. It's not as easy as putting on a car seatbelt. The Colossus nose is pointed upward, so the seats are tilted ninety degrees. Getting in place means wiggling and wriggling on your back into the contour seat with your legs higher than your head. The straps are padded across the shoulder and come down across the chest similar to a helicopter pilot's harness. They are worn tight for safety and not for comfort. The head and helmet padding is more than adequate to keep your head from uncontrolled rag doll shaking with the intense vibration from the thirty one big engines in the booster stage. Launch Control pans both decks and a commentator introduces each one of the crew. The commentator points out that the youngest, Alexei Ivanov, Sophia Brewster, and Jacob Petrov, are the only space rookies on the mission.

Coby has the two-way audio feed off so that unplanned remarks are not broadcast at this historic event.

Elena speaks her mind, "Will everything we've done to prepare and all the supplies we've sent ahead be enough for our survival?"

Coby senses that this is a good opportunity to open the feed and speak to the world, "CASSI open Coms please. Launch Control, Commander Brewster has a few words."

CAPCOM Steve Fishman replies, "Go ahead Commander Brewster."

"Thanks Steve. I would like to say a few words to my crew and to anyone out there who may be interested and listening. All of us have chosen this path to take humankind to new homes beyond Earth. Leaving Earth for Mars is a big deal for each one of us. We do have mixed feelings but we are committed and excited to be leaving for a new life. There are regrets for those of us leaving but it is perhaps more traumatic for the families and friends we leave behind. It's both a sacrifice and an honor to leave Earth to establish a colony on Mars. I won't sugar coat this. 'Mars is more hostile to life than anyplace on Earth.'[58] Yet, with our technology, Mars offers us all the resources that we need. The biggest challenge everyday may just be survival until we get established, dug-in, and self-sufficient. Are we sufficiently prepared and trained? I say categorically-Yes! We owe gratitude to the thousands of people around the world-- especially the brightest engineers who make this journey possible. We've trained for every possible contingency. Most of us are space hardened veterans. We have supply reserves to get us beyond the next resupply ship arrival in 2037. Meanwhile, Trevor Brown and his wife Mandy Shields will be using their combined expertise to begin growing our food crops and ultimately allow us to be self-sufficient for food. We will make our own air, water, propellant, and be able to manufacture most of our high-tech needs.

We owe a debt of gratitude to the *Arcadia 1* crew who paved the way for us at *Arcadia Base* and we mourn the loss of Barry

---

58 Attribute: Neil deGrasse Tyson

Peterson. We have run safety audits, redesigned many systems, and have redundancies to insure our safety. History, fate, and exploration are calling. We're ready to go."

"Well said Coby. Mission Control wishes you Godspeed. Our hopes and prayers are with you. We have a record three million people watching from all the beaches and Causeways around the Cape. The weather is clear and warm. T minus three minutes and counting. The room has been polled and all stations say you are go."

"CASSI, please report our flight systems status."

"All systems, power, propulsion, flight control, and life support are nominal. The methane header tank pressure is one percent below nominal but in tolerance. *Taurus* is go for launch."

There are affirming looks shared couch-to-couch on the Command Deck and Deck Two. Couples are holding hands. All of them are trying to maintain composure for the internal cameras. Alex and Sofi share their thoughts silently mind to mind, "Awesome, awesome, awesome!"

"T minus 10, 9, 8, 7, internal power and engine sequence start, 3, 2, 1, ignition and one hundred percent power. Liftoff! We have liftoff of the first Mars colony crew in Colossus ship *Taurus* at 10:16 AM from Pad 39C!"

The ride is smoother than the veterans have experienced in any previous launch system. G-forces climb to 3 g's at Max-Q, maximum dynamic pressure, when the big ship passes the speed of sound. In six minutes, the *Taurus* is in low Earth orbit and closing in on *Propellant Depot Alpha*.

"Okay crew, helmets off and stowed. Welcome to microgravity, our reality for the next six months. You can unstrap and try out your space legs. We've got six orbits to take in the view before TMI."

Trans Mars Injection, TMI, is the big engine burn that launches Taurus beyond Earth escape velocity on its Hohmann transfer orbit to Mars. It will take six hours to rendezvous with *Propellant Depot Alpha* and another two hours to complete refueling to prepare for the big burn to Mars.

The veterans manage well in microgravity, as natural as a walk in the park. The rookies, Sofi, Alex, and Jacob, have a bit of trouble, randomly bouncing off the bulkheads until they manage to grab the backs of their seats. Alex has his arm around Sofi's waist to help her.

Both the Command Deck and Deck Two have panoramic windows. Everyone, especially the rookies, are awed at the huge panoramic view of Earth below. They could see the Canary Islands in the deep blue Atlantic framed by puffy white cumulus clouds. In the same view they saw Spain, North Africa, and the entire Mediterranean with the boot of Italy. These last views of Earth will fill their heads for a long time to come.

Sofi is in Alex's head again, "Look at all these places we've never been, places we've only seen in our history graphics. Pictures can't do it justice. What are we missing?"

Alex looks into her eyes, "We won't miss it. We'll have a whole new planet to explore. Wait till you see this panorama of Mars!"

One the second orbit, Jacob looks a bit green. Oleg comes to the rescue just in time with a barf bag specially designed to catch the space sick projectiles so they don't mess up the new ship.

Alex pleads, "Oleg, we need a few more of those over here…"

On the third orbit, Abby is in the galley and gets on the intercom. "We've got simple eats in the galley. Make sure you get down here in the next hour and get some nourishment. That goes double for you greenies. I've got a special drink for you called *The Right Stuff* that'll help with your nausea and keep you from getting dehydrated. Remember CASSI and I see all and know all about your nutrition."

The galley on *Taurus* is ample sized but no way can it fit everyone at a sitting. The galley can comfortably accommodate six or seven of the crew at a time. The schedule will naturally sort itself out over time. Sitting in a space ship is a euphemism. There are no seats in the galley per se. There is a communal table with handholds around the sides and toe holds below. The table has elastic bands across it to help hold things down. Duct tape and Velcro are very useful to hold food bags and utensils to any nearby surface.

On the fourth orbit, with Coby and Vik monitoring on the Command Deck and Sofi and Alex observing, CASSI brings *Taurus* in for a rendezvous with *Propellant Depot Alpha*. Docking is tail first at the propellant bay connections of the depot.

Coby comments, "Nice driving CASSI."

"Not bad for my first time out with my learner's permit."

Vik adds, "Yeah and I taught you everything I know on *Altair*."

"And you know I'm a fast learner."

The *Taurus* will take on fuel to top off with a 1100 MT full propellant load. TMI and minor mid-course corrections will use 800 MT and landing on Mars will use about 190 MT leaving a reserve of 110 MT of propellant. It takes two hours to complete refueling.

"Houston, *Taurus*. Houston, *Taurus*. Refueling is completed and we are undocked with *Alpha*. All propellant pressures in header tanks and mains are on the money. We are ready for TMI when we align with the launch corridor."

"*Taurus*, Houston. Roger that. You've got the hopes of the whole world with you."

On the sixth and final orbit coming up on the California coast, Coby requests, "CASSI, please give me an update on the TMI launch corridor."

"TMI corridor alignment confirmed. TMI initiate in ten minutes and twenty three seconds."

"Thanks you CASSI. Crew, this is not a drill. Please get strapped into your couches. We have TMI in ten minutes. Repeat TMI in ten minutes. Get strapped in now. We are going to Mars!"

Abby and Ellie appear on the Command Deck and help each other strap in. The rest of the crew glides to their designated couches and work in assigned buddy pairs to get strapped in. It's not so easy in microgravity. There is some bumping and giggling on Deck Two.

"Where's Elena?"

Abby responds. "I last saw her in the galley two hours ago."

Ellie says. "I'm not her keeper. I don't know where she is."

Arcadia Colony Ship *Taurus*
June 23, 2035
Mission Elapsed Time 00:08:50:13 ·

On the intercom, "Thanks for getting strapped in. Elena Petrov please report to the Command Deck- *now*! TMI in five minutes and counting."

About one minute later, Elena appears and glides to her couch. "Sorry about that. I was in the hygiene unit."

"You're an experienced astronaut. You have a watch. Get strapped in now *please*!"

Elena does quickly get into her seat and buckles in. "Sorry Commander."

CASSI reports over the intercom, "TMI in sixty seconds. All power and propellant pressures nominal...Thirty seconds...Ten, nine, eight, propellant pumps spinning up, three, two, one. TMI initiate. Throttling up to full power. The burn will last three minutes and eighteen seconds."

The g-force again builds up to 3 g's. Coby notices tears in Ellie's eyes. He doesn't know if it's joy or regret.

Ellie looks at Coby and smiles. "This is just pure raw emotion with us making the biggest life change of any humans in history."

Alex and Sofi see the Texas coast and Houston slipping by below. Again they share their thoughts silently mind to mind, "That *was* our home. Awesome, awesome, awesome!"

Trevor and Mandy are ecstatic and holding hands. Mandy says to him, "Smooth. It's a good ship."

Trevor replies, "Mars is calling. *Arcadia* has our names on it. Let's pray that everything goes smoothly all the way out."

CASSI reports over the intercom, "Burn complete in three, two, one, shut down. Fuel pumps are powered down and being purged."

Microgravity returns instantly.

Vik comments to Coby, "The number two inboard engine was under powered at eighty percent."

"That should come out in the wash. We can make up for any trajectory issues on our first course correction burn. CASSI, do you concur?"

"Affirmative. One engine under power at eighty percent still puts the burn as normal. I compensated by burning 5.3 seconds longer than planned. My navigation computation will give us a good course correction scheduled for three weeks from now. The next item on the check list is solar cell deployment."

Coby has another concern. "We've only addressed the trajectory to Mars. Both inboard engines need to be at one hundred percent with full gimballing control for a precise controlled landing. Extending a landing burn to compensate is not an option with the surface looming!"

Vik responds, "I hadn't thought of that yet. We can still trouble shoot that number two inboard on the mid-course correction burns and hope for the gremlin to get sorted out."

From Deck Two, Sofi and Alex have been listening on the intercom. Alex nudges Sofi and she nods knowing what Alex is thinking and agreeing to stick her neck out.

Sofi keys the intercom to the Command Deck, "Dad, Sofi here with a suggestion."

"Really? Okay, it can't hurt. Go ahead."

"You're describing the landing specs by the book. We have six engines to work with and each one is throttleable. The outer four have some gimbal control. We can use those at lower power under CASSI's control and should still get a precise landing."

Coby asks, "CASSI, can you compensate on the outer four engines and get us a precise landing even if the number one and two inboard engines are shut down."

"Affirmative. It has never been done but it is just a matter of computation, which I have just completed. Precise control for landing with the outer four engines is possible."

Cobi replies, "Thank you CASSI and thank you Alex and Sofi for the genius suggestion! I think we can sleep better tonight? Let's get a report and analysis off to Houston."

"Affirmative."

Elena audibly gasps, *"Bo-zeh moy!"*

Coby admonishes her, "We have this under control. I'll thank you to keep your sarcastic comments to yourself."

"Y-yes sir!"

Ellie knew when to stay quiet.

Abby has been listening and though concerned knows that the problem will get sorted out in the six months cruise to mars. "Do you think we can get the crew unstrapped and started into cruise routine?"

"Just the thing. Those rookies need more practice with their space legs. I can still smell their space sickness. The intercom is yours. Please make the announcement. Meanwhile, we need to attend to deploying the solar cells."

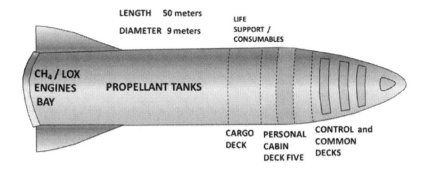

The Colossus Colony Ship *Taurus*[59] (modified for the colony complement of twenty-one people.)

"Crew, we're on our way to Mars! Our trajectory looks good. Let's get everyone unstrapped. Please get your flight suits stowed with your helmets. Your sleeping compartments are assigned on the post in the galley. The compartments are numbered with your names posted on your compartment door. Your sleep shift and exercise schedule assignments are also posted in the galley. It's a big ship but we can't have everyone bumping into each other all the time. Olga and Oleg will assist in handing out the PPKs from storage locker three on Deck Three."

The issue of the size of the ship has everything to do with the number of common facilities. It is just easier to have three sleep shifts of eight hours each. There are twelve personal sleeping compartments on Deck Five: nine doubles and three singles arranged in a torus in the nine meter diameter space. Doubles are naturally assigned to the married couples. Sofi and Alex requested a double. Dao-Ming and Sandy requested a double. The three singles are Elena, Jacob, and Dieter. The sleeping compartments

---

59 Honoring the SpaceX commitment to design, build, and utilize its BFR super-heavy lift rockets to send cargo and humans to Mars: "Becoming a Multi-Planet Species", SpaceX, Web accessed 12 July 2018.
http://www.spacex.com/sites/spacex/files/making_life_multiplanetary-2017.pdf

are the only assigned personal spaces on the ship. The inner core of the torus has four hygiene units. Imagine if all twenty one crew members were awake vying for hygiene units at the same time! There are four TARED exercise machines in two bays on Deck Four along with the spacious entertainment salon, and medical bay. The galley is on Deck Three next to the communications cubicles and library. Deck Two, with the launch couches, also serves as a communal movie theater and observation deck.

Arcadia Colony Ship *Taurus*
June 23, 2035
Mission Elapsed Time 00:10:01:31

Coby begins, "CASSI, please deploy solar cell Array One on the starboard side."

"Affirmative. Solar Array One deployment initiated...Extending boom...Unfolding...Rotating to optimum sun alignment."

"Good. Please test the output circuits."

"Affirmative. Solar Array One generating peak output at ninety eight kilowatts.

"Great show. Now deploy port side Array Two."

"Affirmative. Solar Array Two deployment initiated...Extending boom...Unfolding...Negative on the actuation sequence to unfold Array Two."

"Dammit! Oh sorry CASSI, I'm a bit concerned about that problem."

"Your expletives do not bother me. The Array Two actuator is being a bitch."

Sounding amused with CASSI's remark, "Okay CASSI, let's both curtail the expletives and please diagnose the actuator problem. What do you think Vik?"

"The arrays have been extensively ground tested and successfully deployed on dozens of Colossus missions. This problem is a new one."

CASSI replies, "The AMB, actuator motor box, is the source of the problem. It had a voltage spike at the initiation of the unfolding sequence. I cannot diagnose it further. I recommend an investigative EVA. The ship's batteries are low and we need both solar arrays or cut back severely on power usage."

"Mmm. Okay, put me on intercom."

"Done."

"Crew, this is Coby. We can drop the Commander formality but I do need help from all of you. We were off to a great start with our TMI burn. Up to that point we had been on battery power as programmed but the batteries only last so long. We have one solar array deployed but the second one has a problem that will require an EVA to fix. The first EVA team will be Oleg Ivanov and Olga Sadoski. Harrison Frank and Eve Cain are on deck for a second EVA if needed. Please report to the suit locker area and begin oxygen prebreathing. Meanwhile, we have half of the solar power we need. We need to ration power until we get this fixed. Vik is in charge of the rationing requirements and EVA procedures. "Paul Earhart is Vik's second in command on rationing. I want their requests to be strictly obeyed. Vik, it's yours."

"So, imagine you're on a submarine and you don't want the enemy to hear you. We are all going to curtail unnecessary activity including exercise. This will allow us to go to eighty percent on life support. Turn all lights to dim. Eat only food that does not need to be heated. Entertainment will be on tablets only. No big screen stuff. Turn off any monitors that are not essential. Switch urine and solid wastes to the holding tank with no processing until we get the power fully up. Unnecessary communications to Earth are banned for now. Get a book, lay back and chill out! Even without the second solar panel, this rationing should bring our batteries back up to green. We do hope to have that second solar array up in a few hours. Thanks for your cooperation and patience. Vik, out."

Vik glides down to the cargo deck to the suit locker bay. There is an airlock used for in-space EVAs instead of using the huge cargo airlock. As requested, Oleg, Olga, Frank, and Eve are there prebreathing oxygen with a simple oxygen masks on hose tethers. The pre-breathe routine is necessary to purge excess nitrogen and prevent the bends. The EVA suit is lower pressure and higher oxygen content than the ship atmosphere. The suit-up routine and entire EVA is being beamed to Houston.

"Hey Papa! We're psyched up for this. Our PLSS packs are charged and ready. Our tool belts have been checked. Let's go over the schematics."

Only a handful of the crew has trained for repair EVA's on Colossus. Vik, Oleg, Olga, Frank and Eve are the top among them. Of necessity, the training is generalized since the needed repair intervention can't be predicted. Because of their critical nature, the solar arrays and deployment issues were covered in the training exercises. Vik pulls up schematics for the AMB actuator motor box.

"The traverse from the airlock to the solar array has well marked tether points and hand holds. First you'll need to remove the AMB cover plate. It's just a ninety degree turn to release each of the four retainers. The plan is to remove the motor assembly and power board and bring them back in for repair. The motor needs to have its power cable unplugged and then remove these four bolts. Carefully bag and tether the lot. The power board should pull right out. Again bag and tether it. Any questions?"

"No. I'm good. Olga?"

"No questions. We know the drill. Let's get underway so we can get the power full up. I'm sure the crew is taking this as a bad start on our new life. Or perhaps this is SNAFU."

Eve asks the obvious question. "What is SNAFU?"

CASSI answers, "SNAFU is an acronym that is widely used to stand for the sarcastic expression *Situation Normal: All F***ed Up*. It is a well-known example of military acronym slang."

Eve replies, "Right. Thanks for that not so sugar coated answer CASSI. All we can do is fix one problem at a time. Let's finish getting suited up."

The rest of the crew is keeping a low activity level as requested. Paul is doing a round to check on compliance and the mood of the situation. He glides into the entertainment salon and finds Elena parked watching a video on her tablet and sipping orange juice from a squeeze pouch.

"I'm being good officer. The charge on my tablet will last two days. We had better be back to normal by then."

"No problem Elena. This is just a minor glitch. We've got to expect glitches occasionally and we're prepared to fix damn near everything."

"Yeah. I hear you but I don't like this one bit. The air is already starting to smell stale."

"Easy there. We're all in this together for a long time."

Arcadia Colony Ship *Taurus*

June 23, 2035
Mission Elapsed Time 00:12:28:15

The airlock is cycled and Oleg emerges first, tethering off, and waiting for Olga to egress.

"Okay. Traversing to solar Array Two..."

Olga comments, "This is so much easier than in the tank at JSC. It's like being back on ISS except here we see the Earth and Moon receding below us."

"Yeah. It's beautiful and makes me feel sad all at once...Tethering to the base of Array Two at the AMB box."

Olga replies, "Tethering off and securing in the toe holds."

"Good, let's get the cover off...Turning retainer one...two...three... and four. Olga get the bag open. Here's the cover."

"Got it bagged. I have the wrench for the bolts...God who torqued these down?"

"Careful Olga, Go easy."

"I got this. Three bolts are loose now. Working on four...urrh...uuhhnn! There, I win! Now, bag these bolts as I get them out...That's the last one. Now for the motor assembly... It's already loose...Got it... Please bag it."

"Okay. It's in the bag. Now get the power board and let's get back inside."

"So far so good. The board is just a snug fit in its slot. Mmmhh...Yeah that's snug. One more time...Rrrhh! Got it. *Vot der'mo!* My hand! Take the board!"

"Olga, you're bleeding. I see blood droplets spewing into space with your air! I got the board. Put pressure on the glove tear and the cut."

"I'm okay big boy. Just get me back inside quick. I have a suit pressure alarm screaming in my ear!"

"I've got you. I'm tethering us together. Vik, we have an emergency! Olga cut her suit and her hand. Traversing back...Olga? She's not responding. Oh God, her eyes are rolled back."

"Get her in quick! We're ready for you. Abby's on her way down."

"Almost there!" Oleg unhooks his tether and launches both of them the last five meters clean into the airlock. He takes the impact fending off the bulkhead with a straight arm then rolls to take the rest of the impact with his shoulder. "Unngh, ouch! We're in. Closing the hatch. Cycle us in now!"

Abby takes over. There is an audible hiss. "Pressurizing now. Get her helmet off when the light turns green! Her sensors have a weak pulse... Okay, now!"

Oleg unclamps Olga's helmet and quickly pops it off just as Vik opens the airlock hatch. Olga's skin looks blue. Abby slips into the airlock with an Ambu-bag and trailing an oxygen hose. She begins positive pressure resuscitation. Oleg twists the glove seals to take her gloves off. There is a five centimeter gash on her hand and forefinger that is still bleeding freely. Vik takes Oleg's helmet and gloves off. Harrison and Eve back off to give them room.

"Come on Olga, come back to us...There now breathe in the oxygen...Vik get a sterile pad out of my kit and open the foil pack. Press and hold the pad on the wound. I'll dress it properly later...Breathe Olga!"

Oleg desperately asks, "Will she be alright? I got her back in as quickly as I could!"

Vik replies, "*Moy syn*, you did everything you could. If you hadn't, she might not be with us now."

Abby says, "I see some color returning."

Olga's eyelids flutter then open. She's looking at Oleg. "H-how did I get back in? Did we get the motor and p-power board?" It's hard to hear her through the Ambu-bag.

Abby speaks, "Easy there. Quiet now. Oleg rescued you and yes we have the parts." She removes the Ambu-bag and replaces it with a passive oxygen mask. We need to get her to the med bay. Oleg, please help me move her and keep pressure on that wound."

"I'm with you Olga."

Vik says, "Harrison and Eve, you can drop the oxygen now and come with me to the machine shop to look at this gear. If we can figure out the problem and fix it, you'll be going back out on EVA to replace the gear."

As Abby and Oleg are moving Olga to the medical bay, they are passing up the tunnel past Deck Five and they hear a commotion. "Ignore that. Gotta get her to sick bay!"

On Deck Five, Paul Earhart is confronting Elena. This time he has a problem with her. "Elena, what the hell are you doing?"

"We were told to relax so I felt like curling my hair. I feel better when I look better. Besides, this whole solar array business has me upset."

"You haven't heard upset until I dress you down. Dammit, do you realize that your little curling iron consumes about 1200 watts! You just used up every watt of juice we were asked save. Besides, that little toy is a fire hazard! How in the hell did you get that up here?"

Sheepishly, "In my PPK. A woman can't leave all the necessities behind."

"For an experienced astronaut, I would have attributed you with a little more common sense. Give me that damn thing. You'd better straighten up Elena!"

"Or what, you'll send me home?"

"Elena, you're on report to the Commander."

"Thanks I'd like that."

In the medical bay, Oleg helps Abby get Olga secured and comfortable. "Olga, since you had oxygen deprivation only for a short time, it's serious but it could have been so much worse. I'm going to give you an injection that should help prevent damage and bring you back to your perky self quickly. It was developed at the Harvard Medical School.[60] It has lipid-based microparticles encapsulating a core of pure oxygen gas that delivers oxygen temporarily more efficiently than your stressed lungs can…There it's done."

Olga nods and Oleg kisses her forehead. Vik and Coby have arrived and Abby gives them an update. Vik is sympathetic and gives Olga's hand a squeeze. Then he gives all of them an update on the solar array issue.

---

60 "Oxygen Gas–Filled Microparticles Provide Intravenous Oxygen Delivery", Science Translational Medicine, 2012, Web accessed 25 Aug 2018. http://stm.sciencemag.org/content/4/140/140ra88

"I worked with Harrison and Eve on the drive motor and power board. The bad news is that both of them are fried. The good news is that we do have spares on board and the two of them will do the EVA to install the parts. We'll begin that EVA in one hour."

"If you'll excuse us now I need to attend to her laceration. Cleansing, stitches, and antibiotics and Olga will be as good as new."

Arcadia Colony Ship *Taurus*
June 24, 2035
Mission Elapsed Time 01:13:42:53

Harrison and Eve have completed the second EVA installing the solar array actuator motor and power board. Now both solar cell arrays are operating and generating two hundred kilowatts of electrical power for life support and all other needs on the ship. Olga is discharged from sick bay- just another day as an astronaut. Life aboard the *Taurus* is settling into a hopefully uneventful routine that will last another six months and seventeen days.

The entertainment salon and library are occupied. Abby checks into activity on the Deck Four exercise facilities. She's pleased to see that all four of the TARED exercise units in the two exercise bays are in use. Each crew person has to do two hours per day in assigned shifts to maintain muscle tone and prevent bone loss. The experience is intended to be a joy rather than something painful to be endured.

The TARED units have evolved since *Aquila*. There are the same single user activities with immersive VR experience to climb, swim, or fly in an almost limitless selection of places- the most thrilling places Earth has to offer. Now there are similar activities, except swimming, to explore Mars in VR. Abby recommends a balanced mix of both planets for mental health. The VR experience has expanded to a multiplayer realm in the same selection of environments that include athletic games. Among the popular list there is two-person racquetball, two or four-player tennis, and soccer with up to four real players mixed with avatar players generated by the software. Abby is tickled to see Alex and Sofi giggling enjoying a brisk swim on reefs in Hawaii according what she reads on their TARED. Ellie and Tracy Dixon are playing tennis in the opposite bay.

On the Command Deck, Coby is completing a systems check review with CASSI. Elena appears from below and announces her arrival.

"Hello Commander. CASSI alerted me that you wanted to have a word."

Without turning toward her yet, "Hello Elena. Good of you to come." He turns around and his smile turns into a stifled gasp.

"Wow. What have you done to your hair?" He sees that her shoulder length hair is now a neat one centimeter crop.

"Oh not much. I cut it off to be more practical here in microgravity. You haven't seen me like this but after you left on *Aquila*, I chopped off my hair for convenience on ISS."

"Are you sure it has nothing to do with the incident yesterday with Paul?" He hands her the curling iron back sans power cord. "What's gotten into you? You are somehow different and not just the hair. There are many reasons you were selected to join this colony. Your demonstrated career professionalism is high on that list."

Sobbing, "You say nothing of our son Jacob? He's a reason I'm here. I love you *moy medved*. I have since Baikonur."

Coby holds her for moment and wipes the tear droplets from her eyes.

"I love you too Elena but *only* as the mother of our son. Nothing more- it can't be, just as you've said many times. Keep the past in the past."

"*Chert poberi!* I know dammit! I never meant for you to hear those words. It was easier for me when we were a half a world or millions of kilometers apart. Rafaela is a very lucky woman to have you *moy medved*. But now, we'll share a life so close together yet still apart. I'll keep my feelings to myself and yes above all be professional."

Kissing her forehead, "Thanks for your candor Elena. Make me glad you're part of this colony. That's what I ask of you. Jacob is already my pride and joy as much as Sofi. "

Arcadia Colony Ship *Taurus*
July 13, 2035
Mission Elapsed Time 20:09:17:46

Sofi and Alex spend five to six hours a day in the library studying. They are continuing the same programmed curriculum they started back home in El Lago when they were three. The online learning series allows them to learn at their own pace. They often get help and advice from their parents or any of the adults on board. Sometimes they get more help and advice than they would like. They can best relate to Jacob since he's closer in age and he has plenty of time and patience for them. They also exchange video files to interact with teachers back on Earth.

They are both at a university junior standing in coursework. They've completed four terms of calculus through differential equations and linear algebra. Sofi is better at these abstract concepts and tutors Alex where he needs help. CASSI also interacts with them especially for visualization of concepts like *n-dimensional* space. They have chosen aerospace engineering and are getting course instruction from MIT. At age twelve next year, they will still not be the youngest to have earned bachelor degrees.

Alex explained to his parents, "The degrees don't matter to us. What does matter is the fun of learning stuff that we can use to make life better for us on Mars."

Mission Elapsed Time 20:12:30:51

Coby has been giving Sofi and Alex about an hour a day on the Command Deck systems and assigning course work on astrogation, Colossus ship engineering and maintenance, and life support systems. At 12:30 MET, Coby invited Ellie, Vik, Abby, Jacob, and Oleg to join him with Sofi and Alex in the Command Bridge."

"Thanks for coming. I have an important announcement."

Sofi says, "Such drama. What's this all about? We didn't do anything wrong."

"On the contrary, Sophia Accardi-Brewster and Alexei Denton-Ivanov, in recognition of your dedication and mastery of ships systems and navigating in space, in recognition for your suggestion for the alternative landing solution for Mars, I hereby appoint you as honorary Deputy Commanders of the Colony Ship *Taurus*."

Their simultaneous reply, "Way cool! Can we eat lunch now?"

Mission Elapsed Time 20:13:08:26

On Fridays, Abby, Ellie, Olga, Tracy, Mandy, and Eve gather at 13:00 in the entertainment lounge for an informal wives club. Others know that their giggling and chatter is not to be joined or endured by any other ears. The voyage has been underway for three weeks and everyone is settled into a routine.

Olga brings up what would be unspeakable between the men-- sex in microgravity.

"When Oleg and I got together, even before we were married, he taught me everything I know and enjoy about being together. We thought that being together in space was going to take things to a new height but we end up thrashing and bumping off the bulkheads."

They all laughed and Tracy, Mandy, and Eve had to agree with the description of the awkward sessions they've had.

Tracy said, "Without gravity, it's just not natural and ends up in frustration."

It's Abby and Ellie's turn to laugh. Ellie explains, "Don't fight it girls. The sleep compartments are padded. It's all about arm and legs holding each other to become one. Then don't forget your hips and physics! Equal and opposite actions do the job."

More giggles.

Abby adds, "Yeah, I call it the pretzel. Vik and I struggled a bit at first but practice makes perfect. Alex and Sofi are a testament to that and to bad pills."

Ellie continues, "I'm looking forward to Mars' point four g gravity. That should make Coby feel like he's superman!"

That got full on laughter and agreement on the expectation. They hadn't noticed that Elena had drifted to within earshot from the library area. Elena growls, spins around, pushes off the nearest bulkhead, and disappears in a cloud of virtual smoke.

Eve asks, "What's got her knickers in a bunch?"

Ellie replies sheepishly, "Jealously has fertile ground in Elena. Let's keep our eyes and ears on her."

Mission Elapsed Time 20:15:28:14

Jacob has found that Sandy Conklin is a willing and able tennis opponent. They play two or three sets on the TARED VR system several times a week. He enjoys spending time with her and they are often seen together in the galley or in the library. What Sandy takes as innocent friendship, Jacob thinks could be something more. What he doesn't concede is that Sandy spends much more time with Dao-Ming and that they are lovers. They aren't interested in a lover's triangle even though that might be the fodder of pulp fiction. Sandy tries to be gentle with him when he gets too cow eyed. She's sympathetic to the fact that Jacob has no real match his age in this small colony group.

"You just need to cool your jets Jacob. You're a very handsome man with a bad case of testosterone overload. I enjoy your company and I sincerely hope that our future colony arrivals have better prospects for you."

Jacob says, "In fact, my hopes for finding a girl who can appreciate me are not as dismal as it might seem. The *Arcadia Beta* colony launches next month and arrives in May next year. The colony ship includes the well-known Jennings family. Sam and Paula Jennings are PhD Space Systems and Hab Engineers who were very influential in our colony design. Their daughter Tracy Jennings is my age and just graduated with her BS in Astrobiology from Princeton. She hopes to have her masters by the time they arrive next year. We met during the joint mission simulation last year. We text and exchange vid messages every day."

"Love will not be denied even across millions of kilometers of deep space."

Kennedy Space Center Pads 39C, 39D, and 39E
Cape Canaveral, Florida
August 14-15, 2035

The Mars *Arcadia Beta* supply ships *Castor,* and *Pollux* and Colony Ship *Gemini* launch. Their refueling is completed at *Propellant Depots Alpha, Beta, and Gamma.* The Mars launch window is not optimal and the transit time is 276 days for the supply ships and 281 days for the colony ship with twenty one international colonists. Among the colonists is the well-known Jennings family and Jacob's big love interest, Tracy Jennings. *Gemini* is under the Command of Paula Jennings.

Arcadia Colony Ship *Taurus*
August 15, 2035
Mission Elapsed Time 53:13:32:16

Commander Coby Brewster personal log:

We are fifty-three days outbound toward Mars. The Mars Arcadia Beta supply ships *Castor,* and *Pollux* launched yesterday and the Colony Ship *Gemini* launched yesterday to join us and will comprise the other half of our international Mars colony-*Arcadia Beta.* We've been in contact with them and with the first Mars landing crew *Arcadia 1* returning to Earth aboard the *Arcturus.* Today at 14:01, we'll actually pass within five hundred kilometers of each other like two ships passing in the night. I have had some long video conferences with Commander Trent Granger.

"We left a light on for you. The base is in good shape for our crew which is down to nine persons. You will not immediately be able support your twenty-one persons on the existing life support. The number two Sabatier reactor is temperamental. We've never been able to get it up to one hundred percent capacity. I'm ready to get back to Earth to have a cold beer. Jees, Brewster, I hope your family and crew are happier than this bunch…"

Ironically Granger has not allowed our people to have direct contact with his crew. We would have liked to hear about their experiences from all sides. Granger will allow his people to appear on screen without audio when we make closest approach. It should be an emotional event for both sides.

At 13:45, the entire Arcadia crew is gathered on Deck Two. After people gathered, lights are extinguished on the deck with only a few dim red LED lights marking the transfer tunnel. The observation panoramic viewport is turned with the ship in the direction of the approaching *Arcturus* ship. It is expected to appear in the constellation Virgo, an inconspicuous constellation conspicuously marked with the first magnitude star Spica. The closest approach of the two ships is today at 14:01 with a relative passing velocity of ten thousand kilometers per hour. Even knowing exactly where to look, the *Arcturus* ship is only visible for five minutes, starting as a dim but slowly moving speck of light. The *Arcturus* crew appears on a big flat screen panel as the *Taurus* crew is seen on *Arcturus*. There is waving and cheering but no audio is broadcast.

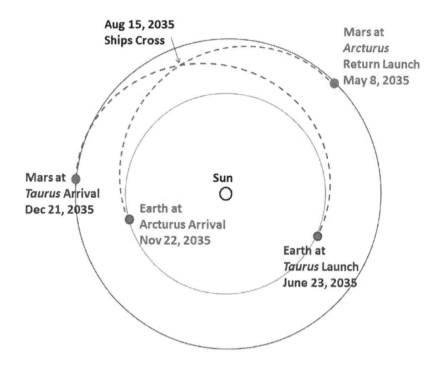

Hohmann transfer orbit diagram of the Taurus ship outbound to Mars, crossing paths with the Arcturus ship returning to Earth.

Ellie speaks out, "There she is just five degrees left of Spica! Thank you crew of *Arcturus* for laying the foundations of our new home. The labs back on Earth are eager to get your Mars rocks!"

Elena is emotional but reserved. "Godspeed crew of *Arcturus*. Get home safely." Her eyes glisten with the sparkle of tears.

Sofi speaks out. "I'm so awed at seeing that ship. They've *been* to Mars. I wish I could meet them and speak to them to know what it's really like."

Alex is touching her mind. "I can feel them. They're celebrating going home in a way you wouldn't expect. I sense that they'll be glad to get out from under the thumb of Commander Granger, their Captain Bligh. On the flip side, I sense that our people have huge respect for your father Coby and for our family that's central to our colony. I hope we don't screw it up."

Sofi winks and returns the thought, "I've got your back."

At closest approach, *Arcturus* appears as bright as Venus, and then just as quickly as it approached, it fades to invisibility.

Arcadia Colony Ship *Taurus*
August 15, 2035
Mission Elapsed Time 122:10:29:34

The BSF Incident

Coby just passed through the tunnel to Deck Five intending to get ready for some sleep. "Oh God! What's that smell? It's as bad as a twenty year old brick shithouse! CASSI, please report."

"I can't smell Commander but I can report that sensors read trace amounts of hydrogen sulfide, methanethiol, and dimethyl sulfide. We are just now getting a breakdown report in the SWRRP[61], solids wastes recycling reactor process."

"*Great.* The big-shitter-fail! How do we get so lucky? We haven't had this kind of issue since ISS."

Just then Ellie glides in to get ready to join Coby for sleep. "Oh my! That's not right!

"No, it's not right! There is an issue with the SWRRP unit." On intercom, "This is Coby. Megumi and Satoshi please report to Deck Five. Megumi and Satoshi please report to Deck Five."

"Thankfully, it seems that the sleep compartments are not occupied. Nobody on this sleep cycle has come down yet but us. I

---

61 Solids Waste Recycling Reactor Process, SWRRP, pronounced "SWIRP".

think we're sleeping on Deck Two tonight. We can wear earplugs, turn off the lights, and sleep under the stars in the panorama window."

"Amazing. You can be romantic even in adversity! But it could be a long night before we can rest. We gotta get this sorted out first."

Megumi Hirakata and Satoshi Fukoshima are best qualified to work on this recycling system with their expertise in space hab systems. Although they would prefer to use their talents on a more glamorous project, it's not the first time or the last that they are called on do some high tech plumbing work on waste systems. Without this expertise, the crew survival could be in jeopardy. All life support systems are critical.

Megumi and Satoshi floated in and reacted immediately to the problem.

Satoshi spoke first. "Ah. Oh! Something tells me why we're needed down here. You're going to appeal to our expertise in hab systems and hygiene systems. We are *so honored* Commander!"

"Yeah. I knew you'd be thrilled but this is mission critical. We'll have a mutiny if we don't come up with a solution soon. CASSI sees a fault in the SWRRP processor."

Megumi replies, "No doubt. Well here's the score. We have four hygiene units and the two waste Sabatier processors take care of the liquid waste so there is redundancy for that. But there is only one SWRRP processor. We can bypass all of it to a holding tank until we get the SWRRP sorted out. The problem is that the holding tank is not large enough for twenty-one people for very long."

Satoshi suggests, "The issue is not urine. That can be collected in the normal funnel system we use all the time. It will go to the Sabatier, no problem. For fecal collection, we should

188

use our low tech back-up system. We have a big supply of plastic bags with adhesive strips to stick to your bottom for fecal collection just like on Apollo. The bags have germicide and odor control chems. I do suggest that we push a high protein, low residue diet. Powdered eggs and synthetic steak ought to work. Meanwhile, anyone can use the hygiene units for number one while we attack the SWRRP."

Coby says, "Have you read Mutiny on the Bounty? Trent Granger seemed to have his issues on *Arcturus*. I have to hope our crew takes this in stride."

Ellie is unflappable. "No problem my Commander. It'll be like a camping trip. Let's just get that damned SWRRP fixed soon! Get us to the potty bag supply and Coby and I will go distribute them to the troops up on Deck Two with the news. It's a good thing there aren't a lot of stones lying around there."

Coby adds, "We'll be back soon to check on what you can find out about SWRRP. I'm prepared to roll up my sleeves and help where I can."

Ellie, not to be out done by a man, says "I'm in too. We have lots of moisturizing hand sanitizer for an after party. "

"Thanks Coby. Thanks Ellie. We should be able to sort this out soon. We have a big supply of the bio-active bugs needed to get the SWRRP going again once we figure out the mechanical issues."

Coby and Ellie return about thirty minutes later. Coby reports, "Well, the troops took the news in stride, sort of. I only had one crumbled juice bag hit me in the head. It's better that a stone."

Sofi and Alex poke their heads in and sheepishly asked if they can go to use a hygiene unit. There seems to be a few more heads in line behind them.

Ellie puts on her motherly smile. "No problem! Don't mind the fragrance. We're still working on the SWRRP down below."

Megumi pokes her head up from the crawl space. She's fitted with a respirator. "We've figured out the problem. There is a stirring mechanism that has three broken paddles. The manifest says we have four spares but they're nowhere we can find just yet. We can 3D print replacements but it will take at least eighteen hours to do that and get it running again. This is a good trial run of what life will be like at *Arcadia*."

During the remaining time of the *BSF Incident*, until the repairs are completed, Deck Two is designated as a quiet dark zone like the sleeping lounge at Schiphol Airport in Amsterdam. They have the stars to lull them to sleep instead of happy cows by a quiet canal that you see on a video loop in Schiphol. Video calls home to Earth are filled with funny stories of life on the colony ship.

Arcadia Colony Ship *Taurus*
December 7, 2035
Mission Elapsed Time 166:22:14:29

Commander Coby Brewster personal log:

I've had a sleepless night again. We are outbound towards Mars and two weeks from arriving. My mind is taking time to reflect. The Colossus ship is a well-tested machine. There have been nearly one hundred successful launches and only one minor failure. To date, there have been six robotic Colossus Mars landings and one crewed landing and all were successful. Ours will be the seventh Colossus landing on Mars and I'm hoping and praying for a successful landing. We still have one big issue to sort out. The inboard number two engine issue could complicate the landing. We still have one more short burn tomorrow to help troubleshoot the bad engine.

Meanwhile, we still observe days of the week to keep us connected to Earth. On Sundays as a routine, we gather in the entertainment lounge and pick a movie to watch. Old movies about missions to Mars are popular with the crew. All of those movies seem to end in disaster. Movies we have watched several times include *Species II with* a crew on Mars that has an alien ooze to infect the first man to walk on Mars. On *Mission to Mars* the crew ship is struck by meteor storm just before Mars atmosphere entry. The crew ship on *Red Planet* is damaged on arrival by gamma ray burst. Then things go from bad to worse when a military robot named AMEE runs amok. In *The Martian,* the hero, Mark Watney, is stranded alone on Mars during an epic sandstorm. The National Geographic docudrama epic *Mars* lasts for a whole week of binge viewing if you want to subject yourself to Seasons One and Two. Their first catastrophe is having a circuit board failure on entry causing them to land seventy five kilometers beyond their base without all necessary life support and supplies. My personal favorite-- their commander dies of the internal injuries he sustained in the hard landing.

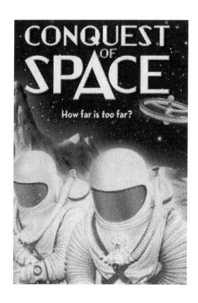

The Conquest of Space is a typical disaster film about the first interplanetary flight to Mars. The ship is manned by a crew of five who encounter many dangers that nearly destroy the mission. Credit Paramount Pictures. Based loosely on the 1949 book by Willy Ley and Chesley Bonestell7.

This fascination with Mars disaster movies on our journey is like flying on a plane from Boston Logan and watching *Flight 93* about the ill-fated plane hijacked by 9-11 terrorists.

God knows we'll have our challenges setting up the colony and keeping it running. There's already been one fatality on Mars. On Aquila, we had *Logan's first law* to keep us on our toes. *Space is always trying to kill you.* I think the corollary to that is that *Mars is always trying to kill you.* During our training, we learned to always be vigilant watching for any possible thing that could go wrong. Find it and fix it before it kills you. We have sensor alarms and backup systems so that everything is redundant. I would think that with me being a seasoned commander and all the time that I've spent in space I would spend less time worrying. But that's not the kind of person I am, especially when we have twenty-one souls on board. Almost half of them are family and the rest are dear friends.

Ellie has been especially helpful to me and the rest of the crew. But as with any family and any friendship, inevitably there can be squabbles. We have resources to help smooth things out. We have two fathers, three mothers, one psychologist, and two Chaplains to serve as peacemakers.

Arcadia Colony Ship *Taurus*
December 8, 2035
Mission Elapsed Time 167:08:21:07

"The orbital dynamics of getting to Mars on an Earth scale is analogous to hitting a golf ball from Paris, while on a moving pickup truck, to Pebble Beach in California and making a hole-in-one."[62]

Coby, Vik, Abby, Ellie, and Elena are on the Command Deck minutes before the final mid-course correction burn. The previous two mid-course correction burns besides keeping them on a very precise trajectory, had also been used to troubleshoot the number two inboard engine. It was determined that number two inboard still could not get to more than eighty percent power. All of the finely tuned landing software is based on the two inboard engines working at one hundred percent power and balanced perfectly to perform as the landing retrorockets. Gimbal control could not compensate for the imbalance in power. Thanks to Sofi and Alex's suggestion, CASSI, Vik, and the best experts back on Earth have fine-tuned the solution to use the four outboard engines at fifty percent power for the landing retrorocket thrust. These four engines do not have the degree of gimbal control that the two inboard engines have but the four

---

62 Attribute- Tory Bruno, President and Chief Executive Officer, United Launch Alliance, Congressional testimony July 25, 2018

working together can theoretically get the job done. The software updates have been uploaded and this final mid-course correction burn though very short, will be able to test the software. Only those on the Command Deck plus Sofi and Alex are fully aware of the significance of the retro-fire issue.

"*Aldebaran* and *Pleiades* are on the money to be down waiting for us when we land. All of *their* readings look good. We'll have to make do with the hand we are dealt."

"On intercom please. All crew are confirmed strapped in for the mid-course MCC-3 burn. Prepare for some g-forces. CASSI, please give us the count."

"MCC-3 burn in ten, nine, eight, propellant and fuel pump pressures nominal, three, two, one. Burning four outboard engines at fifty percent... Shut down in three, two, one, engines shutdown. Analyzing data…The burn is precise. The software control functioned as advertised."

"Whew. Okay, let's put that in the bank for landing. CASSI, please send a report with data dumps to Houston."

"Affirmative. Report and data are sending now."

Later that day, Olga visits Abby in the medical bay. She has been feeling nausea. Abby has a knowing look and runs a urine test.

"The sex lessons we laughed about a while back must have worked for you. My dear Olga, you are about two months pregnant!"

"Oh my God! That's wonderful news! I can't wait to tell Oleg! Uhh, by the way, seriously do you have anything for the nausea?"

Arcadia Colony Ship *Taurus*
December 21, 2035
Mission Elapsed Time 181:10:03:46

The entire crew is gathered on Deck Two for a briefing. Commander Brewster begins, "Two hours from now, we'll encounter the upper reaches of Mars atmosphere. Most of you have experienced reentry into Earth's atmosphere. This should be a smoother ride. Many Colossus ships have preceded us and put it down on the dime on their landing pads. The two robotic Colossus Mars Arcadia colony supply ships, *Aldebaran* and *Pleiades* landed at Arcadia Colony Base four days ago. They'll be our Christmas gifts this year and for the next two years until the next supply ships arrive. I need all of you in flights suits with helmets for the landing. Be fully suited and in your assigned couches at 11:30. Any questions?"

Oleg, a qualified pilot with access to ship's records, asks, "Not to alarm the others, but I've seen reports that say we are coming in with the inboard engines shut down and using the outboard four at fifty percent power for our retro-propulsion. Has this ever been done before?"

Vik replies, "You all *do* have the right to know about this. We have computer simulated this a hundred times and we had a real test on MCC-3 a few days ago. We worked tirelessly with Houston and have a robust software control program uploaded. It works just like the standard retro-thrust with the two inboard engines at one hundred percent. There is no reason to worry."

Coby interjects, "You've all seen too many Mars movies. This one has a happy ending. We'll be down at Arcadia by 12:09, about two hours from now. You'll be glad you spent so much time on the TARED these past months. Mars gravity is calling.

Any more questions?... No? Okay then, happy landings to all of us!"

Sofi looks at Alex tells him with silent thoughts, "I can sense that Dad is worried but he has confidence in everything they've done to make this work. I can see *Taurus* setting down gently as she has done in a thousand sims."

Alex returns a thought and smiles, "Papa is not worried. That's all *I* need."

Arcadia Colony Ship *Taurus*
December 21, 2035
Mission Elapsed Time 181:11:59:13

Coby speaks, "CASSI, please open Coms to *Mars Basecamp* and Houston."

"Affirmative. Coms channel open."

"*Mars Basecamp* and Houston, *Mars Basecamp* and Houston, this is *Arcadia Colony* Ship *Taurus.* We are one minute from atmospheric entry. We'll raise you from the other side."

"CASSI, on intercom please. All crew are confirmed strapped with helmets on for atmospheric entry. Prepare for some g-forces. CASSI, entry corridor readouts please."

"Reading the homing beacon at Arcadia. Entry corridor optimal. Entry heads up angle engaged... Atmosphere contact confirmed."

All of them feel a slight vibration in the ship and an occasional bang of control thrusters keeping the ship precisely oriented nose up and belly first into the atmosphere at 12,000 kilometers per hour. G-forces build gradually. All of them see ionization as a blue-white aurora tinged with yellow flames streaking by the panoramic windows. Minutes pass with the crew silently watching the spectacle. Ellie is biting her lip and she has a death grip on the arm rests. Abby's eyes glisten with diamond tears of joy mixed with fear. Alex is holding Sofi's hand and touching her mind as a soft feather on her cheek, "Awesome, awesome, awesome!"

More bangs and a feeling of slow rotation. The ionization show subsides.

CASSI announces, "Hypersonic tail first orientation engaged. Retro-thrust in ten seconds… Prepare for deceleration g-force increase."

Suddenly there is a rumble from deep below. Everyone is pushed harder into their couches. The sky above them has turned from the black of space to a pinky orange hue toward the horizon and tinged with blue high above. The big ship wallows on the four outboard engines' retro-thrust. The unconventional solution is in practice. There is a crunch and deep groan from below. The gimbals whine as they adjust the thrust vector to keep the ship on the precise landing corridor. Sofi can sense that her father's worry meter has red-lined. The wallowing gives way to a rock steady rumble that builds as the ship plows deeper into the atmosphere. All of them can see the horizon clearly now as the ship slowly rolls to vertical.

CASSI announces, "Fifty meters altitude. Landing pad Alpha dust is minimal…Ten meters… Touchdown. Engines stopped and purging." The ship creaks, squeaks, and settles on its four landing pads.

Coby shouts into the intercom and transmits, "Good piloting CASSI! Houston, *Taurus*. Houston, *Taurus*. We have landed at MET 181:12:09:13 and it's SOL Zero at Mars *Arcadia Colony Base!*"

.

6

ARCADIA PLANITIA

"I think that space flight is a condition of Nature that comes into effect when an intelligent species reaches the saturation point of its planetary habitat combined with a certain level of technological ability... I think it is a built-in gene-directed drive for the spreading of the species and its continuation."

Donald A. Wollheim, *The Universe Makers,* 1971

Arcadia Colony Ship *Taurus*
December 21, 2035
Mission Elapsed Time 181:12:09:13

Arcadia Planitia- Mars Arcadia Colony Base
Mars Colony Time MCT SOL 00:08:21:36

The Colossus Colony Ship *Taurus* crew just landed after a one-hundred-eighty-one day journey. They are welcomed into the embrace of Mars gentle gravity. The celebration is on:

"Yes! Yes! *Yes!*"

"Whew!"

"Yeah!"

"We made it!"

"Mars is ours! Mars is *ours!*"

"Wahoo!"

"Thank God for gravity!"

Coby is on the intercom, "Congratulations people! Now stay put for a few minutes while we safe the ship. Stay strapped in until I give the word. You can take off your helmets and stow them."

The celebration continues with high fives. Some are laughing. Some are sitting smiling in silent contemplation. Others are weeping openly. Coby has just given word to unbuckle. There are eager helping hands for that. Now there are hugs and kisses. It's a moment they will never forget- the beginning of a new life. They are a small beginning for a new chapter in the history of humanity. Coby and the rest from the Command Deck descend to join those on Deck Two.

They are amazed at the view from the panoramic window facing west toward the rise of the rugged rim of Golombek Crater. The *Aldebaran* and *Pleiades* supply ships sit majestically gleaming on their landing pads to the northwest. The robot dozers have leveled and transformed the base area. The surrounding plains are rugged with the subsurface ice pingos. There are four solar arrays deployed, four kilo-power reactors, the huge ten megawatt SSTAR reactor, two Sabatier propellant reactors, and the first arch constructed greenhouse beyond the two BS-340 Hab modules. A hundred meters to the east of the habs there is a small cairn of rocks marking Barry Peterson's grave. This is *Arcadia Base* as it was established for them by the first humans on the *Arcadia 1 Mission*. They will soon deploy two BS-550 inflatable hab modules with two more ECLSS life support units that are waiting for them in the *Pleiades* supply ship.

Coby requests attention in the hubbub. "Please, let's all meet in the cargo bay in thirty minutes at 0900. Please reset your watches to MCT. The shore party roster was posted in the galley. The shore party will be led by Vik and Abby accompanied by Oleg, Olga, Tracy, Paul, Megumi, Satoshi, Trevor, and Mandy. The shore party will check out the two habs, get the ECLSS systems running, and if the habs check out, we will begin occupation of the habs. Take your hygiene kits to the cargo bay. We'll send them down with supplies and equipment.

"We need everyone down in the cargo bay to help the shore party suit up and egress. The rest of us will remain on *Taurus* today to help in the cargo bay. *Taurus* will remain our home until we get the next two habs up and running. Those remaining will have our first working EVA tomorrow. See you in the cargo bay."

When Coby climbed down the ladder to the cargo bay, most of the crew is already there. The shore party is prebreathing oxygen and suiting up with assistance from the others. Coby assists Vik and Ellie assists Abby.

Coby speaks, "CASSI, please extend the sky crane arms and lower the elevator cables."

"Affirmative. The elevator cables will need to be securely augured in for cargo larger than the crew platform."

"Got it. I helped redesign the system after the sky crane incident with Barry Peterson." Then he keys the mic to the suit radios, "At 0930, five minutes from now, the shore party will enter the cargo airlock. Be careful out there and- welcome to Mars!"

Stepping out of the airlock onto the crew platform and into the sunshine of Mars, they began their descent down the sky crane rails to the red surface of their new home. Clunk, the elevator starts down.

Abby blurts out, "This is glorious!"

Vik replies, "*Bo-zeh moy!* Mars. We can just enjoy this. There is video being sent to Houston but the networks won't cover it except a snippet on the news. No need for a speech from us. Trent Granger and *Arcadia 1* deservedly got all the glory…Here we are! My first boot steps on Mars mean everything to *me*. Here goes! Okay shore party, as you were briefed, our first task is to get *Taurus* on shore power then we enter the habs and get them fit for occupation. These are our new homes. Commander Granger assured us they are ready for us but that was a months ago."

Satoshi is on Mars soil next to Megumi. He bends down and picks up a few Mars pebbles and hands them to Megumi. "We're really here!"

Oleg and Olga are looking at a tablet with CASSI's readouts of the habs atmosphere and ECLSS stats. Oleg reports, "Hab 1 is looking good. Internal pressure and gas compositions are all in tolerance. Hab 2 pressure is good but the atmosphere has some contaminants, meaning it probably smells bad. We'll go change filters and check that both ECLSS units are at one hundred percent. Replacing the big activated charcoal canisters and getting the whole air volume through ECLSS should hopefully clean-up the air in Hab 2."

"Okay, team, the rest of us will enter Hab 1. We'll have to cycle in four at a time in two cycles. Use the CO_2 hose to dust off before you get in the airlock."

When the eight of them are inside Hab 1, Vik reports over the radio, "It's exciting and a bit spooky. The first boots on Mars lived here. They left us a big welcome message! They used precious printer paper to make us a banner: Welcome to your New Home Arcadia Colony! It's signed by each of them with personal notes."

Megumi adds, "There's also a stack of signed *Arcadia 1* crew photos for us. Only Granger's signature is missing. Did he think we were going to sell these on eBay?"

Vik says, "I'll be the canary in the coal mine. I'm removing my helmet."

Abby jumps in, "The readouts say it's good. If anything smells off or if you feel it's not good, get your helmet back on quick! Then I'll help you get a quick recycle to get a full suit full of fresh air."

"Here goes." Vik takes his helmet off with a dramatic flourish. "It's air- yes... Smell? Yes, but it's very subtle. Slightly like a locker room and sweaty socks but the ECLSS filter change should get rid of that. You're all welcome to take your helmets off. Let's have a look at the three decks and see what work needs to be done."

Tracy speaks, "It's like being in a rented RV that even though reasonably clean, all of its surfaces, edges, floors, and appliances are used. Yes, that was *our* honeymoon."

Paul adds, "It's better than Motel Six after a group of construction workers spent the weekend in the room. I should know, I was in the construction crew one summer. Let's go have a look at the upper decks."

The BS-340 habs are rigid inflated cylinders fourteen meters long and seven meters diameter with a wall that's half a meter thick. The wall has more radiation protection than the Colossus ship. The cylinders are set on their sides connected end-to-end with crew access up a ladder to the center air lock. Each hab module has 340 cubic meters of inflated volume with three decks that can accommodate six persons. The lower deck is living and working space. The mid-deck is the galley, recreation, and TARED exercise unit. The upper deck has the sleep and hygiene modules. The modular design allows for movable walls to accommodate doubles or singles.

Oleg reports on the radio, "We have the filters changed out. Both ECLSS units are now running at one hundred percent. We'll go enter Hab 2 to check it out while the atmosphere is recycling."

Vik replies, "Okay Oleg but keep your helmets on. Be careful with Olga. That girl is having my grandchild! We also need to minimize her EVA time radiation exposure." Others not in the loop on the pregnancy news took this as wishful thinking.

"No worries Papa. We're dusted off and in the airlock now…Pressures equalized. Opening the hatch… So far it looks fine on this level. I don't see any souvenirs left behind."

Olga speaks on a closed circuit to Oleg. "I'm going up to check out the upper decks...I'm on the mid-deck in the galley...Eeek!"

"Olga, I'm coming! What happened?"

"Nothing happened. I opened the refrigerator. Yes, they did leave us a souvenir. Someone forgot to dump their leftovers into the recycler. It's gross!"

Oleg is beside her now. "Yuck! No wonder there are contaminants in the air. Let's get this cleaned up. Send the mold monster into the chipper!"

An hour later the shore party is back outside reporting to the crew on *Taurus* that they have the habs checked out and ready to move in. Vik has his team secure the four elevator cable augers for larger loads.

Coby calls down. "Ready below! Here's cargo Module 1A coming from the cargo bay. It's got your first load of supplies and your hygiene kits."

Vik replies. "Ready for it. We'll get it on the power wagon and start the supply chain. It's going to be a long day."

Abby says, "And you thought starting life on Mars was going to be easy?"

"No but I'm looking forward to someday kicking back in my easy chair with grandchildren to fetch and carry for me."

"I like that thought. Dream on."

Christmas Eve
Arcadia Planitia- Mars Arcadia Colony Base
December 24, 2035
MCT SOL 03:07:01:43

Over the next three Sols, the colonists unloaded a prioritized list of pressure sealed cargo modules from the *Taurus*. All EVA's are generally kept shorter than four hours to lessen the acute accumulation of radiation exposure. In the future, fewer EVAs will be necessary when the colony construction is more advanced and when the AI robots are trained to be more facile at construction and maintenance without humans directly involved. The contents manifest determines the priority for unpacking and storage in Hab 1 and Hab 2. Two ECLSS units are unloaded with the assistance of the CARIAN android. The ECLSS units are for the new hab modules. The electrical and plumbing for them are prepped for the installation.

The first shore team is comfortably settled in. They can visualize the colony expanding to accommodate the rest of them who are still living on the *Taurus*.

The *Taurus* is substantially emptied of the highest priority items. The two Colossus robotic supply landers *Aldebaran* and *Pleiades* are there waiting to be unloaded. So much work to do! All of it will be done in due course by the prioritized list. Each ship carries an inflatable BS-550 Hab Module. The BS-550 Hab Module like the BS-340 has three decks of living and working space for ten persons including galley, communications and control, entertainment, sick bay, exercise bay, sleep and hygiene modules.

The colony has a primary store of twenty-seven months of supplies to store on the surface with six months of emergency rations to cover a system breakdown. Supplies are stored in the *Alcyone* consumables module connected to the living habs through an airlock. Additional emergency supplements can be delivered from the orbiting Basecamp. Basecamp is autonomous now that the latest crew just left for return to Earth. There is a scheduled Colossus supply run at each Earth-Mars opposition every twenty-six months. So any additional emergency supplies from Earth will take six to twenty-six months to deliver depending on the Earth-Mars configuration.

The Alnath module is a pressurized and radiation hardened special storage module carried on the *Aldebaran*. It contains biological supplies for near term and long term need. It has the seed bank for potatoes, tomatoes, strawberries, soybeans, spinach, lettuce, radishes, barley, wheat, rye, hops, sugar beets, and corn. In vitro fetus growth technology has advanced to allow an expectation of eventually growing many types of animals. The cryo bank has cryo-frozen fertilized chicken egg-embryos, tilapia, and catfish. There are stores of fertilizers, chemicals for neutralizing Mars soil perchlorates, antibiotics, vitamins, nutrition supplements, calcium, and iron. Future supply ships will carry even more diverse biological supplies including frozen embryos of pigs, sheep, goats, dairy cows, dogs, cats, and humans.

Coby and Vik called a much deserved break in the work at 1600 MCT. "It's Christmas Eve people! We've just unloaded a top priority module from *Aldebaran* marked *Do Not Open Until Christmas*. We're all going up to *Taurus* for a Christmas Eve feast and a special viewing of a movie that we've held in reserve for this occasion."

The special module was connected to ship power to maintain a small freezer unit. In it are twenty-two frozen gourmet Christmas dinners. Certainly not everyone in the crew is Christian but no one is a vegetarian. After six months of dehydrated space food fare, the meal is worthy of a celebration of their new home and the holiday connecting them to Earth. The menu is real turkey, giblet gravy, whole berry cranberry sauce, green beans almandine, and pumpkin casserole with brown sugar crumbles. This is complemented with a precious selection of red and white wine. They manage to cook the meals perfectly in the galley oven and keep them warm until they were served in one sitting in the common spaces. There were no speeches, just lively, happy conversation.

Mandy and Trevor hold hands and give thanks. Then Trevor says, "God willing, we'll have a special meal of Mars grown food for next Christmas."

In the middle of the hubbub Paul Earhart comments, "We knew that this would be hard work and I'm exhausted. The robots can do some of the work. The CARIIN heavy equipment robots are great at digging, hauling, and plowing under CASSI's direct control. The CARIAN androids are good at some of the finer work but again they need CASSI's control. The AI designation is generous. I'd rate CARIAN level of intelligence barely higher than a bag of hammers."

Tracy adds, "For this work, the colony roster should include manual laborers, plumbers, and electricians."

Harrison tops that, "We already have that and they are us. Since ISS, highly skilled astronauts have had to do all those tasks. We have the training, intelligence, and versatility to solve almost any problem. We're exactly complementary to the robots."

Dieter agrees, "Yeah. We're one big happy family of laborers."

They laughed and passed the bottle of red wine to refill glasses.

Coby wanted the lighthearted celebration to continue but felt it necessary to remind all of them. He raps his wine glass with a spoon. "Yes, we've made it! We've come the distance and this is our new home. I want to drink a toast to our success and to all the people back on Earth who have made this journey possible.

They have an uncertain future. We owe it to ourselves and to all of humanity to survive and multiply."

"Hear, hear!" The spontaneous reply goes around the room as they clink plastic glasses.

After dinner, they gathered in the entertainment lounge. They open gag gifts from notables in the *International Space Coalition* and from family connections on Earth. Personal presents between colonists will be shared tomorrow in private.

Then they all watched the promised movie, the silly cult classic film *Christmas on Mars*. The film explores the experiences of the first Christmas on a newly colonized Mars. The lead character, Major Syrtis, is celebrating the birth of the first colonist baby. Sofi and Alex assure them that they have only seen the tip of the iceberg of bad Mars sci-fi movies. "We'll dole these treasures out in future celebrations!"

Oleg stands up and proudly announces. "If fate actually gives us this blessing, Olga and I are having the first baby on Mars for real!" Some but not all of them knew the good news.

Olga interjects, "It wasn't planned, but we landed three months pregnant. We truly believe that this is more important than the first boots on Mars. The children of this colony are the future of humanity on Mars."

Mars Arcadia Colony Base
December 25, 2035
MCT SOL 04:11:22:16

They have a day of rest on Christmas. Christmas music is piped through the intercom. Curiously Megumi and Satoshi especially enjoy the festivities.

"We enjoyed Christmas music at home. Even the street sweeper machines played *We Wish You a Merry Christmas* all year."

Some of them exchange personal presents. Alex, Sofi, Jacob, and Oleg received gold pins flown on *Aquila* from their parents.

Jacob gives Elena a medallion he earned from his first Soyuz flight to ISS. "It's to remind you how much you inspired me to go to space."

Elena is moved and sobs. "I have nothing for you." The scene that makes the rest of them feel uncomfortable.

Ellie changes the mood with an announcement. "There's another special meal from the freezer on *Aldebaran* that we'll serve in fifteen minutes. Now, we're serving hot holiday hors d'oeuvres on Deck Two where we can take in the view of our new home."

Harrison says, "Outstanding! This is better than anything we had on the entire outbound trip. Do we have to wait two years for the next supply ship to hope for such good fare?"

Trevor speaks up, "Not if our new greenhouse and aquaponics units work out. We could be setting a new trend for cuisine on Mars."

"Oh! Look!" Mandy jumps up and knocks over a tray that clatters to the deck as if in slow motion in Mars gravity. "There are two dust devils bearing down on us from the west out of Golombek Crater."

There are gasps around the room.

Harrison is fascinated, "Oh man, that's amazing! Those are some angry looking twisters!"

Coby is concerned but helpless to do anything. "Yeah, they're coming right at us. We'll be safe in here but we would take some good licks if we were outside. Here it comes!"

The dust swirls violently around them. The panoramic window is being peppered by red dust and Martian sand. The ship vibrates.

Jacob says, "Whew! I'm glad nobody is out on EVA in *that*."

Vik says calmly, "Seriously. But, our solar arrays are taking a beating. Thankfully they're redundant with the big SSTAR reactor."

Jacob replies, "Don't be so fast to make them obsolete. That reactor and the kilopower units have to be shut down about once a month for inspection and maintenance. That's when we'll need that solar power. Do you think the habs will hold up to those dust devils?"

Satoshi says, "They are rated for some tough stuff including micrometeoroids. They're securely anchored. They should be okay."

Coby says, "CASSI, please give me a readout from the solar panel arrays. Are any of them offline?"

"Negative. The arrays are all still online and their power output has increased by twenty percent."

"Great! Thanks CASSI. Not only did the solar arrays survive but they got a good dust-off just like the old *Spirit* and *Opportunity* rovers. They ran on solar power instead of plutonium RTGs. JPL Mission Control used to pray for a dust devil to bring life back to the power starved rovers. They were only supposed to last ninety days but *Opportunity* outlived *Spirit* and gave us fifteen years of exploration. The great global Mars dust storm of 2018 virtually shut off sunlight for over two months. *Opportunity* went into hibernation and never woke up."

New Year's Eve
Mars Arcadia Colony Base
December 31, 2035
MCT SOL 12:23:58:43

About a dozen of the colony extended family are staying up to watch a replay of New Year's Eve Celebration on Times Square in New York. There isn't a lavish celebration like they shared on Christmas Eve but there are snacks and hot chocolate to help them endure watching the snow flurries on Times Square. Coby and Ellie are there with Sofi. Vik and Abby are there with Alex. They wanted their kids to stay connected with Earth customs. The hectic years of training and with their young age, Sofi and Alex had never had the experience of ringing in the New Year by actually staying up until midnight. They wanted to share the joy of experiencing the event with them for the first time. There is music and dancing and an ecstasy of the moment on Times Square. The excitement grows as the crystal ball atop the building at One Times Square drops forty three meters in the last minute before the New Year begins. The ball reaches bottom and what seems like all of humanity explodes in celebration. It's an emotional scene that Sofi and Alex will never forget.

Mars Arcadia Colony Base
January 2, 2036
MCT SOL 10:08:19:21

Commander Coby Brewster personal log:

We have only unloaded smaller high priority items *from Aldebaran* and *Pleiades*. The first major objective for this week is to unload and begin installation of the two inflatable BS-550 Hab Modules and spare ECLSS life support service module systems. Each ship is carrying one hab. These cargo ships are now specially modified to unload cargo as large as one hundred metric tons like the SSTAR reactor and maintain safety and stability. The big, auger anchored, four cable sky crane and expanded stabilizer pads made the job almost routine. The robotic CARIAN and CARIIN units are used extensively in the operation. The more the robots can be used and trained on the ground, the less the colonists are exposed to industrial accidents and EVA radiation exposure time.

The BS-550 Hab Modules, Hab 3 and Hab 4, are sixty percent larger than the BS-340 modules, Hab 1 and Hab 2, already installed for *Arcadia 1*. Each BS-550 has three decks of living and working space for ten persons including galley, communications and control, entertainment, sick bay, exercise bay, and sleep and hygiene modules. The habs are interconnected in a T-shaped configuration in plan view. The *Arcadia Beta* colonists, arriving in May, will add two more BS-550 modules, Hab-5 and Hab-6, increasing the Arcadia Base capacity to fifty-two.

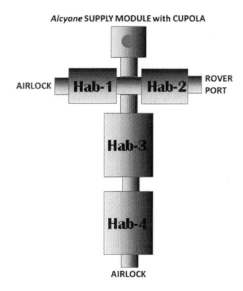

Alcyone SUPPLY MODULE with CUPOLA

AIRLOCK | **Hab-1** | **Hab-2** | ROVER PORT

Hab-3

Hab-4

AIRLOCK

We held a lottery of sorts by family, married couple, and single status to determine who will occupy which hab and unit. The big move-in will happen on SOL 15, January 5th. It's really important to everyone to have some ownership of a table, chair, bed, sink and toilet. Also, having gravity has actually relieved some of the crew stress. The standout odd-lot arrangement is that all of the singles, Elena, Jacob, Dieter, Dao-Ming, and Sandy, will be sharing Hab-2, one of the original BS-340 habs. I don't expect trouble. Elena has been on an even keel recently. Now she'll have two chaplains and a psychologist sharing the hab to keep tabs on her.

Our near term construction plans will make the habs more radiation hardened with 3D sintered regolith arch covers. Future expansion will go underground for radiation protection on par with what the Earth's magnetic field and dense atmosphere affords all life on the blue planet. Earth does not stop all radiation. There is a fine balance of beneficial radiation. Our human vitamin D synthesis requires some ultraviolet exposure. Over geologic time scales, evolution is fueled by chance mutations caused by radiation. Too much radiation causes tissue and DNA damage that the body cannot repair and then the chances of developing cancer increase exponentially.

The first phase of colony development is ensuring survival. Our twenty year plan promises Earth-like parks and lakes and ever better developments on the future horizon. Some visionary plans feel Earth-like familiar and some seem fancifully fit for another planet.

The second major objective for this week is to unload from *Pleiades,* a shiny new six passenger pressurized Mars Exploration Rover now named MER-2. The rover already on Base from *Arcadia 1*, MER-1, is a two passenger version with two EVA suitports. These ports allow an astronaut to step into their suit from inside the rover, have the PLSS life support unit seal the back and port, and egress in less than ten minutes. The astronaut can exit and enter the rover without bringing harmful Mars dust and dirt inside. The rover is designed to require little maintenance with an expected ten year lifespan.

The new six passenger MER has four suit ports and is capable of science excursion sorties covering hundreds of kilometers and up to two weeks. EVA's will only be necessary when the rover instruments and manipulator arms aren't adequate for the exploration science task at hand. This rover has a docking port that mates to a hab module so the rover can be entered from the hab without going EVA. I've promised Sofi and Alex that Vik and I will take them for an overnighter rover trip when the rover is checked out and hectic construction pace eases. I really, really try to keep my promises.

The third major objective for this week is to unload a big beast from the *Pleiades* affectionately called the *HORTA.* It's a large, one and a half meter AI robotic CARIIN boring tool for mining ice and in the process excavating underground tunnels and habs. Why is it called the *HORTA*? Horta was a minor Etruscan goddess of agriculture- think horticulture, and here we have a machine delivering life giving water. It's also a place name of several cities in the Mediterranean region. But, the real reason the name *HORTA* stuck is that it's affectionately named after a tunneling creature on the planet Janus VI from the original *Star Trek* series.

A kilopower nuclear reactor on the *HORTA* is the power source for both the boring operation and most importantly, for melting the pulverized ice. Insulated cargo modules surplused from unloading the cargo bay will be converted to become water tanker wagons. The water will be delivered to the Sabatier reactors and to the aquaponics greenhouse.

Up until now, the ice mining operation has been like strip mining on Earth using a CARIIN backhoe and auger. The near surface ice is dirty with fifty percent or more regolith mixed in. SHARAD orbiting ground penetrating radar shows us that the best, cleanest, thickest ice in Arcadia Planitia starts ten meters down. We'll start our tunneling project from a nexus adjacent to the surface habs. We'll use our structural engineering expertise to design adequate structural support as we tunnel and make living space. Sintered regolith walls will be added for insulation. Like any construction project, the electrical, data, and plumbing lines have to be engineered. We have the expertise. Living in ice underground sounds cold! We'll have water circulating solar panels to deliver water heat. This will be supplemented with electric heat as needed at night or when the Sun is dimmed by dust storms. The whole system will be thermostat controlled through CASSI.

What will we do with the three Colossus ships that brought us and our supplies here? The *Taurus* and then the *Aldebaran* will be refueled to be returned to Earth at an unspecified future date.

There is an industrial laser on *Pleiades* that will eventually be used to dismantle the giant ship for precious scrap metal and electronics.

These early operations make it seem like we have all of this colony business figured out. The reality is that we are figuring it out one step at a time. *We* are fueled with an abundance of hope.

Mars Arcadia Colony Base
April 15, 2036
MCT SOL 116:20:31:42

CASSI addresses Coby in his micro-earpiece worn 24/7. "Commander Brewster, incoming text files from Houston marked for your eyes only"

"Give me a summary please CASSI."

"The text says that there has been encrypted traffic between Dao-Ming Cai and the People's Republic of China. Houston interprets it to be of grave concern. I have decoded the encrypted message and have determined its source and author. My report file and evidence are in your inbox."

"Thank you CASSI. I'll share this with Vik and we we'll deal with it accordingly."

After the dinner hour, the entire colony group is assembled in the *Alcyone* module to watch an astronomical event. *Alcyone* is now a consumables storage and common area with an observation deck outfitted with a cupola dome. Coby asks, "Where's Elena? She's part of our happy family."

Dieter replies, "She went back to our hab saying that she didn't need to join the gathering."

"Well, what can I say?" Coby begins, "We've come a long way and have much to be thankful for. Our little colony is growing. Twenty one Arcadia Beta colonists arrive next month. Oleg and Olga's baby is due in June. Now, Tracy and Paul have an announcement."

Paul looks at Tracy with a big smile and nods to her to speak, "Yes, well, true to what Coby said, we have much to be thankful for. Paul and I are expecting our first baby in November!"

There is a short round of applause and then the others close in to give Tracy a hug and shake Paul's hand in congratulations.

After the hubbub starts to die down Trevor nudges Mandy, "Mandy and I have an announcement of our own. "There are surprised looks around the room. "No, no, not that! We aren't pregnant. We want to announce that the greenhouse started by *Arcadia 1* has been completely restarted using our hydroponics methods. We have lettuce, bell peppers, tomatoes, cucumbers, and peas coming in."

Mandy continues, "The second greenhouse we set up in January is our trial for growing crops in treated Martian soil. We have a start on our root vegetables- radishes, turnips, beets, potatoes. So far so good but we don't expect harvest from the second greenhouse for a few weeks. Meanwhile, we're planning a communal dinner on Sunday nights and serve our fresh greens."

"Hell yes!" Harrison blurts out. "Sunday night is salad and a movie night!"

Trevor adds, "This is just the beginning. We have more greenhouses to put up. The aquaponics unit will be started soon. It'll take about six months per brood to mature the tilapia. Then we'll start up our poultry unit."

Dieter replies, "Oh man! It'll be good for our souls to get some fresh food. Our food stores are nutritious but it gets dismal after months and months of it."

Ellie says, "Great news Trevor. We'll *all* enjoy the fresh produce grown on Mars. Now Sofi and Alex want your attention."

Sofi begins, "Thanks Mom. Well, Alex and I have been studying Mars' moons."

Alex finishes her sentence, "Yah, Phobos and Deimos. Phobos is the closer and bigger one. "

"It's also the faster one, crossing our sky in four hours. It's so close it almost looks as big as our old Moon."

"Deimos takes over two sols to cross. Tonight there's a special conjunction."

"Yah. In just ten minutes Phobos will cross paths with Deimos."

"It happens only once every Mars year from our location."

"Alex and I invite all of you to come up to the observation deck to see it."

In a few minutes they were gathered under the acrylic dome. Most of them hadn't been up here at night. It was used often to getaway and look at the whole perspective of sky, Mars vistas, and the lay of the growing Base. The view is a respite from the walls of the habs even though they decorated to make the spaces homier.

Abby says, "Oh, I've missed the stars. We used to enjoy the observation deck on *Taurus* and the cupola on *Altair*... Look there they are- just a few degrees apart!"

Ellie agrees, "Nothing could be as beautiful as going EVA over Bennu and getting time to look at the Milky Way. I feel a connection to Phobos and Deimos. They're actually gravity captured asteroids- C-type just like Bennu."

"Mom, quiet please! Just *look* at the beauty of this event. They'll cross paths in about fifteen seconds."

Alex says, "There it goes. *Fear* is eating *Fright*."

"Phobos is swallowing Deimos. Wow!"

Coby adds, "While we contemplate Phobos and Deimos, fear and fright, I want to remind all of you that the nuke impactor *Vishnu* speeding to deflect *Shiva* has its close gravity assist flyby of Jupiter tomorrow. We'll have some grand first row seats of the Jupiter maneuver relayed to us. Let's have a moment to remember the peril that Earth is in if this nuke fails."

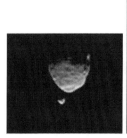

Phobos and Deimos photographed by NASA/JPL rover Curiosity on left and by the HiRISE camera on NASA's Mars Reconnaissance Orbiter on right.

Exploring Golombek Crater
MER-2
May 1, 2036
MCT SOL 132:07:18:21

The expedition team is seated and buckled in the rover ready to leave on an epic exploration journey. The straps are more like a car seatbelt than the stout harnesses in the Colossus ship. They will experience some jolts to be sure. Today begins the first long duration and longest distance sortie of any human or robotic rover exploration on Mars. The six passenger Mars Exploration Rover-2, MER-2, has been checked out on shorter excursions since it was unloaded from *Pleiades*. The check-out runs were over-nighters ranging up to ten kilometers from base. The kilopower reactor onboard can last almost indefinitely.

MER-2, even with the abundance of view port windows, provides radiation protection beyond what the habs afford the colonists. The hull has a thick hydrogen rich polyethylene and layered aluminum, titanium, and tantalum foil insulation and the windows are hydrogen rich polycarbonate infused with tantalum to absorb radiation. Layered tri-metallic Z graded foil attenuates electromagnetic radiation. Tantalum is an efficient absorber of high energy protons and neutrons.

This expedition is planned to last one week. Today MER-2 has provisions for six people for two weeks and a recycled air supply that can last for weeks longer. The expedition is being led by Ellie Accardi. It's an honor she earned as the astrogeologist who rocked the world on the *Aquila Mission*. She's been waiting for years for a chance at this first in person real human science exploration of Mars. Their objective, Golombek Crater, promises to reveal some deep exposed layers of Mars' geologic history. The rim wall of Golombek Crater lies twenty kilometers to the west. The crater is nearly one hundred kilometers in diameter so they'll concentrate only on what they can access in the planned week long sortie. Their communication link and GPS navigation will be facilitated by recently commissioned commercial orbiting satellites. The two man MER-1 rover will be on standby at Arcadia Base if a rescue is necessary.

The rest of the expedition roster includes Oleg, Tracy, Dieter, Sofi, and Alex. Oleg is an experienced pilot and engineer. Tracy is an engineer and physician. Dieter is an electrical and computer engineer. Sofi and Alex qualify as newbie engineers and get the ride because of Ellie's influential status. Elena lobbied to come but Ellie vetoed it. Coby agreed. Having Elena that close to Ellie for so long could be a recipe for disaster.

The four adults have space suits fitted for the rover's four suitports. Sofi and Alex will not be going EVA from the rover since their only space suits will not fit the suitports. Their non-suitport spacesuits are brought along in case of emergency. There are six respirators to get all of them through the first moments of an emergency depressurization while they get a chance to suit up.

The resident AI on the rover was to be named CARI with the 'R' standing for 'rover'. The AI program is related to CASSI and a direct descendant of the CAMI AI they used on EVAs during *Aquila*. Ellie insisted that the CAMI AI remain with the name CAMI. She had a personal connection to CAMI during *Aquila* exploration. On an EVA, CAMI was an extension of Ellie's eyes and hands.

Ellie had personally worked with astrogeologists back on Earth to lay out the EVA route and planned EVA and science stations. The route will include laying a series of seismic sensor and geothermal probes to better understand what makes Mars tick. There are specific geologic sampling sites and objectives with the highest priority of looking for mineral resources and signs of past or present life on Mars. Ad hoc site opportunities are expected and welcomed. That's the first rule of exploration!

Ellie gets the sortie going at 0730 sharp. The video and audio feed is going to Houston and all interested networks on Earth. "Coby, love you my Commander. We're getting underway now. This will be one for science!"

"We're with you every second and kilometer. *Be safe!* Come back to us with something that previous probes on this planet missed. You and CAMI have a stellar history!"

Sofi gets on the channel, "Dad, thanks for letting us go on this expedition. This is gonna be the coolest adventure *ever!*"

"You bet-ya! Now you and Alex mind your Mom and help her keep an eye on things."

"You bet-ya!"

MER-2 lurches forward and a low hum turns to a whine as the rover accelerates to twenty klicks per hour. Ellie veers around a solar array and points the rover west toward Golombek.

Oleg says, "Okay there. Easy does it!

"Right. I'll let the expert drive. CAMI please take over the autopilot and use the GPS waypoints to get us to Objective 1."

"Affirmative Captain Accardi."

"CAMI, please just call me Ellie. Everyone does."

"Affirmative."

Alex and Sofi giggled. Alex is in her head, "Way cool!"

The sun is at their backs. The going gets rough a few hundred meters out of Arcadia Base. Their progress slows sometimes down to a walking pace. Forty-five minutes and twelve kilometers later they arrive at Objective 1, which is a tilted ridge of layered rock that geologists call a hogback. The layers are brown, red, orange, and buff colored. They install the first seismic sensor and geothermal probe at the base of the hogback.

Sofi to Alex, "This is *really* Mars. It's so good to get out of the hab."

Alex to Sofi, "Yah buddy. I was going stir crazy. It's sure gonna be a tease to not be able to go out on EVA."

"But we're going on the camping, RV, science, most awesome trip of a lifetime!"

Ellie comments, "This ridge looks so much more *Mars* than on the HiRISE imaging. The layers on this ridge are from the ocean, *Oceanus Borealis,* that existed here in the northern hemisphere about four billion years ago. We are about four to five kilometers below the mean elevation of Mars."

Sofi blurts out, "Wow! Maybe we we'll find Atlantis over the next rise!"

"It's no joke. Every kilometer, every meter, every centimeter we explore is a discovery of something no rover and no human eyes have seen before."

Alex bites on that. "Do ya think that some non-rover, non-human eyes might have been here?"

"Ah hem! That's enough of *that* or we won't get any sleep tonight. Creeepeee…"

Oleg says, "How about an EVA?"

Dieter and Tracy, "Yah!" "Let's go for it!"

"Not so fast. We'll only go EVA when we find something so interesting that we can justify the radiation exposure. The rover is equipped to get the job done. Just watch and learn."

For Ellie, this work will be similar to working on asteroid Bennu while strapped in and operating the deep space MMU. A big difference is that since Mars has stronger gravity. They won't need to be harpooned in place to get sampling work done.

For geologic and instrument sampling, MER-2 has a manipulator arm, an instrument arm, and a coring tool. Like the deep space MMU on *Aquila* and the Mars Curiosity rover, the instrument arm on MER-2 is equipped with a ChemCam laser, APXS alpha proton X-Ray spectrometer, RAD-D (radiation detector measures alpha, beta, gamma, and x-rays), and GHLI Geologic Hand Lens Imager, all legacies of the successful NASA robotic rovers. The rover also has an array of high resolution panoramic to telescopic cameras.

"CAMI, please do a panoramic photo documentation of Objective 1."

"Affirmative... Completed."

"CAMI, please record these sample locations I will point out with this 100 mW green laser."

"Please proceed. I am recording."

"Okay, as I point I will dictate the photo and sampling designations. Layer 1-A...Layer 1-B...Layer 2-A...Layer 2-B... Layer 3-A...Layer 3-B...Layer 4-A... Layer 4-B...Core 1...and lastly Core 2."

"Sample locations have been recorded."

"Thank you CAMI. Now I want each of those spots photographed with the lens Zoom 1 and with the GHLI. Sample each spot twice at one centimeter separation with the ChemCam, APXS, and RAD-D instruments."

"Affirmative. Estimating that the survey will take approximately one hour."

"Please begin. We'll be standing by."

CAMI operates the instrument arm methodically. For a few of the samples, CAMI readjusts the position of the rover...

The crew have a snack and continue their off color speculations about sci-fi Mars.

"What do you think about that big face on Mars?"

"Very funny. You know that was debunked when the MRO returned the first hi-res images of the knoll in Cydonia. It was a kind of optical illusion of low resolution imaging and oblique lighting that got so many tongues wagging. It was the catalyst for the movie *Mission to Mars*…"

CAMI announces, "The photo and instrument survey of the sample spots is completed and recorded with your name designations."

"Great CAMI. Now for some rock sampling. Please try to get a small rock sample from each sample spot with the chisel and grab sampler on your manipulator arm. Then bag and digitally tag each sample with the ID chip in the sample bag. Then put the samples in the sample return container SRC-1."

"Affirmative. Estimating that the sampling will take approximately one hour but there is uncertainty depending on the rock hardness encountered."

"I understand. Do your best. Please begin. We'll be standing by."

It was fascinating to watch CAMI operate the manipulator arm as it whirs with the hydraulics and electric motor action. It was most amusing when CAMI announced the sample location was "bitchy and difficult."

Finally CAMI announces, "Rock sampling of the sample spots is completed, bagged and tag recorded with your name designations. Note that sample Layer 2-B was most difficult and only about one cc was recovered.""

"Good work CAMI! Thank you. The last task is to take a fifty centimeter core at the Core 1 and Core 2 locations at the base of the outcrop."

"Affirmative."

CAMI announces, "Cores 1 and 2 are completed. I recorded the locations and the geotechnical torque parameters."

"Excellent! The torque readings are a bonus. We're through at this location. Let's have lunch."

CAMI says, "I will have a ham on rye, hold the mayo. It corrodes my circuits."

"Ha! Precious CAMI! Who's been tweaking your personality?"

"Nobody. I listen and I learn."

Golombek 13
MER-2
May 5, 2036
MCT SOL 136:09:23:14

The rover team documents and samples eleven more sample locations over the next four days working their way along the great west wall of Golombek Crater. Ellie thinks that these locations will reinforce their findings from the first Objective 1 location.

"We have ten times the sample material ever gathered and returned to Earth. This will be a treasure to load onto the next ship we send home. But I get first crack at working on these samples in my new biologically isolated lab. Now we have to find our way into the crater to Objective 13."

She's hoping that the inner crater wall will expose some deeper strata layers. The traverse over the wall is tricky. The HiRISE imagery is not detailed enough to make the descent into the crater without getting into a risky situation with the rover. Oleg launches a drone to get more detailed images to confidently guide the way.

CAMI analyzes the drone images with the MRO digital elevation model to make a route plan with switchbacks to minimize the slope angle that the rover will traverse. If the head down slope exceeds forty degrees and the rover hits a significant bump, the rover could pitch pole head over heels. Not a good situation!

Ellie says, "We have a good route that should keep us out of trouble. But, let's go over the safety briefing again just in case it doesn't go as planned. If we get a big rock bump that pierces the hull, we go for the respirators in Locker 1. Oleg is assigned to the patch kit. If he's incapacitated, the closest one to it needs to get the kit and slap a patch on the hole. Tracy of course is our medic and doctor. Medical supplies are in Locker 2. Now buckle in."

Sofi says, "Wahoo! This is gonna be a ride!"

As they make their way down into the crater, radio beacons are placed at strategic places to insure that they can find their way back up on the same path. The rover doesn't always leave wheel tracks to follow- especially over a rocky path. Their traverse progress is being relayed to CASSI back at Base. The first three switchbacks make it seem like the rover can 'turn on a dime' with its six wheel independent drive. Ellie is gaining more confidence descending into the crater. The fourth switchback CAMI has selected is just ahead. It looks like the first three except there are two large boulders making the planned turn zone a bit narrower. CAMI is driving. Ellie trusts CAMI's driving with rover cams seeing hazards she cannot.

Halfway into the turn, there is a screech and jolt sideways toward the steep drop into the crater.

"Eeek! CAMI, Stop! Status check please."

CAMI replies, "MER-2 is stable. The rear starboard quarter grazed a rock that was not visible from any camera angle. Ellie, do you have first accident forgiveness?"

"Not very funny. Yes, I forgive you. Is everyone okay?"

"Ok."

Sofi says, "I'm okay but I think I wet my pants."

Alex nudges her. "Okay here."

Oleg asks, "CAMI, do we have any damage? Is the hull pressure stable?"

"No damage is detected. There might be a scratch. The pressure is stable."

Ellie says, "Please monitor it and report if there is the slightest pressure drop."

"Affirmative."

"Let's proceed slowly. We're almost down to Objective 13 just above the crater floor."

"Roger. Objective 13 is two hundred meters ahead."

Oleg comments, "The slope is more gentle now. The exposed rock layers ahead are similar to those at Objective 1 but the colors are darker."

Ellie replies, "Yeah, that's our outcrop, Objective 13. It's deeper into the stratigraphy so it's older. The layers are thinner than the other outcrops we've sampled. It looks like the layers are tilted away from the crater at about ten degrees dip. CAMI, park us about in the middle of the outcrop facing towards it and take a panoramic image."

"Affirmative."

Alex says, " Do you think this is even older than four billion years?"

"Relatively, yes. These layers were laid down in roughly the same time period but these are probably a few million years older than what we've studied so far since they are deeper."

The rover is stopped facing the outcrop.

"CAMI, we are ready to do the panoramic photo documentation of Objective 13."

"Proceeding."

Tracy asks, "What do you make of that darkest layer? It's almost black."

"Good observation. That layer looks like it could be mixed shale and limestone. If we were on Earth, I'd say that indicates organic material but here on Mars I'm not sure until we get closer and study it. The Bennu asteroid is nearly black with organic compounds that formed in the early solar system."

CAMI reports. "The panoramic image documentation is complete."

"Please move up closer to the outcrop to within instrument range."

"Affirmative."

Ellie designates the sampling layer spots with the green laser. The nearly black layer is designated Layer 4-A. There are six layers, twelve sampling spots, and two core locations.

"As before, I want each of those spots photographed with the Zoom 1 lens and with the GHLI. Sample each spot twice at one centimeter separation with the ChemCam, APXS, and RAD-D instruments. I would like two one meter cores from the base of the outcrop at C-1 and C-2."

"Affirmative. Estimating that the survey will take approximately ninety minutes."

"Please begin. Alert us if you get any anomalous readings."

It's routine now to hear the instrument arm whirring and working to take readings on the sample sites.

Dieter opens a conversation, "Can you believe we've been on Mars for over five months? We've accomplished so much back on Base. In a little more than a week, we'll see the *Gemini*, *Castor* and *Pollux* ships land. It's another whole new phase of our colony."

Tracy adds, "And a whole bunch of new faces on our island. I'm really looking forward to the change."

Sofi jumps in, "Yeah, and poor puppy dog Jacob is pining over Tracy Jennings. I think he's gonna explode when they finally get together!" That got a laugh all the way around.

"I'd almost forgotten that there'll be another Tracy on Base. I'll be Tracy-D so she can be Tracy-J. But that sounds like android names in a sci-fi movie."

CAMI reports, "I heard that! But I do have a report. I just finished a RAD-D measurement on Layer 4-A. I jumped ahead to it since there were anomalous readings on the RAD-D even before I focused on that layer. RAD-D is being flooded with alpha particle radiation."

Ellie responds, "Really? Really? Really! That could be a sign that we might have found something we want to find but had put it in the fanciful dream file. Could it be a signature of uranium decay? I need a series of ChemCam laser pulses on Layer 4-A specifically looking for organic molecule and uranium signatures. Use the tunable laser spectrometer, TLS,[63] mode and laser filamentation[64] mode."

"Engaging the ChemCam Ellie. Standby…"

The team can see the laser hitting the Layer 4-A spot repeatedly.

"Oh God, I can't stand the suspense. We could be on the verge of something…"

Sofi asks, "What can organics and uranium tell us? Are we looking at the remains of radioactive Martians?"

Alex bites on the bait, "Sure! World War Three on Mars four billion years ago!"

Oleg says, "Chill guys. Ellie may be on to something. I know a bit about uranium prospecting on Earth."

CAMI reports, "Chill guys. I have some initial results. The TLS laser mode has indications of benzene, thiophene, and long

---

63 "NASA Goddard Instrument Makes First Detection of Organic Matter on Mars", NASA, 2014, Web accessed 6 Sept 2018. https://www.nasa.gov/content/goddard/mars-organic-matter

64 "Lasers can detect weapons-grade uranium from afar", Univ. of Michigan News, Web accessed 6 Sept 2018. https://news.umich.edu/lasers-can-detect-weapons-grade-uranium-from-afar/

chain hydrocarbons. The laser filamentation mode has slight indications of U-235 and stronger indications of U-238."

Ellie responds, "Oh my. That's all I can say. OH MY GOD!"

Oleg wants to tamp it down a notch. "Ellie, I can see where you're going with this but we're gonna need comprehensive samples to send to Earth and for you to study in your lab. We've trained for high priority EVA geology work. I think this is screaming for just that."

"Okay, okay. I'm thinking a million things at once here- not the least of which is getting these samples back to the lab. Okay, methodical field work fist. CAMI, please send a preliminary report back to Base and to Houston."

"MER-2, MER-2, this is Arcadia Base, Coby speaking. I'm hearing you on the open channel and share your excitement. Do the job safely. Don't push it. Then get back here *safely*. We miss you. Over."

"Arcadia Base, MER-2. Roger, Coby. We'll finish up our work here, which will require an EVA, and then head back to Base. Mars has surprises around every corner, rock, and boulder! We miss you too. MER-2 over and out."

"CAMI, please finish the routine instrument and rock sampling of the designated layer sampling spots. Bag and tag the samples and put those in SRC-2."

"Affirmative Ellie. Starting over on sample spot Golombek Objective 13 Layer 1-A."

"Team, let's get some early lunch while CAMI is finishing the instrument and sample work. We will go EVA at 1300 to get a first-hand look at this site and take more samples."

Sofi asks, "What's all the excitement? I know all of this is for science which is way cool but I'm missing the connection between some organic molecules and some traces of uranium."

"Sorry Sofi dear. In my excitement I left you out of the loop on some of the details. I think Oleg knows where I'm headed with this. The uranium could be an ore deposit that someday we could use to process for our nuclear reactor fuel needs to help us be more independent of Earth. But the organics could be so much more than that. In this geologic setting, the organics aren't likely to be abiotic or unrelated to life like we find in carbonaceous asteroids and meteorites. This could be a sign of past life on Mars."

Sofi replies, "I hear you but I still don't get the connection between organics and uranium."

Oleg jumps in. "Let me explain what I know about uranium and uranium prospecting on Earth. Our solar system condensed from the remnant gas clouds of some long dead star that went supernova and spewed all manner of elements including heavy metals like uranium into our local space."

"Okay we get that. Astronomy 101."

Alex adds, "Not to forget heavy elements from the collision of neutron stars. Astronomy 102."

Ellie is trying hard not to laugh watching the exchange.

Oleg continues, "Okay wise guys, let's think about the chemistry 101 of uranium. It has a chemical life aside from being highly purified in a fuel rod. Uranium can be found in several geologic settings but what may relate to what we have here is that uranium is precipitated under reducing conditions caused by reducing matter like carbonaceous material in the sandstone.[65] On Earth, the carbonaceous matter could be from plant debris, logs, marine algae, or stuff like dinosaur bones. Seriously, petrified wood and dinosaur bones are often radioactive with uranium."

"Way cool! But what do you mean by reducing, Mr. Chemistry?"

"Well, let's start with uranium that's dissolved in ground water. The most common soluble ionic forms are U3+, U4+, U5+, and U6+ meaning it has had three to six electrons stripped from each uranium atom. *Oxidation* is the loss of electrons or an increase in *oxidation* state. *Reduction* is the gain of electrons or a decrease in *oxidation* state. When the soluble uranium ions mix with organics it gets reduced to an insoluble form that precipitates as U3O8. So that's how we get radioactive dinosaur bones."

Ellie adds, "We sure don't expect dinosaur bones here but I sure do want to find out what made the organics. This could be as big as finding the tarsus on Bennu." Sofi says, "So that's why you leapt at a black organic layer spewing radiation. I get it and I'm excited too!"

Alex can't help himself. "I still want to find dinosaurs on Mars."

After lunch CAMI reports, "I have finished with the instrument documentation, sampling, and two one meter cores. All samples are bagged, tagged, and stored in SRC-2."

---

65 Spirakis, C.S., 1996, The roles of organic matter in the formation of uranium deposits in sedimentary rocks, Ore Geology Reviews, Volume 11, Issues 1–3, June 1996, Pp. 53-69, Web accessed 7 Sept 2018. https://doi.org/10.1016/0169-1368(95)00015-1

"Excellent. Great work CAMI. You make geology field work seem easy. Now it's our turn. Team, let's get on prebreathing oxygen and slide into our suits for an EVA. I want take as many large rock samples as we can pry loose. Sofi and Alex, I'll ask you to latch our PLSS packs and the back hatch when we port out, just like we've practiced."

Sofi replies, "Got it."

Alex finishes, "We can do it."

Dieter and Tracy port out first. Ellie watches how Sofi and Alex tender them to the final port seal.

"Okay Ellie and Oleg. We're standing by for your egress."

Ellie and Oleg slide into their suits and Sofi and Alex latch their PLSS packs and port seal. Sofi taps on Ellie's port to give her the signal to hop out.

"MER-2 radio check."

Sofi replies, "We read you. Find something awesome out there."

Ellie goes to the equipment locker and takes out two field hammers, rock chisels, sample bags, and the SRC-3 storage box.

"Okay, let's get to work on the outcrop. I want to sample the black organic layer, Layer 4, Layer 3 above it, and Layer 5 below it. Go for rock samples about fist sized. Use the electronic tags to label the sample location. We'll probably need the hammer and chisels to break the rocks loose but be very careful. If you have to get heroic, have CAMI nudge up and hold the chisel with the manipulator arm. A missed hit with the hammer could do more than smash a finger, it could rip a suit."

Oleg says, "First I want to look at that little fender bender we had with the rock up there…Looks okay. Like CAMI said, it's just a scratch."

Ellie says, "That dark limestone in Layer 4 is finely laminated and looks like a stromatolite on Earth."

Tracy asks, "So what's a stroma-err-stromabolite?"

"Oh, sorry. A *stromatolite* is a fossil of layered cyanobacteria or blue-green algae. They're larger than most bacteria and have a thick cell wall that can be seen in fossils that are fairly common in Earths' rock record. They do photosynthesis and fix limestone and organic matter in the layers preserving the evidence of their cellular life. They've been found going back over 3.5 billion years[66] and still live in places like Shark Bay in Western Australia. God, if we could only be so lucky to find stromatolite fossil evidence from *here*."

An hour later, they have about twenty kilograms of rock samples from Layers 3, 4, and 5 stored in SRC-3. "MER-2 we're ready for ingress. Tracy and Dieter first. Ports 1 and 2."

Tracy says, "Ready for ingress. I'll need a hand to get latched in."

Dieter says, "Got you latched. My turn…"

"MER-2, Ports 1 and 2 are ready to unlatch inside."

"Okay Mom. Got it."

"Oleg, help me latch."

---

66 "Bacteria: Fossil Record", Univ. of CA Museum Paleontology, Web accessed 9 Sept 2018. http://www.ucmp.berkeley.edu/bacteria/bacteriafr.html

"Got you. Now I can get up myself…Latched in. MER-2, Ports 3 and 4 are ready to unlatch inside."

"Got you Mom."

MER-2

May 5, 2036

MCT SOL 136:14:51:29

With all four back inside the rover, Oleg says, "CAMI, recheck our pressure seals from the suitports."

"Affirmative, pressure seals are rechecked. Cabin pressure is stable."

Ellie says, "Thank you CAMI. We've had a very successful expedition. No need to push our luck. Let's start making our way back up the crater wall. We've got good sunlight for three more hours. We'll overnight on top when we've gotten those switchbacks behind us."

Mars Arcadia Colony Base

May 7, 2036

MCT SOL 138:10:14:32

"Arcadia Base, MER-2. We're knocking on your door. We'll be ready for docking in five minutes."

Anticipating the rover team's return, Coby and Vik are standing by the radio. Coby replies, "Welcome home team! From the sounds of it, you've had quite an eventful trip! I have a short request for you before you dock."

"No rest for the weary travelers. Go ahead Coby. What can we do for you?"

"While you're out there, please go and check that Landing Pads Beta, 5, and 6 are clear and ready for our new arrivals."

"Roger that. We'll use the compressed CO2 on the rover to give them a dust-off. It won't do to have the landing ships sand blast us."

"We've been in radio contact with *Gemini*. They're eager to get here. She's due to arrive on schedule May 22nd, in just over two weeks with the supply ships *Castor* and *Pollux* arriving a week earlier."

Most of the colonists are gathered in Hab 2 when the rover port opens. Coby and Vik are first to receive the returning expedition team. Coby scoops up Sofi and kisses Ellie just as Vik gives Alex a big bear hug.

Alex says, "It was awesome Papa. Boy it's good to be back and out of that rover. It was starting to smell." Sofi is agreeing silently.

Vik replies, "Yeah, almost as bad as your hab room!"

Mars Arcadia Colony Base
May 12, 2036
MCT SOL 143:08:04:23

Ellie has had extensive consultation with ARES at JSC in Houston and the NASA Astrobiology Institute. The NAI has ten teams including about six hundred scientists from many institutions in the US and international partner organizations. It's hard to say if there is more excitement here on Mars or with her colleagues on Earth regarding the samples from Objective 13 in Golombek Crater.

Dr. Kikuko Nakahara of ARES says, "We have to wait for more than two years before you can get a sample return to us. So it's all up to you to give us some results from the equipment you've got there on Base. But for God's sake, keep the lab biologically isolated."

There is an eight minute two-way radio delay while Mars and Earth are still relatively close after opposition. Most of the colonists are crowded into the communication room of

"I hope you and everyone else who's on this radio link are sitting down. With lab assistance from Mandy Shields and Trevor Brown, it's taken us a few days to get the first samples processed with thin sections and preliminary optical and SEM microscope results. CASSI please send the preliminary report now. The report has my text conclusions, photomicrographs, and SEM microprobe analyses. Yes, we have complete biological isolation."

"Ellie, I have sent the report to ARES, Houston."

"Thank you CASSI. That report will be beaming to you while I continue to describe what I've seen and found.

Let me first review the controversial report on the Martian meteorite ALH8001 from forty years ago. What are the chances of smacking a piece of Mars loose, having it land on Earth, then being found in Antarctica and that very rare piece of Mars having a sleuth's load of possible evidence of fossil life? [67] [68] Few found

67 McKay, D S et al, 1996, Search for Past Life on Mars: Possible Relic Biogenic Activity in Martian Meteorite ALH84001, Science, 16 Aug 1996, V.273, Issue 5277, pp.924-930, Web accessed 9 Sept 2018.
http://science.sciencemag.org/content/273/5277/924

68 "Mars Life? Twenty Years Later, Debate Over Meteorite Continues", Space.com, 16 Aug 2016, Web accessed 9 Sept 2018. https://www.space.com/33690-allen-hills-mars-meteorite-alien-life-20-years.html

the evidence to be a convincing argument for fossil life. If had come from Earth, the bar might not have been set so high.

The analysis focused on carbonate that had formed in basalt from the primordial crust of Mars. The carbonate apparently formed around four billion years ago, when Mars had surface water, higher atmospheric pressure, and higher temperatures. In it, they found some small tube-like structures, in the size range of Earth nanobacteria at only 100-200 nanometers. The found PAH polycyclic aromatic hydrocarbons that could be associated with life. They found strings of magnetite associated with some of the tube-like structures. This is similar to some modern bacteria. Each of these pieces of evidence taken alone is not convincing but taken together, the *possibility* as claimed becomes plausible.

So if you are sitting down, I'll continue with my results. First, I have found convincing evidence of well-formed stromatolitic layers in carbonates from the samples from Golombek 13. The photomicrographs show sheets of colonial cell walls from ten to forty microns in size. Second, there are PAH organics and uranium associated with the cell structures. Third, there are magnetite crystals inside the Mars cells like Earth based bacteria that align with the Earth's magnetic field to aid orientation to higher levels of light and oxygen. Cyanobacteria in stromatolites on Earth put significant oxygen into Earth's atmosphere from about two and a half billion years ago. Fourth, the Golombek 13 carbonates are light in the C12 to C13 carbon isotope ratios compared to inorganic chemically precipitated carbonates on Earth. We know that photosynthesizing organisms, such as algae and plankton, preferentially uptake C12 during photosynthesis giving such a light carbon ratio.

No, a living Martian didn't come out and shake my hand, but ladies and gentlemen, I believe we have found very convincing evidence of fossil life on Mars! Gibson and McKay were right!"

She gives Mandy and Trevor hugs. Coby gives her a sensuous kiss of congratulations.

Sofi says, "That was a long way to the crater and a long way around the block to explain it but that's really cool!"

Ellie says, "What's even cooler is that we don't know if life formed on Mars first and was spread to Earth by meteorites like ALH8001!"

Alex says, "Chickens and eggs and cyanobacteria!"

"What's left is to find life underground on Mars. Life adapts to live in the harshest environments on Earth where bacteria and even pin worms live to almost three kilometers below ground in billion year old water at nearly the boiling point. There's warmth and water underground on Mars. We suspect that that's what's causing the seasonal rises in methane in the atmosphere."

In 2018, the MSL [Curiosity Rover] data revealed a baseline level of CH4 (~0.4 parts per billion by volume [methane ppbv]), with seasonal variations, as well as greatly enhanced spikes of CH4 with peak abundances of ~7 ppbv. What do these CH4 revelations with drastically different abundances and temporal signatures represent in terms of interior geochemical processes, or is Martian CH4 a biosignature? Discerning how CH4 generation occurs on Mars may shed light on the potential habitability of Mars. There is no evidence of life on the surface of Mars today, but microbes might reside beneath the surface. In this case, the carbon flux represented by CH4 would serve as a link between a possible subterranean biosphere on Mars and what we can measure above the surface.[69]

"Arcadia Base, Houston. Arcadia Base, Houston. We have received your data transmission and your verbal report. Your visual reports from the crater had the science team here buzzing. Now they are somewhere between shock and wild jubilation. Congratulations Arcadia! What will the news nets think of this?"

---

69 "Methane on Mars and Habitability: Challenges and Responses", Astrobiology, Published online and web accessed 19 Sep 2018. https://doi.org/10.1089/ast.2018.1917

7

ARCADIA BETA

"When the history of our galaxy is written, and for all any of us know it may already have been, if Earth gets mentioned at all it won't be because its inhabitants visited their own moon. That first step, like a newborn's cry, would be automatically assumed. What would be worth recording is what kind of civilization we earthlings created and whether or not we ventured out to other parts of the galaxy."

Astronaut Michael Collins, *Liftoff,* 1988

Mars is destined to be populated by peoples of diverse beliefs and politics. From the Colossus ships, the first designated colony addition to Mars Arcadia Colony Base, *Arcadia Beta,* is sponsored by a multinational consortium but funded by the Mars Society, Planetary Society, Explore Mars, Mars One, and the Mars Initiative. The twenty-one colonists are multinational representatives of the consortium. Paula Carter Jennings, the

245

commander, is married to Sam Jennings. Both are renowned engineers on space systems and habitats. Their daughter Tracy is an astrobiologist. There are six other married couples and six single colonists representing nine nations including USA, Russia, China, Japan, Germany, Great Britain, Netherlands, and the UAE. John Meek is the advance liaison of the New Kolob LDS colony. Jameel al-Badie is the advance liaison of the al-Salam al-Jadid UAE colony. Both of these new adjunct colonies will arrive in March 2038.

The *Arcadia Beta* Colony Ship *Gemini* is due to land on Mars On May 22, 2036 after a two hundred eighty one day voyage. The long journey is an extreme test of human endurance. Is there a means of getting there faster? The paramount consideration is the short launch window offered every twenty-six months near the time of Mars opposition with Earth. The crowded launch schedule dictated that the Beta fleet take the longer journey or wait until 2038. The **Beta** colonists voted to take the longer journey and get there in 2036.

Future Colossus ships will add two of NASA's SAFE-400[70] nuclear reactors with each producing 100 kW of electricity to power a VASIMIR (Variable Specific Impulse Magnetoplasma Rocket) [71]engine. The engine is a low thrust, high specific impulse drive that can operate for months in deep space only. This will allow the ship to accelerate all the way to Mars boosting the Mars arrival velocity from 12,000 km/hr. to 18,000 km/hr., still well within the aerodynamic entry capability of the Colossus.

---

70 "Design and analysis of the SAFE-400 space fission reactor," AIP Conference Proceedings 608, 578 (2002); Web accessed 10 Sept 2018. https://doi.org/10.1063/1.1449775

71 "Experimental Research Progress Toward the VASIMIR Engine," 28th International Electric Propulsion Conference, Toulouse, France, 17–21 March 2003. Web accessed 10 Sept 2018. https://spaceflight.nasa.gov/shuttle/support/researching/aspl/reference/iepc03.pdf

The extra acceleration will cut a month off of a normal six month trip.

Mars Arcadia Colony Base
May 16, 2036
MCT SOL 147:19:27:51

Arcadia Beta *Castor* and *Pollux* supply ships are approaching Mars landing after a two hundred seventy six day voyage. It's dusk and it promises to be a good show. The supply ships are arriving in advance of the colony ship *Gemini* carrying twenty one carefully vetted candidates to join the Arcadia colony. Their voyage has taken half again as long as the *Taurus* passage since their launch window was not optimal.

CASSI announces, "The *Castor* and *Pollux* are inbound with entry corridor alignment optimal. Atmospheric contact in thirty seconds...Contact. Seven minutes to landing..."

Most of the colonists are gathered in the *Alcyone* module below the cupola to gawk and watch the big ships land. Elena is conspicuously absent. It's dusk and the ships are drawing crimson streaks on the orange-pink hued Martian sky. The ships are facing belly forward coming in on autopilot control. Now they rotate aft first to present the engines for retrofire. The inboard one and two engines ignite at one hundred percent power. The two big ships are riding on purple columns of flame making little dust from the landing pads but creating roiling clouds of water vapor in their dramatic simultaneous descent to landing on Pads 5 and 6.

Coby goes to the communications console and calls the inbound colony ship, "*Gemini, Gemini,* Arcadia Base. *Gemini,* Arcadia Base."

"Arcadia Base, *Gemini*. Commander Paula Carter Jennings at your service. How did our birds land?"

"Greetings Paula! It was the most glorious synchronized landing you can imagine. I'm sending a vid file of the landing now. Tomorrow, we'll begin unloading and setting up the BS-550 modules. Habs 5 and 6 and new colonists will be a nice addition to our cozy little colony. Jacob, who's standing next to me, sends special greetings to your daughter Tracy. Their reunion will be a bright light for us all. Have a safe journey and happy landings. See you in a few days. Over."

"Thanks for the call Coby. It's been a long journey indeed. We're looking forward to gravity and tasting some fresh veggies from your greenhouses. And yes, Tracy is very eager to see Jacob and sends her special greetings! *Gemini*, over and out."

Mars Arcadia Colony Base
May 22, 2036
MCT SOL 153:06:15:27

Habs 5 and 6 and their ECLSS units have been installed with the assistance of the CARIAN and CARIIN robots for the heavy work. The operation is directed by Vik with Oleg, Dieter, Eve, Megumi, Satoshi, and Sandy assisting in details of electronics and plumbing. Coby insisted that Vik carefully involve Elena. The others see to unloading priority one supply modules.

When invited, Elena commented, "At last I feel like I have some use on this planet. I'm looking forward to having the new colonists join us. Maybe there's someone in their group who will give me the time of day."

The Hab cluster has grown but still has the original T-shape. The central core of each hab is the connector to the next hab with a 2.5 meter walkway headspace. In case of an air leak, hatches can be closed for isolation. Each hab has working, living, and galley space. The Central Medical Bay is in HAB 3 on Deck 1. Future hab, recreation, and communal meeting spaces for Arcadia Colony will be constructed underground in the ice.

The last two days have been harbingers of a big Martian dust storm. The dust in the air has increased steadily so that now the visibility is down to less than five hundred meters. It can only get worse.

Coby reports the conditions to Commander Jennings. "The fine dust shouldn't be an issue with your robotic ship navigation and our landing beacon at *Base* to bring you in without visual. We can send a CARIAN robot out to dust off landing pad Beta with compressed CO_2 again. All we can do then is wait and wish you a safe landing. Godspeed *Gemini*. Over."

"Thanks Coby. We're five minutes from atmosphere contact and twelve to touchdown. *Gemini* over and out."

Just after Coby radioed the dust storm report, an angry reddish brown wall cloud of dust approaches from the east. There are even some flashes of green lightning. As the wall passes, the habs are pelted not just with fine powder dust but with grains of sand sounding like rain and threatening to complicate the ship landing. Coby does not report this to *Gemini*, there is nothing they can do but land and hope for the best. Dusting off the landing pads is a moot point now. The ship landing retrorocket high velocity exhaust may cause damage to *Base* infrastructure by accelerating sand particles to hypersonic velocity. They'll have to deal with that damage after the *Gemini* sets down safely.

All of the *Gemini* colonists are strapped into their couches. Paula, Sam, and Tracy Jennings, along with pilots Jochem Nabers and Elle Zandjans are on the Command Deck.

Paula calls out on intercom and radio beacon to Earth and *Arcadia*, "Reading the homing beacon at *Arcadia Base*. Entry corridor optimal. Entry heads up angle engaged. Atmosphere contact in fifteen seconds...Contact. Hull temperature is seven hundred degrees and climbing." The g-forces climb with a slight vibration in the ship. The blue and yellow ionization fireworks outside the panoramic viewports are mesmerizing.

CASSI calls out, "Reorientation for retrofire in ten seconds...Retrofire begins now in ten seconds...five...retrofire."

G-forces climb to 3-g's. They all find this excruciating after nine months of microgravity. Suddenly, the g-forces abate.

CASSI reports, "We have lost the inboard number one engine thirty one seconds into retrofire." CASSI has the programming patch that *Taurus* used on their landing but it takes precious seconds to initiate. "Taking over the descent control from auto. Shutting down inboard number one and two engines. Switching to the outboard four engines for retrofire at sixty percent thrust. Engaged."

G-forces increase again and a big bass rumble builds as the ship cuts thicker atmosphere. As the ship slowly rolls to vertical only an orange haze and no horizon can be seen.

Paula implores, "CASSI, can we still make Landing Pad Beta?"

"Negative. Unable to bring V-dot and H-dot to zero for a controlled landing at *Arcadia*. I recommend going long to insure a controlled landing."

Tracy tries to stifle a scream. It's not supposed to go like this…

"Go for the emergency alternative Landing Zone B in Golombek Crater. Do you have eyes on the designated place to bring us down?"

"Negative on visual. I have GPS, DEM, and landing radar to bring us down at the alternate."

Colonists who claimed no connection to a higher being say a prayer for deliverance. Sam Jennings holds Tracy's hand for comfort. Paula is engrossed in H-dot, V-dot, fuel remaining, and engine performance parameters and fearing a bad outcome on this landing. The lives of the entire crew and her family depend on the landing skill that CASSI provides in this emergency situation. The simultaneous fine control of throttle and gimbals on the four outboard engines is beyond her manual control even if she wanted to intervene.

The rim wall of Golombek Crater lies twenty kilometers to the west of Arcadia base. The *Gemini* just clears the wall. The crater is nearly one hundred kilometers in diameter. Much of the crater floor is rough terrain from subsurface ice. Landing Zone B is a flat area another twenty kilometers farther from *Base*. It's about one kilometer wide but punctuated with small secondary craters. CASSI allows for rapid horizontal motion (H-dot) of the ship to get to Landing Zone B then slows to pick a landing spot.

CASSI announces, "V-dot five meters per second…three…two…one…Hovering for optimum landing site…Lots of dust…Fuel five percent…Ten meters…five…Touchdown. Engines stopped and purging"

The deceleration g-forces give way to Mars' gravity. The ship groans and settles on its four landing pad stabilizers.

Paula finally gasps on the radio, "Thank God! *Gemini* is down at Landing Zone B. It's gonna be a long walk to *Base*. Good flying CASSI."

"Thank you Commander. I calculated a seventy-five percent chance of a survivable landing."

"*Gemini, Arcadia Base*, Coby here. Copy you down at Landing Zone B. Any landing you can walk away from is a good landing! We'll dispatch our rover. It's at least two days there and back. The rover is designed for six but in this pinch we can stretch it to twelve and bring you back in two runs unless you'd *rather* walk."

"Very funny Coby. We'll standby for the ride. Nine months in this ship, what are a few more days? We'll have to deploy the solar arrays or we'll run out of power soon."

Suddenly the ship lurches and tilts headward. There are several screams.

Tracy utters, "Oh God! What's happening?"

Paula demands, "CASSI report!"

"The landing zone has many small secondary craters. I suspect that landing pad two came to rest on the edge of one which has just collapsed."

"CASSI, extend the stabilizer pads to keep us from tipping over. NOW PLEASE!"

"Affirmative… Extending…Done. The ship should be stable at this ten degree tilt."

"Can we still operate the sky crane at this tilt?"

"Affirmative. The headward tilt will not hinder the sky crane since we are canted toward the cargo bay. However, care must be taken in handling cargo that may have shifted."

"Are we stable so that we can get out of our couches?"

"Affirmative. The stabilizer pads are extended ten meters beyond our center of gravity."

"Please dispatch a CARIAN android to survey our landing pads and the crater we're leaning into. We need eyes down there."

"Affirmative. I will give you a report when we have a survey."

"Okay crew, we've had a rocky landing but we're here. We're safe. We have a rescue underway. You can take your helmets off but stay in your suits until we're one hundred percent sure that we're stable. Welcome to Mars! Unbuckle and celebrate!"

No one feels like unbridled celebration. It's the relief of having a scrape with death. You're alive! Husbands and wives or the ones closest at hand hug and kiss. Paula held Sam as fiercely as he held her.

Paula says "It's not what we planned…"

He interrupts and says, "Shhh. My love, you handled that mess and saved the day. We're safe and unhurt. All I see is some delay in getting to base and some yet to be solved issues of getting our supplies unloaded and moved across some rough terrain."

Tracy says, "Mom and Dad, stop with the next bit of business and be *happy* with me. I can't freaking *believe* what just happened and we're *alive* and we're on *Mars*!"

Paula gives her a hug and Sam kisses her cheek. "Yes! We're here and gravity feels great! Oh and CASSI, thank *you* for getting us down in one piece."

"You are welcome. I acted on the only option open to us when the engine cut out at such a critical moment."

Tracy moves around the Command Deck feeling Mars gravity for the first time out on the tilted deck. Between that and the excitement of landing, she has the jitters and decides to sit for a while with her helmet on her lap.

... The big ship groans and creeks. It starts to tilt slowly at first then faster and faster. The groaning becomes a shriek. The ship is past the point of no return falling faster and faster. Tracy is slammed to the side of her seat. With an explosive crash, the ship hits the rocks below piercing it's hull. There is a huge rush of air as the ship's atmosphere is screaming towards the rent in the hull. Tracy is struggling and screaming trying to get her helmet on. She's gasping for air and losing consciousness. Everyone around her is screaming-- "This is the end!"

Sam hears Tracy scream and nudges her gently awake. "What happened? We were dead!"

"You nodded off and had a bad dream. Here take a sip of water. It'll be at least a day until the rover gets here to rescue us. We can get out of these suits now. The CARIAN recon looks good for the ship's stability."

Mars Arcadia Colony Base
May 24, 2036
MCT SOL 155:10:03:14

For safety and to expedite getting the *Gemini* colonists and the highest priority cargo back to Base, Coby dispatched both MER-1 and MER-2 to Golombek Crater at 0900 on May 22 just over two hours after the *Gemini* landed. Oleg is solo piloting MER-1 and Ellie is solo piloting MER-2. The dust storm is annoying but will not hinder their rescue mission. Visibility is limited to five hundred meters. The Mars GPS system and guide beacons will guide them.
   "*Gemini*, MER-2. *Gemini*, MER-2."

254

"MER-2, *Gemini*, come back."

"We have you on radar and we're five klicks out. ETA is forty-five minutes. The terrain is rough so it's slow going. Let's plan on taking eight of your passengers in MER-2 and three in MER-1. You'll be in spacesuits for egress from *Gemini*. That takes up precious space so we can only allow minimal cargo. A ten kilo PPK is all we can allow. We can fit these in the outer cargo bay on each rover. We'll depress each rover and ingress will be through the side port. It will be tight and uncomfortable but it's the best we can do. Tell those left behind that we'll be back for them in four days."

"Roger. We have our first shore party ready. We'll egress fifteen minutes before you arrive. We have our solar arrays deployed so we have power for life support. Over."

"Great. We'll give you a shout when we're fifteen minutes out. MER-2, over and out."

The situation had been discussed in detail in a three-way conference between *Arcadia Base*, *Gemini*, and Houston. The *Gemini* landed with five percent fuel remaining so it cannot lift off and fly to *Base*. There was a proposal to use the propellant wagon and ferry propellant to *Gemini*. Unfortunately, the arduous trip with tight switchbacks going into the crater eliminates the possibility of towing a cargo wagon in or out of the crater. Only MER-1 and MER-2 can do the job of ferrying passengers and priority cargo.

Getting the rest of the cargo out of *Gemini* will be a longer term issue. What is needed is a Mars hopper transport capable of lifting off and maneuvering to locations up to thousands of kilometers from base. The ideal hopper transport could carry six passengers, a rover, and up to ten metric tons of cargo. Such a vehicle would not fit into a Colossus ship cargo bay unless it was in modular pieces. The soonest that Houston could send such a beast will be in two years in 2038.

Vik suggests, "We can build our own hopper transport. We have a collection of more Colossus ships here that we can refuel and send back in the foreseeable future. I've been thinking about the scrap value of just one of those big ships. Now the *Gemini* is stranded. There's an industrial laser on board that will be just the thing to do the job of cutting up the hull after the CARIAN robots help us dismantle the interior. Two of the *Gemini* engines could be used to power the transport."

Coby agrees, "That's one hell of a project, Vik. *SpaceTrans* never expected to get all of the Colossus ships back. In fact, for deep space missions, the customer buys the ship outright and only gets credit towards a future mission purchase if the Colossus is returned to Earth. We have a small army of qualified engineers at *Arcadia* now. Let's do it. CASSI can be our test pilot so we won't risk any humans getting the bugs worked out. The cargo and the hopper can wait for now. Meanwhile we have stranded colonists to rescue."

Mars Arcadia Colony Base
May 26, 2036
MCT SOL 157:14:23:51

The trip back negotiates the tight switchbacks going up the crater wall. Nine people in MER-2 share tight quarters and one even tighter hygiene facility. Rover ECLSS units are strained to recycle air and water. Their food supplies are monotonous high protein, low residue consumables to minimize fecal collection demands.

After a two day strained and cramped ordeal, the first group of eleven *Arcadia Beta* colonists approaches Arcadia Base. Among them are Sam and Tracy Jennings, couples Jochem Nabers and Elle Zandjans, Julia Levine and Mike Fischer, Chen Zhong and Liao Shi, Fermo Caracci and Liana Vitacco, and LDS liaison John Meek. Paula Jennings stayed behind on *Gemini* to tend to ship stability and putting the ship into hibernation. Now the second group waits for evacuation as the first group reaches *Arcadia Base.*

"*Arcadia Base*, MER-2. We made it and are docking at the Hab-2 rover port."

"MER-2, Base. Got you. We're on our way to greet you."

Jacob was up front to open the hatch. He searches the faces and finds Tracy. She has just turned nineteen. She has short brown hair and stunning green eyes like her mother. Sam takes her hand and urges her forward through the crowd.

There are hugs and greetings in a the crowd crush at the docking port.

Coby speaks above the din, "Welcome to Arcadia Base. Welcome to Mars! Please come in. No need to crowd. You have new Hab quarters and blessedly warm showers. By my nose and seeing your weary faces, you need the showers! There's so much to talk about to get reacquainted."

After they move away from the crowd, Tracy gets a big wet kiss. "Jacob, we're really here! The landing and rescue were not what we bargained for. But seeing your face again makes it all worth it."

Jacob says, "We've talked on vid every day but now you're here and oh so real. Come on. Let me show you around the habs. We've actually got this colony up and running!"

Mars Arcadia Colony Base
May 27, 2036
MCT SOL 157:21:46:13

After the hab tour and more private romancing, Jacob brings Tracy to talk to Elena in her hab room. Her door is open and the light is on. He knocks.

"Mama, Can we have a word with you? "

"Yes, come in. I suppose this is *the* talk?"

"Hear me out and be nice. You remember Tracy from our colony training?"

"Yes I do. I remember that you couldn't keep your eyes off of her."

Tracy blushes, "It's good to see you again. May I call you Elena?"

"Sure, everyone does except Jacob."

"I'm so glad to be here. That nine month trip out made me really appreciate the spacious habs you have here."

"Mama, we have something to talk to you about."

"I know. I'm not a fool."

"Mama, Tracy and I want to be married. Her father, Sam, gave us his blessings. We'll all talk to Commander Paula when she gets here from the *Gemini* rescue run in a few days. We have Papa Coby's blessings. Mama, we'd like your blessings too."

"Well, I'm not blind. I've seen this coming. I'm pretty much alone anyways. No, I won't stand in your way. In fact, why don't you call Paula and get her blessing so you can get married as soon as the last group from *Gemini* arrives? Get it done while you can. You never know what tomorrow brings. You'll certainly have some legacy heritage. What will you call my grandchild? James Tiberius Kirk?"

Tracy would not be insulted. "We were thinking Jean Luc Petrov if we have a boy or Kathryn Janeway Petrov if we have a girl."

"I like this girl already. It's all in the genes."

Jacob is smiling but his cheeks are turning crimson. "Perhaps we'll call Commander Paula today. Thank you Mama. You're *not* alone." Jacob tries to kiss her cheek but she turns away.

Mars Arcadia Colony Base
May 29, 2036
MCT SOL 158:12:33:24

The second and last group of ten *Arcadia Beta* colonists leaves *Gemini* for *Arcadia Base*. This group includes Commander Paula Jennings, couples Seno Masaru and Onishi Suzuko, Dominik Weidmann and Sabrina Kessler, and bachelors Jeff Hendricks, Evgeny Yakovna, Lera Veronochek, Briana Culver, and UAE liaison Jameel al-Badie.

The twenty kilometer traverse across the floor of the crater is rough and slow and uneventful. The crater wall and the climb toward Base are looming. They are following in the red dust of MER-1.

"Oleg, don't get too far ahead of us. This is not a race. Here we go." Ellie says. "Once we're over the crater wall, it's a bumpy but fairly easy run to *Base*. I love you guys but it'll be a great to get out of this rover and into the habs where you can shower and we can stretch our legs. Just ahead is the outcrop Objective 13 where we just found proof of fossil Mars life."

Paula remarks, "I see the black layer that made the news. Imagine this as a tourist site someday!"

The rover is making good progress climbing the lower crater wall.

Ellie adds, "This switchback is the same one that threw us on our first trip down to Objective 13. I think we have it figured out. This is our sixth time running the gauntlet."

CAMI replies, "Yes, I just have to turn eight centimeters tighter to avoid that large rock."

Just then the cliff edge crumbles.

"Ahh! Noo! CAMI get us back up!"

"The port camera shows two port side wheels are dangling over the edge. We've lost traction not only from those wheels but the tilt has the remaining wheels spinning."

The rover is stuck and tilting precariously to the left. The fact is that the drop is not bottomless or straight down. There is a ledge five meters below but even that drop could be fatal with a hull breach and at the very least putting them in a hopeless situation for getting the rover back up.

"MER-1, MER-2. Mayday! Oleg, we need you back here ASAP to help us on this cliff. We are hanging and need a tow line NOW!"

"I see you below me. I'm coming back down for you!"

In two long minutes MER-1 was backed up to them.

Oleg sends, "I'm suiting for EVA to hook up the tow cable. I'm not doing oxygen pre-breathe so I'm pushing normal safety.

But you need help now! I'll be with you in a few minutes. Have all your passengers lean to starboard to stabilize your tilt."

"O-okay...Please hurry! People, you heard him. Lean to the right!"

Oleg has the tow cable attached from MER-1 to MER-2. He stays outside to watch as he directs CAMI on driving both vehicles.

"MER-2, Make sure to keep your people as far right as they can squeeze."

"Got it. You heard Oleg. Sardines to the right."

Since they had shed spacesuits, this removed any last bit of personal space each might have held dear. They are long past noticing that they all need a real shower. Jeff is face to face with Lera. Briana has her front side pressed against Jameel. Both of them apologized and blushed.

"Allah is with us."

The rovers have six independent drive wheels. Oleg directs, "MER-2 CAMI, turn twenty degrees more to the left."

"Affirmative."

"MER-1, CAMI ahead slow...That's it...slowly...MER-2, wheels ahead slowly..."

In MER-2, they feel the tow cable tighten and the rover lurches. There are stifled screams inside. The wheels slide then catch a bit of traction. They crab right and all six wheels are on the rough track.

"All stop! Okay, you're up! I'm going to walk up while we get both rovers around this curve. MER-2 straighten your wheels to follow MER-1...Good. Now all ahead slow...Okay, good...That's it. All stop. We're both in the clear. I'm detaching the tow cable and getting back inside."

Ellie says, "Thanks Oleg. We owe you one."

"All in a day's work. As Papa says, Mars is always trying to kill you. We just stay alert and fight back."

In an hour, they've topped the crater wall and see a glorious red sun setting over the west crater wall. The fact that the west wall is visible is a good sign. The dust storm has abated and their luck is getting them back to Base.

"We'll bivouac here tonight. It's just twenty more kilometers of well-traveled but rough terrain that we'll have to traverse tomorrow."

It's a night of fitful rest and little sleep in the tight quarters. At last the pink sun rises. The dust storm has settled. After a bland breakfast of energy bars they set off to *Arcadia Base*.

Mars Arcadia Colony Base
May 30, 2036
MCT SOL 159:15:07:03

Paula says, "I thought I knew each of you closely from our journey outbound. But, this has been an extreme exercise in lack of privacy and trying to stay sane. Congratulations. We all passed the test."

"Oh Jees. Do we get a reward or earn a new even more extreme test?" Sabrina giggles.

"*Arcadia Base*, MER-2. We made it. Better late than never. We can tell the story to our grandchildren! We're docking to the Hab-2 rover port. MER-1 is standing by to dock after we unload."

"MER-2, *Base*. We read you. We'll be waiting in Hab 2 to receive you. I'm sorry your trip was a bit rocky."

That got a nervous laugh from the rover.

There's a bigger crush of expectation at the docking port than there was with the arrival of the first rescue run. After a clatter and knock at the port hatch, Coby confirms, "Opening the port now…" Seeing Ellie, he smiles and winks. "Welcome Commander Jennings. All of you, welcome to *Arcadia Base*. It's so good to see you again after our training days back on Earth. Welcome to Mars! Come in please. We'll get you settled in your new Hab quarters where you can freshen up. We have real hot water showers. We have new clothes for you that we unloaded from *Castor*. Your PPK's will be retrieved from the rovers by a CARIAN shortly. We have a grand reception planned for you at 1800 in Hab 6. There is a top priority storage module from *Pollux* marked *Special Handling-For Gemini arrival celebration dinner*. We've added special offerings from the greenhouse. The others have been settled in Hab 4. We have you in Hab 5."

Sam catches Paula and says, "Welcome back babe! Follow me to our new quarters. I want to hear all about *your* rescue trip."

Paula says, "Those showers are calling. I've dreamed of the luxury for nine months of only sponge baths in micro-g. Lead on. I'll tell you about the rescue while you lather me up."

"The showers *are* heaven but not as good as I'm imaging making love to you in the embrace of Mars gravity!"

MCT SOL 159:18:00:03

The Arcadia Colony musters an elaborate celebration. It's good for the spirit for everyone. The last celebration at *Base* was at Christmas right after they arrived. All of the *Arcadia Beta* colonists are arriving to the common area and mingling in. Their rescued group is reunited and now officially joins the Arcadia Colony. This is a breath of new humanity into the original colony group of only twenty-one that has been isolated for nearly a year.

The top priority storage module from *Pollux* has many pleasant surprises for their welcome celebration. There are flash frozen filet mignon steaks with cracked pepper gravy, roasted garlic mashed potatoes, six bottles of red, and six bottles of white wine. There's an attached note card that Coby reads aloud: "Congratulations on getting to Mars and getting *Arcadia Colony* started. Enjoy the feast and celebration. You should be supplying the greens by now. Any future libations will be up to your needs and your resourcefulness. All of the people of Earth wish all of you success and happiness. Signed- Jacques St. Martin, acting President of the *International Space Coalition*."

Dieter is tired of microwaved and hot water rehydrated fare. He has fashioned a Panini type double sided griddle that serves the purpose to perfectly cook the filets and many other of their food stores. The griddle exhaust is vented directly to the ECLSS. Tracy D. and Paul handle the rest of the fare including the salad and green beans. There's a serving table but not traditional banquet seating. They do have enough seats brought in for the communal meal.

Dieter announces, "Dinner is served. Welcome to *Arcadia* one and all!"

Sofi and Alex get the honors of being first in line. "Wow! Space food never looked so good!"

"Yeah. Let's get our plates and go huddle in the far corner. Too many adults about and I sense speeches are coming."

After dinner, Olga is sitting and has her hands demurely resting on her eight month baby bump. Oleg gives her a big kiss.

Paula approaches and comments, "Oh my dears, I'm so happy for you two. The last time I saw you, you had just announced that you were getting married."

Olga replies, "Thanks for the kind words. We're very excited but also nervous about playing roulette with radiation. Sofi and Alex are an inspiration seeing how perfect they are after spending conception and six developmental months in deep space."

Sofi laughs and says, "We heard that!"

Olga adds, "You'll remember Tracy Dixon and Paul Earhart. You can thank them for much of tonight's dinner grown in their greenhouses. They're expecting in November."

"Well, that's what needs to happen in a thriving colony. I wish you both all the best on the big day."

Just then, Paula picks up an empty glass and raps it with a fork. Ding-ding-ding! She signals to Sam to join her. Jacob and Tracy are smiling and waiting for the announcement.

Paula continues, "*Arcadia Colony*, I have an announcement. Sam and I are announcing and celebrating that our daughter Tracy will be married to Jacob Petrov here tonight and now."

Elena is staring at Coby looking for a sign of recognition. Ellie notices Elena but knows Coby's attention is on the young couple.

Dieter comes forward after having cleaned up from his galley duty. "As Chaplain for this colony, I've been given the honor of performing this ceremony. Coby and Paula have drafted the first

Arcadia Colony Marriage License for the first wedding on Mars. Jacob and Tracy please come forward…"

"Jacob do you take Tracy to be your lawfully wedded wife?"

"I do."

"Tracy do you take Jacob to be your lawfully wedded husband?"

"I do!"

"Jacob, do have the rings?"

"Yes and I have to say these beautiful rings are polished 3D printed titanium fabricated right here on Mars! Tracy, my wife, I give you this ring as a sign of my vow, and with all that I am."

"Jacob, my husband, I give you this ring as a sign of my vow, and with all that I am."

Dieter finishes, "May the creator of this universe bless this union and bless this first colony on Mars with health and happiness. Jacob, *please* kiss your bride!"

After the ceremony, Sofi and Alex, self-appointed DJs, cued music. It's a Trance-pop group, *Tearra Starzz,* that Coby and Ellie or anyone else had never heard of.

By tradition, Sam, as the father of the bride, has the first dance with Tracy. Soon, Jacob cuts in. By now, Ellie and Coby, Paula and Sam have joined in.

Elena, having had a few glasses of wine, is feeling a bit of courage. She has her eyes on Evgeny Yakovna. He's a rough cut Russian bachelor at least ten years younger. She takes a glass of red wine to him and introduces herself.

"I'm Elena Petrov, mother of that handsome groom Jacob. Glass of wine?"

"Sure. Thanks."

After a few moments, "Would you like to dance?"

Awkwardly, Evgeny replies, "Sure. I-I was an incoming academy recruit and admired you when you were first on ISS. So, why not?"

The dance floor is small to say the least. The music is throbbing in the small space. They bump into another couple.

"Sorry." Elena then pulls Evgeny close, "This is too much noise. Do you want to come join me in my quarters?"

"N-no thanks Ma'am. I've never been with an older woman."

Elena pulls away and makes a scene by purposefully knocking Evgeny's glass of wine from the table. She storms out of the Hab.

Coby apologizes to the young married couple for the scene and adds, "We can't send you on a Honeymoon cruise but we can give you what may be the best thing, what you have lacked for so long- *Privacy*. Since the colonists are not fully settled in and we have the spare room, we're giving you the privacy of the entire upper deck sleeping compartment area of this Hab 6 for your honeymoon. Get lost now!"

Tracy says, "Thank you!"

Jacob is smiling, "We're gone!"

Elena ran to her quarters and slams the door.

Looking in the mirror she says, "What happened to you? Where have the years gone? That bitch Rafaela Accardi took everything from me!" She throws herself on her bed crying… Her subconscious memories of the *Kazan State School* come to her conscious thoughts. I have to have a plan…

Mars Arcadia Colony Base
June 27, 2036
MCT SOL 189:10:12:31

The informal Wives Club continued after their arrival on Mars. It has grown from the original six wives Abby, Ellie, Olga, Tracy D., Mandy, and Eve to now include Paula, Julia, Liao, Elle, Liana, Seno, Sabrina, and Tracy J. They gathered in the *Alcyone* module on Fridays at 10:00. The hatch is soft closed with a *'Meeting in Session'* sign hung on it.

Ellie begins, "Girls, what do we think of Elena's mental state. What can we do to help her? She seems so isolated."

Abby replies, "I go out of my way to talk to her when I get a chance. I've asked her to talk to Dao-Ming or Sandy or Dieter because of their skills as counselors. I do know that Sandy has spent time with her. Sandy seems to think that Elena is getting better."

"God, I hope so. Sometimes I think she's got me in her sights. It creeps me out."

Paula adds, "Don't worry; we've got your back." Then changing the subject, she innocently asks her newlywed daughter, "How's married life?"

"Oh Mom, we're so happy. But Abby, I do wonder if sex can substitute for time on the TARED machine?"

When the laughs and giggles subside, Abby replies, "No but the extra credit never hurts!"

They laughed again till their sides hurt.

Olga interjects with a concerned look on her face, "I just had a big contraction. I-I think my water broke!"

Abby takes charge. "Okay dear. You're in good hands. Sabrina and I will take care of you. Ellie, please page Oleg to go to the Medical Bay in Hab 3. Ladies, I could use some help getting Olga there."

MCT SOL 189:23:44:28

After thirteen hours of labor, a new life arrives in the colony. Oksana Dominika Ivanov is the first baby born on Mars. Olga and Oleg count ten fingers and ten toes on the most beautiful baby on this world.

Making Progress
Mars Arcadia Colony Base
September 20, 2036
MCT SOL 274:09:22:14

Commander Coby Brewster personal log:

The greenhouse, aquaponics, and poultry complex continues to grow. It's managed by Trevor Brown, Mandy Shields, Julia Levine, and Mark Fischer. All of the colonists have a schedule to contribute to the work involved in tending to the crops. Much of the work is done by a specially trained CARIAN android.

The goal is to establish a nearly self-sufficient food supply within two years. The bland taste of their Earth-based food stores is a huge motivator to expand Mars grown food production. Mandy's hot pepper sauce is a big hit! The agriculture complex is expanded from robotically constructed 3D printed sintered regolith arched structures. There are currently five 15 x 65 meter structures and one dome that's producing mature tilapia. Each structure is thick enough to attenuate deadly solar and cosmic radiation.

We don't rely on the sun for growing crops. Powerful LED lights provide the ultraviolet light to drive photosynthesis in the prolific hydroponic farms.[72] Different crop varieties are grown in each of the four greenhouses. The isolation is intended to avoid spreading any blight that might affect one crop. One of the four is dedicated to root crops grown in treated Mars regolith. Experimental plantings of soybeans are showing promise. The fifth arched structure is the poultry farm. Chicken eggs brought in stasis started the operation that is now producing a supply of eggs and meat. The chickens are free range if you can call clucking around their 15 x 65 meter space a free range. Waste from the greenhouses feed the chickens and tilapia and their waste is returned to the greenhouses as fertilizer. The next new greenhouse will be fully underground and dedicated to soybeans.

The one and a half meter AI robotic CARIIN boring tool called *HORTA* is used for excavating the tunnels and habs in the clean ice layer ten meters down. A kilopower nuclear reactor on the *HORTA* is the power source for both the boring operation and for melting the pulverized ice. Insulated cargo modules surplused from unloading the cargo bay have been converted to make water tanker wagons. The water is delivered to the Sabatier reactors and to the aquaponics greenhouses.

Arcadia has now developed a second larger two meter diameter nuclear robotic HORTA for multi-purpose tunneling.

---

72 "Shipping Container Farms" Business Insider,2017, Web accessed 4 January, 2017. http://www.businessinsider.com/kimbal-musk-shipping-container-farms-new-york-city-2016-12

Aside from resource mining, the tunnels are designed for additional living space fitted with airlocks so they can be pressurized.

The underground construction of a common area, hab rooms, and tunnels to the adjunct future *New Kolob* and *al-Salam al-Jadid* colonies is underway. The common area is designated the *Nexus* where tunnels intersect. The adjunct colonies are being laid out three hundred meters north and south of Arcadia Base. Sintered regolith provides the wall insulation from the cold minus 40° C subsurface ice.

The *Nexus* between colonies has a 3D printed surface airlock and rover bay. There is an elevator down to the *Nexus* common room. The surface habs connect to the underground complex with a tunnel and elevator below the *Alcyone* module. *Alcyone* was temporarily disconnected and moved aside to allow the vertical access tunnel to be excavated and for constructing the pressure tight hard connect between the modules.

With the power from the ten megawatt SSTAR nuclear reactor, we're making progress on refueling the five Colossus ships, *Taurus, Pleiades, Aldebaran, Castor, and Pollux* that are sitting idle on their landing pads. They are due to be sent back to Earth at the next launch window in 2038. In time, not only will it be possible to regularly refuel and return BFR ships but we'll be able to export propellant to depots in Mars orbit, at LOP-G, at L2, or wherever there is a market in the solar system. Propellant will be our currency of commerce as humans spread further into the cosmos.

Sofi and Alex have their mothers Ellie and Abby corralled trying to help them build a psycho-electronic interface to CASSI's AI "brain." I've seen too many instances of the space twins having spooky mental communication purely exchanging thoughts and images with one another to have any doubts about their prodigious mental abilities. They have goals of "being able to mentally access CASSI's AI thoughts and enormous memory banks and similarly to interface with the CARIAN robots. Imagine what we can accomplish with that!"

Abby has been indulging them by allowing them access to EEG equipment in Central Medical to record their brain waves. Alex explains, "When the brain wave signal is analyzed with a Fourier transform, it can be decomposed into a number of discreet sine wave signals in specific frequency ranges. We're most interested in beta waves of conscious thought in the 15-40 Hz (cycles per second) range. The activity measured with an EEG is the result of electrical transmission and potential difference of the pyramidal neurons in the cerebrum."

Sofi and Alex have degrees in electrical engineering. Their experimental approach also involves equipment from Ellie's geology lab. Sofi has asked for "extremely low frequency electromagnetic field (ELF) ELA-1000 telecommunications receiver equipment."[73] This is hoped to be the core of their mental interface with CASSI. "ELA-1000 can be encoded on a microprocessor chip so it's miniaturized to integrate with CASSI's or a CARIAN's audio visual interfaces."

All I can say is good luck with that and don't break CASSI!

Vik, Oleg, Dieter, Elena, Jacob, and Sandy have taken the MER-2 rover with a CARIAN android and a kilopower reactor

73 Kulak, A., J. Kubisz, S. Klucjasz, A. Michalec,J. Mlynarczyk, Z. Nieckarz, M. Ostrowski,and S. Zieba (2014), Extremely low frequency electromagnetic field measurements and methodology of signal analysis, Radio Sci.,49,361–370. Web accessed 3 March 2019.

back out to the *Gemini* ship in Golombek Crater. They have established a new, longer but safer route down the wall of the crater. The purpose of the journey is to finish unloading *Gemini* and begin deconstructing the Colossus ship to build Vik's concept of a Mars hopper transport vehicle. The need for the flying transport was driven home by the difficult *Gemini* rescue executed a few months ago. Aside from that incident, rover exploration is impossible over much of Mars rugged terrain. The rocket powered *Transport 1* Mars hopper will open up remote exploration areas.

There is an industrial laser on board *Gemini* that will do the job of cutting up the hull after the CARIAN robot helps dismantle the interior. The transport vehicle is constructed from the *Gemini* salvage including aluminum hull material, hull insulation, electronics, gyro control, and two salvaged Colossus engines with throttle and gimbal control. Structural support is from *Gemini* interior aluminum struts. Structural welds are done by an arc welder expertly controlled by the CARIAN android. Helium is not needed for welding the aluminum as it is on Earth since there is no oxygen in Mars' thin atmosphere to interfere with the hot welds. Propellant tanks are salvaged *Gemini* header tanks that held reserve fuel for landing the Colossus ship. All of them use their expertise to put together the puzzle. Vik commends Elena for her diligent help in working out the electrical and engine connections. Dieter is indispensable for the installation of the electronic and computer systems.

Transport 1 is operated by CAMI's AI computer control with GPS 3D flight and course navigation. *Transport 1* can lift off with the engines at ten percent throttle. The engine gimbal control allows the transport to maneuver in any horizontal direction. The *Transport* has geologic prospecting capability with an ALMS-

LIDAR[74] instrument sent up on the *Gemini*. The cargo bay can carry the two man MER-1 rover for running exploration sorties. At present, the hull pressure integrity is unproven so the pilot and passengers will fly in full space suits.

Vik's concept design for the Mars hopper transport.

They have completed four short hops, without a crew, to test the transport's control and stability. The first hop looked almost as bad as the disastrous incident that happened to Neil Armstrong on the jet engine powered *Flying Bedstead* during his lunar lander training. The machine lost control. Armstrong ejected and parachuted to safety. The lunar module simulating *Flying Bedstead* crashed in a ball of fire. Thankfully that wasn't the fate of the Mars hopper on its first flight. CAMI had a quick learning curve to get the hopper transport under control. The last five short hops have shown that CAMI has it mastered even with ten metric tons of cargo on board.

Vik and Sandy have volunteered to fly the hopper back to *Arcadia Base* loaded with supplies from *Gemini*. Today is the day. They have no more surplus of propellant to salvage from *Gemini*.

---

74 Arcadia multispectral LIDAR (Light Detection and Ranging) a remote sensing instrument using a pulsed laser to measure distances and properties of the reflecting surface.

There is enough propellant on board to get to *Base* with a ten percent reserve. The flight will take less than thirty minutes. Oleg, Dieter, Elena, and Jacob will return to Base in MER-2. That trip will take two days.

MCT SOL 274:11:15:47

Vik and Sandy are helmeted and strapped into *Arcadia Transport 1*. They have finished a preflight checklist with CAMI.

Vik calls on the radio, *"Arcadia Base, Transport 1. Arcadia Base, Transport 1.* We are number one on the runway and ready for takeoff. GPS coordinates for Landing Pad 2 is programed."

Coby responds, *"Transport 1,* Base. Got ya' Vik. I've been expecting your liftoff call. Landing Pad 2 is dusted off and clear. See ya' in about thirty minutes. Have a good flight. This is history."

CAMI calls the count. "Liftoff in five, four, three, engines at ten percent, and liftoff."

"CAMI, please take us to one thousand meters and head for *Arcadia Base.*"

Vik and Sandy's med sensors record their heart rates spiking. Vik reports, "Liftoff is controlled and smooth. What a way to fly! We are pitching slightly forward and leveling off at one thousand meters. We are high enough to clear the crater wall. H-dot is sixty klicks. We are stable and heading for the barn."

"Transport 1, Base. We hear you flying to the barn. Good show."

"Base, *Transport 1.* The crater wall is clear. We have a good view of the *Arcadia Base Complex* on the horizon. ETA eight minutes…"

"The view of Base is spectacular! The habs, the greenhouses, the majestic ships on their pads- that's what we've accomplished and what everyone supporting us back on Earth has accomplished! CAMI, please bring us to a hover here at five hundred meters so we can photograph *Arcadia Base*. Also, give me a fuel reading."

"Affirmative for hovering. Fuel is at fifteen percent. We can hover for five minutes and still have some reserve if you wish."

After two minutes Sandy says, "I have some great shots. Please put us down now so we don't push our luck with this experimental tin can."

Vik agrees, "CAMI, please bring us down to Landing Pad 2 on the programmed approach vectors."

"Affirmative. V-dot fifteen meters per second...ten...five...one. Five meters altitude and touchdown. Engines stopped and purging. People say that any landing you can walk away from is a good landing. How was that Vik?"

"Perfect. You make me look like I know what I'm doing as pilot. You are the best CAMI! Thanks."

"You are welcome. I learned some fine control aspects of this tin can on this flight. It was good for me too."

"Please. Let's not make Abby jealous."

A New Life and a New Challenge
Mars Arcadia Colony Base
November 5, 2036

MCT SOL 320:11:03:42

Tracy Dixon and Paul Earhart are having an ob-gyn consult with Abby concerning Tracy's pregnancy. Tracy herself is a physician so she knows the technical details and possible complications of pregnancy. Tracy and Paul asked for an amniocentesis procedure to check on their baby. Abby had drawn a small sample of amniotic fluid a week ago and ran a genetic analysis on tissue cells in the fluid. Tracy and Paul were expecting to learn the sex of the baby.

"To start, I have some good news for the both of you."

Tracy pleads, "Yes, go ahead. We want to hear all of it."

"The good news is that you going to have a baby girl."

Paul exclaims, "Fantastic!"

Tracy adds, "Oh Paul, we have our Adele! Is there anything else we need to know?"

"Yes. I won't sugar coat this. Adele has a genetic condition that we need to consider and someday soon try to cure."

Paul is angry. "Damn the radiation! What have you learned?"

"Yes, tell us everything."

"Adele will be perfect in every way except that she will have to be very protected from all forms if radiation. She has XP, Xeroderma pigmentosum[75]. Her only hope of survival is to live underground until we can cure this with CRISPR gene therapy. We have the first livable hab rooms completed in the underground complex that we'll all be moving into someday. Yes, the radiation is bad for all of us but it can be deadly for Adele. We'll have special low level lighting since even normal room light can cause the equivalent of sunburn that can cause permanent damage."

---

75 "Xeroderma pigmentosum". Genetics Home Reference. U.S. Library of Medicine. 26 June 2018. Retrieved 28 June 2018.

Tracy turns to Paul. "This is not what any parents want to hear. But, if we follow the strict guidelines, she can still live a normal but sheltered life. We have normal genes and are able to repair the damage to our skin and eyes that we suffer every day from UV and harder radiation especially here on Mars. We produce enzymes that strip out the damaged segments of DNA in our cells, replacing them with undamaged DNA. With XP, Adele won't be able to do that and can develop lesions and cancer from even the slightest radiation."

"Oh damn! Will the underground habs be completely free of the hardest cosmic rays?"

Abby replies, "We've measured the radiation flux at ten meters depth finding that the ice is a good barrier. It will be a safe environment for Adele. Your amniotic fluid has been a natural radiation absorber but we need to get you underground--the sooner the better."

"Are the quarters ready?"

"I've seen to it. All you need is to gather your personal effects and move in. Come with me now and I'll give you a tour."

They walk from the med bay in Hab 3 out to the Alcyone module to the elevator that can just fit three people. Tracy's tummy is pressed into Paul's side.

With a wry smile he says, "If you get any bigger, we won't fit in this elevator."

She gives him a mock punch in the nose. They step out into a modestly small common area that has some Spartan 3D printed chairs and some posters of Earth-side woodland scenes. The walls are curved, polished, and subtly Mars red from the 3D printed regolith insulation.

"Your suites are the first two doors on the left. The main common room, library, and TARED units are farther down. Here, have a look at your rooms."

As they walk in Tracy says, "Impressive! It's so much bigger than our old hab quarters."

"Sure. Down here we have the luxury of making all the space we need. It just takes some time for the equipment to do the job. You can go on the net and design furnishings that might better suit your tastes. Our ample supply of mattresses doubled as radiation shielding when they were carried on *Taurus.* The LEDs are set to a dim, soothing number one setting that is perfect for Adele with XP. There's a control panel on the wall. The temperature is set to a comfortable twenty two degrees."

Paul is anything but complacent. "Sure, I'm pleased with the accommodations but this is no long term life for a growing child. She'll be deprived of the starkly beautiful Mars vistas that we thrive on. You mentioned a cure for XP with gene therapy. When, how, and how long will that take? If we have this condition from a radiation mutation, what future do we as humans have on Mars?"

Abby says, "All good questions. Let's just slow down and talk about that. The quick answer is that we have the means to handle the problem. When Adele is bigger and stronger, say at two Earth years, we'll begin CRISPR gene therapy. She may need repeat therapy every six months or so until we see a permanent improvement."

"What is CRISPR?"

Tracy answers, "It's just an acronym for a long description of some gene therapy magic. The gene-editing tool CRISPR uses a deactivated virus to replace a "bad" gene with a healthy one.[76] It just might work for Adele." Tears are welling in her eyes. "Abby, we can work this out together."

"When your time comes, we'll do the delivery down here where Adele can enter a world free of radiation."

Mars Arcadia Colony Base
November 12, 2036
MCT SOL 327:01:14:37

"Ahhhh-Rrrrhhh-Unnhhhhhh!!

It was a roar, a super primal roar that Paul did not know a human could make. The huge roar is Tracy's pain management system.

Abby coaches her. "That's it Tracy. When the next contraction comes, push with everything you've got."

"I've already given it everything I've got. I've been at this for days."

"You're doing fine. Your hard labor has only been an hour. One more. Adele is almost here."

"Hoo, hoo, hoo…Rrrrrrhhh-Unnnhhhhhh!!!"

"There's her head…There she is! Let's get her cleaned up and let her catch her breath…Here you go Daddy."

---

76 "CRISPR enhances gene therapy to fight inherited diseases", Washington University School of Medicine, 29 Mar 2018, Web accessed 16 Sept 2018. https://medicine.wustl.edu/news/crispr-enhances-gene-therapy-to-fight-inherited-diseases/

Paul is crying as he holds his daughter for the first time, "She's beautiful. So pink and perfect, and, and with tiny freckles."

Abby says, "That's the tiny kiss of radiation from when you were topside. She'll be just fine and she's earned her place in history as the second human born on another planet."

Tracy is tired but not too tired to need her new daughter. "Let me hold her please Paul."

"Of course. Adele, meet your beautiful mother."

It's Tracy's turn to cry. Adele is already nuzzling her breast. With the loose fitting gown, Tracy easily helps her find it.

"Sleep little baby don't you cry. I'll sing you a Martian lullaby..."

The Sortie
Mars Arcadia Colony Base
March 10, 2037
MCT SOL 445:08:03:14

Coby, Dieter, Oleg, and Jacob are gearing up for an exploration sortie east of Arcadia Base. They'll be going about twenty klicks out in the MER-2 rover to do a routine geology reconnaissance. Jacob minored in geology and has been studying about Mars under Ellie. He laid out the objectives and the GPS route from MRO data.

Coby sees Elena working around the PLSS packs in the suit bay. There are four charged PLSS packs that Coby has checked out and has ready for loading into the rover to be connected to the rover suit packs.

"Hi Elena, are you getting ready for an EVA? We don't have anything scheduled."

"Well yes. I fancied that I might join you boys for your Sortie. I haven't been out for a while."

"Jees, Elena. Any other time and I'd be happy to have you along. But I thought I made it clear that this is to be Jacob's show to lead the sortie. You raised him and I think he needs his wings."

"Well, okay. Suit yourself. I'll just stay behind and work on my crochet project."

"As I've always said, there's plenty of satisfying work to do in the greenhouses. They're so much more spacious that the habs. I think the humid air and green growing things are good for the soul."

"Perhaps you're right. Don't worry about *my* feelings. Be *careful* out there. I want my Jacob to come back as happy and healthy as when he left."

The planned two day sortie gets underway at 08:30. The track that Jacob has chosen is rough like most of Arcadia's ice heaved terrain. It's an uneventful straight drive for the first five kilometers then the route requires navigating around some large ice pingos. Jacob is driving using his GPS track for guidance.

Coby starts some small talk. "How's married life Jacob? I haven't really had any alone time with you since you married Tracy."

"We couldn't be happier. Thanks again for giving us a few weeks of privacy in Hab 6. It let Tracy and I get to know one another without thinking that we're disturbing the neighbors.

Oleg teases, "You must be making her happy if she makes that much noise!"

"Julia Levine and Mike Fischer, plus Dominik Weidmann and Sabrina Kessler have moved into Hab 6, so we've both learned to tone it down a bit."

"What's our ETA and exploration plan Commander Jacob?"

"The ETA to Objective 1 is forty-eight minutes taking it easy. That's the entrance to a canyon that should expose some geology that we haven't documented. It's hard to get a good look at it from orbit so I'm really expecting some surprises. We can go EVA one pair at a time. I have Coby and Dieter up first. Then Oleg and I will do some scouting in the rover while staying in close radio contact."

"So we'll add your canyon to the official Mars topographic map as Jacob's Canyon."

"I'd like that if you're serious."

"Indeed I am."

MCT SOL 445:10:07:13

Under a hazy pink tinged sky, the rover passes the stark beauty of the landforms on the traverse to the first objective. The layered cliffs and buttes of Arcadia Planitia bear testament to Mars's geologic history.

Jacob announces while transmitting back to *Base* where Ellie is monitoring, "Here we are at my first objective. The outcrops are very well exposed. I think we can do some valuable science here. I'm getting some good panoramic shots. Let's go with the EVA buddy pair plan. Coby and Dieter, I want you to document the stratigraphy that you can safely reach. Standard field plan: GPS coordinates, photograph, sample, bag and tag. Oleg and I will go no more than one klick farther into the valley to the second objective for a recon then come right back and wait for you to complete your EVA."

What Jacob did not take into account are the minor side canyons that could complicate his naïve but well-meaning plan.

Coby replied, "Got it. We'll begin our oxygen pre-breathe and begin suiting up. Dieter, buddy, let's get to it."

"It'll be good to get a stretch of the legs, pushing the frontiers of science, where no human has gone before!"

MCT SOL 445:10:45:21

Dieter reports, "Egress is complete. Coby, buddy, let's go."

"Okay buddy. Let's start working the north wall then check out that side canyon ahead."

Jacob is elated. "Guys. You've got it. We're going up canyon for the recon. We'll be back in about thirty minutes. We'll be in constant radio contact. Have fun!"

Back at *Arcadia Base*, Sofi grabs Alex and sends him the alarming thought that something has just gone wrong on and EVA with Coby and Dieter. Together they immediately communicate with their recently installed psycho-electronic interface to CASSI.

"Issue an alert to Jacob in MER-2. They must go back and pick up Coby and Dieter. Something terrible has happened."

MCT SOL 445:12:13:13

Coby Brewster's eyes flutter awake. The backup oxygen on his PLSS has come online and begins to bring his suit mixture up to a level that only barely supports consciousness.

"Mayday. Mayday, Altair… Mayday. Mayday, Houston… This is Commander Coby Brewster… Mayday. Mayday, Altair… Mayday. Mayday, Houston… This is Commander Coby

Brewster. I… I don't know what happened to me. Where am I?… Altair,… MMU-1,…Ellie!… Vik, Abby, come in…God! Where am I? …There is hard gravity but it can't be Earth."

Coby struggles to stand supported by a boulder that is waist high. He stumbles and drops back to the ground, lying prone to conserve his strength. Unfortunately, CAMI is not resident in his PLSS pack. He is alone without the senses and intelligence of his AI CAMI.

What is this place? The reddish soil, the distant red rocks and sand dunes, the pink sky, the desert landscape, could be… No, it can't be… Not a bit of vegetation. Not a weed or a mere blade of grass. I have an atmosphere sensor…

Coby keys his wrist pad and readouts appear in his helmet HUD display:

Gravity 0.376 g
Atmosphere 0.0067 bar
Carbon Dioxide (CO2) 95.32%
Nitrogen (N2) 2.7%
Argon (Ar) 1.6%
Oxygen (O2) 0.13%
Carbon Monoxide (CO) 0.08%

"Oh God! I'm on Mars! How can this be? My PLSS backup is barely maintaining supplementary life support and oxygen is dropping fast… Water?… I have about 700 milliliters… Yes, a sip would do right now… All alone and talking to myself."

"Mayday. Mayday, Altair… Mayday. Mayday, Houston… This is Commander Coby Brewster… Mayday. Mayday, Altair… Come in please! This is Coby! I don't want to die alone in this place!" Coby puts his helmeted head down in his hands for a long minute.

"Am I going to die alone in this place? What would Mark Whatney do? He had a hab, potatoes, a rover, and an ERV. He had tools to science the shit out of his survival. I have nothing! Ah damn it, that was only a book and a classic movie. This is real!…"

Coby tries in vain to focus his mind. "What happened to me?…How could I be marooned on Mars? I was just on *Altair* with Ellie, Vik, and Abby…"

Coby struggles to lift his head and catches a glint of sunlight reflecting off of a shiny moving object that just appeared from behind the cliff wall about five hundred meters to his right. He recognizes the object as a version of the Mars Exploration Crew Rover that he had seen when he was at JSC training with his Aquila crew. Coby's vision blurs.

"Mayday… Mayday, Mars Exploration R-Rover…This is Commander B-Brewster… Come in… I—I am f-five hundred meters on your e-eleven o'clock…

"M-Mayday… Mayday, *Altair* …ay …d-day…" He is looking into an expanding black tunnel. *"M-mm…"* He trails off into unconsciousness again in a universe of stars…

"Altair…"

Mars Exploration Rover2
March 10, 2037
MCT SOL 445:12:14:21

"Coby! Papa. Papa! We were reading you loud and clear, and then you faded and we lost contact. This is Jacob. Papa, come back! We lost track of you an hour ago. CASSI issued an alert that you're in trouble. We have a weak signal on you now. We're almost there."

"Oleg, I need you to port out quickly and help him. God only knows where Dieter is in this cockup. How can things go so bad so quickly?"

"Roger. I'm suited and just securing my helmet. Suit check!"

The fast moving rover is about fifty meters off now. The rover whines to a stop in a cloud of reddish Mars dust next to the prone, space suited body. Coby's red commander suit stripes stand out and confirm it's Coby and not Dieter.

"Coby! If you can hear us, Oleg is suited and porting out now."

"Jacob, I'm unlatching. Get the port hatch behind me!"

Oleg jumps down to the surface next to their Commander. He sees Dieter ten meters away. He quickly manages to scoop Coby up in a fireman's carry. He masses one hundred-fifty kilograms with his spacesuit and PLSS pack but weighs only fifty-six kilograms on Mars. Oleg carefully arranges Coby into a fetal position in the auxiliary airlock. He levers the hatch closed.

"Jacob, cycle the lock!"

After the thirty second cycle, Jacob pulls Coby into the rover. He immediately gets Coby's helmet off and fits an oxygen mask over his face.

He gives Coby a shake. "Coby, Papa, can you hear me?"

Oleg has reached Dieter and cannot find any sign of life. He carries Dieter to the emergency airlock and levers the hatch closed.

"Jacob, cycle the lock for Dieter!"

Jacob pulls Dieter into the rover. There are no vitals on his med sensor readouts. He's flatlined. Jacob cannot feel his breath or find a pulse.

Oleg has latched into the rover. "Jacob, I'm ready for the port hatch. Get me in…" Oleg takes his helmet off.

"Dear God, how are they?"

"I think Dieter is dead. Coby is unconscious. His pulse is weak and his breathing is shallow. I have him on oxygen. Apparently they had suit malfunctions and ran out of air."

"I've got to get Dieter's suit off and try the AED to see if the shock can get his heart beating. We don't know how long he's been out."

"*Arcadia Base, Arcadia Base.* Mayday, Mayday this is Jacob in MER-2. We are returning to Base with an emergency! Coby and Dieter had suit malfunctions. Coby is unconscious in the rover and on oxygen. Oleg is using the AED to try to bring Dieter back. *Arcadia Base,* come back."

"MER-2, *Arcadia Base.* This is Vik. We copy your emergency. Abby and a med team will meet you at the rover airlock. What is your return ETA? "

"We are ten clicks out and ETA is about thirty-five minutes pushing it to the metal."

"Push it but get here safe. *Arcadia,* standing by."

"CAMI, take the rover controls, follow our GPS track, and get us back to *Base* as fast as you can go and still keep all the wheels on the ground."

Jacob checks that Coby is still breathing. There's nothing more he can do for him.

"Oleg, let me help you with Dieter. AED is charged. Clear!" The first shock is delivered.

Oleg reports, "No pulse. Give another shock."

"AED is charged. Clear!" The second shock is delivered.

Oleg says, "No pulse. I'm starting CPR."

They take turns every few minutes giving CPR to Dieter and checking Coby's vitals.

After a jolting thirty minutes' drive, CAMI mates the rover to the airlock on Hab-2. The lock is quickly cycled to base pressure. Jacob and Oleg open the hatch to the Hab. Abby, Vik, Ellie, and Tracy Dixon are there to receive them.

Jacob summons, "Quick! Help us get Coby and Dieter out of the rover!"

Abby and Vik jump in. Jacob says, "Coby is unconscious but breathing. Dieter is flatlined. We've used the AED and have been giving him CPR for thirty minutes."

Abby says, "Good job. You've done all you can but I think Dieter is gone. Let me take over."

Vik works with Oleg to get Coby out, "Okay, head and shoulders first. Easy now."

They lay Coby on a gurney and replace his oxygen mask. Tracy adds pulse/ox and cardio-monitors. Ellie cradled his head and kissed him. "Coby, I love you. Don't leave us. I need you. We need you!"

Abby takes charge. Her eyes are glistening with raw emotion. "Dieter is gone. Let's get Coby to sick bay NOW!"

Mars Arcadia Colony Base

Central Medical Bay
March 10, 2037
MCT SOL 445:16:38:46

Abby addresses those gathered in the room: Ellie, Vik, Jacob, Oleg, and Tracy. "Coby is in a coma. He has hypoxemia from his suit failure. His blood oxygen is severely low at seventy three percent. That's low enough to begin organ failure. He is not breathing well on his own. I'm going to put him on a respirator and put him on an IV sedative to keep him comfortable while he recovers from the hypoxia. Hyperbaric oxygen would be better but we aren't equipped for that. I need to clear the room while I do this. Ellie, please stay and give Coby support."

Trying to control her composure, she squeezes his hands. "I couldn't leave if you ordered me. God! Coby, find your strength. You need a deep rest. Dream of us, dream of Sofi and Alex, dream of Jacob and Tracy, and then fight like hell and come back to us!"

Coby was the Commander on the outbound colony trip to Mars and he has been the Colonial Commander and Governor for the first two year term, until December 21, 2037. Succession is decided by a majority vote of colonists age sixteen and over but to be ratified by the *International Space Coalition.*

Vik takes Abby's and Ellie's hands and solemnly says, "As second in command, with Coby incapacitated, I have to take the role of acting Base Commander and Colonial Governor. We have to attend to some unpleasant business. I need a small volunteer shore party to bury Dieter next to Barry Peterson. Mars has claimed a second human life. We pray that Coby will recover. We must investigate why we had two simultaneous suit failures. I smell the stench of sabotage. If that proves to be the case and when we find a suspect, we'll have to convene a council to deal with criminal justice. We've always hoped and many have prayed for Mars to be Utopia. Unfortunately, Utopia only exists in the minds of fiction writers. We still have to deal with the reality and consequences of human prejudice, hate, and irrational passion."

Oleg responds, "I volunteer for the shore party to attend to Dieter and I'll be first in line to investigate the suit failures. It could have been me out there."

Jacob follows, "I'm in with you. It was *my* expedition. I'm responsible. We *will* get to the bottom of this. Sandy Conklin was close to Dieter and she's a chaplain. She should join us to say the right words as we bury Dieter."

Mars Arcadia Colony Base
March 11, 2037
MCT SOL 446:09:23:04

Vik, Oleg, Jacob, and Sandy egress from the airlock on Hab 1 and lay the body of Dieter Schwartz on a rover wagon as his makeshift funerary caisson. Vik directs a CARIIN robot to pull the wagon to the grave site next to Barry Peterson one hundred meters east of the Hab complex. The CARRIIN makes short work of digging a grave through the regolith into the crystal blue ice. Dieter Schwartz is laid to rest with a ceremony presided by Sandy Conklin as Chaplain. The CARIIN completes his burial and mounds up a cairn of rocks on the grave. They place a memorial plaque fabricated overnight commemorating Dieter's sacrifice as the second fatality on Mars. They solemnly walk back to Hab 1 and complete the EVA.

Vik says, "Thank you Sandy for you eloquent words for Dieter."

"It comes with the job and I really did care for Dieter as a human being."

"We have the ceremony recorded and relayed to Houston. Our next task is to examine the suits Coby and Dieter were wearing on their ill-fated EVA. Sandy you can be excused. Jacob and Oleg are with me in the examination since they were the engineer's on Jacob's science sortie. Let's go to the suit locker in Hab 2. Their suits are marked as evidence."

Vik plugs umbilicals into the marked suits. Jacob and Oleg do the same with their own suits.

"CASSI please run diagnostics on Suit 1, Commander Coby's, and Suit 13, Dieter's."

"Affirmative. Working...Both suits have commands in their life support scripts to dump primary and secondary oxygen at fifteen minutes into the EVA."

"The dump command would have to be entered under a secure login. Whose login is responsible?

"There is no login signature to read. The login protocol was overridden with a backdoor script."

"Do we have a video recording in the suit bay for twenty four hours prior to the sortie departure?"

"Negative. The camera was disabled."

"Dammit! We have attempted murder and no solid evidence on who did it. Even if we go CSI and try to get prints, there would be a mash of most everyone's prints around here."

Oleg says, "I have the same dump command in my suits. This would have happened if I went EVA."

Jacob adds, "I don't see that command in my suit. Maybe the perpetrator did not have time to get to mine."

Oleg offers, "Commander Coby was in here an hour before we departed. Maybe he saw someone."

Vik laments, "Coby is still in a coma. He can't be a witness. It literally could have been anyone in *Arcadia Base*. The *Arcadia Beta* group is less known to us. Our group is like family. What deranged mind and what deranged motive drove this heinous act?"

Jacob averts his eyes laden with tears. "Mama Elena has become like a stranger even to me. I don't know where her mind is but she certainly has no motive for *this*."

"CASSI, please restore the camera in here and keep a record of everyone's whereabouts until we get to the bottom of this. Alert me if there is any suspicious hack into our life support systems."

"Affirmative. Please accept my condolences on the EVA incident. I apologize for failing to record the sabotage."

"Thank you CASSI. I don't find fault with you."

Mars Arcadia Colony Base
Central Medical Bay
March 14, 2037

MCT SOL 449:10:13:41

Ellie has spent most of the last four days sitting by Coby. Their daughter Sofi has been a comfort and strength to her mother. Jacob has been there often holding his father's hand as he lies comatose and hopefully healing. Elena appeared briefly. Ellie saw that her eyes were darting about wildly. Elena felt she was crowding the room and promptly left.

Ellie, Jacob, and Sofi are in alone in the room with Coby. Sofi is probing Coby with her mind. She sees images of the deep dream he's having--the deep space vehicle Altair; the comet; a strange vent; bewilderment... She sends her thoughts, "Papa! Papa! This is me Sofi. Please come back to us. We're so worried about you!"

Coby's eyes flutter open and looking bewildered. He slowly shakes his head. Ellie presses the intercom call button. "Abby, come now! Coby is waking!"

"Coming Ellie!"

"Coby, it's me, Ellie. You're going to be OK now. That tube in your mouth is a respirator. Don't fight it!" She is gently holding his shoulders and looking deep into his eyes. "Be calm Coby. We're here. It's OK now." Coby nods but has a look of panic on his face.

Abby arrives. "Let me have some space with him. Welcome back Coby. Can you hear me?" He nods yes. "I'm going to gently remove the respirator. Be calm. OK, gently now... There it's out."

Coby coughs and splutters. "W-Where...? How...?"

"You're in sick bay. You had a suit failure. You've been in a coma for almost four days."

More coughing. "Sick bay, w-where...? We were on Altair..."

"Your suit failure caused severe oxygen deprivation. You may be confused after the coma. We're on Mars in *Arcadia Colony Base*. You were on a science recon with Dieter, Jacob, and Oleg. Jacob and Oleg rescued you and brought you back in the rover."

"But we were on Altair... Where is Vik? When is this? Who are Jacob and Oleg?"

Fighting back tears, Ellie takes over. "Slow down, Coby. You're weak and confused from the coma. We are on Mars. It's 2037, thirteen *years* after *Aquila*. Vik is coming to see you now. Jacob is right here. He's your son with Elena. She's also in the colony. Oleg is Vik's son from before *Aquila*."

Coby sees a young freckled girl of about twelve holding his hand and Ellie's. "Who is this?"

"Oh God, Coby! This is our daughter Sofi. Take it slow. You'll remember."

Coughing, "S-Sofi? This is so overwhelming! Yes, you were there in my dream. Then I was here. How?"

Vik arrives and the room makes way for him to see Coby. Giving his shoulder a big squeeze, "Coby, welcome back. Everyone in the colony has been so worried."

"Vik. We were on *Altair*. I'm trying to r-remember...Sofi..." Coby's eyelids flutter and close.

"OK. Coby's had quite enough for now. Back out of the room and let him sleep."

8

THE COUNCIL

"It may take endless wars and unbearable population pressure to force-feed a technology to the point where it can cope with space. In the universe, space travel may be the normal birth pangs of an otherwise dying race. A test. Some races pass, some fail."

Robert Heinlein, *I Will Fear No Evil,* 1970

Mars Arcadia Colony Base
March 16, 2037
MCT SOL 451:08:05:13

Abby enters the small curtain draped space in the Central Medical Bay.

"Good morning Coby. Good morning Ellie. How's our patient today."

"Good morning Abby. I'm feeling stronger but my mind is still a fog. I don't remember anything since *Aquila* and the comet vent."

"That's OK. Please don't worry. Your brain is still recovering from the hypoxia. You've been our mainstay all these years. It's our turn take care of you for a while. We'll all work with you to fill in the gaps. Meanwhile, I'd like to move you back to your own quarters. I'll still be taking close care of you but your family will do better and you'll do better being in comfortable, familiar, safe, surroundings."

Ellie agrees, "Great. The sooner, the better. It's hard to sleep in here!"

MCT SOL 451:10:22:01

Elena looks into the mirror and sees a young, beautiful visage instead of her growing wrinkles, graying hair, and dark circles under her eyes. Her paranoid delusion is that she's been subliminally activated, now twenty-nine years after her indoctrination at the *Kazan State School* in Russia. There she was trained in allegiance, social etiquette, manipulation, and *kompromat*. It served her well over the years. Her mantra is, "I will faithfully support and die for Russia and FKA over the *Coalition*."

In some twisted logic, it's Elena's mission to eliminate Coby who not only spurned her but was an obvious threat to Russia's prestige and dominance in space. Russia had asserted that dominance and gained respect by being the only country capable of sending a crew to ISS for eight years from 2011, when the ill-fated space shuttle retired, until 2019 when the damned US commercial space program began sending crews to space. Elena's first attempt to kill Coby failed. Dieter was a necessary casualty of her mission. Besides, he deserved to die for being party to the insult of not including her on the science sortie. She had covered her tracks so there can be another chance to kill Coby. Equally important, she must kill that bitch Rafaela Accardi who took Coby from her. Not only that, but the whore has all the glory of discovering life beyond the Earth. The Earth showered her with accolades. No wonder Coby foolishly fell for her. She vows not to fail this time.

Elena's new plan to kill both Coby and Ellie is to extract a large cylinder of gas from the Sabatier reactor with an odorless, deadly mix of compressed carbon monoxide, carbon dioxide, and hydrogen. On a timer set for their sleep schedule, the gas will feed into the life support system of their living quarters downstream of the ECLSS atmosphere processing. No one would suspect the odorless gasses. Today is the day. Coby is back in his own quarters recovering.

MCT SOL 449:12:17:34

Elena was aware that Dao-Ming Cai had sent some encrypted radio traffic to the PRC. With her backdoor super-user access, she flagged a recent encrypted message to sow seeds of discord and deflect from her devious plans. The message flag mysteriously appeared in Vik's email as urgent. Fifteen minutes later he finds it.

The apparently anonymous text planted by Elena says, "There has been encrypted traffic between Dao-Ming Cai and The People's Republic of China. Houston interprets it to be of grave concern. CASSI has decoded the encrypted message and have determined its source and author. The report file and evidence are in your inbox."

Vik summons Dao-Ming Cai. Sandy Conklin, her partner, appears with her. When confronted, Dao-Ming freely admits to the exchange.

"My mother is gravely ill with cancer. To get direct communication, I had to use government channels which of necessity are encrypted. I used customary party salutations to get the communication about my mother. I would never intentionally jeopardize my standing in this colony. I love Sandy. My being on Mars in this colony is the only way that I could have this freedom to love her and to be who I am."

Sandy, respected as a Chaplain in the colony, regrets more than anyone the loss of Dieter, the other Chaplain on the original colony. "I love Dao-Ming. Our relationship could get her the death penalty in China. Mars is our choice for freedom. I can vouch for her character and her concern for her mother. She told me about her angst over the encrypted transmission to get through to her mother."

Vik says, "I'm sorry to hear about your Mother. I hope she recovers. Please clear encrypted traffic with me before you send it. We're on high alert. If you'll excuse me, I'm being summoned the Coms station."

MCT SOL 449:13:13:01

Elena suits up and egresses from the Hab 1 airlock with an empty oxygen cylinder. Since the *Base* is on heightened alert, Jacob is on watch at the Coms station. CASSI sends an alert that there has been an unauthorized egress. Elena's face is clearly visible on the video surveillance. He sends a message to Vik with the news. Momentarily Vik joins him.

"Jacob, I'm going to stay here on Coms. I want you to carefully follow Elena and be careful that she doesn't see you. Keep your radio on a closed circuit to me and keep me informed about what she's doing."

In the library, Sofi senses the threat. She nudges Alex and gives him a troubling thought. "Auntie Elena has gone rogue out the airlock. She means to harm our families."

"Yeah. I'm feeling that too. Jacob is going out to stop her! There's nothing we can do but wait. I've been getting bad vibes from Elena for a while. This is the strongest read yet. God, I hope no one gets hurt."

"People *have* been hurt! I'm feeling sure now that she sabotaged Dad's and Dieter's suits."

"Yeah. Got that loud and clear! Pure, raw, gut sickening hate."

In ten minutes, Jacob is egressing with his tool belt and HUD readout giving range and bearing on his mother. In the short time she was outside alone, Elena had loaded the toxic gas mixture from the Sabatier reactor into the cylinder. She lugged the big cylinder to the ECLSS outside Ellie and Coby's Hab living quarters. She feels her full strength as she carries it in Mars 0.4 g. The thought crossed her mind that Vik, Abby, Sofi, and Alex shared Hab 1. Collateral damage is acceptable in war. She snaps the quick connect inlet fitting from the cylinder to the ECLSS downstream location. The timer is already set and the gas valve will only open when her timer goes off at midnight when her intended victims are asleep. All that's left is to cover the cylinder with a surplus scrap of aluminum to keep it from being discovered before the job is done. Even if she is caught later she will have the satisfaction of knowing her mission succeeded. She cackles to herself. No one can hear because her radio transmitter is off.

Jacob finds his mother loading a gas cylinder at the ECLSS inlet T-valve. She sees him and has no choice but to defend herself and her plan. She uses the large spanner wrench from her tool belt as a weapon and swings it full force at Jacob's helmet.

"Die!"

Her aim is not true and the wrench hits Jacob's helmet with only a glancing blow that nearly stuns him with whiplash and the booming sound. His helmet is intact. He's dealing with a killer. He dives and tackles Elena to the ground. Jacob reaches into his tool pouch and grabs two zip ties that always on hand along with duct tape. Restraining his struggling mother, he quickly zip ties her hands together. He manually clicks her communication control and his to broadcast to all channels. He rolls Elena over and looks deep into her wild eyes. There can be no doubt that she knows who is restraining her.

"Nooo! What are you doing, you bastard?"

The word bastard never cut so deep.

"Mama, what the *hell* are *you* doing? What is that gas cylinder you've attached to the ECLSS lines? That leads to Coby and Vik's family quarters. Are you trying to kill them? Dammit! You are!" He reaches down and uncouples the gas connection.

Elena tries to kick his legs out from under him. "Bastard! Bastard! Bastard! Nooo!"

Jacob opens Coms, "Emergency. Possible life support breach on Hab 1! Repeat. Possible life support breach on Hab 1!" He zip ties her ankles and wraps duct tape around her wrists and ankles to make doubly sure she doesn't get loose. "You may be my mother but you'll have to answer for this. How can you do this to the colony? Murder?" He opens coms again. "*Arcadia Base* Coms, this is Jacob Petrov. I need security at the Hab 1 airlock. Repeat. I need security at the Hab 1 airlock. I have a prisoner attempting to poison Hab 1 through its ECLSS. CASSI, send me a CARIAN unit instructed to assist me. We must get the prisoner to the airlock. This as a medical emergency. Do you copy?"

"Jason, this is Vik at Coms. Affirmative on security at Hab 1 airlock!"

CASSI adds, "Affirmative on CARIAN assistance. ETA thirty seconds. The unit is directed to obey your commands only and to transport your medical emergency to Hab 1 airlock."

Vik keys his intercom key, "Abby and Oleg, this is Vik. Meet me in Central Medical stat!"

Both immediately respond, "We're on our way!"

Sofi nudges Alex and gives him an imperative thought. "Let's get our butts to Medical and see what's goin' on."

"I'm with ya!"

There is a small crowd gathering in Central Medical. Vik, Abby, and Oleg are in the middle of the crowd. Ellie is standing aside with Sofi and Alex.

Vik's booming voice takes command. "I need all of you to back off. Let us handle this emergency. Abby, get the heavy tranquilizer pen and three Tasers from the security vault."

"I'm on it. Keep the crowd way back."

Sofi steps toward Vik. "Alex and I need to talk to you, private, NOW!"

"Oleg, keep the crowd back. Okay, Ellie, Alex, Sofi, give it to me quick."

Alex leans in close to his father, "I'm not joking. You know Sofi and I have telepathic senses sometimes. We both read horrible thoughts from Auntie Elena. She sabotaged Coby's and Dieter's suits and is trying to poison our families in Hab 1."

"God, it's worse than I suspected. Keep this quiet for now." Keying the intercom, "All personnel, evacuate Hab 1. Repeat, all personnel evacuate Hab 1!"

Ellie says, "Oh God! Sofi and Alex, let's move back and let them get on with it."

Outside Hab 1, the CARIAN android arrives. Jacob is relieved. He bends down and turns off Elena's coms completely so she will not interfere with the android.

"CARIAN, good timing! I need your help to carefully carry this medical patient to the Hab 1 airlock please. She's having uncontrolled convulsions."

The CARIAN is a remarkable two meter high humanoid robot with tremendous strength and able to work indefinitely in the Mars environment with only a daily recharge.

"Affirmative. I will handle the patient."

The CARIAN lifts Elena effortlessly and supports her thrashing body in a fireman's carry as programming required for a medical emergency with no suspected spinal injury. It takes two agonizing minutes to get Elena's thrashing, space-suited body to the Hab 1 airlock.

Jacob commands, "CASSI, please open the Hab 1 airlock and cycle us through quickly."

"Affirmative. Airlock opening...I confirm your ingress with the CARIAN and medical patient. Ten second carbon dioxide dust purge...Cycling the airlock...Atmospheric pressure equalized...Opening airlock to Hab 1."

MCT SOL 449:13:28:14

Vik, Abby, and Oleg are there waiting as the airlock opens. The imposing CARIAN is carrying Elena as she thrashes ever more violently. Now that her space suit is embraced with full atmosphere in the Hab, her wailing cries can be heard muffled through the suit.

"Eeee! Ahhhrrr! No! No! Damn you all! No! Die! Die! Die!"

Abby commands, "Vik, get her helmet off. Be careful of her teeth. Hold her head to the side so I can get this trank pen into her."

Vik gets Elena's helmet off. Elena shrieks louder. "Let me finish! Die! Die!"

Vik holds her head to the side and cups his hand over her mouth. Abby quickly reaches into Elena's suit and jams the trank pen home into her shoulder.

"Bitch! What wasss thaa…?"

Elena is out cold.

Vik speaks, "Well that was fast work. That's how Commander Helen Craig took care of Trask on ISS when he went off the rails and sabotaged Altair. "

Abby replies, "Except all she had to do was send her little problem, Trask, back down to Earth. We have to sort out what we're going to do with our alleged murderer on Mars. She's our problem, not Earth's"

"I hear you, but first things first. Oleg, help Jacob out of his suit. Abby, you and I will get Elena out of her suit. That means removing the restraints. We'll need to have restraints for her when she wakes up. We'll make her quarters a jail room." Abby replies, "Not so fast. I need to observe her vitals in sick bay first."

"Do you have restraints in sick bay?"

"Of course. We've never needed them but I have restraints suitable to keep her immobilized. The heavy tranquilizer will have her out for about twelve hours. I need to observe Elena and Jacob for signs of decompression sickness. Haldane can't be ignored. Neither of them had done an oxygen pre-breathe procedure. Jacob, I'm not going to admit you to sick bay but I want you to report to me for checkups every six hours for the next day. Let me know immediately if you have any joint pain. It might mean decompression sickness"

"Got it. I don't want to be around sick bay when Mama wakes up. Hell hath no fury like Mama when she's pissed off. How can you keep her quiet?"

"I can keep her mildly sedated for a few days until we figure out a better solution. I have a supply of RIPP protection masks if needed. With the mask, she'll be able to breathe easily but any scream will be muffled and more importantly, she won't be able to bite. She'll be on a catheter and an IV to keep her hydrated. I'm going to need Tracy Dixon to help cover her around the clock. I have Coby to take care of also."

Vik says, "The CARIAN can stand guard if we need some quick forceful action. We can't otherwise put up a round the clock security detail. We need to have a constant video file of our patient for the record- especially when she awakens from the trank."

"We need to figure out some longer term solution. Our cozy little colony has gotten complicated. We can't live without law and order. Coby can't help us now."

"The incident with Robert Trask at the start of *Aquila*, raised the problem of encountering a criminal or a dangerously psychotic individual in space. Our situation cannot have the same solution so far from Earth. I'm may be acting Commander and *de facto* colonial Governor but what we need is a government not a dictator. I'm calling a *Council of Principals* today. I also need to communicate with Houston and the *Coalition*."

MCT SOL 449:19:01:32

Vik calls the first *Council of Principals* for 19:00 in the Underground Habs Common Room. Elena is still unconscious. Tracy Dixon is watching over her in Central Medical with the CARIAN standing guard. Coby is still sleeping. Jacob, Sofi, and Alex are sitting with him.

Key persons assigned to the formal *Council of Principals are* Vik, Abby, Coby (in absentia), Ellie, Paula and Sam Jennings, Eve Cain, John Meek, and Jameel al-Badie. The council one day will be the *United Arcadia Council* and include two council members from each colony and at least one from each member nation. This first *Council of Principals* session is based on seniority and further includes the three lawyers on Mars: Eve Cain, John Meek, and Jameel al-Badie. The long term goal of having lawyers in the Mars colonies is to help form colonial government. The time has come.

Vik opens. "Ladies and gentlemen, welcome to the first session of the *Council of Principals.* We'd planned to get around to this in due course but now we have the serious business of criminal justice on the table. We are preparing for the criminal trial of Elena Petrov for one count of first degree murder and six counts of attempted first degree murder. This session is being recorded for broadcast to Houston and the *Coalition.* They have been apprised of the situation and are in support of the formation of this council. We have eight present. The *Coalition* will have two votes in our business that will be exercised only if we are at a stalemate. Any comments?"

Ellie speaks up. "From what I gather from the twisted thoughts Sofi and Alex have read from Elena, it seems that Coby and I were the intended targets of Elena's wrath. Dieter was collateral damage. Everyone in Hab 1 could have been killed. We need justice. I move that Eve Cain serve as a prosecuting attorney and Jameel al-Badie serve as a defense attorney. Both have degrees in criminal justice. I move that we seat a jury of six of Elena's peers. I further move that Vik act as judge."

Vik calls for a vote and Ellie's motions pass unanimously without the *Coalition* vote.

Jameel speaks. "The first thing we need to have a fair trial is to gather evidence. I'm sorry to say that the testimony of Sofi and Alex's thought reading Elena's motives cannot stand as evidence."

John Meek adds, "We do have the solid evidence of Elena's actions today. We'll need to test the contents of the gas cylinder. We do have evidence that Coby's and Dieter's suit life support was sabotaged but as yet no proof aside from circumstantial evidence that Elena did it. I move that we postpone the trial and judgment until we have gathered more evidence."

Vik calls for a vote and John's motion passes unanimously without the *Coalition* vote. He continues the discussion.

"What can the colony do with a criminal- an alleged murderer? We came to Mars to make a second home and better place for humanity. However, circumstances will inevitably bring out the dark side of human nature. The colony must protect its citizens. If we deem that Elena is guilty of murder and six counts of attempted murder of all the residents of Hab 1, what are our options? Execution? Form a penal colony? We have tough choices for our stretched resources."

Eve speaks, "We have the *Coalition Charter* as our *de facto Constitution*[77]. Wisely, the *Coalition* had the foresight, with some guidance by John, Jameel, and me, to cover cases of criminal justice. Article IV Section 13 expressly states that there can be no imposition of the death penalty for any crime. Incarceration by whatever means available is our only recourse."

Sam confers with Paula then she speaks, "We have an unused lab module unloaded from the *Pollux*. The lab module is twenty meters from Hab 6. It currently has an airlock and a small ECLSS unit for life support so it can be self-contained. Power and communication cables have been run. Add a bed and microwave and it's fully habitable for one prisoner *if* we have a conviction."

Ellie adds, "We really have come to this point in our history. As for communications to the confinement module, I suggest that we make it text only to a stand-alone tablet in the Coms Bay. We can control the life support systems through CASSI. Our theoretical prisoner should have no capability of accessing *Base* systems. I move that we make these modifications to the lab and call it CM-1 for Confinement Module 1."

Vik calls for a vote and Ellie's motion passes unanimously without the *Coalition* vote.

"Thanks for that bit of progress in this unfortunate business. We don't have the resources or desire to start a penal colony. We don't want a police state. We need deterrence. Our euphemistically named CM-1 will provide safe but austere solitary confinement. God help us if we need more than one. Further deterrence measures that we have in stock are Tasers and trank pens. Today's business with Elena will make the necessity

---

77 "What NASA's simulated missions tell us about the need for Martian law" The Conversation, 12 October 2017, https://theconversation.com/what-nasas-simulated-missions-tell-us-about-the-need-for-martian-law-84790

for deterrence perfectly clear. This is not intended as a threat, John and Jameel, we need you to communicate to your colony groups that our larger scale colony defense is provided by the industrial lasers that arrived on *Gemini*. All of these things are secure. The *Coalition* is working with SpaceTrans to insure that no other weapons will arrive with the LDS and UAE colonies. Your liaisons on Earth have ratified this condition as a concession to your alliance with *Arcadia Base*."

Jameel says, "We're aware of the conditions and have accepted them. The situation could become more complicated when other groups and nations send independent colonies. There are rumors that China intends to do just that by establishing a colony on the opposite side of Mars from Arcadia."

John adds, "That'll be a good day. Think of the trade opportunities. We can all benefit from the diversification. On that note, I move that we adjourn and gather evidence for the prosecution and defense of our prisoner."

Vik calls for a vote and John's motion passes unanimously.

Mars Arcadia Colony Base
March 17, 2037
MCT SOL 452:01:13:04

Tracy Dixon is on watch in Central Medical with Elena still tranquilized from the trank-pen. Her vitals are good. Jacob reports from Hab 1 that Coby is occasionally awake and responsive and then nods off. That's to be expected. Coby has a long way to go to recovery but she thinks his chances of that are reasonably good.

The CARIAN reports, "Doctor Dixon, the prisoner-patient Elena Petrov is awake and moving."

"Oh, so she is! Thanks CARIAN." She steps over to Elena. Her eyes are glazed and unfocussed. Her vitals are stable.

Tracy keys the intercom to raise Vik and Abby. "Vik, Abby, sorry to disturb you. Elena is waking up. Please come to sick bay."

Abby responds to the call. "Okay, I expected her to come around just about now. We'll be down in a few minutes. I need to get dressed first."

Elena tries to speak. "W-where...am...I? I- I can't move. What h-have you done to me?... No! I wasn't finished!"

Just then Vik and Abby arrive with Ellie in tow. They all look disheveled from sleep.

Abby asks, "How's our patient?

"Get me out of here! Now! Ellie you should be dead! Die!!"

Vik says, "Sorry Elena. We can't release you. You are being charged with six counts of attempted murder. That gas cylinder was tested and had enough poisonous gas to kill all of us in Hab 1. In the matter of Dieter's death and Coby's attempted murder, you are the prime suspect."

"Yes! I did that! I need Coby and Ellie dead! No one else matters. Let me out of here-NOW!!"

Ellie speaks out, "What *exactly* did you *do* to Coby?"

"Why do you ask? Of course I hacked their suit PLSS packs. I did not hack Jacob's, my dear boy. Oh God! He took me down. Bastard! Let me go! I need to get to Jacob!"

"No. We can't just let you go. You are most definitely under arrest. As soon as this afternoon, you will go on trial for murder and attempted murder. Jameel al-Badie will serve as your defense attorney. He will speak to you in the morning before your trial."

"Trial? Hah! What a sham. You have no right, no laws. No justice! Jameel doesn't even belong to this colony. I need him to be dead too! Die! Die! Die!"

Abby interjects, "Elena, you can have a tranquilizer or the mask. Vik's right. We've heard all we need from you for now. You need some more sleep. This will do." Abby injects a sedative into Elena's IV…

"No! Let me out nowwww…"

Vik speaks, "CASSI, please send Houston the evidence report including the video of Elena since she regained consciousness and confessed to Dieter's murder and attempted murder of Coby."

"Affirmative. The file is collated and sending now."

"Thank you CASSI."

"Glad to be of service."

Elena is back under sedation and the colony is safe from her rage for now. Vik decides that the trial will proceed at 1300. They have the evidence and confession compiled. Abby relieves Tracy and takes over watch on Ellie with the CARIAN. Vik walks with Ellie back to Hab 1 to look in on Coby and then get some needed sleep.

Ellie says, "A few short days ago, this colony was a happy place with an even brighter future. How did we let one deranged person put us in this bad place?"

"We're *still* in a *good* place. Facing a crisis like this was inevitable. Just emigrating to Mars does not change human nature. We have the legal basis to handle this. Houston and the *Coalition* are firmly behind our ad hoc *Council of Principals* and they have all the evidence now, including Elena's confession."

"We just need to get Coby back on his feet and to be mentally with us."

"If he doesn't find his memory, I'll spend all the time necessary to help re-educate him and help make him whole."

"Thanks Vik. We're all going to work together."

They walk into Coby and Ellie's suite and find Jacob, Sofi, and Alex sitting with Coby in the main living room. Coby is smiling and listening to Sofi describe their glorious trip to Mars.

Mars Arcadia Colony Base
March 17, 2037
MCT SOL 452:13:00:51

Vik convenes the *Council of Principals* trial session at 1300 in the Underground Habs Common Room. Elena is awake and only mildly sedated. She is moved to the Common Room in a wheel chair with padded restraints. The CARIAN is her guard and attendant. She's wearing a RIPP protection mask and appears only slightly less scary than Hannibal Lecter. Her wild protests are reduced to muffled grunting sounds. Her eyes are sunken with dark circles. She is unbathed, unkempt, and raises an odor that only can be described as sweat and hate.

A jury of six is seated and includes Paula and Sam Jennings, Paul Earhart, Sandy Conklin, Mike Fischer, and Elle Zandjans. Paula is the jury foreman. There are twenty additional colonists present. Among them, Sofi and Alex, who were collateral attempted murder victims, are seated behind Ellie on the opposite side of the room from Elena. Jacob has brought Coby in a wheel chair. While he still has no memory of events since *Aquila*, he knows Elena and he knows that her actions nearly killed him.

Vik is presiding. "It is with no joy that we are convened for the trial of Elena Petrov for one count of first degree murder and six counts of attempted first degree murder. Eve Cain will serve as the prosecuting attorney and Jameel al-Badie serve as the defense attorney. Both have degrees in criminal justice. I am serving as judge. John Meek is observing as impartial counsel. These proceedings are being recorded and broadcast to Houston and the *Coalition*. The jurors will now read the written affirmation aloud."

Simultaneously, "I solemnly and sincerely declare and affirm that I will give a true verdict according to the evidence."

Eve Cain calls Jacob Petrov as a witness to describe the events that occurred on SOL 445 during his science sortie that led to the death of Dieter Schwartz and near suffocation of Coby Brewster. Next he describes the events of SOL 451 where he apprehended Elena with the cylinder of poison gas she had connected to the Hab 1 ECLSS. CASSI acts as a technical witness to describe how Dieter and Coby's PLSS units were sabotaged and describe the poison gas contents of the cylinder: odorless hydrogen, carbon monoxide, and carbon dioxide. CASSI replays Elena's confession of all of these events with her prime targets as Coby and Ellie. Eve Cain describes that Dieter's murder and the other attempted murders were collateral victims "that did not matter to Elena."

At that pronouncement, Elena gives a loud but muffled cackle under the mask.

Jameel al-Badie, the defense attorney, can only bring a case of innocence by reason of insanity. He calls Dao-Ming Cai, a psychologist, as a professional witness. She describes the Elena she knew from their training days back on Earth and then how Elena had progressively grown withdrawn and sullen. Dao-Ming had several times attempted to reach out to Elena but was rebuffed. Dao-Ming presented Russian FKA files recently sent on Elena outlining the fact that she had attended the *Kazan State School* in the Republic of Tatarstan in her late teens. It's an academy where they taught women "sparrows" the art of sexual entrapment.

"The FKA claims no secret purpose for Elena. They express great pride in all of the Russian professionals represented in the colony. We think the early sparrow training was part of Elena's own subconscious and misguided rationale for her past relationship with Coby that spiraled over many years into the completely irrational deeds these past days. I can come to no other conclusion than that Elena Petrov is criminally insane. Hope for her rehabilitation is nil."

Elena thrashes and gives a muffled scream.

Vik instructs the jury. "The prosecution has presented evidence for the charges including Elena's confession. The defense has mounted a case for innocence by reason of insanity. We will adjourn while the jury deliberates. John Meek, the impartial counsel, will be available to the jury to discuss legal issues. We will reconvene when a verdict has been reached."

MCT SOL 452:19:00:13

The jurors have reported that they have reached a verdict. Vik reconvenes the *Council of Principals* trial at 1900. Elena has been bathed and fed but is still restrained and wearing the mask.

"Paula, has the jury reached a verdict?"

"We have. Being bound by the *Coalition Charter* and the precedent of law, while the defendant has been proven to have committed the crimes as charged, we find the defendant not guilty by reason of insanity."

The room erupts in gasps and murmured protests.

Ellie blurts out, "God no!"

Elena laughs under the mask.

Vik calls for order. "We have no choice but to accept the verdict but that does not mean Elena walks free. Eve, please explain the consequences of this verdict."

"I've had to brush up on some law here. From one of my Georgetown texts: *When a party successfully defends criminal charges on grounds of insanity, the consequences vary from jurisdiction to jurisdiction. Usually, the defendant is committed to a mental institution. On the average, a defendant found not guilty by reason of insanity and committed to a mental institution is confined for twice as long as is a defendant who is found guilty and sent to prison.* So what does that mean for the defendant? By the charter, we do not have the death penalty on the table. First degree then carries life in prison without the possibility of parole. First-degree attempted murder means a life sentence with the possibility of parole but that is overridden by the murder charge. The bottom line is that we must confine the defendant for life."

Vik directs, "CARIAN, please remove the prisoner's mask so that she may speak freely."

"Affirmative."

Sofi and Alex are feeling the charge of Elena's wrath. With android dexterity, the mask is removed. Elena bites the android's finger with such force that a snap is heard. The titanium finger is unharmed.

Elena spits out a bloody tooth. "I need you all to die and *go to hell.*"

"We've heard enough! Replace the mask!"

The CARIAN replaces the mask as blood drips down Elena's chin.

Vik announces, "We obviously don't have the resources to run a prison or mental facility. We have repurposed an unused lab module unloaded from the *Pollux* and placed beyond Hab 6. It has an airlock and ECSS unit for life support. Power and communication cables have been run. It has a bed, microwave, hygiene facilities, and a one month supply of consumables that can be restocked through the airlock. It's fully habitable for one mental patient prisoner. We call it CM-1 for Confinement Module 1. The inner airlock controls have been bypassed. We will provide no EVA suit for the prisoner so there is no possibility of escape. This is not a pleasant outcome but we have no other choice."

MCT SOL 452:21:13:08

A CARIAN moves Elena to the solitary lock up in CM-1. The suit worn for the short walk to CM-1 is removed by the CARIAN after they cycle through the airlock. She finds the consumables. She has text only communications to the Coms Center so there is no possibility of hacking the *Base* systems to cause mayhem. For some diversion and entertainment, there is a standalone tablet that Elena can use to view movies, do research, or write. The tablet is nearly indestructible. It has an AI program that Elena can interact with for mandatory therapy sessions.

"Get out of here you damned metal monster! I don't need you!"

"As you wish. I can be summoned by text communication."

The CARIAN cycles out and Elena is alone.

Mars Arcadia Colony Base
March 20, 2037
MCT SOL 455:09:13:28

After three days of solitary and sending threatening rants by text, Sofi and Alex are alarmed by sensing Elena's resolve. They immediately report it to Vik and Abby. A CARIAN will take several minutes to get to CM-1.

Elena sends a final text message. "I have been alone and unwanted as a member of this colony. I will not be missed. May you all rot in hell! Goodbye."

Elena has spent much of the last three days digging into the airlock controls to reconnect the wiring. Now that her work is complete, she walks into the airlock and triggers a rapid depressurization. She opens the outer hatch, steps onto the red soil of Mars. After five unsteady steps, she collapses from asphyxiation in the ultra-thin, ultra-cold carbon dioxide atmosphere. Her eyes freeze with a terrible look of hate. Her last gasp brings a froth of blood from the pulmonary embolism in her ruptured lungs.

"CARIAN, this is Abby. Have you reached Elena?"

"Affirmative. I found the prisoner dead outside the CM-1 airlock. My medical sensors detect no sign of life. What shall I do with her."

"Oh God, please take her back into CM-1 until we can tend to her."

MCT SOL 456:08:11:13

Jacob, Vik, and Oleg witness Elena's burial. Sandy Conklin says a few words as Chaplain. Elena is buried next to Barry Peterson and to Dieter Schwartz, her murder victim.

Jacob has the last word. "You were wrong Mama. *I* will miss you."

EPILOGUE

...I say a multi-planet species, that's what we really want to be...It's really being a multi-planet species and having civilization and life as we know it extend beyond Earth to the rest of the Solar System, and ultimately to other star systems. That's the future that's exciting...

Elon Musk, *YouTube,* June, 2016

Mars Arcadia Colony Base
April 1, 2037
MCT SOL 467:10:44:32

Coby Brewster personal log:

I have recovered physically and have essentially recovered my memory through therapy. My family and dearest friends have spent many long hours with me recounting the missing years. I have enjoyed listening to the emotional accounts of our accomplishments, celebrations, and occasional downfalls that have been lost with my brain injury. The events they describe are part of me again and the tapestry of the life of our colony seems whole again.

I do not want to take back the role of Base Commander and Colonial Governor. Vik handled the Elena Petrov crisis with aplomb. Not only did we survive the crisis, we now have a more solid legal foundation to take our colony to the future especially with next year's arrival of the LDS and UAE colonies. A special election retains Vik in the role of Base Commander and Colonial Governor. The election was ratified by the *Coalition*, the LDS, and the UAE yesterday. Vik will be in the role for two years before the *Council* votes either to reelect him or replace him. By the current *Charter*, there are no term limits. I feel that the *Charter* will evolve with Amendments as we grow and encounter the need to adapt just as the US Constitution is reinvigorated with its Amendments.

The pall of sadness that rocked the colony with Elena Petrov's death has nearly been forgotten with the flow and chatter of busy life here. I have been busying myself with time in the greenhouses. I'm finding lots of company there with others seeking the therapy of the simple joy of helping our crops grow.

The brightest light of hope is that there are four births due this month and four more in the next three months. Megumi Hirakata is in the first stages of labor today with Satoshi Fukoshima by her side. Eve Cain and Harrison Frank are due mid-month. Julia Levine and Mike Fischer are due the following week. Jochem Nabors and Elle Zandjans are due the week after that. Jacob Petrov and Tracy Jennings baby is due the third week of June. Abby, Tracy Dixon, and Sabrina Kessler are keeping busy with the OB-GYN demands! This will bring our colonist count to fifty. Another sixty will be added with next year's arrival of the LDS and UAE colonies.

Oksana Ivanov will celebrate her first birthday by Earth years on June 25th. Adele Earhart is doing well with her XP condition and thriving in the underground hab. Her long term outcome with CRISPR gene therapy is promising. Elle Zandjans' baby boy has been diagnosed with the single gene defect phenylketonuria (PKU). Perhaps this is another radiation induced mutation. Abby is confident that they will also be able to treat it with gene therapy.

When I look at Sofi and Alex, I can't help but think that the exposure to microgravity and higher levels of radiation have challenged the human genome to adapt and evolve faster than in the cradle of Earth. Their phenomenal growth, intelligence, and apparent clairvoyance are beyond my understanding. Abby is studying it and has a ground breaking AMA journal article in the works with Tracy and Sabrina as coauthors.

New Kolob and al-Salam al-Jadid Colony Arrivals

Mars Arcadia Colony Base
March 5, 2038
MCT SOL 805:09:21:07

Coby Brewster personal log:

We have six colony ships arriving this week! *New Kolob* arrives March 7th and *al-Salam al-Jadid* arrives March 12th. SpaceTrans dramatically expanded their Colossus launch capabilities to meet the August 21-24, 2037 window to get these four supply and two colony ships launched to Mars. Each colony ship is carrying thirty persons: ten mission specialists and twenty colonists. The additions of sixty persons will more than double the head count in Arcadia. Functionally, *New Kolob* and *al-Salam al-Jadid* will be adjunct colonies connected by tunnels to the original central *Arcadia Base*. They will govern themselves and have representation on the *Council of Principals*. The future council will be expanded to become the *United Arcadia Council* headed by the Arcadia Base Governor, Vik Ivanov, as *Council* Secretary-General and Ambassador to Earth.

Each of the three adjoined colonies will receive another increment of forty persons launching in the September 2039 window and arriving in May 2040. John Meek and Jameel al-Badie are urban planning architects that have been hard at work on robotic colony construction in preparation for the big arrival of the new colonists.

John Meek has been the architect for the construction work for the *New Kolob* Colony. He's looking forward to the arrival of the Temple Hab on the *Canaan* supply ship. He explained to me that the Angel Moroni is represented as a golden statue on top of the Salt Lake Temple. Joseph Smith recounted that the Angel Moroni visited him on numerous occasions beginning in 1823. According to Smith, the angel Moroni was the guardian of the golden plates, which Latter Day Saints believe were the inspiration for the Book of Mormon. The Temple Hab will have its own golden Moroni incorporated at its apex. The colony living quarters and Commons Rooms are lift connected underground below the Temple Hab. The *New Kolob* colonists believe the colony follows prophesy by reaching a place closer to the throne of God.

Jameel al-Badie has been the architect for the construction work for the *al-Salam al-Jadid* Colony (السلام الجديد : *The New Peace*). The *Sheik Mansour Arcadia Mosque and Cultural Center* has been constructed underground at the center of the colony. The HORTA ice miner bored an underground dome fifteen meters in diameter at its base. The reinforced upper dome has a two meter skylight made of 3D printed clear polycarbonate that extends just above ground level and adorned at its apex with a crescent moon finial. The interior of the dome is adorned with a 3D printed mathematical tessellation of interlacing eight-pointed stars. The basal wall circumference is white except where elaborate Arabic calligraphy of *Quran* scripture is 3D printed in black embellished with gold. The cultural center and library is an adjacent large oval space. Extending beyond that are the family living quarters.

Mars Arcadia Colony Base
March 17, 2038
MCT SOL 817:22:34:21

Coby Brewster personal log:

New Kolob Colony has two Colossus supply ships, *Canaan* and *Moab*, and their first colony ship, *Provo*. They successfully landed at Arcadia on March 7th. The *al-Salam al-Jadid* Colony also purchased three Colossus ships. *Dubai* and *Sharjah* are supply ships. The *Abu Dhabi* is their colony ship. They successfully landed on March 12th. The colonists stayed on board their respective ships for four days after landing until the new ECLSS units and critical supplies were unloaded and installed. Today is March 17th and St. Patrick's Day. We held a huge celebration to welcome the new colonists.

There is no space that could safely hold our burgeoning number of colonists without overloading the nearest ECLSS air handling capacity. We mingled between the underground nexus meeting hall, the Arcadia Base Commons Room, the *New Kolob* Commons Room, and the *al-Salam al-Jadid* Cultural Center. The green beer had to stay at *Arcadia Base*! Neither the LDS or UAE groups appreciated that libation but the *Arcadia Base* group thoroughly enjoyed this offering from the greenhouse. We did make a big hit with the fresh salads, tilapia, and some of the first of our poultry product. All of these were seasoned delicately with our Mars grown herbs.

In the time I spent mingling, I learned some interesting things about our new colonists that is not for everyone to know but will serve me well to understand their cultural dynamics. The *al-Salam al-Jadid Colony* is populated by a few families with ties to royalty. They are exclusively Sunni Muslims. Two are princes accompanied by four wives each and children over age sixteen. The UAE age of majority is age eighteen. Their colonists include highly educated engineers, teachers, musicians, a physician, and a cinematographer to document our achievements.

UAE petroleum and investment wealth has long supported efforts in developing asteroid mining start-ups and off-Earth colonization. They have educated people to support these efforts.

Their leader is Sheikh Humaid Bin Muhammad bin Farhad Al Hasan who will represent the colony affairs along with Jameel a-Badie. Jameel appears to cower in fear of Sheik Humaid's power. Jameel is more secular than his fellow colonists. He's celebrating the arrival of his wife, Layla Mohammed. She is the only UAE woman in sight. The other women stay in seclusion. Other than Layla, only the adult men from the UAE colony participated. This is the way of *their* world.

The *New Kolob* colony likewise has engineers, teachers, musicians, a physician, a geologist, and an accomplished artist. The music and art will be an exceptionally welcome addition to our world on Mars. Perhaps art will blossom in *Arcadia Base* if and when we get more leisure time. Survival and keeping up with our fast pace of growth has been all consuming. The vision of a million humans on Mars seems a long way off!

John Meek has a slightly loose adherence to LDS doctrine and enjoyed the green beer. After a few drinks, he confidentially explained some facts to me. The President of the colony, Elder Henry Young, is age sixty and married to his second wife Julie. She's twenty-two years old and a BYU grad. Henry's first wife died. He left grown children back on Earth. Julie married out of social pressure. She's awed by Henry but doesn't feel deep love for him. Elder Todd Scott is twenty-three. He finished his mission, graduated BYU, and has a nineteen year old wife, Ruth. They had been family friends in their Stake church group. Everyone knew they would marry but they were not in love. There is gossip (shhh!) that Todd and Julie are having an affair. Todd looks over his shoulder suspecting Elder Young is after him.

Mars Arcadia Colony Base
March 19, 2038
MCT SOL 819:11:14:21

Coby Brewster personal log:

Today, Vik held the first joint meeting of the *United Arcadia Council* with delegates from the two new colony adjuncts. I attended as one of the *Arcadia Base* delegates along with the original *Principals*. John Meek and Jameel al-Badie gave an inspiring presentation of their architectural vision of an Earth analog eco-park featuring hundred meter domes connected by large arched colonnades with an intersecting transept. The domes will mimic Earth's four seasons. They propose snowboarding on Mars in the Winter Dome!

The Summer Dome will be the largest and is expected to be the most popular. It will offer a respite from the ever subdued lighting on Mars. Everyone can revel in noon sunlight supplemented by LED lights, swim in the reservoir lake, and sunbathe on the lake's sandy shores. The lake is a reservoir of water from excavated Martian ice. The lake will be surrounded by botanical gardens full of fragrant flowers nurtured by the humidity from the lake. I can imagine birds and butterflies flitting about to remind us of Earth. The geodesic dome is inspired from the successful mosque dome. It will involve 3D printing and robotic construction. The triangular polycarbonate panels will be manufactured from ISRU processes involving Mars carbon dioxide and water. The polycarbonate will be designed to filter harsh radiation. The metal girders can be sourced from ISRU aluminum alloy and recycled Colossus hulls.

I was taken in by the vision and was daydreaming of a clothing optional natural scene like Vik, Abby, Ellie and I had at Itchetucknee so many years ago just before Aquila. Where did the years go? Vik and I are long since grey haired (wiser?) old men.

Just then, Sheik Humaid broke the reverie with an outburst. "*La!* How can you envision our people mingling in this dome concept? "

Jameel responds. "My design was inspired by Sheikh Mansour bin Zahid Al Majed and his 2018 bio-dome concept that we built in the Emirates."

"*La!* I'm in charge here! There will be no domes for swimming and fornicating."

Vik stands and puts a stop to it. "*Nyet! Prosite ser!* Excuse me! You are *guests* of the *Coalition!* We established *Arcadia Base* and made your presence here possible. You are bound by the *Coalition Charter* and we have the enforcement ability to back that up. You don't. Jameel will have to apprise you of that reality. You have representation but cannot *control* the *Council.*"

Sheik Humaid responds, "*Ana asif.* My apologies Viktor Ivanov. I am a stranger in a strange land. Perhaps our people will learn to adapt or perhaps one day we will have flourishing independent, strong colonies."

"I remind you that you stand for *New Peace.*"

"*Aiwa.*"

Mars Arcadia Colony Base
June 12, 2040
MCT SOL 1635:10:35:28

Coby Brewster personal log:

SpaceTrans has constructed paired manufacturing and launch facilities in Japan, Korea, China, India, and the UAE, on schedule to make the Mars launch window in 2039. Colossus colony ships launched with colonists from those nations at an increasing cadence. A total of twenty four Colossus ships launched in the window from September 27 to October 3, 2039 with one colony ship of forty colonists and three supply ships from each launch center in Japan, Korea, China, India, and the UAE. *Coalition* and LDS ships launched from the US. Each of the four new colonies will be dependent on the established facilities of *Arcadia Base* until they can develop some degree of independence. The four new adjunct colonies from Japan, Korea, China, and India have been constructed three hundred meters from *Arcadia Base* to the west, southwest, southeast, and east of *Arcadia Base* with tunnels connecting back to the nexus. The ships landed on their individual new landing pads from April 28 to May 3, 2040.

This is a successful realization of making Mars colonization open for a wide sector of humanity. A sobering detraction from that ideal is that there were massive riots in India during the selection of their colonists. During the Colossus launches from India, masses of people tried to break through the heavy gates of the SpaceTrans launch facility driven by the insane thought that some lucky few of them could barge on board and be whisked out of their overcrowded suffering. Over two thousand people died in these riots and stampedes.

On a brighter note, the total number of people on Mars in May 2040 is has grown to four hundred eleven including the thirty one births we've had to date. This is an almost unimaginable growth since we first arrived almost five years ago. We'll begin building adjunct colonies in a larger circumference ring around *Arcadia* to accommodate the arrivals coming in the July 2042 and September 2044 launch windows. Also in 2044, we'll establish another Arcadia nexus three hundred kilometers southwest of here in Arcadia Planitia. The new colony nexus will be called *Erebus Montes Base*.

We've been criticized for the current colonies being from elitist countries and individuals. The reason for this is rooted in the still extremely high cost and necessity for a high proportion of the colonists to have needed skills and professions. The goal of having a million humans on Mars by 2079 is still a long, long way from reality.

Our communications systems have grown along with our system of trade and barter. Free trade is the carrot for maintaining a mostly harmonious cluster of colonies.

Tasers and trank-pens are still the best deterrence of smaller altercations. The only time that we needed a trank-pen was when Elena had her unfortunate meltdown. Since then we've only had one brawl between teen boys from the LDS and UAE colonies. It was quickly defused and treated with really strong parental discipline. Ouch!

We brought to Mars not only our instinctual curiosity to explore but also our baser animal instincts. Ultimately when Mars population grows, we will undoubtedly see some of "man's inhumanity to man" and we'll need to deal with it. We'll need to have defensive and even the offensive ability to deal with man's innate bloodthirsty belligerent nature. "The best defense is a good offense" is an adage that has been central to military strategy since General George Washington. Because of these realities, there can never be a true Utopia.

The stick for large scale defense measures are the industrial lasers mounted on armored rovers stored in secret bunkers below Arcadia in case of need in a future conflict. Each rover will soon be fitted with a ballistic missile capable of hitting any place on Mars or any threat in Mars orbit. God forbid that there is a future conflict needed these weapons. We have the second home for humanity to protect.

The *Coalition* has redoubled its oversight on all SpaceTrans Mars launch manifests and inspections to insure that only the *Coalition* has any weapons for possible conflict on Mars. All bets are off for any future colonies that may be launched independent of SpaceTrans and the *Coalition*. Mars and anywhere beyond Earth is open territory if you can get there.

I believe that having just two homes for humanity is not enough to ensure our long term survival. Perhaps the next objective for spreading humankind into the solar system would be a place like Titan, the largest moon of Saturn. There is no lack of resources there including water ice and it rains liquid methane. Ha! Who needs a Sabatier reactor on Titan? For resources like aluminum, titanium, iron, other heavy metals, and rare earth elements though, we have to look to asteroids and the inner solar system where the physics of the formation of the solar system endowed a wealth of these elements. This underscores to the need for a lively economic trade system from the inner solar system to the outer solar system as we expand.

Mars Arcadia Colony Base
November 20, 2042
MCT SOL 2526:23:16:43

Coby Brewster personal log:

Sofi and Alex have finally reached age eighteen and will be officially married today. It seems kind of superfluous since their inseparable connection has been undeniable and has only grown stronger since they were toddlers. This was a day of celebration the likes of which we've not seen since the LDS and UAE colonies arrived. If any of these groups find a reason to let down barriers and celebrate, it's for a wedding. This is not just any wedding. It's the daughter and son of *Arcadia's* founders!

The wedding ceremony took place today at the colony nexus with as many high ranking leaders and entourage as we could safely fit into the space. Our own Sandy Conklin performed the non-denominational ceremony. The couple was stunning in garments they designed and made. They stood a head above the crowd with Alex at two meters tall and Sofi only a few centimeters less. The space twins have come of age! How their conception and gestation in deep space might have given them their special gifts is beyond all understanding.

"Alex do you take Sofi as your wife?" They answered simultaneously "I do!" and that was the ceremony. Speeches went on for a while.

After mingling in receptions in each of the colonies' common areas, Sofi and Alex made a getaway for a honeymoon they had planned for a while. They wanted some space and took Rover 3 out for a two day sortie. No messages, just a GPS track and life support data streams to assure us they were okay. They agreed: "No EVAs!"

As they were getting into the rover, Sofi gave Ellie and me hugs and kisses and said, "We need this time to get away from all the voices in our heads and see a few Martian sunrises where no one has been before."

Mars Arcadia Colony Base
November 23, 2042
MCT SOL 2529:02:33:13

Sofi and Alex personal diary:

After the wedding reception, we drove away slowly into the Martian night to the east toward the coming dawn. CAMI has the helm steering by our selected waypoints. The stars are brilliant and the voices are fading behind. We are surrounded by the soft warmth of synth-down comforters and in each other's arms caressing and exploring as we have so many times before.

Tonight is different. We let go all the way and are inside one another so completely that we are joined physically and mentally as one being. Nothing can come between us.

On the second night out, we are sleeping in a natural embrace dreaming like two contented cats. We've never forgotten watching the 2036 New Year's Eve celebration shortly after we arrived on Mars…

Now it's New Year's Eve Times Square December 31, 2078. People are wildly intoxicated as the trance group plays their bizarre version of Auld Lang Syne. The Crystal Ball is dropping to 2079. People are dancing, kissing, and crying. The ball reaches bottom. There is a terrible white flash in the east brighter than a million Suns.

Sofi wakes up and nudges Alex. "W-what?"

They both scream out in disbelief. "Nooo! It's not supposed to end this way!"

What can be done to make sure it doesn't? How will the next chapters in the survival of humanity unfold?

GLOSSARY OF TERMS

AI artificial intelligence

albedo proportion of the incident light or radiation that is reflected by the surface of an astronomical body

AMB solar array actuator motor box

APXS alpha proton x-ray spectrometer instrument

arcminute 1/60th of a degree

arcsecond 1/60th of an arcminute; 1/360th of a degree

astronomical unit average distance from the Earth to the Sun-- approximately 150 million kilometers

AU Astronomical Unit- average distance from the Earth to the Sun--approximately 150 million kilometers

basalt a dark, fine-grained volcanic rock rich in iron and magnesium

biosignature element, isotope, or molecule that provides scientific evidence of past or present life

CAMI Cybernetic Artificial MMU Intelligence

CAPCOM Capsule Communicator- NASA jargon for communications link between flight control and astronauts.

carbonaceous containing carbon and carbon compounds

carbonate a mineral containing the carbonate ion $(CO_3)^{2-}$

CARIAN (sounds like Carrie Ann) Cybernetic Artificial Robotic Intelligence- Android

CARIIN (sounds like Karen) Cybernetic Artificial Robotic Intelligence- Industrial

CASSI Cybernetic Artificial Space System Intelligence

CCD charge coupled device that takes an image in a digital camera. Analogous to the retina in your eye.

CH4 methane

ChemCam instrument for laser spot analysis of elemental composition

chondritic a meteorite containing chondrules

chondrules round particles in a meteorite or asteroid from the original solar nebula that formed the solar system

CM-1 Confinement Module 1

CNSA China National Space Administration

Coalition / ISC *International Space Coalition*- the international partners of the *Aquila Mission* and signatories of the International Space Treaty of 2018: NASA, FKA, ESA, JAXA, CSA- later expanded to other countries.

CRISPR clustered regularly interspaced short palindromic repeats of DNA that can be used to edit genes within organisms

CSA Canadian Space Agency

CT-1 Ceres Telescope 1

CT-2 Ceres Telescope 2

cyanobacteria bacteria that obtain their energy through photosynthesis and produce free oxygen

Delta-V Orbital change in velocity in km/sec

DEM digital elevation model

DIANNAO Diànnǎo- Chinese AI Computer controlling navigation, life support, and communications functions.

EDL Mars Entry Descent and Landing- a traditionally difficult and dangerous phase of the mission

EEG electroencephalogram

ELF extremely low frequency electromagnetic field

ELT Extremely Large Telescope

ESA European Space Agency

extant still in existence; surviving; opposite of extinct

f 24 optical focal ratio--focal length of primary light gathering lens or mirror is 24 times its diameter; narrow angle, high magnification view

f 4.8 optical focal ratio--focal length of primary light gathering lens or mirror is 4.8 times its diameter; wide angle

Fourier transform a mathematical decomposition of a complex signal into frequency components

GEO Geosynchronous Orbit--orbiting at the same point over the Earth at an altitude of about 36,000 km.

GHLI geologic hand lens imager

gimbal rocket engine with freedom of movement to vector thrust about both the pitch and yaw axes for steering

GWh gigawatt-hour or one billion watt-hours

H-dot Horizontal velocity in meters per second relative to the ground

helo slang for helicopter

Hohmann transfer Hohmann transfer orbit uses the lowest possible amount of energy in traveling between Earth and Mars

HWN Hurricane Warning Network

Hz Hertz or cycles per second of a sine wave

ICF Credit *Interplanetary Coalition Fund Credit*--One credit for one metric ton of propellant or food exported

ISRU In situ Resource Utilization- e.g. mining water ice on Mars to produce water, oxygen, and hydrogen

JAXA Japan Aerospace Exploration Agency

JIQIREN Chinese AI robot

JWST James Webb Space Telescope

KBO Kuiper Belt Object- an minor solar system body orbiting the Sun beyond the orbit of Neptune

klick slang for kilometer

Kuiper belt Large region in the cold, outer reaches of our solar system beyond the orbit of Neptune harboring millions of small, icy objects from the beginnings of the solar system. It includes dwarf planets such as Pluto.

L2 2nd Lagrange point of stable gravity balance between the Earth and the Moon

LAX Los Angeles International Airport

LEO Low Earth Orbit-- for example the International Space Station at about 400 km altitude.

LH2 liquid hydrogen

LHB Late Heavy Bombardment- from 4.1 to 3.9 billion years ago, the inner solar system planetary bodies suffered a huge influx of impactors. Evidence of this is the huge circular impact basins and mare on the Moon. Computer modeling implies that a shift in orbits of Uranus and Neptune sent the impactors to the inner solar system.

LOP-G Lunar Orbiting Platform- Gateway (to the Moon or deep space)

LOX liquid oxygen

LRO Lunar Reconnaissance Orbiter

magnetite an iron bearing mineral with magnetic properties

Mars launch window Earth-Mars: Lowest energy Hohmann transfer is achieved by launching before Mars opposition and arriving just after opposition. Launch windows occur about once every 26 months.

MarsNet Mars planet wide information network

MAV Mars Ascent Vehicle

MGS Mars Global Surveyor

micron one millionth of a meter

MIRV-ICBM Multiple Independently Targetable Reentry Vehicle- Intercontinental Ballistic Missile

MITL Martian Interplanetary Trade Liaison

MOLA Mars Orbiting Laser Altimeter

MRO Mars Reconnaissance Orbiter

MT Metric ton= 1000 kilograms

MT1 Mars Telescope 1

MT2 Mars Telescope 2

MT-SDOT Mars Telescope Shiva Debris Operations Team

nadir the point on the celestial sphere directly below an observer

nanometer one billionth of a meter

NASA National Aeronautics and Space Administration

Oort Cloud cloud of predominantly icy comets and planetesimals beyond the Kuiper Belt at distances ranging from 2,000 to 200,000 AU beyond the Sun.

organic molecule molecule of a carbon compound. May or may not be related to life.

oxidation loss of electrons or an increase in *oxidation* state of an element or compound

PAH polycyclic aromatic hydrocarbons (e.g. benzene rings)

Pan-STARRS twin 1.8 meter telescopes at the Haleakala Observatory on Maui used for finding asteroid threats to Earth

PASCI (sounds like Passy) Pan-STARRS Astrometric Computing Intelligence

polycarbonate thermoplastic polymers containing carbonate groups in their chemical structures e.g. Plexiglas

ppbv parts per billion by volume

pyros small explosive devices on a spacecraft designed to sever connections in a programmed sequence of events.

RAD-D geologic radiation detector

reduction gain of electrons or a decrease in *oxidation* state of an element or compound

REE rare earth elements-- set of seventeen chemical elements in the periodic table, including the fifteen lanthanides, as well as scandium and yttrium. Used in high tech electronics, ceramics, and metallurgy.

reflector telescope a telescope that uses a precise concave mirror to collect and focus light onto a secondary mirror to be imaged at an eyepiece or camera

RIPP a restraint mask that prevents a prisoner from biting and spitting e.g. Hannibal Lecter

Ritchey–Chrétien a reflector telescope that has a hyperbolic primary mirror and a hyperbolic secondary mirror

Roscosmos / FKA Roscosmos State Corporation for Space Activities

Sabatier reactor Propellant factory on Mars using hydrogen from water and CO_2 from Mars atmosphere to make methane fuel

Shēn Kōng Yóuxíng *Deep Space March* Super Heavy Lift Vehicle--Chinese clone of the Colossus ships

Shiva Shiva, the Destroyer, is the third god in the Hindu triumvirate. Namesake of the KBO threatening Earth.

SNAFU Military jargon- Situation Normal: All F***ed Up

SSTAR Small, sealed, transportable, autonomous reactor powered by uranium fuel rods, delivered from Earth capable of sustained 10 megawatt electricity output.

stromatolite a fossil of layered cyanobacteria or blue-green algae

SWRRP Solids Waste Recycling Reactor Process, SWRRP, pronounced *"SWIRP*

TCI Trans Ceres Injection rocket burn

TLS tunable laser spectrometer instrument

TMI Trans Mars Injection rocket burn

UAE United Arab Emirates

VASIMIR Variable Specific Impulse Magnetoplasma Rocket

V-dot Vertical velocity in meters per second relative to the ground

Vishnu Vishnu, the Savior, is the second god in the Hindu triumvirate. Namesake of the missile sent to divert the KBO threatening Earth.

zenith the point on the celestial sphere directly above an observer

DRAMATIS PERSONAE

Mars Arcadia Colonists in June 2035- Launch to Mars

GENDER	NAME	AGE in 2035	NATIONALITY	PROFESSION(S)
male	Coby Brewster	65	USA	Pilot; Engineer (Aero/Elec/Habs)
female	Ellie Accardi	51	ITALY	Astrogeologist / Astrobiologist
male	Vik Ivanov	66	RUS	Pilot; Engineer (Aero/Elec/Habs/Comp)
female	Abby Denton	51	USA	Flight Surgeon/Ob/Gyn/Oncology
male	Alexei Ivanov	10	RUS/USA	Student Engineer (Aero/Elec/Habs/Comp)/Astrophysicist
female	Sophia Brewster	10	Italy/USA	Student Engineer (Aero/Elec/Habs/Comp)/Astrophysicist
male	Oleg Ivanov	41	RUS	Pilot; Engineer (Aero/Elec/Habs/Comp)
female	Olga Sadoski	39	RUS	Engineer (Nuclear/Solar/Electric.)
female	Elena Petrov	54	RUS	Pilot; Engineer (Aero/Electric.)
male	Jacob Petrov	18	RUS/USA	Pilot; Engineer (Aero/Comp/Habs/Geology)
female	Tracy Dixon	41	USA	Engineer (Nuclear, biomed.); Physician
male	Paul Earhart	45	France	Engineer (solar electric; chemical)
female	Megumi Hirakata	25	Japan	Engineer (Agriculture /Habs)
male	Satoshi Fukoshima	40	Japan	Engineer (Space systems /Habs)
female	Sandy Conklin	24	USA	Engineer (Robotics/3D Printing); Chaplain
female	Dao-Ming Cai	26	China	Engineer (Robotics/AI/VR); Psychologist
male	Trevor Brown	29	Britain-Afro	Astrobiologist; Aquaponics
female	Mandy Shields	28	Britain-Afro	Astrobiologist; Aquaponics
male	Harrison Frank	27	Canada	Engineer (mech. /civil / electric.)
female	Eve Cain	25	USA	Engineer (Habs); Lawyer-Space Law/CJ;
female	Oksana Ivanov	born 2036	Martian	
female	Adele Earhart	born 2036	Martian	
male	Travis Frank	born 2036	Martian	
male	Filip Petrov	born 2037	Martian	

KEY

male	Married
female	Married
male	Single

OTHER PLAYERS		
NAME	PROFESSION	ROLE
Dr. Kikuko Nakahara	Astrogelogist	sample researcher Aquila
Dr. Daniele Lorenzo	Astrogelogist	sample researcher Aquila
Dr. Grant Jeffries	Astrogelogist	sample researcher Aquila
Dr. David Moreau	Astrobiologist	sample researcher Aquila
Matteo Russo	Astronomer	Shiva discovery
Kelsey Leech	Astronomer	Shiva discovery
Bruce Bouchout	Astronaut	Director Mars Orbiting Camp
Ben Kirk	Astronaut	NASA Flight Operations Director
Dr. Shirley Hansen	Physician	NASA Flight Surgeon
Emily Collins	Publicist	Coalition PR Secretary
Kate Turner	Correspondent	GNN Science Reporter
Dr. Harold Draper	AI Programmer	MIT Project PI for CASSI Development
CASSI	AI Computer	Cybernetic Artificial Space Systems Intelligence
CAMI	AI Computer	Cybernetic Artificial MMU Intelligence
PASCI (Passy)	AI Computer	Pan-STARRS Astrometric Computing Intelligence
CARIAN (Carrie Ann)	Robotic AI	Cybernetic Artificial Robotic Intelligence- Android
CARIIN (Karen)	Robotic AI	Cybernetic Artificial Robotic Intelligence- Industrial
HORTA	Robotic AI	Robotic Ice boring machine

ARCADIA 1-- FIRST MARS LANDING		
Trent Granger	Astronaut	Cdr. Arcadia 1, first boots on Mars
Serena Solis	Astronaut	Pilot Arcadia 1
Barry Peterson	Astronaut	Arcadia 1-engineer, first fatality on Mars
Tom Decloux	Astronaut	Arcadia 1 engineer, Chaplain
Lisenka Savelievna	Astronaut	Arcadia 1 engineer
Denikin Andreevich	Astronaut	Arcadia 1 astrogeologist/astrobiologist
Kerstin Nemetz	Astronaut	Arcadia 1 Flight Surgeon
Cloe Lenza	Astronaut	Arcadia 1 engineer
Kaga Hikaru	Astronaut	Arcadia 1 engineer
Takahashi Shigenaga	Astronaut	Arcadia 1 engineer

ARCADIA BETA COLONISTS

Paula Jennings	Commander	Engineer (Space systems /Habs)
Sam Jennings	Pilot	Engineer (Space systems /Habs)
Julia Levine	Colonist	Botanist Agronomist Aquaponics
Mike Fischer	Colonist	Botanist Agronomist Aquaponics
Chen Zhong	Colonist	Engineer (solar electric; chemical)
Liao Shi	Colonist	Engineer (solar electric; chemical)
Jochem Nabers	Pilot	Engineer (Space systems /Habs)
Elle Zandjans	Pilot	Engineer (Space systems /Habs); Counselor
Fermo Caracci	Colonist	Engineer (mech. /civil / electric.)
Liana Vitacco	Colonist	Engineer (Robotics/AI /3D Printing)
Seno Masaru	Colonist	Engineer (Agriculture /Habs)
Onishi Suzuko	Colonist	Engineer (Agriculture /Habs)
Dominik Weidmann	Colonist	Planetary Geologist; Psychologist
Sabrina Kessler	Colonist	Engineer (Nuclear, biomed.); Physician
Jeff Hendricks	Colonist	Engineer (Materials Science,3D Printing)
Evgeny Yakovna	Colonist	Control systems and Thermodynamics
Lera Veronochek	Colonist	Robotics and AI
John Meek	Colony Liason	PhD Urban Planning/IPE/Space Law
Briana Culver	Colonist	Robotics and AI
Jameel al-Badie	Colony Liason	PhD Urban Planning/IPE/Space Law/CJ

NEW KOLOB COLONISTS

Elder Henry Young	Colonist	President of the Colony
Julie Young	Colonist	Artist
Leah Fielding-Meek	Colonist	Cinematographer, wife of John Meek
Elder Todd Scott	Colonist	Musician
Ruth Scott	Colonist	Musician

AL-SALAM AL-JADID COLONISTS

Sheikh Humaid Bin Muhammad bin Farhad Al Hasan--	Colonist	President of Colony
Layla Mohammed	Colonist	Artist, wife of Jameel al-Badie

Sheikh Mansour bin Zahid Al Majed	Pres. United Arab Emirates, Emir of Abu Dhabi

ABOUT THE AUTHOR

Doug Cook is retired from a thirty-four year career as a petroleum geophysicist. A career highlight was participating in ten years of deep-water submersible oil seep studies in the Gulf of Mexico. Imagine the submersible as a spaceship exploring extreme life forms in the deep ocean. Astronomy and astrogeology are Doug's life passions. He is a member American Association of Petroleum Geologists (AAPG), Chair AAPG Astrogeology Committee, Society of Exploration Geophysicists (SEG), VP Colorado Springs Astronomical Society, member of the Planetary Society, National Space Society, and Adjunct Astronomy Professor PPCC. He has two daughters and lives in Colorado with his wife Elizabeth.

doug@aquilamission.space

OTHER PUBLICATIONS:

Cook, Doug, 2019, Mars In Situ Resources and Utilization for Human Settlement, AAPG 2019 Convention Abstracts

Cook, Doug, *The Aquila Mission,* CreateSpace, 2018. Print

Kenkmann, T., Sundell, K., and Cook, D., 2018, Evidence for a large Paleozoic Impact Crater Strewn Field in the Rocky Mountains, Nature *Scientific Reports,* V 8, Article no: 13246. https://www.nature.com/articles/s41598-018-31655-4

Sundell, K.A., M.H. Poelchau, D. Cook, T. Kenkmann, 2018, The Douglas Crater Field, Wyoming, USA: Discovery of an Unexpected Crater Cluster at the Carboniferous-Permian Boundary, 81st Annual Meeting of The Meteoritical Society 2018 Moscow (LPI Contrib. No. 2067), Abs. 6149

Kenkmann, T., Sundell, K., and Cook, D., 2018, Exhumed Paleozoic Impact Crater Strewn Field near Douglas, Wyoming, USA: Evidence from microstructural analysis, satellite, and drone imagery, 49th Lunar and Planetary Science Conference, Abstract 1469.

Kenkmann, T., Sundell, K., and Cook, D., 2018, Discovery of a Paleozoic Impact Crater Strewn Field near Douglas, Wyoming, USA: Evidence from Microstructural Analysis, Satellite, and Drone Imagery, Abstract to the EGU General Assembly 2018, EGU2018-6010

Cook, D., 2018, Near Earth Objects (NEOs): Population Distributions, Origins, and Implications on Earth Impact Threat and Asteroid Mining Resources, AAPG 2018 Convention Abstracts

Cook, D., and K. Sundell, 2017, AAPG Total Solar Eclipse Field Guide: Leaders Dr. Harrison H. Schmitt, Dr. James

Reilly, Dr. Kent Sundell, Doug Cook, Don Clarke, and Karl Osvald

Cook, D., 2017, Asteroid Mining: the State of the Industry and our Future in Space, AAPG 2017 Convention Abstracts

Cook, D., 2016, A Bold Proposal for a Crewed Deep Space Mission to Rendezvous with and Sample an Asteroid and a Comet, New Worlds Space Settlement Symposium 2016 Austin, TX Proceedings

Taylor, D., K. Pomar, S. Rahati, C. Reid, A. Henderson, F. Lu, M. Ferguson, and D. Cook, 2016, Chronostratigraphic Framework and Gross Depositional Environments of the Shu'aiba Formation in the Under-Explored Eastern Rub' Al-Khali Basin, Saudi Arabia, GeoArabia GEO 2016 Convention Abstracts

Cook, D., Bohmail, A. Rademakers, M., 2016, Exploration and Commercialization of Tight Gas Reservoirs in Saudi Arabia, AAPG ME Exploring Mature Basins Geosciences Technology Workshop Abstracts; Workshop Co-Chair Douglas Cook, Saudi Aramco.

Cook, D., 2016, A Bold Proposal for a Manned Deep Space Mission to Rendezvous with and Sample an Asteroid and a Comet, AAPG 2016 Convention Abstracts

Kenkmann, T., Afifi, A. M., Stewart, S, Poelchau, M.H., Cook, D., Neville, A.S., 2015, Saqqar: A 34 km diameter impact structure in Saudi Arabia, Meteoritics & Planetary Science 50, 11:1925-1940.

Neville A. S., Cook D. J., Afifi A. M., and Stewart S. A., 2014. Five buried crater structures imaged on reflection seismic data in Saudi Arabia. GeoArabia 19:17–44.

Neville, A., A. Afifi, and D. Cook, 2012, Possible Impact Structures in Saudi Arabia, AAPG 2012 Convention Abstracts

Cook, D., A. Norton, and A. Neville, 2008, Petroleum Systems and Recent Exploration of the Permo-Carboniferous Unayzah and Devonian Jauf Reservoirs in Eastern Saudi Arabia, AAPG 2008 Convention Abstracts

Cook, D., et al, 2008, Petroleum Systems and New Plays in Frontier Exploration in Northwest Saudi Arabia, AAPG 2008 International Convention Abstracts

Lawrence, Paul, Tom Harland, David Tang, Douglas Cook, Geraint Hughes, Ravi Singh, Greg Gregory, Abdel Fattah Bakhiet, and Abdel Ghayoum Ahmed, 2008, Regional Hanifa Reservoir Fairways in the Eastern Province of Saudi Arabia: An Integrated Approach, GeoArabia GEO 2006 Convention Abstracts

Xiao, H., Knowlton, A., Rademakers, M., and Cook, D., 2006, Structural Styles in Eastern and Central Arabia, GeoArabia GEO 2006 Convention Abstracts

Cook, D, and C. Tsai, 2004, Use of Model Based K-L Filtering to Attenuate Interbed Multiples in Seismic Reflections of the Devonian Jauf Reservoir, Eastern Saudi Arabia, GeoArabia GEO 2004 Convention Abstracts

Cook, D., 1992, Stratigraphy of Pleistocene Upper Slope Sands, Gulf of Mexico, An Analog for Deep Water Exploration Offshore Nigeria, Nigerian Association of Petroleum Explorationists Tenth Annual Proceedings *Best Paper Award

Roberts, H., D. Cook, and M. Sheedlo, 1992, Hydrocarbon Seeps of the Louisiana Continental Slope: Seismic Amplitude Signature and Sea Floor Response, GCAGS Trans., Vol.42:737-749 *GCAGS Levorsen Best Paper Award

Sheedlo, M. and D. Cook, 1992, 3D Seismic Imaging and Direct Observations of Sea Floor Features on the Upper Slope,

Green Canyon Block 184 Federal Unit, Gulf of Mexico, AAPG Convention Abstracts

Cook, D., et al., 1992, Stratigraphy of Pleistocene Upper Slope Sands in the Green Canyon Block 184 Federal Unit, Gulf of Mexico, AAPG 1992 Convention Abstracts

Cook, D. and P. D'Onfro, 1991, Jolliet Field Thrust Fault Structure and Stratigraphy, Green Canyon Block 184, Offshore Louisiana, GCAGS Trans., V.41:100-122

Cook, D. and P. D'Onfro, 1990, Jolliet Field Thrust Fault Structure and Stratigraphy, A Deep Water Development Milestone, Green Canyon Block 184, Offshore Louisiana, Abst., AAPG Bull., V.74/5:633

Randazzo, A. and D. Cook, 1987, Characterization of Dolomitic Rocks from the Coastal Mixing Zone of the Floridan Aquifer, Sedimentary Geology, V. 54:169-192

Cook, D. et al., 1985 Authigenic Fluorite in Dolomitic Rocks of the Floridan Aquifer, Geology, V13:390-391

Made in the USA
Columbia, SC
15 February 2023

12208965R00196